Not a Sparrow Falls

Matt 10:31

Lynnette

THE WYLDHAVEN SERIES

by Lynnette Bonner

Not a Sparrow Falls – BOOK ONE

On Eagles' Wings – BOOK TWO

Beauty from Ashes – BOOK THREE

Consider the Lilies – BOOK FOUR

A Wyldhaven Christmas – BOOK FIVE

Songs in the Night – BOOK SIX

Honey from the Rock – BOOK SEVEN

Beside Still Waters – BOOK EIGHT

OTHER HISTORICAL BOOKS

by Lynnette Bonner

THE SHEPHERD'S HEART SERIES

Rocky Mountain Oasis – BOOK ONE
High Desert Haven – BOOK TWO
Fair Valley Refuge – BOOK THREE
Spring Meadow Sanctuary – BOOK FOUR

SONNETS OF THE SPICE ISLE SERIES

On the Wings of a Whisper – BOOK ONE

Find all other books by Lynnette Bonner at:
www.lynnettebonner.com

Not a Sparrow Falls

Lynnette BONNER
USA Today Bestselling Author

Not a Sparrow Falls
WYLDHAVEN, Book 1

Published by Pacific Lights Publishing

Cover design by Lynnette Bonner of Indie Cover Design, images ©
Depositphotos_232384046 - Flare
Depositphotos_67237793 - Badge
Depositphotos_21219423_DS – Texture
AdobeStock_606424995 – Décor and Dividers

Other images generated by Lynnette Bonner using Midjourney and Adobe Photoshop.
Book interior design by Jon Stewart of Stewart Design
Editing by Dori Harrell of Breakout Editing
Proofreading by Sheri Mast of Faithful Editing

ISBN: 978-1-942982-07-4

To All who are Hurting:

People fall. They wound with words or actions that cut deep and leave scars.
But know this...
There is One who never fails.
He loves you more than any other.
So much so, that He even knows the number of hairs on your head at any given moment.
He is constantly good and loving.
He notices when sparrows fall, yet loves you more.
He is worthy of your heart.
Worthy of your service.
He created you because He wanted to deeply and intimately, as a closest friend, fellowship with you.
Do you know Him?

If not, but you would like to know more please visit:
www.peacewithgod.net

MATTHEW 10:29-31

Are not two sparrows sold for a penny? Yet not one of them will fall to the ground outside your Father's care. And even the very hairs of your head are all numbered. So don't be afraid; you are worth more than many sparrows.

Chapter One

Early August, 1891
Boston, Massachusetts

Charlotte Brindle, seated at the desk in her bedroom, leaned her elbows on the blotter, propped both hands against her throbbing forehead, and stared down at the rows of newspaper advertisements before her.

She scrunched her eyes shut against the memory of what she'd seen in town this nooning. Her stomach roiled at the images. Kent Covington, the man she'd intended to marry, was not who she'd thought he was.

Why was she never enough?

Be anxious for nothing, but in everything by prayer and supplication, with thanksgiving, let your requests be made known to God; and the peace of God, which surpasses all understanding, will guard your hearts and minds through Christ Jesus. Had she really read those words from the book of Philippians only this morning? She huffed a breath. How did one go about being anxious for nothing in a situation like this? *By prayer and supplication...* She gritted her teeth. Fine.

"Lord, rip his head off."

She could almost picture the Lord's disapproving frown. It looked a lot like Pastor Sorenson's would, had he heard her say those words. She sighed. Right. That probably wasn't the kind of prayer and supplication the verses referred to. Another set of verses, ones Pastor had spoken on just this past week, came to mind. *But I say to you who hear: Love your enemies, do good to those who hate you, bless those who curse you, and pray for those who spitefully use you.*

Her focus angled toward the ceiling. "I just want someone to love me. To really love me. Is that too much to ask?"

She waited. But no peace that surpassed understanding crept in to soften the blow her heart had taken today. Instead a restlessness churned inside her. A burning desire to get as far from Boston as possible. Was that the Lord speaking? Why did it have to be so hard to determine the Lord's will for one's life? She'd thought she knew. And now this...

She sighed and forced her eyes open. Her agitated fingers had loosed several of her dark curls, and she went to work repairing the damage. She thrust the hairpins in with deft fingers and then used her silver hand mirror to assess her hair in the larger mirror across the room. Satisfied the job was done well enough to keep Mother from fussing about her appearance, Charlotte returned to the task at hand.

She'd snuck the newspaper from Father's study and needed to put it back before he discovered it was missing and asked Mother where it was. The last thing Charlotte wanted right now was to answer a bevy of Mother's questions over why she'd needed the paper, for Mother surely wouldn't understand, nor be amenable to, her desire to escape the stuffy confines of Boston.

Well, if the truth were told, it was more an escape from the perfidious Kent Covington than it was from Boston. How far was far enough that he wouldn't come looking for her? Any place would suffice, she supposed, so long as she could convince Mother not to give him her forwarding address.

The headache flared with a vengeance. How likely was she to be able to keep her destination a secret? Not very. For Mr.

Covington had Mother firmly in his corner. His reputation was so stellar Charlotte wondered if Mother would even believe her if she told what she'd seen. On second thought, of course Mother would. And then she would remind Charlotte that all men were faithless flighty creatures, and point out how much money the man brought to the relationship, and advise her to set aside her qualms.

Then Charlotte would spend the autumn declining proposals from the man and facing down Mother's ire afterward. She shuddered. If she thought speaking of what she'd seen this morning would change Mother's mind, she would go to her posthaste and tell all! But truly all Mother cared about was the number of dollar signs attached to the Covington name.

In the newspaper, there were advertisements for everything from women's corsets (complete with rather shocking illustrations of skimpily-clad women modeling them) to Coca-Cola, "The Ideal Brain Tonic—Specific for Headache."

After reading that particular ad, Charlotte briefly toyed with sending Rose right down to the corner store for a bottle to ease the throbbing in her skull, but then she would have to explain to Rose why she had Father's paper, and the maid never could keep a secret.

Again, the desire to simply get as far from Boston as possible churned through her. She remembered another of Pastor Sorenson's oft-quoted quips. "A ship that is moving is easier to steer." Very well. She would make a move and trust the Lord to steer. *Lord, I only want Your will, so please guide my steps.*

"There!" A small printed piece without any imagery caught her eye, and Charlotte straightened, lifting the paper for a closer look. A town out west in the new state of Washington was looking for a schoolteacher, but the address to respond to was right here in Boston!

Without another moment's thought, Charlotte took up the fountain pen, pulled out a sheet of her favorite rose-scented stationery, and penned her interest in the position.

She'd already been offered a teaching position here in town, but she hadn't accepted it yet, thank heavens. Mostly because Mother had objected so strenuously, stating she was concerned about Charlotte taking a carriage into the heart of the commercial district every day. In truth, Charlotte wondered if Mother wasn't hoping to be a grandmother before the end of the year. The thought made Charlotte even queasier. And now there wasn't a chance under heaven that she'd be taking that school, because that would mean remaining in Boston, where Mr. Covington could, and would, continue to call.

After inserting the stationery into an envelope, she promptly called for a carriage and rode into town herself. The late-summer day was warm, and she enjoyed the breeze cooling her brow. She untied the ribbons on her hat and pulled it off, tipping her head against the seat to catch the strongest gusts. Someone was sure to glimpse her through the window and report her scandalous behavior to Mother, but she couldn't bring herself to care at the moment. The air wafting in her curls was doing wonders for her headache. Or perhaps that was simply the relief at having found a position to apply for which would take her far from here?

Benedict pulled the carriage to a stop, and Charlotte quickly replaced her hat and tied the ribbons as he opened the door and held out a hand to help her down.

"Thank you, Benedict. I know a trip into town twice in one day is not what you expected."

He gave a stiff little bow but, as usual, made no reply.

Charlotte sighed. Mother's silly rule about the male servants speaking as little to her as possible wore very thin most days.

Father was only a banker, a very well-to-do banker, but it wasn't like they were part of some European royal court where her reputation could be tarnished by a simple word spoken here or there.

"You know I'd never report you to Mother for speaking to me, don't you?"

Benedict only offered a dip of his chin, his eyes darting up and down the street.

Charlotte gave up. He was afraid that one of Mother's upper-echelon friends might see them and turn him in.

The post office loomed before her, but she couldn't seem to get her feet to move. She stood quietly, staring up at the doors. The letter in her fingers trembled, and the pain in her stomach, which had been a tiny crimp up to that moment, threatened to roll over into all-out nausea. Charlotte closed her eyes and tapped the envelope against her palm. She envisioned the brick facade of the school down on Tremont Street. It was a good school that would allow her to stay home and at the same time give her some independence. Yet her independence would end the moment the school day came to a close and she walked back through her parents' front door. It would especially end the moment Mother wore her down and talked her into letting Mr. Covington come calling again, for well she knew Mother's powers of persistence and persuasion.

Behind her, Benedict shuffled his feet and cleared his throat softly.

A moving ship...

Lifting her chin, Charlotte took the stairs up to the double doors and strode inside. She was a grown woman, after all. Independent and in full possession of her faculties. And this was almost the twentieth century! Surely a woman ought to be able to make up her own mind about whom she ought to marry?

She slapped the letter on the counter so firmly that the attendant startled.

Charlotte felt her face heat. "My apologies. I'd like to buy a postage stamp for this, please."

Early August, 1891.
Seattle, Washington

Patrick Waddell sat at a window table of the O'Shanigan's Pub and Eatery.

A middle-aged woman with mouse-colored hair and rolls around her midsection set a plate of greasy chicken and potatoes before him and topped off his mug of ale. She plunked one hand on an ample hip. "You a stranger to these parts?"

Waddell kept his expression bland. He was wise enough to recognize a gossip when he saw one. "Just passin' through."

She gave him a nod. "Best food in the city. We'd be obliged if ye'd spread the word."

She scurried to the next table before he could reply, but as he glanced down at the puddle of oil forming beneath the soggy gray chicken, he strongly doubted any word he might spread about the place would be the kind O'Shanigan wanted getting about. He grimaced. He used to be able to tolerate grease when he was younger, but now that his years had rolled past sixty, it caused him no end of chest pains whenever he ate too much of it.

But just this once, he'd let a complaint remain silent. He wasn't here for the food. No sir. Not the food at all.

He glanced out the window. Across the street stood the Pacific Federal Bank, and just visible in the side alley he could make out the wagon that was unloading all the cash that should tomorrow, on payday, be doled out to various city workers. A satisfied smile nudged his lips. *Should.* Because tomorrow a lot of city workers were going to be severely disappointed by their lack.

He sipped his ale. Pretended to eat. Waited.

His patience was rewarded when thirty minutes later, the wagon pulled out of the side alley. All the cash had been delivered.

Waddell pulled his pocket watch from his vest and consulted it. Fifteen minutes till the schedule started. He stood, dug out his wallet, and deposited several bills on the table. He tipped his hat to O'Shanigan, then stepped out onto the porch. Arms folded, he leaned against the wall in the shadows cast by the roof.

A few minutes later, the door of the pub opened and two other men emerged.

Waddell consulted his watch. Ten minutes till the schedule started. "You ready?" he asked quietly, not really looking at the two.

From the corner of his eye, he saw Horace Crispin nod enthusiastically, glee stretching his lips. He reached into his coat pocket and withdrew his flask, swishing a goodly amount around in his mouth before spitting it out. Next he poured a splash into one palm and patted it against his cheeks like he was going courting.

Lenny Smith's smile was less enthusiastic, but he too indicated the affirmative.

"Right then, to your places." Waddell stepped off the porch and strode in the direction of the mercantile next door to the bank. Behind him he heard Horace's and Lenny's footsteps moving in their respective directions. Satisfaction curled through him. Honestly, as long as they followed directions for the next ten minutes, he didn't care what happened to them after that. He bit down on a grin. He sure would like to be a fly on the wall when those two and the others woke up and realized they'd done all this for naught.

It was no trick at all to slip into the back room of the mercantile when right on schedule, Lenny dropped the glass chimney of an oil lamp in the front aisle, and Chalmers, the mercantile owner, hurried forward with a broom and dustpan to clean it up. Waddell's first worry was that Chalmers's wife might be working on inventory in the back, but providence must be smiling down on him today, because she was nowhere to be seen.

It took him a full twenty seconds to pick the lock on the door that linked the mercantile's back room to the bank's back room. He was getting slow. His hands weren't as steady as they used to be.

Waddell's second worry had been that not all the bank personnel would move out front when Horace created his diversion, but when he poked his head carefully around the door, not a soul was in sight, and he could hear Horace's bellowing even from here. "What's a man gotta do to get money from his account 'round these parts!"

"But, Mr....Higgenbaum, did you say your name was? We don't *have* an account registered under your name." The bank employee sounded quite distraught.

"Balderdash, I tell you!" Horace screeched. "I've had an account here for years!"

Waddell grinned as he soft-footed his way farther into the room. Here was where the entire plan could go awry. He held his breath as he stepped over to where he could see the vault, and then he eased it out on a big grin. Just as he'd been informed, the bank was slow to relock the vault door after large deliveries. And it still remained open, as inviting as you please.

Out front, he could hear Horace ramping up his complaints. Patrick hurried to the back door and pushed it open a crack. He had chosen Tommy Crispin, Horace's younger brother, specifically for his mission for one very key reason. The boy was simple. And that would serve Waddell's needs just fine tonight.

He smiled at the boy. "You got my bags, Tommy?"

Tommy nodded vigorously. "Just like Horace an' me been practicin'."

"Good lad. Hand them here, and then go wait behind that bush by the fence."

Tommy pulled the gunnysacks from beneath his shirt. A large grin split his face. "We gonna trick them bankers good, ain't we, Mr. Waddell?"

"Shhh!" He glanced over his shoulder, feeling a tick of anxiety over Tommy's excitement-raised voice. Thankfully, no one seemed to have heard. "Yeah, we're gonna trick them, but we have to be very quiet, or the trick won't work. Got me?"

Tommy's eyes widened. "Got you." He pressed one finger to his lips, lowering his voice. "Be quiet, or the trick won't work. Got you." He nodded.

"Good lad. Now go wait behind the bush. I'll call you when I'm ready for you to come back."

"Behind the bush. Call when you ready fo' me." Tommy nodded and trotted in the direction of the thick laurel that grew at the back of the bank lot.

Patrick eased out a breath and hurried into the vault. He glanced at the stack of bills that the bank employees had already started to divide into payroll for individuals. Three hundred thousand dollars didn't look so large when you saw it all stacked together. Less than fifty pounds of cash.

Footsteps in the adjoining room jolted him, and he pressed his back against the row of lockboxes at one side of the vault. His skin prickled, and he reached inside his jacket and wrapped his palm around the handle of his Colt, holding his breath. But whoever had come into the back room kept on going out the back door.

Patrick eased out a sigh. They were likely going for the sheriff. That meant he only had a couple more minutes of distraction from Horace.

With a snap, he shook open one of the gunnysacks and started stuffing cash inside. Thirty seconds and the first bag was half filled. Another thirty put the rest of the cash into the other bag.

He darted a longing glance at the lockboxes. If only he had a little more time, he could pick a few locks, but getting greedy might cost him his life. Besides, deposit-box locks were a mite trickier than a door's. It might take him longer than was prudent to get the boxes open. So with a fortifying breath he poked his head out to give the back room a quick glance.

Empty.

Good. He hurried to the back door and repeated the scan.

The back of the building was also empty.

Here again was a critical moment where the plan might skew off course. The blasted train couldn't seem to stick to a set schedule. It might be coming through at any minute. Or it might be thirty minutes from now.

First he had to get rid of Tommy.

As fast as his age-hampered joints would let him, he scuttled across the road to the laurel where Tommy had been instructed to hide. When he pushed behind it, the boy was sitting on the ground with his arms curled around his head, rocking himself in that peculiar way he had.

Patrick's heart clenched. This lad, of all of them, didn't deserve his double cross. Rolling his eyes at his own sentimentality, he reached into one of the sacks and withdrew two twenty-dollar bills.

He bent and touched Tommy on one shoulder. "Hey, Tom. You done good. Real good, you hear?"

Tommy's face split into a wide grin. "I done good?"

"You sure did. And because you did so well..." He held up the two bills for the boy to see.

Tommy's eyes lit up, and his mouth dropped open.

"You like those chocolate bars that Magnusson sells in his shop, don't you, Tommy?"

A vigorous nod preceded "I sure do!"

Patrick tugged the boy to his feet and tucked the two bills into his front shirt pocket. "Well, you've earned yourself some chocolate. Why don't you go down to Magnusson's and buy a couple bars, but then you take the change and go back to the camp, hear?"

"Take the change and go back to the camp." Tommy nodded.

"Good lad." Patrick glanced through the leaves of the bush. All clear. He pushed Tommy out into the open. "Go on now. I'm gonna meet you all back at the camp too."

Tommy took several steps and then turned to face the bush with a huge grin. "I'm gonna buy you some choc'late too, Mr. Waddell."

"That's fine, Tommy. I'll like that real well. Go on now." He held his breath. Sometimes the boy got stubborn about cutting off conversation.

"Go on now." Tommy nodded and then darted down the alley on the other side of the mercantile.

Patrick eased out a breath and clambered up the berm of the railroad tracks just behind him. Once on the other side of the tracks, he crouched down and set to running. He needed to hightail his old hide to the top of the hill before the train arrived. The crest was the only place the train would slow enough for him to jump aboard.

As he ran, he grinned between puffs for air. He wanted to leap and whoop, but only allowed the grin. Blast but the boys were going to be furious when they figured out he wasn't going to arrive back at camp after all.

One week later
Wyldhaven, Washington

Sheriff Reagan Callahan sat, feet propped on the corner of his desk, paper open in his hands. He whistled low.

Someone had made off with nearly three hundred thousand dollars from Pacific National Bank in Seattle. And they'd pulled the job off in broad daylight.

Seattle was less than fifty miles away. He lowered the paper and glanced out the front window of his office. Thankfully, Wyldhaven didn't have a bank for him to worry about. But they did get payroll for Zeb's loggers that came through once a month. He'd need to have a word with Ben King about varying up their routines with the cash.

Speaking of Ben. The postman-cum-accountant for Zeb's logging crews was coming this way now.

Reagan dropped his feet to the floor, crossed to the stove, and poured a second cup of coffee. He handed it to Ben when he walked through the door, and Reagan motioned to the seat across from his desk.

"Thanks." Ben sank into the offered chair. He set a telegram on the desktop and slid it toward Reagan's chair.

Reagan lifted a brow and resumed his seat, pulling the yellow paper closer to him.

"You know my father is sheriff over in Cedar Falls. He sent this our way just a few minutes ago."

Reagan felt his stomach roll into a knot at the words of the message. "So, it was Patrick Waddell who robbed the bank? And then he double-crossed his gang and absconded with the cash all on his own?"

Ben nodded grimly. "Seems that way."

"How did your pa come on this information?"

Ben shrugged. "Aw, you know Pa. He always seems to know someone who knows someone. This time it was his friend Sheriff Blanchet from Seattle. Seems there was a young simpleton who ended up with forty dollars. Two twenty-dollar bills whose serial numbers matched two from the cash that was stolen. Story the boy tells is that Waddell gave them to him and told him to buy chocolate bars. He also slipped up and mentioned that his brother, Horace Crispin, had been helping Waddell plan the robbery. They were all supposed to meet back at their camp, but Waddell never showed up." Ben folded his arms. "Pa says the boy's being taken care of by an elderly widow in Seattle. But even though he's been questioned several times, that was all he seemed to know."

"And did Sheriff Blanchet go to this camp?"

Ben nodded. "But of course the gang had hightailed it before he arrived. No one was there."

Reagan lifted the newspaper in a deliberately exaggerated motion and then dropped it into the trash receptacle by his desk. "Why do I read the paper when I have you, Ben?"

Ben chuckled. "After all our years of friendship, you'd think you would have learned by now. I'm always the one with the good scoop."

Reagan chuckled. He and Ben had been fast friends for a good seventeen of Reagan's twenty-five years. "Tall tales is generally more like it."

Ben winced and thrust a hand over his heart. "Hey, my tall tales saved your sorry blond hide from getting tanned a time or two. Remember that time you dipped Betty Lou Harrick's ribbons in your inkpot? Who took the blame for you that time?"

Reagan laughed. "I don't know if my pa ever did believe that you were somehow able to cross the room, dip her ribbons, and make it back to your desk without Miss Flaherty seeing you."

Ben stood. Rubbed his backside. "I can still feel the licking I took for you that day. Pa knew how to whip but good."

Reagan angled him a look. "You owed me that one. There was that little incident before that where you prevaricated about me erasing your homework from your slate. I had to sit in the corner with the dunce cap on all day."

Ben laughed. "I'd almost forgotten about that one." He stretched his back into an arch, his face turning serious as his focus dropped to the telegram once more. "I best return to work. Just thought you'd like to know."

Reagan nodded. "Yeah. Thanks, Ben."

Pondering the news Ben had brought, Reagan stared out the window as Ben returned across the street.

A thought jolted through him. Hadn't he heard Lenny Smith mention the name Horace Crispin once? He scrubbed his fingers over his jaw. Yes. He was certain he had. Lenny was a regular over at McGinty's Alehouse.

This could mean nothing good for his town in the months to come. Nothing good.

But if he could catch the gang... And if he could get more proof than just the word of a simpleton, well, that would go a long way to getting this gang locked up for a good long time.

He stood and lifted his hat from the hook by the door. Maybe it was time to mosey on down to McGinty's and hang out for a while.

Chapter Two

All week long, each time the front bell rang, each time the postman arrived with the day's mail, each time she saw a flutter of movement on the front walk, Charlotte felt her stomach clench. She was doing a terrible job at trusting the Lord to steer, she knew, but what would she do if she didn't sense any sort of direction after some time? It was rather unnerving not knowing what method Mr. Heath, the man she'd written to about the job, would use in responding to her letter.

Surely the Lord wouldn't ask her to remain with an unfaithful man? No. He wouldn't. So that would mean leaving Boston. It would take time, but she would figure out what to do next.

On the two occasions that Kent had come to call, she had pleaded ill—which was rather close to the truth when she'd contemplated having to speak to him—and remained in her room.

Charlotte had just about given up on hearing back from Mr. Heath.

But a week later at dinner, Mother had just rung the bell to indicate the staff could clear away the china, when James stepped into the room. Always formal, James clapped his hands to his sides and stared at the far wall as he spoke. "There is a gentleman at the door to see Miss Brindle. Shall I show him in?"

Charlotte suddenly wished she hadn't indulged in the gravy

for her potatoes. Her hands trembled, but she forced her excitement into the fingers she wove into her serviette below the table, keeping her face stoic.

Mother blinked and pinned Charlotte with a curious look. "Who is it, James?"

"A Mr. Zebulon Heath, madam."

"Zebulon Heath? We don't know—"

"I'll see him," Charlotte blurted out, her eagerness momentarily getting the best of her.

James remained where he stood until Mother finally waved a hand of permission for him to see the man at the door to the parlor.

Charlotte's lips twitched with humor. The butler clearly understood just exactly which Brindle buttered his bread.

When James left the room, both Mother and Father stared at Charlotte. Father's eyes narrowed in that specific way he had of ferreting out truth from even the most reluctant of subjects.

The longer they all looked at one another, the more Mother's face reddened. "You haven't gone and done something rash to avoid poor Mr. Covington, have you?"

Charlotte sighed and dropped her serviette by her plate. There was nothing for it, she supposed, except to out and tell them the truth. "Indeed. I've applied for a teaching position out west."

"Teaching out west!? Oh dear Lord have mercy!" Mother leaned against the back of her chair, tipped her face to the ceiling, and flapped her serviette before her face.

Charlotte resisted a roll of her eyes. Mother should have been a thespian. "Mr. Zebulon Heath was the man I wrote to about the position. The address was right here in Boston."

Father's face remained passive, jaw hardened. The only

sign that some emotion coursed through him was that he kept flipping his silver table knife end over end, a gesture unlike him. "Is this really wise, do you think, Charlie?"

"Oh, Burt!" Mother was out of her chair and pacing the room now, but still flapping her serviette like a windmill in full storm. "How many times do I have to tell you she's a *lady* now. You really must stop calling her Charlie! And Charlotte, he's right!" Mother threw up her hands. "This is most unwise. *Most. Unwise!*" She paused and plopped her hands onto her hips. "You are going to throw away a perfectly good match, and with not even a sniff of a good reason lingering in the air! Just like you did with poor Senator Sherman."

"Come, Etta. We all know that Charlotte declined Senator Sherman's suit only after I found him with my secretary in his...private quarters."

Charlotte felt her face blanch at the reminder and quite literally bit her tongue to keep from blurting the truth about Kent. Perhaps because she wasn't quite ready to hear it herself, and *she'd* been the one to see him! She gritted her teeth. She had more than a *sniff* of a good reason. She'd gotten an eyeful. An eyeful that wouldn't soon be banished from her memory.

Mother spun away and resumed her pacing. "Nevertheless, he would have made a fine match. Just as Mr. Covington would. Oh for the day when children were good, and obedient, and listened to the wise counsel of their elders!" Mother pinned her with a glower. "As ever, you are acting on impulse. What's happened? You are running from something!"

Willing away the quaking at her center, Charlotte ignored Mother and answered Father's question. "You've always told me I'm only young once. And talking to the man won't create a sealed contract. Can't I at least hear what this Mr. Heath has to say? According to his advertisement, he's the town's founder." She tipped her head and gave Father the look that was half-pout, half-pleading—the same look that had gotten her just about everything she'd ever wanted from him since she was six years old.

Father sighed and set down his knife. "You may speak to him, but only if I'm present."

"Bertrand Brindle! You can't seriously be thinking of letting our only child run off to the West where she might—" Mother's face, which had until that moment been quite rosy, turned a shade of white that could have rivaled the bone china on the table. "Oh Lord have mercy! She could be killed by wild Indians!"

Father's lips thinned, and he leveled Mother with a glower. "This is 1891, Etta. We're almost to the twentieth century. I hardly think wild savages are still roaming about."

"And when they were acting savage, it was mostly because we were taking their land and impinging on their way of life," Charlotte added and then wished she hadn't, because that brought Father's ire into focus on her.

"Well, what about her lung condition?" Mother's voice might have been mistaken for a squeaking hinge.

Charlotte dare not let Father think too long on that question. "I only have trouble with my lungs on the rarest of occasions, Mother. I'll be fine." She transformed her features into her pout-plead and waited for him to confirm his answer.

With a sigh, he stood and ran one hand over his thinning gray hair. "As I said...you may speak to this man, but not without me present."

"Oh, Bertrand!" Mother collapsed into her chair, looking rather like a damp dustrag someone had forgotten to take to the laundry.

But Charlotte had lived with her long enough to know

that by tomorrow Mother would be planning some women's luncheon or plotting over which latest dress pattern to have her dressmaker try, so Charlotte bounced out of her seat and threw her arms around her father's neck. "Thank you!" It was the first good news she'd had all week.

Father patted her shoulders and smiled thinly. "Let's not get too excited until we hear what he has to say. Etta, ring for tea to be sent to the parlor."

Mother grumbled and whimpered under her breath, but she did lift the bell and ring it.

Father was doing his best to hide his humor when he turned back to Charlotte. "Shall we?" He motioned for her to precede him from the dining room.

The man waiting for them in the parlor was not like she had expected him to be at all. She had imagined a town founder to be a robust man, likely in his late thirties or early forties, and since he was from the West, maybe a touch unkempt. But the man seated on the settee was sixty-five if he was a day. His beard was long and pure white but neatly trimmed. And he was so frail it seemed a good stiff Boston breeze would knock him right off his feet. A silver-headed walking cane rested against the settee beside his leg, and a top hat with a pair of black gloves lay on the side table next to him.

Father strode over and extended his hand. "Bertrand Brindle."

The man stood briskly. "Heath. Zebulon Heath. It's a pleasure to meet you." He pumped Father's hand with gusto, and Charlotte's image of him being able to be blown over by a breeze dissipated. He actually seemed quite spry.

Father swept a hand toward Charlotte. "This is my daughter, Charlotte."

Charlotte curtsied and dipped her head. "Mr. Heath."

Mr. Heath bowed. "So you are interested in the teaching position I advertised?"

Charlotte blinked at the rapidity of his get-down-to-business approach. But she supposed it wasn't a bad thing to cut right to the chase. "I am. But I have a few questions first." Suddenly nervous, she pressed her hands together and resisted the urge to fiddle with her skirt, for Miss Gidden, her finishing-school mistress, would surely chastise her for such a display of nerves.

Mr. Heath smiled and, when Charlotte sank into the wingback chair across from him, resumed his seat. "Please, ask me anything."

Charlotte twisted her fingers together in her lap.

Before she could form any words, Father injected, "I presume you know that this will be Charlotte's first teaching position?"

A kind smile lit the man's rheumy blue eyes. He didn't look at Father but instead addressed his answer directly to Charlotte. "Everyone has to start somewhere, Miss Brindle."

Charlotte nodded her thanks for his thoughtfulness and rushed ahead before Father could jump in again. "How many students will I have?"

Mr. Heath steepled his fingers together and leaned forward. "I only just founded Wyldhaven this spring, and we haven't had our first year of school yet, but a rough estimate is fifteen children."

"Will there be more than one teacher?"

Mr. Heath shook his head. "The schoolhouse will be one room. We'll assess the need for change before each school year."

A thrill of excitement zipped through Charlotte. A school all her own, where she would be in charge of all the lessons! What could be better? Maybe the Lord had indeed directed her to Mr. Heath's advertisement. She nearly forgot what her other questions were, but remembered another in the nick of time.

"Will there be supplies? Or will I be in charge of procuring those?"

Mr. Heath smiled. "We'll do our best to make sure the schoolhouse and teacherage are properly supplied. But anything you choose to bring can be reimbursed."

Another thrill traipsed through her. Her friend Bonnie Blythe had to supply all her students with pencils and writing books at her own expense! And that was at a school right here in Boston!

Rose entered the room with a tea tray, and there was a lull as each of the three accepted a cup of tea.

Rose served Charlotte first and subtly pointed to a specific cup. Regular tea gave Charlotte raging headaches, but Mother stocked a special blend she could drink without problems. Charlotte was grateful the maid had been delicate about pointing it out. It wouldn't do for Mr. Heath to start off thinking her sickly.

As soon as Rose departed, Mr. Heath was right back to business. "Do you have any other questions, Miss Brindle?"

Charlotte's mouth was dry at the thought of her next question. But it was a valid one, and not something she should be embarrassed about asking, so she forced the words past her tight throat. "What is the salary being offered?"

"We are prepared to offer fifty dollars a month in addition to room and board."

Charlotte's eyebrows lifted at the very generous sum. Most of her friends who taught in Boston were receiving thirty dollars a month and had to provide their own living and eating arrangements.

Father cleared his throat. "While that salary is very satisfactory, Charlotte's mother is concerned for her safety. What can you tell us about your town... What is the name of it again? Wild Haven, did you say? That doesn't sound very civilized, if you'll pardon my saying so."

"Wyldhaven, yes. All one word and with a 'y' instead of an 'i.' And I can assure you"—Mr. Heath raised a hand like a witness in a courtroom—"that Wyldhaven is the most civilized of places, Mr. Brindle. I like to describe it as 'a little piece of New England blooming on the wild frontier.' We already have a post office, a very dedicated sheriff, a seamstress, a boardinghouse, a mercantile, and several other buildings about town. If you'll permit me..." The man cleared his throat, reached into the inner pocket of his black coat, and pulled out a pamphlet, which he held out to Charlotte triumphantly. "This will tell you a little about the Wyldhaven I have dreamed of building for quite a goodly sum of years."

Charlotte studied the drawings on the little brochure, and her excitement grew. The streets of the little town were cobbled, and there was even an arched cobblestone bridge over a pretty little creek. Streetlights graced pavered walkways that lay before several stone cottages. And the schoolhouse sat in a field right next to the creek.

She closed her eyes for a moment and imagined listening to the burble of water over stones, the twittering of birds, and the droning of pollen-laden bees as she taught with the windows open on a spring day. A happy sigh slipped from her lips. Best of all, Mr. Kent Covington wasn't in that picture at all.

She smoothed one hand over the brochure and turned her focus to Mr. Heath once more. "When would I need to start?"

Mr. Heath rubbed his hands together. "Well, I'm in Boston on business for a few weeks longer, but if you wouldn't be averse to it, I'd like to see you return ahead of me so the school year can start on time. The students are very eager to begin learning." He smiled at her.

Charlotte wanted to blurt out that she would take the job right then and there, but instead managed a restrained, "Do you have any questions for me about my experience, Mr. Heath?"

The man smiled at her. "I hope it won't offend you to learn that I've been looking into you all week, Miss Brindle. I've spoken to several of your previous teachers, and a— Miss Gidden, was it?—at the finishing school. And I'm quite satisfied that you are just the candidate we've been looking for in a teacher. The job is yours if you want it."

Charlotte tried not to let the flattery go to her head, but failed miserably. "That means a lot to me, Mr. Heath. Thank you."

Father fidgeted nervously. "When do you need a decision, Mr. Heath?"

"Well, if we can make this work, I would like to procure tickets for next Saturday's train."

Father's face turned a little paler. "That's very soon."

"I understand," returned Mr. Heath. "But it is nearing the end of summer, and leaving on Saturday would give Miss Brindle a couple weeks to settle in before the school year started."

"Thank you, Mr. Heath." Charlotte wanted to be candid with the man. "I have another offer from a local school I'm considering." She didn't add that the salary was considerably less by the month or mention the drawback of one Kent Covington also residing in Boston. "But I will let you know my answer within the next two days. Will that suffice?"

"Absolutely." Mr. Heath stood and stretched out his hand. "Miss Brindle, I believe that if you compare Wyldhaven, the little piece of New England blooming on the wild frontier, to any other town, you'll find it will be the far superior place to settle one day. And we hope you'll grace us with your excellent teaching skills."

Mr. Heath gathered up his cane, hat, and gloves, and James saw him to the door.

By the level of exhilaration coursing through her, Charlotte knew that she'd already made up her mind. Now all that remained was to convince Mother and Father. Well, Mother really, for Father would roll right around to seeing things her way with little need for theatrics. At least he would if one Mr. Covington wasn't involved.

She looked at him, pouring all the sincerity she was feeling into her next words. "I don't want to marry Mr. Covington, Father."

Father swallowed and fiddled with his cup on its saucer. "Yes. You've made that abundantly clear this past week."

She pressed her luck. "And how would you have felt if you hadn't wanted to marry Mother?"

He spun the cup again. "Truth is, I didn't want to marry her."

Charlotte gasped softly. She'd never heard that before!

Father clasped his hands between his knees and stared across the room at nothing in particular. "And truth is, I can't say we've been happier for our decision to follow our parents' wishes." He blinked and returned his focus to her. "So for my part, I'll not stop you."

Charlotte's heart lurched. Was he saying he hadn't been happy with Mother for all these years?

Father must have seen her questions in her expression, because he rushed on. "Don't get me wrong. Your mother and I have come to love one another. But that didn't make our early years any easier."

She couldn't deny her relief at that confession.

Perhaps one of the reasons Mother was lobbying so vehemently for Charlotte to accept Kent was due to the fact that he could provide for Charlotte in a way Father hadn't been able to in the early years of their marriage? Maybe Mother thought that would make Charlotte happier than she herself had been. But Charlotte was, as of last Tuesday morning, utterly certain she would never be happy were she to marry Kent.

So Father's consent gave her a thrill of joy. For his consent was certain guarantee that Mother's would follow. Charlotte almost squealed with excitement. She had set out to move, and the Lord had steered. She was going on an adventure!

But no more had she turned to look at Father, with the intent of thanking him for seeing things her way, than Mother stepped into the parlor followed by none other than Kent Covington himself.

Charlotte's elation gave way to sudden anger, with dread fast on its heels. The evening ahead was not going to be pleasant. But she must stick to her guns. Just the sight of Kent brought to mind the scene that had set her on this path in the first place and made a cold sweat break out on her palms.

Mother's face was still a little pale, but she forced a smile, and Charlotte could tell she was trying to act like her world had not just been turned upside down by her only daughter.

"Look who just stopped by, darling."

Charlotte stood and offered the expected curtsy. "Mr. Covington."

Kent strode to her side and took her hand, then raised it to his lips. "*Kent*, please. How many times do I have to tell you, hmmm?"

Charlotte extracted her fingers from his, willing her stomach not to pitch like a wind-tossed sea. It was the intimate look in Kent's eyes that firmed her decision in mortar. *Of all the deceitful...* She resumed her seat and indicated that he should do the same. “Actually, I’m glad you are here. I’ve something to tell you.”

Across the room, Mother gasped and then whimpered a little, but busied herself taking up her crocheting.

Kent bounced a frown between Mother and her but then returned his gaze to Mother. “Are you well, Mrs. Brindle?”

Mother pegged her with a dark look. “I have been better. However, I thank you for asking.”

Charlotte sighed and looked to her father for help, but he was standing with one elbow resting on the mantel, staring across the room while he absently stroked one finger across his mustache.

Naught for it but to press on then. Charlotte took a breath and willed Kent to hear the truth in her next words. “Kent—Mr. Covington—I’ve decided to take a teaching position...out west.”

He lurched to his feet. “You’ve what?!”

“Bertrand, you really have to do something!” Mother reached for the green bottle of smelling salts she kept on the table next to her chair.

Kent set to pacing before the settee, but Father was still in his own world somewhere.

Charlotte pressed on. “Yes. I was just speaking to the town’s founder. I leave on Saturday’s train.”

Kent tapped one finger to his lips as he paced. “Mr. and Mrs. Brindle? I wonder if I might have a word alone with Charlotte?”

Charlotte clenched her hands in trepidation, but she would get no rescue from her distraught parents, so she resigned herself to the coming confrontation. Perhaps it was best this way. She would tell him what she knew, and then he’d be forced to acknowledge the inevitability of her choice.

Mother thrust her crocheting back into her basket and stood. "Yes. Please do!" She swept to Father's side and took his arm. "Come, dear."

Mother and Father had no sooner closed the door to the parlor than Kent was down before her on one knee. "Charlie, I'm begging you...don't do this. Marry me?"

Charlotte eased a breath between her lips, working up her nerve. "I saw you."

Kent blinked. "Saw me? Whatever are you speaking of?"

"A week ago this morning."

"A week ago..." His face paled, and he lurched to his feet.

Charlotte nodded. "Yes. You had asked me to meet you for lunch, you'll remember. And I had turned you down. But then I decided, why not? Mother and Father have been set on our union, and I had prayed and prayed. They kept urging me to accept you, and I was tired of fighting that battle, I suppose. So I came to meet you." She relished the way he swiped one hand down his face in distress. "And I was going to tell you yes, that I would marry you." She swallowed and made a concerted effort to slow her breathing as her emotions ramped up. "However, I arrived a little late because on my way into town, we found Mrs. Douglas tottering along the middle of the street. Benedict stopped, and we gave her a lift to her daughter's brownstone over on Dearborn." Charlotte looked down, plucking at a small thread on one sleeve. Her mouth was so dry she could barely force the next words past her lips. "When I arrived you were just getting into your carriage, so I had Benedict follow you."

"Charlotte please." Kent's face was almost a perfect match for Mother's lace curtains now.

But she couldn't stop. She pressed ahead, needing to hear herself say the words. Needing Kent to hear her say the words. She gave a dry laugh. "Do you know...when you went down that alley, I was actually naïve enough to think there must be a little diner tucked back in there that you hadn't taken me to before. Despite the fact that he's not supposed to speak to me, Benedict tried to warn me. But not even he could find the words to tell me the only thing at the end of that alley was a *whorehouse*." Her voice rose as her anger increased.

"Charlie, please keep your voice down." Kent cast a furtive glance toward the parlor door as he breathed the request.

But Charlotte's fury was in full roil now, and she wasn't going to let him off so easily. "'Madame Dubois' was all the sign said, so I followed you inside."

"You what?" Kent took a stumbling little step to one side.

"And I'm astonished to confess that before I walked in the door, despite the lowly surroundings, I was still sure it must be an eating establishment I'd simply not heard of. I trusted you that much." Her whole body trembled.

Kent sank into one of the wingback chairs and cradled his face in his palms.

Charlotte nodded. Good, let him feel the horror of being caught. "I'm not surprised you didn't notice me considering you were already trailing that girl in the red—well, I suppose I could be generous and call it a dress. Anyhow, you were already following her up the stairs when I stepped inside. Considering where your eyes...were focused. Where your hands..." Her voice warbled to near uselessness, and she found she could no longer remain seated. She lurched to her feet and set to pacing. "Do you want to know the image that won't leave me?" She didn't wait for him to reply. "I keep remembering that woman's eyes. She looked back as you were nearing the top of the stairs, and the only emotion I saw on her face was dread." Her hands fisted at her sides. "And you would prefer a woman who *dreads* your touch to a woman who would have willingly given you all?"

"Charlie, I wouldn't—" He reached toward her, but she took a step back, shaking her head.

"Don't! I count it a mercy that I decided to follow you that day." She thrust her chin into the air. "I'll not marry you. I'm going out west. Honestly"—she threw up her hands—"I don't know what God wants of me anymore. But this will give me an opportunity to help some children who might otherwise not have a teacher this year."

Kent staggered to his feet and took her by the shoulders. His mustache twitched, a sure sign of his irritation, as he clasped her hand to his chest. She could feel his heart beating a tympani beneath her fingers. "Charlie, there's not a man alive who doesn't have his needs met by such a woman once in a while."

Charlotte's irritation flared. She yanked her hand from his grasp and slapped him. Hard. "Then there's not a man alive who I will ever consider marrying!" She stomped away, then spun to face him from across the room. Her palm had left a red mark across his cheek.

That felt good. Oh that she'd had the opportunity to do the same to Senator Sherman.

Shoulders slumped, Kent put his hands on his hips. "Setting that aside, you know what I'm offering you here. Just because you saw...what you saw doesn't mean it's not God's will. And I hope you know that money is not an obstacle to anything you might want to accomplish? Marry me, and then you can help all the poor western waifs that you want to! Just...*please*...don't throw away all that we've worked to build because you think you are going to find a man who will never stray a bit. Because it's simply not going to happen!"

Charlotte pivoted on one heel and thrust a finger toward the door. "Get out!" She willed him to just accept the situation and excuse himself. She was done with this conversation!

He started toward her, but she lifted one hand, and he stopped.

"Don't make this more difficult. I may not know exactly where God is taking me from here. But one thing I do know. God would not have me marry a man who does not have a relationship with Him."

"Charlie...you would accuse me of being a heathen?"

She lifted her chin. She would. But she was too emotionally charged at the moment to converse logically about it. So all she said was, "I've made up my mind, and it won't be changed."

"Charlie..." Kent raised his hands, palms out. "I'll be faithful once we've spoken our vows—I swear it. I'll even go to church with you every Sunday, if that's what you want. Just don't run off like this!"

She pinned him with a look that she hoped conveyed her disbelief in his promise. How gullible did the man think her to be? "Please leave."

His posture sagged. "Charlie..." But apparently he'd run out of arguments, because he offered nothing more. He paced to the fireplace and took up a position much like Father had just abandoned a few moments ago, elbow on the mantel and fingers absently twirling his mustache as he stared into vacancy.

After a long stretch of silence, he focused on her. "All right. I'll let you go. But as fervently as you vow that you don't love me, I vow that I *do* love you."

Charlotte narrowed her eyes. *Just not enough to be faithful, apparently.*

"I won't give up on us, Charlie. I won't." He fumbled in his coat pocket for the pencil and notebook he always carried there in case he should come across a news story for the paper. "I'm going to write to you every week, so give me your forwarding address."

"I've decided not to let you write to me."

He winced.

Charlotte folded her hands together, unable to feel bad about her decision. She didn't care that it must feel like cruelty to him.

"Charlotte, don't do this. Please, I'm begging you." The sheen of moisture in his eyes brought the first prick of regret, but she stamped it out before it could bloom. He'd brought this on himself.

She lifted her chin and smoothed her hands over her skirt's front. "I'm sorry, but I really feel a clean break will be the best."

She hadn't thought he could appear any more dejected than he already did, but she'd been wrong. As he stuffed the notebook and pencil back into his pocket and dragged his feet from the room without saying another word, she felt a little pity for him. But the pity was far outweighed by the relief coursing through her.

She closed her eyes and inhaled slowly, savoring the moment. She had no doubt that someday Kent would find a woman who would be swayed enough by his money to turn a blind eye to his wandering. She was only glad that woman didn't have to be her.

Chapter Three

Wyldhaven, Washington

Liora Fontaine curled onto her side on her bed and drew her knees to her chest. Across the room, her broken triangle of a mirror angled in just such a way that she could see her face. She closed her eyes against the loathing expression reflected back to her.

For today, it was done. The night was over. At least Ewan McGinty didn't make her serve clientele past closing.

Would there ever come a day when she didn't hate herself at the end of a shift? When she could look in the mirror and be proud of what she saw? Or if not pride, at least feel something north of repugnance?

Girl, why can't you ever amount to anything? She remembered the words as clearly as if they had been spoken to her only moments ago. They had been accompanied by a backhanded blow that had cracked across the side of her head, jarring her eardrum with ringing.

She flinched. She could still to this day feel the sharp slice of pain as her ear split open. She reached up slowly and fingered the scar hidden by the swoop of hair. She remembered the words. She remembered the blow. She remembered the blood that had gushed down the side of her neck and across her shoulder. But she never could seem to remember what her infraction had been that particular day.

With a grunt, she rolled to her back and stared at the ceiling, still hugging her knees.

Trash, that's what you are. Nothing but trash. I curse the day you came squalling into the world!

Tears seeped from the corners of her eyes.

And here she was proving him right, yet again. Just like she had every single day of her life. If only that job at the restaurant in Seattle had worked out. But when the bank had been robbed two weeks back, she'd known bad luck had caught up with her again. And sure enough, Mrs. Pendergast hadn't been able to pay her for the month of work she'd already done. The final kick had come when she'd called Liora to her office to say she'd lost near everything in that robbery and had to let Liora go.

How was it the man could afflict her, even without knowing he was doing so? It was the way of life. At least where Liora's seemed concerned. Nothing ever went right.

At least this way she'd be able to get Ma back on her medicine as soon as she got her first paycheck.

She tugged the blankets to her and curled them around her head.

She had a whole twelve hours before she would be expected downstairs again, and she planned to spend them in the oblivion of sleep.

Charlotte had forced herself to wait a full day before penning her acceptance letter to Mr. Heath. Her hand had trembled to the point of near uselessness as she'd written it, but written it she had.

After Senator Sherman had betrayed her, she'd been nearly overcome by despair for months. But not this time. Because she'd learned the futility of despair. Come to realize that despair was naught but a lack of trust in God. This time she would shake it off, and she wouldn't think about it. She would put all her efforts into teaching the children of Wyldhaven. That was one way God could bring good out of this.

So for the next week she immersed herself in a flurry of activity. Much to Mother's horror, she disenrolled from the finishing school and let Miss Gidden know she wouldn't be returning. Mother recovered from her pique in record time and insisted on taking her in to buy several new dresses, which meant fittings and the choosing of accessories, and more fittings after the first adjustments had been made.

All week she added to her list of school supplies that Father had promised he would ship to her, since she wouldn't be able to take them on the train. For despite Mr. Heath's assurances that all supplies would be provided, she found her excitement couldn't be quenched without the purchase of at least a few luxuries for her future classroom. A phonograph and several waxed cylinder records. A brand-new stereoscope and a set of slides that she would use in her history classes. Another set of slides to bring geography to life. Besides those, there were books, some artwork for the classroom walls, and several sets of flash cards for different subjects.

There was a bevy of good-bye luncheons and teas that Mother insisted on putting together.

And in between it all, Charlotte put up with Mother, who fussed and wheedled and cajoled in an attempt to change Charlotte's mind about leaving. Thankfully, Father seemed to have resigned himself to her departure, and several times he gave Mother a sharp rebuff that tempered her pestering. Otherwise, Charlotte felt sure she would have gone raving mad before the day of her departure arrived.

Now as they stood on the train platform, Mother had turned her fretting in another direction. "Do you think you have enough dresses, dear?"

Charlotte hoped her smile didn't appear too thin. "Rose packed both trunks to the gills. I'm certain I'll have enough."

In the distance the train whistled, and Charlotte wanted to jump up and down in relief.

Father pulled his billfold from his back pocket and extracted several large bills. "I want you to take this, Charlie. You never know when you might run into an emergency."

Charlotte accepted the bills and kissed his cheek. "Thank you, Father. I'll be fine. Don't worry about me." She folded the money and stuffed it into the bottom of her reticule.

"I know you will, darling." He bussed her cheek. "Your mother and I are just going to miss you, is all."

Mother sniffed and dabbed at her eyes, and Charlotte drew her into a hug as the train chuffed into the station. "I'll write to you every week. I promise!"

Mother squeezed her tight. "See that you do! And don't hesitate to come back home if you change your mind. I think Father and I may have pushed Mr. Covington on you overmuch. We promise not to do that again. We only want what's best for you."

Charlotte's heart softened. Perhaps telling her parents what she'd seen, which she had done the moment Kent had stormed from the house last week, had been the right thing after all. "I know you do."

All around them, passengers bustled off the train and streamed past them into the station.

Mother put her at arm's length. "Are you *sure* this is what is best for you right now, Charlie?"

Charlotte almost smiled at her mother's use of the childhood nickname she'd insisted Charlotte was too old for now. "I'm very certain, Mother. And I promise to come home if things get to be too much for me."

"It's just...it's the *Wild West.*"

Charlotte swallowed and wished Mother would quit talking like this might be the last time this side of heaven that they saw one another. She squeezed Mother's hand. "You've seen the pictures of Wyldhaven. It's a most civilized place with lots of amenities. I'm going to be just fine!"

Mother sniffed and dabbed her eyes, giving a nod. "I'm sure you will. The Lord will watch over you." Her face crumpled, and her words pitched into the high squeal she got when she was doing her best not to cry. "He'll have to because your father and I won't be there to do it!"

Father folded his arms and scuffed one toe against the platform, blinking hard.

"All aboard!" the conductor called in a loud voice.

Charlotte glanced around to see where the entry to the car was, and that was when her gaze collided with Kent's. He stood just down the way, his hands thrust into the pockets of his slacks. He looked like a little boy who had just lost a puppy.

Charlotte's lips pressed into a thin line, but she couldn't be so rude as to ignore him altogether. She lifted a hand of farewell toward him. He returned the gesture, and she was thankful to see that it didn't look like he planned to come any closer. She would pray for him. The thought surprised her. Only a week ago she might have gladly confronted him with a knife if one had been available to her. But...she eased out a breath. He was obviously a man in need of true repentance.

She returned her focus to her parents and reassured, "Yes, the Lord will watch over me." Charlotte pulled first her father and then her mother into another hug.

Mother clung to her tightly, and Charlotte had just begun to fear she would never be released when Father took Mother's elbow and gave it a tug. "Come, Etta. Let's get Charlie aboard before she's left without a window seat. I know she's going to want to watch the countryside pass by."

As Mother reluctantly let her go, Charlotte gave him a grateful smile. He knew her so well.

She blew a final kiss to Mother, tightly squeezed Father one last time, and then she was inside the car and settling into a window seat about midway down. Relief at being free of Kent Covington coursed through her. The relief was quickly followed by the emotion she'd been keeping carefully tucked away for the past two weeks since she'd caught him in the bawdy house. What was so wrong with her that both men who had shown an interest in marrying her couldn't seem to stay away from other women?

The train started forward, and her hands trembled as she waved good-bye to Mother and Father, who still stood on the platform. When they were out of sight, she curled her fingers into fists to stop the trembling. *Deep breath in. Ease it out.* If she wasn't careful, she was going to work herself into a full-blown breathing attack. And wouldn't that be something were she to die before the train even crossed the state line?

Forcing herself to relax, she pulled out the brochure for Wyldhaven and smoothed it open on her lap, carefully studying the pictures of the little town.

A little piece of New England blooming on the wild frontier. There was absolutely nothing to be anxious about. What a grand adventure this was going to be!

Reagan Callahan strode down the street toward Dixie's

Boardinghouse. His day had started out with a trip to the logging camp to collect statements about a fight that had taken place between two crewmen the evening before. He had yet to put a morsel of food into his stomach, and just the thought of a hot bowl of Dixie's beef stew had his mouth watering.

Behind him and across the street, a door banged open. "Sheriff?"

He squelched a groan, giving Dixie's a longing look before turning to see what Ben King wanted this time. "Yeah?"

Ben held up a telegram. "Got something you will want to see."

"Can it wait till after I eat lunch?"

Ben's head tilted. "It's a telegram from Lionel Schantz, sheriff down in Ellensburg."

Reagan grunted. Ellensburg was a city a few days southeast of Wyldhaven. And what with all the doings last week... Reluctantly, he changed direction and crossed the road to meet Ben. He took the telegram from his fingers with a sigh that didn't do much to disguise the grumbling of his stomach.

Ben's gaze dropped to his midsection, and his lips quirked. "Sorry, man."

Reported to me P. Waddell may be on Wyldhaven stage.

Reagan's pulse spiked. He pinned Ben with a look. "You get anything other than this?"

Ben shook his head. "Nothing."

Reagan scrubbed a hand over his jaw. Ellensburg was two days from here. The stage would stop for the night in Cle Elum. But Cle Elum didn't currently have a lawman. So that left only Shantz and himself. "Wonder if that sheriff would go after him? You know anything about Schantz?"

Again, a shake of Ben's head. "Not much. Never met him.

Only hearsay here and there. But from what I've heard, as long as the trouble is leaving his city, he's not going to stir the pot. Especially in this case where it sounds like someone came to him afterward and reported they saw a man who might be Waddell getting on the stage. It could be anyone."

Reagan rubbed his jaw. That was likely true enough. Still... He glanced toward McGinty's Alehouse. This could be an opportunity to round up the rest of the Waddell gang, if they played their cards right. If it really was Patrick Waddell on that stage, then so much the better. They would get the whole gang. But if it wasn't him, a trail of honey could still be squeezed out to attract the rest of the crew.

With a sigh of resignation, Reagan tucked the telegram into his shirt pocket and clapped Ben on one shoulder. "I guess today I'm giving up a bowl of Dixie's stew in favor of a plate of Ewan's greasy chili."

Ben's face scrunched into a sympathetic twist. "Sorry."

Reagan grinned. "Comes with the job, Ben. Sacrifices."

Ben chuckled and headed back into the post office while Reagan went in search of his deputy, Joseph Rodante. A plan was coming into place, but he'd need some help to pull it off.

Most of Wyldhaven's residents were honest, upstanding citizens, and Reagan Callahan couldn't complain any about the many quiet days he had on his job. But for the entire week he hadn't been able to shake the feeling that Lenny Smith might have ties to Waddell's gang. And so it was that twenty minutes later, after a brief powwow with Joe, Reagan found himself in McGinty's Alehouse settling onto the barstool next to Lenny.

"Evening," he said.

"Sheriff." Lenny gave him a nod before shifting his gaze away and lifting his glass with an unsteady hand.

Reagan tapped the bar with two fingers as though drumming the bass line to the bawdy-house song Liora Fontaine was banging out on the tinny piano in the corner. Liora pursed her ruby-red lips at him and raised her blond brows seductively. He looked away as though he hadn't noticed. Nothing but trouble there. He'd been careful to maintain a strictly polite but distant relationship with her since she'd come to work for Ewan two weeks ago, but Liora was nothing if not persistent.

Ewan stepped over and wiped the counter in front of him. "Sheriff. What can I get you?"

"I'll take a bowl of your chili."

Ewan's mustache lifted into a near straight line. That was as much of a smile as anyone ever saw on Ewan. "Good and fresh this time. I only made it three days ago. Coming right up."

Reagan thanked the Lord Almighty that he hadn't gotten that telegram a day later. He'd always thought if he died in the line of duty, it would be from a bullet, not from a meal in a questionable eating establishment. A moment later when Ewan placed the steaming bowl in front of him, he offered what he hoped passed as a smile of thanks and not a grimace of dread.

Beside him, Lenny studied him with a curious furrow in his brow. "Don't you normally eat down to Dixie's, Sheriff?"

Reagan picked up the spoon Ewan had dropped on the bar by his bowl and chipped off some crusted remnants. He slanted Lenny a look. "Always good to mix things up once in a while, don't you think?"

Lenny's brows nudged toward his hairline. "There's mixing things up, and then there's suicide."

Reagan chuckled and wished Lenny's attempt at a joke didn't cut so close to his own feelings on the matter. He gingerly sampled a bite of the red beans and coughed. "Well, Ewan puts enough red pepper in his chili to kill anything that might make a man sick, I suppose."

Lenny slurped his beer. "True 'nough."

"And you seem to have survived."

Lenny smirked. "I never eat here. Only drink." He lifted his mug in a sloppy salute.

At that moment, Deputy Joseph Rodante burst through the batwing doors, calling, "Boss! Boss! You gotta come quick. It's Patrick Waddell!"

Reagan thanked the good Lord for the timing. Hungry as he was, he didn't think he'd have been able to choke down another bite of Ewan's concoction. That stuff was hotter than Satan's breath. He leapt off his stool and pretended to shush his deputy even as he noticed the jolt that shot straight up Lenny's spine.

Liora left the piano and wrapped both hands around Joe's upper arm, leaning in to smile coyly.

Joe's face turned crimson. He swallowed and fixed his focus back on Reagan. "Boss!" Joe stage-whispered just like they'd practiced. "Somebody saw him, and he's supposedly going to be arriving in town on tomorrow's stage!"

Reagan was proud of the kid for staying on task. "That's enough, Joe! I said quiet now. If we aim to catch this rattler, we have to keep our wits about us! Liora, if you'll excuse us..." He rushed Joe out the door, and they hurried to the alley.

Joe rubbed at his arm as though trying to dismiss the feel of the woman who'd just been clinging to him. "Think it'll work?"

"It will if he's the man I think he is," Reagan replied, peering carefully around the barrel he'd squatted behind. The road in front of the saloon still lay empty.

"And if Liora doesn't turn her charms on Lenny next."

Reagan smirked. The kid sounded a trifle jealous. For one long minute, he feared they'd overplayed their hand, but Lenny Smith didn't disappoint him—well, other than to prove that he was the outlaw Reagan had suspected him of being—and a moment later he bustled out of the alehouse, looked both ways, and hurried down the street.

Reagan batted Joe with the back of his hand. "Don't lose him. I'll meet you at my ma's place at midnight."

"You got it, Boss."

"And Joe?" Reagan waited till he had the younger man's full attention. "Don't try to be a hero. Tomorrow's soon enough to capture these buzzards."

"Understood." With that, Joe disappeared around the back side of the saloon. Reagan knew he would run down Second Street and pick up Lenny's trail on the other side of the river.

Wherever the outlaws were camped out, it was certain Lenny was going to let them know that their chance at revenge was arriving on tomorrow's afternoon stage.

Reagan stepped out of the alley and rubbed his hands in satisfaction. Not only could he finally head to Dixie's to get a decent meal, but by this time tomorrow he might have the entire Waddell gang locked up in his jail.

That made for a good day, in his book.

Chapter Four

Charlotte stepped out of the coach house and set her traveling bag by her feet. She hoped her trunks were still attached to the stage. The driver had assured her the evening before that they would be fine, but the farther she got from civilized society, the harder it was for her to let her things out of her sight each night.

This town of Cle Elum was so uncivil that a man had asked for her hand in marriage before she'd even reached the coach house the evening before! She shuddered at the memory of his roving gaze. Thankfully, he'd been good natured about her curt refusal.

At least, according to the coachman, this was the last town she would need to stay in before she arrived at Wyldhaven this evening. She couldn't help but be thankful that Mr. Heath's brochure showed he had founded a civilized and respectable town as opposed to those she'd been forced to stay in for the past week on her travels west. Why, the boardwalk beneath her feet was cracked in so many places she practically had to search out where to place each step.

She arched her back and pressed her hands into the ache. Even the beds in the train cabin she'd used for the first several days of the journey had been preferable to the lumpy mattress she had slept on the evening before.

A breeze wafted to her from the open plains on the far side

of town, and she crinkled her nose. *Cattle.* Yet another thing to be thankful for about her destination. She doubted logging would be quite as odiferous as the cattle business seemed to be.

Down the street, it appeared that not too far in the past a fire had taken out several buildings. One was still boarded up. And construction had begun on two others. Two muddy little boys darted by, rolling a wagon wheel before them. Charlotte's heart churned. It was a Thursday morning. Shouldn't those two little ones be in school? A smithy's hammer banged from the building on the corner across the street, and that was where the two boys stopped. At their call, the smithy came out and set to examining the wheel. Would those two boys be attending a school this year? Did they even have a school in this town?

She searched the street but didn't see one.

The coach was coming her way, however. And she supposed that bringing education to the waifs of Cle Elum was not her job. As she picked up her bag, she made a mental note to make sure she personally invited every Wyldhaven family with children to attend her school. There were too many families these days who didn't see the value in education. It would fall to her to change that way of thinking. Yet one could hope that in a civilized town like Wyldhaven purported to be, there wouldn't be a need for such convincing.

An older man in top hat, who had also been on the stage from Ellensburg with her yesterday, stopped beside her, a scantily clad woman clinging to his arm.

"Now, Mr. Waddell, don't you be forgetting me, all right?"

"Trust me, Wanda. A man doesn't easily forget a night like last night."

Charlotte felt her face heat in shock, even as the woman tittered seductively.

But there was something false in the sound of it that made Charlotte look their way.

The woman swirled her finger down the older man's chest and leaned closer to him to whisper, "Neither does a lady."

Above his shoulder, Charlotte caught a glimpse of the woman's face. It was flat and expressionless until she pulled away from him far enough that he could see her, and then a pretentious smile bloomed.

Charlotte swallowed and concentrated on tugging her traveling gloves more firmly into place. Why would a woman give herself to such a life if she hated it as much as evidenced by Charlotte's glimpse of the woman's true emotions?

Another memory flashed into her mind. The image of the woman Kent had been prodding up the stairs that fateful day in Boston. The expression that had flashed across that woman's face just before they disappeared at the top of the stairs was clearly one of aversion. Much as she wanted to revile such women and name them home wreckers, dream crushers, life stealers, she couldn't help but have a touch of sympathetic curiosity about what would make a woman fall so far as to give up everything, even her own body and personal happiness, just for a bit of money.

The coach pulled to a stop before them, and Charlotte was glad to see that her trunks were indeed still strapped to the top. The older man left his companion behind and held out a hand to help Charlotte climb the coach steps. Reluctantly, Charlotte accepted his assistance, but she withdrew her hand from his the first moment she possibly could, for his touch sent a shiver of revulsion through her. The man probably had an unsuspecting, faithful wife waiting for him back home!

Would that have been how her life turned out? If she hadn't followed Kent into the city that day? If she had gone ahead and married him? Would it have been her destiny to sit at home and wait for him to return? Her lot to ignore the scent of another woman on his clothes when he arrived? Her portion to make excuses for him to her children?

How had she allowed herself to be so severely deceived by the man?

Mr. Waddell settled onto the seat across from her and laid his hat and gloves on the bench beside him. His gaze slipped over her.

Charlotte felt her eyes widen in outrage. The man was three times her age if he was a day! And he'd just left a woman of the night standing at the stage stop! Charlotte gritted her teeth. She was to be stuck with him in this stage for how long?

Chuckling, the man tilted his head into the corner of the coach and closed his eyes, seemingly unaffected by her disdain.

Charlotte eased out a tremulous breath. The fiend!

Was immorality taken so lightly in the West? Why, even Kent, when she'd confronted him, had asked her to keep her voice down. But this man, it seemed, didn't care a whit that his indiscretions had been noted.

Oh, she needed a distraction. She dug through her reticule for her book. The day was long, and the roads grew rougher the farther they went. When they stopped for lunch, Charlotte's eyes widened at the sight of the road they'd been traveling. The path couldn't really be called a road at all. It was more like a stretch of ruts that had been cleared of timber.

The stage driver plunked a basket down on the ground and laid out a soiled cloth. "Have a seat." He handed each of his two passengers a hard-boiled egg and a tomato. There was some sort of meat in the basket, but Charlotte doubted she would have the courage to try it.

She frowned at the scanty meal cupped in each palm. There

didn't seem to be a place to sit that wouldn't muddy her dress, so she chose to remain standing.

She bit into her tomato and scanned the forest around them. Other than the sounds of the two men rather noisily consuming their own provisions, everything was silent. Would there really be a lovely little piece of New England at the end of this journey? A town with cobblestone streets and stone cottages? One with streetlamps and flowerpots abloom with color on each corner? She had to admit that if she hadn't seen the depictions on the brochure with her own eyes she would be in serious doubt about her destination right now. Everything out in these parts seemed so rough, and rugged, and unattractive.

All too soon the coachman urged them back to the carriage. Thankfully, Mr. Waddell seemed to have finally registered her pique and taken it to heart, for he'd hardly given her a second glance all day. Charlotte's other consolation was that this was her last day of the trip. Tonight she would sleep in a comfortable bed in what would be her own cottage, at least for the duration of the school year.

As the afternoon wore on, the road grew even worse, if that was possible. Charlotte massaged her fingers into the aching muscles of her jaw. She realized it had been clenched for most of the day. As much as they'd been jostling she might lose a tooth before arriving in what was promised to be an idyllic replica of New England.

The coachman thumped on the roof of the carriage. "Wyldhaven just over the next ridge!"

A sigh of relief slipped free. Even the man across from her seemed to relax slightly at the call.

Whap! A gash tore through the carriage's sidewall. A gaping, splintered hole exploded through the roof. Half a moment later, the loud reverberations of a gunshot rent the air!

"Whoa!" the driver yelled.

Before the coach even came to a full stop, Charlotte had cowered against the floor and curled her arms around her head. Across from her the older man had also lunged to the floor. He yanked the cushion off his seat, folded it in half, and then pinned it with his carpetbag to the side of the carriage, where the bullets seemed to be emanating from. He curled his body into as tight of a ball as he could behind the flimsy barrier.

Charlotte scrambled to follow his example.

For a moment they lay in silence, the only sounds cutting through the stillness, the sharp puffs of their breaths.

Then the *zing* of another bullet shot above the coach.

Charlotte flinched, though she already lay coiled so tightly it could hardly have been counted as a movement at all.

Her reticule, pinned beneath her cheek, rustled, and she was reminded of the brochure it contained.

Charlotte would have snorted if the unladylike propensity hadn't been so thoroughly expunged from her at finishing school. If this welcoming committee was standard fair for Mr. Heath's town, she would be on the first wagon bound in an eastward direction this very afternoon!

Except... Disappointment curled through her. Was she to be a failure not only at finding a man who could remain faithful, but at making her own way in the world also? Retreat might sound heavenly right about now, but it would prove true Mother and Father's concern that she might not be cut out for life in the "Wild West." Going back would also mean dealing with Kent, and she'd almost rather face this hail of bullets than face him.

Still, if this was what life in the West was like on a daily basis, she just might have to swallow her pride and crawl back home with her tail between her legs. Providing she lived that long.

The report of another shot made her stomach pitch.

The coach jostled, and she heard a soft thud on the back side of the carriage, then footsteps darting away and the crash of underbrush.

Perfect. The coachman had just abandoned them!

Hadn't one of the positions Mr. Heath so proudly proclaimed he'd already filled in Wyldhaven been that of sheriff?

Where's your sheriff now, Mr. Heath? She was certainly going to have a few complaints to lodge with the sheriff about the way citizens were welcomed to the town he was employed to keep safe!

If he was like any of the men in her life lately, he was probably entertaining himself with some bawdy house woman right about now. Charlotte pressed her lips together. The bitter thought didn't make her like herself all that much. That wasn't the kind of person she wanted to be, always suspicious and suspecting people of doing wrong. After all, there were good men in the world. Father was a prime example of that.

Still... She couldn't deny that having just one of those good men show up right about now wouldn't hurt her feelings any.

She angled her gaze up to the bullet hole torn in the sidewall of the stagecoach just above her head. Wouldn't Miss Gidden be aghast to see her now, sprawled on the floor of the stagecoach in such an unladylike fashion, and with her skirts all a mess from dust and dirt, and her hat likely askew. Yet somehow acting the lady had been the furthest thing from her mind when the bullets had started flying!

From outside a deep, gravelly voice called, "We know you're in there, Waddell. Why don't you come on down and face us like a real man would?"

Charlotte's gaze darted across the interior of the coach to her fellow passenger. The older man's top hat had fallen between them. One of his gloves remained on the bench behind him. The other had somehow become draped over his shoulder, as though a malnourished ghoul clutched at him from beyond the grave. And his shock of white hair stood from the peak of his rather pointy head like the comb of a rooster.

He met her look and pressed one finger to his thickly whiskered lips.

Charlotte nearly rolled her eyes. As if she planned on calling out.

He inched closer to the side of the carriage, lifting his head above his makeshift barrier for the first time since the ordeal had begun. He pressed one bloodshot eye to a bullet hole, peering into the field next to the road. He looked first in one direction, then craned around to study a different angle.

Charlotte couldn't help but contemplate that the man had to be slightly crazy. Because she felt certain that any movement the men outside might witness would draw another hail of bullets.

Unless... Surely they wouldn't shoot at a woman? And it was obvious their disgruntlement wasn't with her, because they were calling Mr. Waddell's name.

Another bullet whined overhead.

Charlotte cringed and thought fondly of the litter-laden streets of the commercial district back home where she could be, even now, preparing her lessons without so much as a whiff of gunpowder in the air.

Well, this was certainly a fine mess she'd found herself in! But it was no more than Mother had direly warned her about in the last days before her departure. For when Mother had noted that her warnings about wild Indians had taken no effect, she'd changed tactics and started talking about all the outlaw gangs she'd heard about over the years. Charlotte had dismissed the stories out of hand. Those were the types of things that happened in uncivilized towns, not towns like the one Mr. Heath had promised his to be.

Charlotte gritted her teeth. She hated the thought of admitting that Mother had been right. But she hated even more the thought that she'd traveled all this way only to die on the threshold of her destination. She was thirsty! And tired! And she hadn't traveled thousands of miles squashed between ill-groomed and ill-mannered men to be killed in a volley of lead only moments before she might experience the joy of a hot bath once more. Wyldhaven was just over the next rise, and she meant to get there.

She needed to set her mind to coming up with a plan. She had students to teach, and hot baths to take, and drat if her temper wasn't starting to get the best of her!

Her mind went once more to Mr. Heath's promises. Stone cottages and picket-fenced yards, a new millinery shop and students eager to learn. All these things he had averred. Not one word had been said about the potential drawbacks of Wyldhaven's welcoming committee!

What should she do? She couldn't think with her mouth so parched! What she wouldn't give for a good cup of tea right about now.

That did it. "Don't shoot!" she called.

Across the coach, Mr. Waddell jolted so high off the floor one might have thought she'd jabbed him with a hatpin.

Charlotte ignored him and fought her skirts until she could gain her feet. "I'm coming out! I'm the new schoolteacher for Wyldhaven, and if you shoot me, you're going to have to deal with Mr. Zebulon Heath himself." She prayed these hooligans didn't know that man would still be back east for several weeks yet.

Heart pounding in her throat, she cringed and waited for a bullet to end her thirst, but all around hung nothing but silence. Slowly, she eased open the door of the stagecoach and thrust her empty hands into the breezy August air, then carefully peered outside.

"I'm coming down now, and I'll thank you not to put any holes in my brand-new day dress, gentlemen."

She threw in that last word as an afterthought. *Gentlemen indeed.* There was nothing gentlemanly about this lot, and that was of a certainty.

From his prone position behind the log just inside the forest, Reagan Callahan almost cursed. This was a complication he hadn't seen coming! He could hear the brush all around him rustling and knew the men of his posse were all probably wondering what to do now, as well.

Blast it! Why hadn't Zeb wired ahead that the teacher was coming? As far as he knew, no one in town even knew Zeb had hired a teacher!

But there she was, big as life. Well...not so big—a tiny little thing with the craziest feather contraption atop her head that he'd ever seen. And she was standing right smack in the center of a feud betwixt members of the most dangerous outlaw gang in this area.

Everything they'd planned had been rolling along just as smooth as butter until that schoolmarm had stepped off the stage a second ago. She was bound to be taken hostage by one side or the other if she didn't get herself out of there and right quick.

As though the very thought had conjured the action, Waddell leapt from the coach and wrapped one arm around the schoolmarm's neck. So he *had* been aboard.

The lady squeaked rather loudly, but Reagan would give her points for not falling all to pieces like he'd halfway suspected a woman of her obvious station and privilege might have.

Reagan clenched his fist.

Using her as a shield, Waddell pressed the muzzle of his six-shooter to her temple. "You all just listen up real good now." Waddell's eyes darted around wildly. "I'm going to climb on the back of one of the stage horses, and I'm going to ride on out of here, nice and peaceful like. I'm not going to hold it against you, Horace, that you rounded up the boys and brought them here to bushwhack me—especially on account of my double-crossing you like I did. But lest you want this here pretty slip of a gal to be left along the trail one piece at a time, I suggest you all back off and just let me go on about my business."

"Aw, blazes, Waddell. We just want our money back! Whyn't you let that teacher lady go and just split the money with us fair and square? Then we can all go our separate ways with none o' us holdin' no grudges 'ginst t'other."

The schoolteacher nodded rather vigorously for having a pistol pressed to her head, feathers swaying. "Yes, I think the man has a very reasonable solution to this whole misunderstanding!" Her voice was amazingly calm, despite the agitation revealed by her movements.

"Just one problem, boys." Waddell slapped a feather out of his face and dragged the lady toward the horses.

Don Brass, the stage driver who had plunged off the seat and disappeared into the brush a moment ago, now peered out from behind a tree on the other side of the gully, rifle in hand.

Reagan would have admired the man if he wasn't so concerned about the safety of his own men.

Beside him, Joe shuffled in the brush. "He starts shooting, and one of us is likely to get hit."

Reagan nodded. "My thoughts exactly."

"Should I brush him back a bit?" Joe held up his rifle.

Reagan shook his head. "Taking a shot will let them know we're here. We're just going to have to take our chances. Don's a smart man. I don't think he'll make a move unless he has a clean shot."

Waddell tightened his grip around the teacher's neck, carefully keeping her positioned between himself and his former crew. He lowered the gun for just a moment to snatch a knife from the top of one of his boots.

Joe motioned that they should run down the hill and save the teacher. "Right now while Waddell's attention is divided!"

But Reagan held up a hand to still him. Joe's biggest weakness, which would abate with experience, was that he tended to rush headlong into things without thinking them through first. There was too big a risk of the woman getting hit by a stray bullet from either side if they all ran in, guns blazing, right now.

If only he'd had more time to react after she stepped off the stage. Now the only solution would be to wait till Waddell and his crew split up, and try to rescue her from Waddell once he and the lady were alone.

Waddell freed the closest horse from its traces with a quick slice of his knife and put the animal between himself and his former crew, then threw the schoolteacher across its back.

Waddell peered beneath the large roan's neck. "I mean it now, Horace. You all stay back. I don't have the money anymore anyhow. I gave it to my daughter on account of her daughter who's ailing something fierce and needs a surgery at the hospital down Seattle way."

Reagan frowned. Waddell didn't have a daughter!

Carefully keeping the horse between himself and the disgruntled outlaws in the field next to the coach, Waddell led the animal back into the brush.

"You ain't got no daughter!" Horace called after him.

But there was no reply.

"Go!" Reagan whispered as he motioned for Joe and the posse to move on down the hill and capture the three men who still remained in the field. "I'll get the teacher." Interestingly enough, even though Lenny had led Joe to the gang's hideout and from there they had trailed the men here, Lenny hadn't shown up for today's confrontation. Lenny might be smarter than Reagan had given him credit for. What better way to take over the gang than to send most of the key leaders into what he knew was going to be a trap?

As Reagan leapt onto his mustang, rifle in hand, and spurred it toward the ridge where he would soon hopefully be able to see Waddell and the teacher below him, he heard one of the men in the field whine.

"We oughta've just shot the teacher and taken away his shield."

Horace cussed him good and sound. "You know what they do to women killers 'round these here parts?"

"Can't be much worse'n what they do to bank robbers."

"Speaking of which..." The sound of several Winchesters cocking accompanied Joe's dry words.

That was followed by lots of cussing from the outlaws, and Reagan knew that Joe and the men had done their jobs. At least something had gone right tonight.

Now if he could just keep Mr. Heath's newly hired teacher from getting her hide filled with lead.

Chapter Five

Charlotte wanted to cry, but really there would be no profit in it at the moment, hanging practically upside down as she was, draped over the horse. The ground sped by at a stomach-sickening pace and much too close to her face, thank you very much! Besides, much of her effort at the moment needed to go simply toward breathing, since the ridge of the horse's back kept ramming all the air from her lungs. She only hoped her lungs wouldn't take this moment to seize up altogether, like they were wont to do occasionally. That would be yet another of Mother's dire predictions coming true.

Somewhere a ways back, a bush had stolen her hat, and now her hair hung like a brown curtain in front of her face no matter which way she turned her head. She couldn't use her hands to move it out of the way because she was too busy using those to hang on to whatever part of the horse or Mr. Waddell's boot she could grab or prop her hands against. One moment she propped them against foreleg or boot to keep from falling, and the next she grabbed mane and lifted herself up a bit to aide in breathing, and she was never quite sure which need was going to necessitate the most urgent action moment by moment.

"You are a horrible—*oooff!*—fiend, Mr. Waddell!"

Waddell slapped the reins against the horse's flank, urging

the poor beast to go faster. "That isn't the first time I've been told so. Now shut up so I can think."

"If my silence is going to aid in your escape, then"—she paused to readjust her balance—"you had better believe that I'll do just as much talking as I possibly can!" She spat out a hank of hair that had jostled into her mouth on that last word and tried to think of something else to say. "So do you have a wife?"

"A what!?" Waddell pulled the horse to a stop for a moment and turned them in a circle as though assessing their location. "No, I definitely don't have a wife. Why?" He chuckled maniacally and urged the horse forward again. "Are you volunteering for the position?"

"Of all the—most certainly not!" Charlotte propped her hands against the rippling brown of the horse's foreleg and tried to catch a full breath, to no avail. "I was only asking to make conversation. So what did you think of the statehood?"

"Lady! Be quiet!"

"It's just that Washington became a state just a couple years ago, and I wondered what a man such as yourself thought of it because—"

"Lady!" Waddell jerked the horse to a stop once more. But this time he grabbed a handful of her hair and wrenched her neck back. He stripped one of his gloves from his hand with his teeth. "I don't want to hurt you, but I said"—he crammed the glove into her mouth—"I needed silence." He released her and urged the horse forward again.

Charlotte tried to spit the glove out, but it was too large to budge. She felt a nip of panic begin to set in as the need for more oxygen tightened her chest. She put all her concentration into breathing and hanging on.

How was she to have known the man was so dishonorable?

Despite what she'd seen of him in Cle Elum, and despite the lingering look he'd given her when he climbed aboard, he'd seemed at least close to a gentleman when they'd been in the coach together. He with his top hat and coattails, and she attempting to read the perfectly tragic tale from Mr. James Fenimore Cooper about *The Last of the Mohicans* between jars and jostles. And then he'd held a gun on her! A real gun! And stuffed her mouth full of sweaty leather!

She probably should have been quiet when he asked her to. The edges of her world started to turn black, and Charlotte wasn't at all certain it had to do with lack of oxygen this time.

"Ma! Didja hear?" Twelve-year-old Zoe Kastain slammed open the door and practically stumbled across the kitchen threshold of their cabin in her excitement to share the news she'd just heard in town.

At the sideboard where she stood chopping potatoes, Ma jolted at the loud interruption. She turned a look of exasperation on Zoe. "Child! I do declare! How many times have I told you that ladies do not go about yelling and bumbling? One of these days I'm going to end up chopping my finger off when you bound in here like that! Walk *properly.* Speak *quietly.* And only then will I hear what you have to say. Now go on." She motioned with her knife toward the door. "Go out and then come back in and try again."

From her place at the table where she was shucking peas, Belle grinned and crossed her eyes.

Zoe squinted back at her. But that was as far as she let herself go. She dare not reveal her irritation with her sister's propensity to needle her every imperfection, for then she'd only receive another lecture from Ma about her temper. Instead, with slow purposeful steps, she retreated out the door, closed it behind her, counted to five, and then quietly opened it and stepped back into the kitchen. She carefully folded her hands before herself, lifted her chin in an elegant air, and spoke ever so quietly.

"It seems that Mr. Heath has gone and hired a teacher."

"What!?" Belle practically screeched in her excitement and almost spilled all the peas on the floor when she lurched out of her seat.

Even Ma dropped her knife and spun toward her, enthusiasm sparkling in her forget-me-not blue eyes.

Belle rounded the corner of the table. "We get to go to school? How did you hear? When will the teacher get here? Is it a man teacher? Or a woman?"

Fully confident that all the power now lay in her hands, Zoe sealed her lips and purposefully smoothed imaginary wrinkles from the apron of her pinafore. She let the silence stretch, pressing her lips even more tightly together lest in her excitement the words should spill from her before she'd eked out every satisfaction at making her family wait for the news.

"Ma! Make her tell!" Belle pleaded.

Ma only smiled, took up her knife, and set to chopping once more. But she did lift one brow at Zoe.

Zoe had to admit to a little relief at the silent command. For much as she was enjoying torturing her older sister with her knowledge, it was also self-torture to withhold it. She burst out, "Deputy Rodante just done—"

"I don't know why you call him Deputy Rodante as though we haven't known him almost all our lives, Zoe. Just call him Joe. It's not as though we aren't going to know who you are talking about." Belle ended her interruption with a huff.

And for some reason, Ma looked like she was trying real hard not to bust up laughing.

Zoe frowned. She was missing something, but couldn't quite figure out what it might be. At any rate, she was not to be put off sharing her juicy news. She brushed Belle's concern away. "Well, anyhow, Joe come into town not more'n fifteen minutes ago. He said the sheriff was trying to arrest the Waddell gang, when to everyone's surprise, a woman stepped off the stage and said Mr. Heath done hired her as teacher!"

Belle squealed and clasped her hands over her chest in rapture.

"Course that was right afore Patrick Waddell took the lady hostage!"

Even Ma gave a satisfactory gasp at that information.

Zoe nodded firmly. "Joe done said she was a real lady too. All frills and lace. Sheriff Callahan is after finding her right now. Her and Waddell."

"All frills and lace?" Belle's voice sounded a little like someone had her throat in a tight grip. "Did he say anything else about her looks?"

Zoe's nose wrinkled. "Belle, if ya don't beat all! Why would Joe say anything else about her looks? He was just telling that she'd been taken captive!"

Belle seemed satisfied with that information. She nodded primly and paced to the window. "Probably has to dress in frills and lace to enhance her appearance. And she's probably about as helpless and useful as a newborn mouse too!" Belle continued talking, but the rest of the words were muttered beneath her breath so that Zoe couldn't hear what she was saying.

A glance at Ma revealed she was fighting laughter again. But even through her humor, she managed to ask, "Did they catch any of the outlaws?"

"Sure 'nough! Joe and the posse had them down to the jail just a bit ago. They captured three o' that no-good gang. Just not Waddell himself. Leastwise, not yet."

Belle's hands were still clasped over her heart as she stared out the window into nothingness. "Reagan will save the teacher. I know he will."

Ma gave Belle a sharp look. "You may be fifteen, young woman, but he's still your elder and the sheriff. It's Sheriff Callahan to you, and don't you be forgetting it!"

Belle's cheeks turned a bright pink. "Yes, ma'am."

Zoe never liked the tension that often stretched like a clothesline between Ma and Belle, so to get everyone's mind on something else, she stepped forward, took both of Belle's hands, and leaned far back, twirling her sister in a circle. "We're gonna have a teacher! We're gonna have a teacher!" she chanted.

But Belle wasn't so quick to be thrilled. She pulled away and sank into her seat at the table. "Oh, I hope Reag"—her eyes darted to Ma—"the sheriff is going to be okay! And what if the teacher is killed before she even arrives?"

Zoe swallowed at that. Truth be told, she hadn't even considered that possibility. Best she run straight to her room and ask the good Lord to keep the lady safe.

Reagan kept an eye on Waddell and the teacher down in the gulley as he followed them from the top of the ridge. He'd grown up in these mountains, and he knew that if Waddell kept to his current path, he was going to run into the middle fork of the Snoqualmie River just around the next bend. Then he'd have the man right where he wanted him with no place for him to escape.

Reagan spurred his mountain-bred mustang ahead, urging it to quickly take the trail down to the gulley just before the river. He waited behind the outcropping of the rocky cliff, and then when he heard Waddell's horse pass, he stepped his black out onto the trail behind him. With a large outcropping of rock to both Waddell's left and his right and the river blocking the trail before him, Reagan had the man effectively cornered.

Here the river ran into a deep pool before plunging down the mountain. It tumbled away in a swift cataract that descended in a rush of white water through a cut toward the west.

The sound of his Colt six-shooter cocking was loud in the stillness. "Better just hold up right there, Waddell."

The teacher whimpered softly. She tried to glance his way, but a thick snarl of her brown hair seemed to be hampering her efforts to see who he was.

Waddell, who had been surveying the river while scratching the back of his head, spun his horse around to face him.

The teacher wiggled, gasped for a breath, then slumped across the horse in front of Waddell as though the life had just gone out of her.

Something clenched tight inside Reagan. Was he already too late? "Give it up, Waddell." His voice portrayed calm, as though he hadn't a care in the world. He made sure to keep his gun aimed at Waddell's chest, where no bullet would be in danger of hitting the woman.

Waddell lifted his hands slowly, but the tug that put on the reins caused the coach-trained Clydesdale to back up several quick paces, and its hind hooves slipped over the embankment into the edge of the river.

Startled, the horse whinnied, and the whites of its eyes showed as it lunged forward, hooves scrabbling for purchase.

Waddell, already partially off balance due to sitting so far back to make room for the teacher, lurched to gain a better hold of something, but the Clydesdale's lunge forward had unseated him, and with a loud curse he toppled from the animal into the river.

For one suspended moment, he righted himself and stood upright, but the current whipped his feet out from under him, and the last thing Reagan saw of him was his top hat disappearing into the white-water rapids.

In the blink of an eye, Reagan was off his mustang. "Whoa there. Easy." He held out one hand to the wild-eyed Clydesdale.

The teacher still seemed to be unconscious, but the Clydesdale was in danger of plunging both itself and the teacher into the swift current if it didn't calm down.

Slowly, Reagan took a step toward it. "Easy now. Come on. That's it."

After a whuff of his hand, the horse snorted, and bobbed its brown head, hooves prancing in agitation.

A moan emanated from the teacher, who squirmed slightly.

The horse's ears twitched back, and the muscles along its haunches bunched as it prepared to buck the unfamiliar deadweight from its back.

Reagan leapt forward, and at that very moment the horse raised up to paw the air!

He lunged farther to grab the woman—and caught nothing but a handful of green skirts!

With a quick jerk, he pulled the teacher toward him and clasped her tight before she could strike her head against the ground.

Freed of its burden, the Clydesdale barreled past him and bolted up the trail.

Reagan glanced down, realized he had a hold of the teacher's legs and had clutched her to himself quite upside down, and scrambled to right her into a prone position in his arms. Now what was he to do with her?

He gazed down into a face that was slack and much too pale. Noting the gag stuffed in her mouth, he pulled it out and tossed it aside. Her hair was a wild disarray of dark curls and broken twigs. It tumbled over his arms in a curtain of tangles. And her lips had a bluish-purple tint to them, like the stain summer blackberries left when you ate them straight from the bush. She had less color than the last corpse he'd seen.

"Miss? Can you hear me?" He patted her cheek, hoping to bring her back around.

Her eyes fluttered open.

"Can't...breathe," she murmured.

His heart thudded hard against his ribs. Had he rescued her only to have her die in his arms? What would Doc Griffin tell him to do?

She clutched at him and struggled to pull herself upright.

He lowered her feet to the ground but kept his arms about her to steady her. She was tiny, with hardly any meat on her bones. And fear flashed through the green of her eyes.

He should have thought to reassure her. "I'm here to help. Not hurt you."

The teacher slumped against his chest with her head tucked into the space just below his shoulder.

A protective urge zipped through him, and he gritted his teeth. It was a good thing for Waddell that he'd been swept away by the river.

Being upright seemed to help her breathe, and he could feel the warmth of her little breaths puffing against his neck as he soothed one hand up and down her spine and gently brushed her wild hair back from her face. "You're all right now, miss. I've got you. Just breathe easy."

He really ought to be going after Waddell. But he couldn't very well leave the lady here in the woods on her own. Especially when she was having trouble breathing. Tracking down Waddell would have to wait till tomorrow.

The first thing Charlotte noticed was the blessed stillness. No more jarring. No more getting the breaths knocked out of her. The next thing she noticed was the warmth of the cotton twill, and the thump of a steady heartbeat, beneath her cheek. The third was the tight band cinched around her lungs.

Oh no. Not now. She struggled to stand straighter and was thankful that whoever had her seemed to be helping and not hindering her attempts. After a moment the constriction around her lungs eased for one breath but then clamped down with even more fury.

She tightened her fingers into a handful of the shirt beneath them and did her best not to panic. But as the fist around her chest clamped down until only the barest amount of air could get in, she felt the tremble of terror on the verge of taking over. Had she truly heard Waddell falling into the river and being swept away? Yes, she was quite certain of that. Relief eased some of her tightness.

"You're all right now, miss. I've got you. Just breathe easy." The voice floated around her, a soothing tenor. Fingers brushed her hair back from her face with gentle caresses. And the tender ministrations kept her from tipping over the edge of panic. A hand massaged softly up and down her back.

"Breathe in with me. Ready? One. Two. Three."

The chest beneath her cheek lifted in a deep inhale. She tried to follow the example.

"That's right. Good. Now out. One. Two. Three."

Charlotte pursed her lips and forced herself to breathe out.

"Beautiful. Again. With me now. Breathe in. One. Two. Three... And...out. One. Two. Three."

And just as quickly as the attack had come upon her, the band around her lungs released, and blessed oxygen streamed in.

She took several more breaths, afraid to move for fear of reinstigating the attack.

"Are you okay now, miss?" The tenor voice was less ethereal. The muscled chest beneath her cheek and the scents of leather and spice, more tangible. The gentle hand sweeping over her spine, more concrete and comforting. She could contentedly remain exactly where she was for the rest of the afternoon.

Her thoughts flitted to home and settled on Kent. At this very moment she could be back in Boston declining yet another call from that man. She could be safely ensconced in the parlor near a warm fire while sending James to the door with her regrets. Why oh why had she given all that up? And yet, she was honest enough to admit that what brought Mr. Covington to mind at this precise moment wasn't regret—it was comparison.

She took herself back to the last time she'd been this close to Kent. Had she ever stood quietly in his arms, just so, and let him hold her? She couldn't recall. And now as the cozy scent of leather and spice wafted all around her, she tried to recall what exactly the cloying odor that always followed Kent had been. Something acridly sweet and touched with the smell of tobacco from the club he frequented—a smell that repulsed her each time he drew near, yet somehow she'd never realized.

But this fragrance that now enveloped her... She pulled in another slow inhale. It spoke of comfort and home and protection. An aroma she could revel in all day long and never tire of! But suddenly the impropriety of the fact that she was alone in the woods, wrapped in a strange man's arms, washed over her. Alluring scent or not. Asthma attack or not. Neither Mother nor Miss Gidden would allow for such a contravention of the rules.

Forcing herself to step back, Charlotte smoothed her hands down her skirt and then lifted her focus to take in her rescuer. Her breath threatened to stop again, but not because of her asthma this time.

The man's eyes were the bluest of blues, and a scruffy stubble along his jaw that should have made him look unkempt did no such thing. The scruff only added to his attractiveness, heightening the pleasant angles of a handsome face and drawing her attention to full lips that made her fingertip itch to trace them.

At this very moment those lips quirked up at the corners in curiosity and humor.

Charlotte felt the burn of humiliation that she'd been caught staring. She spun away from him and did her best to straighten her appearance. She gathered her tresses into one hand at the back of her head and lifted her chin as she worked as much debris as possible from her hair and knotted it into a quick bun with the few remaining hairpins left to her.

All the while, her rescuer stood off to one side, his Stetson pushed back on his head and his arms folded across a broad chest.

Finally put together the best she could be under such circumstances, Charlotte looked to the man and offered a slight curtsy. "Miss Charlotte Brindle, sir. And might I have your name also, for I'm sure Mr. Zebulon Heath will want to be thanking you in a monetary way for coming to my rescue and facing such danger to your person."

The man snorted. "Zeb would have had my hide if I didn't come to your rescue, ma'am." He stretched out one hand. "Name's Reagan Callahan. I'm the sheriff in Wyldhaven."

Charlotte placed her hand in his and was dismayed to note that her hand was practically engulfed by his broad muscular one. She glanced around, but there was not a building or another living being in sight. How could she have been so negligent? What if the man whose arms she'd been reveling in had been one of the outlaws who had attacked their coach? She could have been in rampant danger, and all she'd been able to think about was the alluring scent of him!

Her pique with herself spilled over onto the man. "Sheriff of Wyldhaven, you say? So it's likely your fault that I find myself in this situation at all, isn't it? Why were those men allowed to roam the countryside and shoot at people!? You surely knew what they were up to, or you wouldn't have been so near!"

The sheriff's brows lifted, and his arms settled into a tighter fold across his chest, which irritatingly drew her gaze to the bulge of strong biceps and made her mouth even more dry than it already was.

The sheriff's lips thinned. "Had we known you were on the coach, miss, rest assured we would have handled things differently."

She tipped up her chin, not entirely sure that fact should let the man off her hook. But for the moment she was too tired to carry on the argument. "You didn't know I was coming?"

The sheriff shook his head.

Charlotte's chin lifted a fraction higher, if only to keep the tears of weariness—and relief at her sudden safety—away. "Well, Mr. Zebulon Heath has hired me as the new schoolteacher. I wonder if you might be so kind as to show me to my place in town, Sheriff Callahan? I'm dreadfully parched and could really use a spot of tea. And thank you, by the way, for..." She swept a gesture toward the place where only a moment ago he had smooth-talked her lungs into cooperating.

He dipped a nod and turned to his horse, which Charlotte just now noticed had stood quietly behind him the whole time. He withdrew a canteen. "I'm happy to show you into town, Miss Brindle. But there's no need to wait to slake your thirst." He thrust the container toward her.

Charlotte eyed it dubiously. How many other people had the sheriff rescued and allowed to drink from his canteen? She studied it for so long that the man finally withdrew it, uncorked it, and then offered it back to her, giving it a little tantalizing shake before her face. The water sloshed temptingly inside.

"The water's perfectly safe, I assure you."

Charlotte's thirst finally outweighed her worry over cleanliness, and she took the canteen. The first drops of water to cross her tongue were like the first breaths of air she always felt the moment her lungs released a clench. Heavenly. She tipped the canteen higher and guzzled so thirstily, she was embarrassed when some drizzled out the corner of her mouth and cascaded off her chin. She caught the drips and swiped them away as she held the canteen back toward him. "Many thanks, Sheriff."

There was a hint of humor in his gaze when he banged the cork back into place. He only dipped a nod of acknowledgment to her appreciation, but he did stretch one hand toward his horse. "Shall we head into town, then?"

She eyed the regular saddle with a twist of her lips. Were she to try and ride the horse, her humiliation would be complete. Just the thought of how she would look astride the large black set her cheeks to blazing. "I'll just walk back to the stagecoach, Sheriff."

"I'm afraid the stagecoach won't be going anywhere until they are able to bring in another harness and track down the loose horse. And it's a fair piece on into town. Five miles or better."

"Five miles? But the stage driver said Wyldhaven was just over the next ridge."

The sheriff tilted his head and rubbed a hand over the stubble of one cheek. "That's true, I suppose. You'd have been in town in less than thirty minutes traveling by coach as you were."

Something inside her tightened up in dread. "And on foot?"

The sheriff propped his hands on his hips, a gesture that said he was doing his best not to lose his patience. "Depends on how fast you walk. But with you riding and me walking...a little over an hour or so."

Charlotte considered her options. Her shoes were highly inappropriate for a long walk such as that. She'd wanted to arrive in the height of fashion to give the best impression possible. As it was, she would already be arriving in town with her head most improperly bare, her hair likely far short of passable, and her skirts as dusty as a maid's apron. So what was one more black mark on her good name? She gave a huff. "Fine. I'll climb aboard. But I'll need to ride sideways. Will your mount tolerate that?"

The sheriff's lips twitched in a most ungentlemanly way. "He won't throw you, if that's what you're asking."

"Very well. I'll need a stump or a hillside or—"

Her sentence cut off in a squeak as the sheriff's hands settled around her waist, and he practically tossed her up into his saddle. His horse shied to one side, and she felt herself starting to slide off the far side.

"Oh!" She was saved from a tumble by the sheriff's hand wrapping around her ankle.

Her face heated at the shocking feel of it. Impropriety seemed to be the order of her day.

She grasped the saddle horn with both hands and scooted herself into a position that offered the best balance available to her without the aid of the leg hook that a sidesaddle would have.

Sheriff Callahan kept hold of her ankle and maneuvered her foot into the stirrup before he stepped back. "All set?"

She lifted her chin. "I will be lucky not to tumble off and break my neck."

He offered not the slightest hint of sympathy. "Yes. Well, let's wait to do that till we are closer to town and our Dr. Griffin. Out here you're likely to die before I can return with help."

She gasped her outrage.

He gave her a startled look. "It was meant for humor, Miss Brindle. I apologize if I offended."

"How about we just get me to my cottage, Sheriff, where I can have a nice hot cup of tea?" *And a bath.* But she wouldn't mention such a thing out loud to the man. Even if "faux pas" did seem to be on today's menu.

He blinked at her. Opened his mouth. And then must have changed his mind about whatever he'd planned to say, because after that he merely bent and retrieved his horse's reins and started at a good clip down the trail.

Chapter Six

For nearly the whole hour into town, Reagan considered, and then tossed aside, all manner of explanations to prepare the teacher for the fact that she would have no *cottage.* But blamed if he knew *where* Zeb planned to house the woman, and none of his conceived explanations seemed as if they would adequately satisfy the elegant, and obviously entitled, woman riding so primly, and with such careful balance, on his mountain-bred mustang.

About halfway back along the trail he found her hat, but it appeared that the Clydesdale had stepped on it. Whether that was when it was coming or when it had fled after bucking Waddell, he couldn't tell. He picked it up and tried to reshape it, but one of the feathers was broken in the middle. When he handed it up to her, she sucked in a small breath.

Her lips that had just a few minutes ago been blue enough to bring to mind death were now more the color of ripe raspberries—the kind that made a man want to taste and see if they were as sweet as they looked.

Startled yet intrigued by the thought, he folded his arms and studied her. She futilely attempted to prop the broken feather up, but the moment she pulled her hand away the shaft flopped to the side again. A shimmer crept into the vibrant green of her eyes, and when she blinked, one tear caught in her long dark lashes. He had a feeling her tears were less about the ruined hat than about the culmination of what must have been one very bad day.

He plucked the hat back out of her hands and shucked his Bowie. A quick slice severed the shaft of the broken feather at its base. He tossed it aside, fluffed the feathers that remained, and offered it back to her with a little bow meant to lighten the moment. It took a few moments for her to respond, but as she accepted the hat from him a second time, her lips did curve into a soft smile. Their hands brushed against each other, and her skin was smooth and soft beneath his fingers. He swallowed and pulled away lest he be tempted to linger.

Her eyes shimmered again, but she bit that pretty bottom lip of hers and lifted her chin, and this time no tears spilled over. He was glad at least for that fact. Because he'd been trying to comfort her, not make her cry again. Guilt pressed in. Maybe tears in a woman of her breeding were inevitable after a day such as this?

The trouble was, her near future held more bad news. He turned and started off toward town again, unable to voice something that would only bring her more disappointment.

So it was that the outskirts of the livery yard had come into view before he'd so much as said two further words to the lady. But when he led her into full view of the main street, which stretched off to their left, he heard her give a sound that was half gasp, half grunt.

He tried to put as much enthusiasm as he could muster into his next words. "Welcome to Wyldhaven, Miss Brindle."

Her horror was evident in the widening of her eyes and the gape of her jaw. "There must be some mistake, sir!"

He almost chuckled at her propensity for sounding so arrogant, when he had a feeling that was the furthest thing from what she actually was. "No mistake, miss." He turned to look up at her.

Face pale, she had one hand pressed to her collar and wore a look of such stricken shock he feared she might at any moment lack the strength to maintain her balance.

He reached up and plucked her from the back of his steed, feeling his concern mount. "Are you well?"

She blinked, rubbed the hollow at the base of her throat, and glanced at him as if to acknowledge that in some nether region of her mind, she'd heard him speak, but her focus returned immediately to the town.

He followed her gaze, scrubbed the back of his neck, and tried to see the place as she might be seeing it. He supposed Wyldhaven did fall a little closer to the side of "wyld" than "haven." Zeb had only decided he had need of a town for his logging crews this past spring. Reagan had arrived when both the post office and the mercantile were still nothing more than floor joists on foundation, and each building had gone up in record time. Other than those two buildings, the only other three in town besides the livery were his jail, McGinty's Alehouse, and the boardinghouse—each of which had also been quickly erected with an eye for service rather than aesthetics.

The town was not without its softer touches, however. Why, Dixie Pottinger even had curtains at the windows of the boardinghouse, and Ben King had hung a flag outside the post office. Though now that Reagan looked at it closely, the flag had seen better days. He probably ought to recommend Ben replace it with a new one.

"I fear there has been some mistake, Sheriff." The woman's voice was barely audible.

He frowned down at her, wondering whatever she could mean.

"This can't possibly be the right place. You see, I was to be the teacher for a town called Wyldhaven. In the newly formed state of Washington?" She said the words slowly, as though speaking to a simple-minded child.

Reagan's frown deepened. Had the woman gone addlebrained? He stretched a hand out to indicate the buildings on either side of the street. "Yes, ma'am. As you see before you."

"Oh mercy." She made a funny little whimpering sound. "There's not possibly *another* town called Wyldhaven around these parts, is there?"

Reagan propped his hands on his hips. "Miss, I assure you this is the town founded by the very man you mentioned earlier, Mr. Zebulon Heath."

"But..." Words seemed to have failed her, and the starch seeped out of her spine.

His dread of leading her to the boardinghouse grew stronger. But there was nothing for it but to do so. He'd already been out of contact with Joe for too long, and he needed to send a wire reporting the possibility of Waddell's death or escape to the towns downriver. He also needed to round up a group of men to ride downriver with him to see if they could find the outlaw, whether dead or alive.

So dread or not, he forced himself to action. He placed a hand gently on Miss Brindle's back and nudged her forward, gesturing down the street to the boardinghouse. "I'll escort you down to the boardinghouse now. That's where you'll be staying until Zeb gets back to town and can determine a more permanent residence for you."

The woman muttered something under her breath, snatched up two fistfuls of skirts, and stepped out ahead of him in the most graceful fit of anger he'd ever had the privilege to witness.

Reagan resisted the humor that begged to lift his lips. He

was just glad to see that the starch hadn't gone out of her for too long.

Charlotte didn't care if Miss Gidden would call her footfalls "less than delicate" right at the moment. She didn't care that the sheriff had said something about a boardinghouse and not her cottage. She could settle into her cottage tomorrow. All she cared about was putting an end to this never-ending nightmare of a day.

Halfway down the street, she realized she didn't know where she was going. She stopped so abruptly that the sheriff, who had been keeping pace behind her, almost ran into her. Angling out of his way, she motioned for him to take the lead.

He took two steps past her, then stopped and opened a door with the arch of one brow.

She felt her face flush as she realized he'd thought she had stopped so he would open the door for her. She hesitated before passing through. "I'm sorry. I didn't—I just realized I didn't know where I was going and..." She let the words trail off, weariness, seemingly bone deep, weighed down her shoulders.

His frown said he didn't understand why she was apologizing. Her shoulders sank a little farther. So maybe he hadn't been thinking anything close to what she'd assumed.

In how many ways could she continue to make this day worse? "I thought you thought..." She sighed. "Never mind. I'd really just like to go to my room."

When she would have started forward, he touched her elbow, and she stalled once more. "My granddad use to say, 'Every sunrise comes with a new perspective.'"

She nodded. "Yes. Some rest will definitely do me some good, Sheriff. Thank you." She stepped inside.

A dark-haired woman stood behind the counter. She smiled prettily. "Good evening, Sheriff."

"Dixie." He swiped his hat from his head and swept it in a gesture toward Charlotte. "This here is the new schoolteacher, Miss Charlotte Brindle. Miss Brindle"—the hat swung back the other way—"Miss Dixie Pottinger."

Surprisingly, the woman's smile grew when it transferred from the sheriff to her. Normally, in the presence of a handsome man, eligible women grew all muddleheaded and flirtatious. But apparently not Dixie. Charlotte liked her immediately.

"You must be exhausted. I've a room all prepared for you." She lifted a key from the back wall and held it out.

Charlotte took it, and a wave of gratefulness washed through her.

"Would you like a plate of dinner before you go up?"

Charlotte shook her head. "I'll be fine. Thank you."

The sheriff plunked several coins and a few bills onto the counter. He replaced his hat and tugged the brim in her direction. "Good evening to you, Miss Brindle. Dixie." With that, he exited, leaving the bell above the door clanging the news of his absence.

Dixie tucked the money away in a box before she stepped from behind the counter. Lifting her skirts, she nodded toward a set of stairs along the back wall. "If you'll follow me, I'll show you to your room."

It wasn't until Charlotte was standing in the middle of her room with the door finally shut on all other human interaction that she realized she didn't have even one of her bags. Even her traveling case had been abandoned aboard the coach when Mr. Waddell had kidnapped her.

The reminder brought a fresh wave of tears, and this time she didn't suppress them.

She flounced to the bed and collapsed atop it, hugging the pillow like it was a long-lost friend. She used it to at least partially muffle her anguish. Oh, whatever in the world had made her think she could survive, much less make a difference, in the wide, wild west? This certainly couldn't have been the leading of the Lord, could it?

"Lord, when will I ever learn to truly hear Your direction?" This had obviously been a big mistake. She would just go back home. Mother and Father would forgive her for running off half cocked. And they'd already promised not to push a suit with Kent further. Decision made, she relaxed a little. "I'll be home by this time next week."

They were the last words she snuffled before the oblivion of sleep claimed her.

Either the cold or the pain woke him, and Patrick Waddell couldn't tell which. The ground beneath him felt stony, and from the way he was shivering, it had likely been sucking the heat from him for several hours. His clothes, still soaked from his encounter with the river, weren't doing anything to help him stay warm.

Something dug painfully into his cheek that was pressed to the ground. He brought his hands toward his chest and tried to push himself up, but his right arm screamed pain from every quadrant. He cried out and let it go limp. He waited for the waves of agony to subside a little.

When he felt like he might be able to move without blacking out, he gingerly used his left hand to push himself upright. So this was what misery felt like. He winced and gasped and groaned his way to a sitting position, then he sat as still as he could with his eyes closed, concentrating on banishing the pain roiling seemingly through every pore of his body. He cradled his right arm against his chest.

He was a blamed fool. That arm was broken, certain sure.

Cocky, that's what his ol' pappy would have told him back in the day. You only get caught when you get overconfident. He should have taken that money from the bank heist and gone back east. Set himself up with a pretty little plantation in Virginia, or maybe the Carolinas. But no. Not him. Because he'd gotten too smug thinking he was insignificant enough and the land big enough to hide him. But someone must have spotted him. Someone who knew who he was. Someone who'd reported him to not only his old gang but to the law as well.

A roil of anger so strong it was almost able to warm him surged. Someone had betrayed him. And *that* was why he'd be staying around even when the smart thing would be to take this second chance and hightail it to a region that knew nothing and cared nothing about one Patrick Waddell.

Taking a fortifying breath, he cracked open first one eye and then the next. The light pinched some at first, but it only took him a moment to adjust. He was in the middle of a rocky shelf that stretched toward the wood from the riverbank. He didn't remember crawling out of the water, but he must have, because the river lay below him a good few feet.

Cautiously, he felt of himself all over. Thankfully, the only thing that seemed to be broken was his right arm. There was also a nasty gash at the side of his skull—probably where he'd cracked his head against a rock when he was tumbling down the river rapids.

He'd somehow maintained possession of his one glove and both boots. But all his other gear was gone, including his hat. He cursed. He'd liked that hat. It made him look dignified. Despite that, it was the least of his worries.

He squinted toward the sky. The sun hung low in the late-afternoon position. If he was going to survive the night, he needed a fire, and he needed to shuck these wet clothes and get into something warm.

But how was he to accomplish that without his things? No matches. No dry clothes to change into. He'd been forced to abandon his bags on the stage when that fool of a schoolteacher had shocked him with her temerity.

A crooked grin tipped up one side of his mouth as he haltingly lurched to his feet. Cursing, he froze and let the throbbing subside.

While he waited, he concentrated on the pretty picture that schoolmarm had made sitting all prim and proper across from him in the coach. He chuckled then. She'd been even prettier, green eyes snapping at him, when he'd yanked her head back to gag her.

He stumbled a few steps forward, and that was when he realized that he must have whacked his leg a good one too, because it was aching to beat the band.

He was in trouble, and that was the truth of it.

Charlotte Brindle bolted upright in bed, hoping beyond hope that yesterday's nightmare had been nothing more than exactly that. But one glance around the boardinghouse room confirmed that the nightmare was indeed reality. She flopped back on the bed and stared at the water stain that marred the ceiling.

She had to think hard to remember anything that had happened after her first glimpse of the town yesterday evening. She very vaguely recalled arriving in the foyer and meeting the proprietress, though she couldn't recall the woman's name at the moment. Charlotte would need to find her and offer payment for the room. *Wait.* She had a hazy image of the sheriff plunking some money onto the front desk and the pretty proprietress scooping it into a box. *The sheriff paid for my room.*

"Oh!" She lurched upright on the bed and covered both cheeks with her hands, her face heating at the impropriety of that!

She would make amends for that oversight on her part first thing this morning! But last night the thought hadn't even crossed her mind.

Slowly, she scooted to the edge of the lumpy mattress and settled her feet against the rough planks of the wooden floor.

She would take care of her morning's necessities and then decide what to do first about tracking down her bags and also about Mr. Heath's deceptions. But a quick scan of the interior of her room proved that Wyldhaven was going to fail to live up to Mr. Heath's promises in yet another way. This was the 1890s! Any town billed as a "little piece of New England blooming on the wild frontier" ought to at least have modern amenities like indoor plumbing!

Oh, whatever in the world had possessed her to abandon the beautiful water closets of Hyde Park for employment, however philanthropic it might be, on the wild frontier? Why oh why hadn't she listened to Father when he'd urged her to reconsider? Her disregard of Mother's warnings, she could easily forgive. But Father was a levelheaded man. She always listened to Father. Well…almost always. She groaned and rose to commence her search.

She found the water closet—a shared one—down the hall, and after finishing her ablutions, she stepped out onto what *should* have been the boardwalk in front of the hotel. Had she even noticed the evening before that there was none? In addition to the cobbled streets and picket fences and small stone cottages, Mr. Heath's brochure had clearly shown boardwalks lining the streets.

But now as Charlotte's kidskin boots sank into the mud in front of the hotel, and she surveyed the main street of Wyldhaven, her mouth gaped. Only years of finishing school reminded her to snap it shut again.

This was deception in its most blatant form! She fumbled for her reticule and withdrew the incriminating evidence. She smoothed the parchment against her skirt and held it up to study it as though to make sure her memory had not failed her. Her gaze snapped from the brochure to the town and back again. There was no mistake. This town couldn't possibly be the one portrayed on the pamphlet in her hand.

Moisture started to soak through to her feet. She lifted one muddy boot and shook it slightly to dislodge a clump of red-brown muck on the underside. Lifting her skirts, she soft-footed her way to a drier patch of ground in a spot of sunshine pooling between the boardinghouse and the building next door.

Everywhere she looked, she saw nothing but brown. Brown buildings, brown watering troughs, brown mud. As if to emphasize that last, there, just down the way, were two men with their shoulders to the back of a wagon heavily loaded with tools, trying to dislodge it from the muddy ruts it had sunk into. They had obviously made a mistake when they drove their wagon off the corduroyed portion of the road.

Off to her left Charlotte could hear a river bubbling. And a rather rickety-looking split-log bridge spanned from one embankment to the other.

From across the bridge, a little girl heartily skipped toward her, her ginger-and-sunshine pigtails bouncing against her shoulders. At the end of a string, a juvenile mongrel bounded along in front of the girl. Despite the fact that it was filthy like everything else in this town, the pup was rather cute with its flopped-over ears, large black spots, and one brown patch over intelligent, alert eyes.

The child raised her arm above her head and waved wildly. "Morning to ya!" she hollered, doing her best to keep up with the dog, which kept lunging at the end of the lead.

Charlotte turned to glance behind her, certain the child must be greeting someone else.

But the child's next words proved her certainty false. "You must be the new schoolteacher!" She gave a little bounce on the balls of her feet.

As she noted the girl's obvious enthusiasm, Charlotte almost felt guilty for her uncharitable thoughts about the town. Yet she'd definitely been deceived. Perhaps if her expectations hadn't been so high...

"My name be Zoe Kastain. My pa's one of the buckers who works for Mr. Heath. We live over yonder." She waved her hand back in the direction from which she had just come across the death trap of a bridge. "We're right excited to have a new schoolteacher in town. None of us even knowed Mr. Heath was gonna get us a teacher!"

"Yes. Well...here I am." Charlotte couldn't seem to force any fervor into her sentence. Still, the child seemed thrilled to see her, and the least she could do would be to take a moment to make the girl feel cared for. "Perhaps you could show me the schoolhouse?"

"Schoolhouse?" The little girl's freckles deepened to a shade of dark brown. "Well, I'm not sure exactly which building Mr. Heath plans on us using for the schoolhouse. We don't got no building set aside just for school use, ya see."

Charlotte lifted her hand to her throat. "Well, perhaps we could use...the church building for school?"

The smattering of freckles across the little girl's nose crinkled into tight dismay. "Ma'am, I don't mean to be impertinent, but ya sure are new around here, ain't ya?" The child swept her hand down the street before them, encompassing the five buildings they could see. "What ya see is all there be. This here is Wyldhaven. Ain't no other buildings in town."

"But Mr. Heath said..." Charlotte glanced once more at the brochure. Her dread was mounting by the moment. And yes there it was as clear as the ink on the parchment. Just across the river over an arched cobblestone bridge—that obviously also didn't exist—stood a building labeled *Schoolhouse.* Yet when Charlotte glanced across the river, there was nothing in that space but an empty, *brown* field.

Zoe's pup, who had been sniffing the corner of the hotel, suddenly seemed to notice Charlotte, and with a suspicious *woof*, bounded to her side. He was larger up close than he had seemed from across the street. After sniffing nearly the entire perimeter of Charlotte's skirt, he must have decided she was harmless and someone on whom to lavish his love, for with a happy yip and a wag of his tail, he leapt up to give her a slobbery greeting, tattooing her skirt with several gooey paw prints.

"Oh!" Charlotte gasped.

"Jinx, get down!" Zoe yanked on the rope, tugging the exuberant puppy back from Charlotte. Her face turned watermelon pink as she set her heels and held the high-spirited dog in check with all her strength. "I'm right sorry about that," Zoe puffed. Her nose crinkled at the muddy splotches on Charlotte's green watered silk. "I guess Pa done named Jinx here rightly. He done said 'that pup is nothing but hijinks waiting to happen.' And it's sort of just stuck."

"Yes. Hijinks indeed." Charlotte tried not to let her irritation come through in her tone, but feared she'd failed miserably. She plucked a handkerchief from her reticule and swiped it at the mud, which only succeeded in smearing it further. Her skirt was positively ruined! And she without even one clean outfit to change into. Whatever was she to do?

But before she could decide how to proceed, a sharp whistle and the crack of a whip drew her gaze down the street. Several steers pulling a triangular-shaped stack of logs taller than Charlotte would have ever imagined possible came around the far building and onto the street. Midway up the stack of logs, one protruded slightly farther out than the rest, and upon this stood the driver, a burly man holding the longest whip Charlotte had ever seen.

The leather strap cracked loudly over the back of one of the bulls, and the man yelled, "Get on now!"

A cat that had been sunning itself in a splotch of golden warmth in the middle of the street yowled in terror at the sound of the whip, shot straight up into the air, and dashed for safety down one of the alleys.

Jinx, as if to prove his owner correct about his name, darted around Zoe, wrapping the rope securely around her ankles, and then lunged after the cat.

Whomp! Zoe landed flat on her stomach in the mud. "Jinx!" Zoe let go of the leash to clamber to her feet as she surveyed her totally brown dress front with a frown of disgust.

Without so much as a backward glance, Jinx gave a happy yelp and bounded down the street after the cat, totally oblivious to the heavy load of timber and hooves rolling at a fast clip down the corduroyed center of the road.

Charlotte saw in an instant that the wagon was so heavily loaded down with logs the driver was not going to be able to stop it, and the puppy was so set on his destination that he had no idea of the danger he was running full tilt toward.

"Oh dear Lord, have mercy!" Charlotte snatched two handfuls of her skirts and tore off after the pup, giving several unsuccessful attempts at stomping on the rope trailing behind him. "Jinx, you stop this instant!" She put her very last ounce of effort into speed and, with one last pounce, felt the satisfaction of the rope beneath her boot.

Jinx hit the end of the rope with a yelp and came to a rather undignified halt. And not a moment too soon. The wagon trundled past while Charlotte still stood, panting to catch her breath.

Jinx gave a little yippy whine and settled onto his haunches, his gaze still fastened on the alleyway where the cat had disappeared a moment earlier.

"Thanks ever so much for saving Jinx's life, Miss Teacher." Zoe appeared at her side, tears making murky tracks down her face. "I don't rightly know what I'd'a done had I lost him."

Charlotte sighed, extracted the rope from beneath her foot, and handed it back to Zoe. "It's Miss Brindle, and you're welcome. Anyone would have done the same."

Zoe's blue eyes grew wide in her mud-splotched face. "No, ma'am. I don't think ya be right on that account."

"Well, you're welcome then. Now if you'll excuse me, I need to find the sheriff." She folded the muddy side of her hanky in and stuffed it back into her reticule. She would have to wash everything later.

"Right. And I need to run back home and change 'fore I go to Mrs. Callahan's to work."

Mrs. Callahan... Charlotte felt the words like a bucket of cold water to the face.

Sheriff Reagan Callahan was married.

Chapter Seven

Charlotte gritted her teeth as she watched Zoe dash back across the bridge.

Of course he was married. Why shouldn't he be? And yet yesterday he had seemed so…well…*not.* Oh, was she forever to be such a terrible judge of a man's character? She cast her mind back over all their interactions. *The man is a positive scoundrel!* He had held her, and soothed her, and even paid for her room at the boardinghouse! And all while his wife waited for his return and probably fretted over his safety!

Zoe stopped on the other side of the bridge, cupped both hands to her mouth, and yelled at the top of her lungs, "The sheriff is likely in his office this time o' mornin'."

Forcing a smile, Charlotte waved her thanks. She cast an inspection over the town once more. Frustration was beginning to become a very familiar feeling! At least it shouldn't take her long to find the sheriff's office. She lifted her skirts and rotated right there in the middle of the street, surveying the signs on each building.

She saw that the place where she had stayed the night was called *Dixie's Boardinghouse.*

Dixie, that's right.

Next to Dixie's was a building labeled *McGinty's Alehouse and Rooms.* Across the street was a building simply labeled *Merkantile* that had Charlotte grumbling beneath her breath about the very blatant need for education in these savage lands. Next to the mercantile was a tall, narrow building with *Post Office* engraved into a placard that hung on squeaking chains above the doorway. Finally her revolving gaze landed on the building labeled *Sheriff's Office and Jail* on the same side of the street as Dixie's Boardinghouse.

Jaw clenched, she headed that way. At the very least, the sheriff needed to know what a crook the man who was luring people to this town was, and in addition to that, perhaps he could find her the first stage headed back home.

Sure enough, Zoe had been right. Through the front window she could see that the sheriff had his boots propped on one corner of his desk, a steaming tin cup in one hand, while he perused a folded-over section of a newspaper. Behind him, two jail cells held three men in various states of repose, presumably the outlaws who'd nearly gotten her killed yesterday.

Without bothering to knock, Charlotte barged through his door.

The sheriff jolted so high that he sloshed hot coffee from his tin cup onto his hand. He hissed and plunked the cup onto the desk, shaking the liquid onto the floor. "Miss Brindle." He winced and swiped the back of his hand against his denims. His words were louder and decidedly more hostile after that. "What can I do for you this morning?"

The three men in the cells came to attention.

"Well, if it ain't the lady that caused us all to be caught," one groused.

"Quiet!" the sheriff commanded. "We would have arrested you all whether Waddell took a hostage or not."

Charlotte determined to ignore the foul outlaws and focus on the reason she was here. She folded her arms and pondered the best place to start. *How could you let me think you were not married* just didn't seem the best footing to begin on, especially not with three ill-groomed hoodlums looking on. Besides, in reality the man had done nothing terribly improper. It was the strange circumstances that had dictated yesterday's improprieties.

She decided to start with the boardinghouse fee. "I would like to reimburse you for the expense of my stay last night."

"Ohhh! Where did she stay, Sheriff?" There was more than a little innuendo in that question, but then the outlaw pushed it further. "Ain't it generally t'other way around? You payin' her?" The men guffawed heartily.

Charlotte felt her face pale.

"I would like to reimburse you for the expense of my stay last night," one of the outlaws mimicked.

The sheriff was on his feet in a heartbeat, and before she could even blink, a gun appeared in his hand.

He stalked a few steps toward the cells. "Would be a shame if my gun accidentally discharged and took a few pieces of flesh out of your sorry hides, now wouldn't it, boys?"

All three men lifted their hands to indicate they wanted no part of that, and sank onto their respective cots.

The sheriff holstered his pistol and returned to his desk. He waved his hand and picked up their conversation as though there had been no interruption. "Think nothing of it. Once Zeb returns, the fee will likely be part of your salary. I'll get reimbursed."

If he could ignore those men, then she could too. Charlotte reached for her reticule. "But I can reimburse you now."

The sheriff picked up his coffee. "I said don't worry about it." He lifted the cup to his lips.

Charlotte suppressed the pucker that wanted to perch on

her brow. "Your wife likely won't appreciate you spending money on me."

Once more hot coffee sloshed out of the sheriff's cup. This time it drizzled down his chin and onto the front of his shirt. "My wife!?" The sheriff sputtered and swiped at the liquid before plunking the cup back down on his desk. "Who told you I had a wife?!"

Another round of guffaws emanated from the cells.

Charlotte darted them a look of irritation, feeling a little light headed. Her gaze turned to the street where she'd just been talking with Zoe, and the pucker did settle into place this time. She looked back at the sheriff. "You don't?"

"No! I don't!" The sheriff's tone indicated his thankfulness to the Almighty over the fact.

How *did* she get herself into these predicaments? "It's just that...I met Zoe Kastain just now, and she said she worked for 'Mrs. Callahan.'"

A glint of humor started in the sheriff's eyes, spread to his lips, and then burst forth in a full volley of laughter.

Charlotte didn't see what was so hilarious. She folded her arms and gave the man her best glower.

Which only made him and the outlaws laugh harder.

Charlotte lifted her chin. "Did I misunderstand her?"

Sheriff Callahan finally managed to contain his amusement. "The Mrs. Callahan Zoe referred to is my mother, not my wife." He leaned back in his chair and folded his arms, a definite twinkle in the blue eyes he leveled on her.

An unaccountable relief washed through her. "Oh. I see." The relief was immediately followed by pique. Why should she care whether the man was married or not? She wouldn't even be here for but a few more hours!

"Was there anything else I could help you with this morning,

Miss Brindle?" His back-to-business tone of dismissal raised her temper a few notches.

"Yes, as a matter of fact, there is." She slapped the brochure onto the desk in front of him, propped one hand to the side of it, and then gave it an extra stab for good measure. Tapping the picture of the town with eyebrows raised, she indicated he should give it a good look himself. "Did you know, Sheriff, that this...*this!*...is what Mr. Heath is using to lure unsuspecting patrons to this, this—" She gave up on an apt word and settled for a sweep of her hand in the general direction of the street, and the buildings to the south of the sheriff's office, and then to the prisoners behind him.

The sheriff picked up the brochure and gave it a once-over, one golden eyebrow arching upward. After a moment he dropped the brochure back onto his desk, lifted his hands in a *what do you want me to do* gesture, and then folded them on the desk before him. And if she wasn't mistaken, a twitch of humor still quirked one corner of his lips!

That did it! The anger that had been on slow simmer roiled up and spilled out of her mouth. "You think this is funny, do you? Your town founder is out there *lying* to people—*deceiving* them into coming here! And all I get from the sheriff—the same sheriff who'd set a trap for those ruffians that nearly got me *killed* yesterday as I was arriving—is a smirk and silence?" She felt quite proud that she'd managed to speak the words through unclenched teeth.

"I believe she called us ruffians," one of the outlaws said in feigned hurt.

The sheriff rubbed one hand over a jaw that had seen the use of a razor sometime between when she'd left him last evening and now, and studied her with those blue eyes that brought to mind the waters of the Neponset River back home. "I'm not sure what you expect me to do, miss. I'm not saying that I believe Heath is doing the right thing with this." He tapped the deceptive drawing of the main street on the pamphlet before him. "But I don't doubt that he fully expects the town to look just like that one of these days, and I also don't see that there's much that I can do about it."

"Well, forgive me!" Charlotte adjusted her lace day gloves. Her irritation mounted as she noticed the fingers on her right hand were a ruin of mud, likely from the dog's lead. She gave the sheriff the best cowing look she could muster. "Forgive me for thinking that you, a man of the law, would want to do something about his deceit. Deceit that pertains to your town nonetheless. But I can see that I was wrong. Well, never mind that." She snatched up the brochure and stuffed it back into her reticule, then folded her hands before her and lifted her chin primly. "I would like my cases. They were on the coach yesterday. And I would like the first ticket on a coach out of town this morning, please."

The sheriff rubbed the back of his neck and eyed her with lowered brows. "I'm afraid there's no coach coming through here until next week this time, miss."

Despite herself, Charlotte's jaw dropped for the second time that morning. No *more coaches for...for a whole week?*

"And your bags haven't been retrieved just yet. Though Don, he's the stage driver, is working on it. He found his missing horse, and the stage should arrive by midmorning to drop off the bags."

Her hopes momentarily soared, but the sheriff must have seen it in her expression, for he held up one hand.

"But from here the stage travels farther west to Seattle. Then it comes back through here on its way east again next week."

Dejection slumping her shoulders, Charlotte strode to the window overlooking the street and stared at the dilapidated little buildings across the way. She had had such high hopes for her time in Wyldhaven. She had anticipated school lessons, and Christmas plays, and an Easter pageant. She had envisioned the children at the front of a theater. She had planned out a cotillion to raise funds for schoolbooks, and perhaps even some historical reenactments to teach the children history.

But all of that envisioning had now been shattered. Because any group of people who would allow themselves to live in such a rundown, dilapidated, degraded place obviously would not be the type who would enjoy cotillions and theater.

Charlotte fiddled with the brooch at her throat as she stared out the window and pondered her next move. Every option she considered was a little blurry around the edges—not quite graspable.

How had Mr. Heath deceived her with such totality? She was more than a little perturbed at her own naivety. How could she have been misled so easily? It was her hurry to get away from Kent, that was what it was. She'd obviously been so set in putting space between them that she hadn't even questioned Mr. Heath's promises.

She dropped her eyes closed. All she wanted to do was to go back home. Yet now the sheriff claimed she had no way to escape for an entire week! Whatever was she going to do?

She would not cry. She simply wouldn't. She blinked, fast and furious.

She heard the sheriff's boots thudding across the floor behind her and felt him come to her side. "I think you'll like Wyldhaven if you give it a chance, Miss Brindle. The people here come from hardworking folk, and ever since they heard yesterday that a teacher came to town, there's been nothing but excitement in the air." From the corner of her eye, she saw him tilt his head and prop his hands on his hips. "You all right, miss?"

She spun away from him, only offering a view of her back. "Yes. I'm quite fine, thank you." She tugged at her gloves again. Miss Gidden would be lambasting her of a certainty for the nervous gesture. "I'll just return to my hotel room. I've got some pondering to do."

The sheriff hurried past her and beat her to the door. He put his palm on the handle but didn't open it. Instead he looked up into her face. "If you'll pardon me, I was set to come by and see you here after a bit anyhow. You see, as soon as Miss Pottinger—Dixie, she's the one that runs the boardinghouse, who you met last night—well, as soon as she heard you were the new teacher in town, she sent out the word, and there's set to be a gathering this afternoon. Folks are all a-jitter to meet you." He tilted her a pleading look. "Can I come by to escort you to the gathering at half past noon?"

Charlotte swept a gesture down herself. "I don't have anything clean to wear."

"I'll make sure your bags get delivered to your room just as soon as Don gets them here. Should be well before noon."

"I really believe the best thing will be for me to simply return to Boston, Sheriff. This town is not what I thought it would be."

"I see. But the word's already gone out. So if we are to cancel the social, I need to let everyone know."

Charlotte sighed. She wouldn't be staying. So she ought not to go down and get people's hopes up. Yet what better place to tell them all at once what a crook their town founder was and let them know she wouldn't be staying. Yes. She would go.

She could even use the opportunity to offer them her apologies for leaving them high and dry in need of a teacher once more.

"Half past noon will be fine, Sheriff."

"Very good, Miss Brindle. See you then." The man swung the door open and offered her a parting smile.

Charlotte pulled in a little breath. The man's smile was positively dazzling. It crinkled the corners of his eyes and etched dimples into each tanned cheek. He had even, white teeth and a solid jawline that led to a thickly muscled neck and broad shoulders.

The sheriff cleared his throat. "Will there be anything else, Miss Brindle?"

She forced her eyes to the street outside. "No, Sheriff. Nothing else. Thank you." She swept through the door with as much dignity as the step down to the muddy street would allow.

Behind her, she heard an outlaw cackle. "I do believe she's sweet on you, Sheriff!"

Were her cheeks as red as they felt? How did she manage to entrench herself in these awkward situations with such regularity?

Sweet on him indeed! Only three weeks ago she'd been set to marry a different man! She wasn't about to dive into that pool again. Much less so soon!

Patrick Waddell woke with a groan.

Wretched misery. He cursed.

He tucked his left hand into his armpit and scooted farther into the patch of sunshine that thankfully was warming the morning. He'd spent the night shivering and gasping in pain each time he moved.

He'd tried to get a fire going, but with his right hand out of commission, he simply hadn't been able to rub the sticks together fast enough to make it work, even though he'd routinely lit fires that way in the past. After a time, he'd given up and concentrated on splinting his arm. But the ties he'd needed to hold the splint in place had cost him part of his shirt. After that he'd been too exhausted to do much but shiver and try and sleep.

It had been a torturous night.

Then this morning the sun had thankfully been out. Now that he'd caught a few hours of shut-eye, he needed to do something about finding food. His stomach growled at just the thought of it. He hadn't eaten since that measly meal the coachman had provided yesterday at noon. Just a few more minutes here in the sun to rest and dry out a little more, and then he'd be on his way. On his way to where, he wasn't quite sure. Maybe he'd be able to find a patch of blackberries. They ought to still be in season round these parts.

He must have drifted off, because the next thing he became cognizant of was voices. *Female* voices. He kept his eyes closed and stayed real still.

"Is he dead, Ma?"

"Hush, Zoe. Of course he's not dead. When was the last time you saw a dead man's chest rise and fall like that?"

There was a pause. "I ain't never seen a dead man."

"You *have* never seen a dead man."

Another pause. "Ain't that what I just said?"

"*Isn't*—never mind. Here let's see if we can wake him—"

Since he was already awake anyhow, he opened his eyes. They were leaning over him, a pretty middle-aged woman with hair the color of the frost-dusted pumpkins that used to grow in his mother's garden of an autumn, and a younger version of herself still in pigtails. The older woman was reaching out to touch his shoulder.

She leapt back when he opened his eyes. "Oh! Land sakes of mercy!" She pressed one slender hand to her chest with a startled laugh. "You about scared the stuffing right out of me, mister." She rubbed her hands in worry. "You look like you've seen the wrong side of luck lately. What's your name?"

Patrick scrambled to think what he ought to do. The stupor of sleep still fogged his thinking. He blinked his eyes and gave his head a little shake, but that produced a moan when shards of fire shot through him from the gash. He didn't want to move. He didn't want to talk. He just wanted to lay here and die.

When he didn't answer, the woman's eyes widened. "Oh. I'm sorry. Maybe we should introduce ourselves first. I'm Susan Kastain and this"—she swept a gesture to the little girl by her side—"is my daughter Zoe."

The fog had cleared a little more now, and Waddell realized two things. These people might be what kept him alive. And he couldn't tell them his real name. He hadn't managed to get more than a few miles from the town of Wyldhaven. At least that would be his guess. And since the sheriff of that town had been the one to confront him at the river, it was a pretty good guess that the people of that town would have heard his name.

"Name's..." He bit his lip. What name should he use? "Hank Sherman." That was a combination of his father's name and his mother's maiden name. Shouldn't be too hard to remember that.

"Well, Mr. Sherman. It's a pleasure to meet you. When was the last time you ate?"

His stomach rumbled at the mention of food. How long had he slept? He'd been hungry earlier, but right now he was so hungry and full of pain his stomach probably feared his throat had been cut. "I can't rightly say when I last ate, but I could sure swallow a bite or two." He gave what he hoped was an ingratiating smile. "I have been better a time or two, yes, ma'am."

They gave him a sympathetic look. "I can see that. Can you walk? Our cabin is just about half a mile from here. If you can make it, we'll walk. Otherwise I'll send my husband back for you with the wagon?"

He sucked in his cheek.

Even with a fake name, word would quickly get around that this family was housing a sick man with a busted-up arm and a gash on his head. It wouldn't take the sheriff more than two seconds to put two and two together and come up with four. So much as he might like to lie abed and have this soft-on-the-eyes woman take care of him for a few days, that wasn't in his best interest.

A wagon, on the other hand, might be just the thing he needed to help him escape. Get him a ways from here where he could hole up for a while and recuperate before he took to investigating who had set him up back there like that.

He knew Horace. He wasn't smart enough to have figured out on his own that he was going to be on that stage at that exact time. Someone had told him. And whoever it was would soon pay dearly for betraying him.

Now he squinted at Mrs. Kastain and did his best to look sickly, which he guessed he didn't have to try too hard for. "Not sure as I can make it walking. My leg is busted up pretty good. Would you mind sending your husband with a wagon?"

She touched his shoulder gently. "You just lie here and rest. He'll be back for you within the hour. And we'll have hot vittles for you once you get to the house."

His stomach rumbled. He surely did wish he was going to be able to take her up on her offer of hospitality. He surely did. "Thank you, kindly, ma'am. Sure would do me some good if you might send some bread with your husband?"

She smiled. "Of course. You must be starving. I'll do just that. I made a big batch of fresh biscuits just this morning."

He closed his eyes and relaxed. Now he just had to come up with a plan to get the wagon away from the husband once he got here.

Chapter Eight

Reagan Callahan escorted Miss Charlotte Brindle from his office back to the boardinghouse.

She gave him a frosty curtsy, holding her muddied skirt as though it were the cleanest of royal silks. "Good day, Sheriff."

He tipped his hat and offered a slight bow. "Good day, Miss Brindle. I'll be back at noon to escort you to the gathering." But most of his words were spoken to the door that had just been closed in his face.

He put one hand to the back of his neck and surveyed the street with an amused sigh.

The woman was positively one contradiction after another. Miss Brindle was clearly accustomed to having her way. And yet there were moments when he glimpsed a softer side to her.

This moment had not been one of those. She was most determined to leave Wyldhaven behind at the first possible opportunity.

A grunt slipped free. As far as he was concerned, the next stage heading east couldn't arrive a moment too soon. Too bad the townsfolk were so excited at the prospect of having a new teacher, because he didn't foresee her changing her mind about going back to Boston. And when it came down to brass tacks, that was probably for the better.

Women like her, all poised and proper, were not the kind

who could make it in the West. Were she to stay, she'd likely contract some illness within a fortnight. Not to mention, how would a little bit of a thing like her handle the older male students, such as the Nolan boys?

No. Miss Charlotte Brindle was definitely not the kind of teacher Wyldhaven needed. What Wyldhaven required was either a man who could handle himself or a sturdy spinster with some grit and stiffness in her spine.

What had Zeb been thinking, soliciting a woman like Charlotte Brindle to be Wyldhaven's teacher? With such a slip of a gal, anything could happen! And with the capture of several key members of the Waddell gang, and the news that Waddell himself might be dead, the town was liable to soon be overrun with every manner of journalist and riffraff outlaw hopeful the West had to offer. Not to mention warring factions within the remaining contingent of the Waddell gang who still remained at large.

Reagan was likely going to have his hands full over the next week, and Miss Brindle didn't strike him as the type who would follow instructions and stay in the safety of her boardinghouse room. He needed to come up with a plan to keep her out of harm's way until the next stage came through.

Maybe Ma would have some ideas on how to keep her away from trouble for the week.

He started down the street toward his mother's dress shop. Who knew part of his job as sheriff would entail babysitting a tenderfoot city girl from back east. A tenderfoot with a pair of green eyes that had a way of reaching inside a man and making him stand at attention. He sighed and turned down the alleyway between the jail and McGinty's Alehouse.

Ma ran her dress shop out of her home at the end of Pine

Street, and women from miles around came to her for their clothing because she was right good and charged a fair price.

Zoe Kastain was sitting on Ma's porch darning a pair of socks, her scoundrel of a dog lying in the swatch of sunshine next to her. Ma paid the Kastain girls for piecework when she had it.

"Zoe." Reagan tipped his hat to the girl, then nodded at the pup. "Jinx here wouldn't know anything about why our new schoolteacher had muddy paw prints all over her skirt, would he?"

Zoe's face turned a shade redder, and she paid particularly close attention to the sock in her hands. "He were only tryin' ta be friendly like."

Reagan grunted his disapproval.

Zoe lifted her gaze to his then, a pending tale sparkling in her sea-blue eyes. "She saved Jinx's life!"

Reagan stilled with his hand on Ma's front door. "She what?"

Zoe nodded and looked satisfied that her words had stopped him. "The new teacher saved Jinx's life! Took off chasing a cat, he did! And knocked me clean off my feet!" She glanced down at the dog whose head now rested on his paws, his ears laid back, as if he were highly cognizant of their conversation. "Bad dog!" The dog's ears pressed even closer to his skull. "Jinx near 'nough darted beneath Leonard Palmeroy's oxen hauling a full load! But ya should have seen Miss Brindle!" Zoe's eyes lit with pure admiration now. "She lifted her skirts and dashed after him like there was no tomorrow! Stomped on his leash just in time to save his life! And that was *after* he'd jumped on her and muddied her skirt. In my book that makes her all right." Zoe leaned down from her chair and ruffled a hand over the dog's head. "She saved yer life, didn't she, boy?"

The dog leapt up, tongue lolling and ears once more upright in seeming happiness that his scolding was over.

Reagan would have liked to have seen the petite Miss Brindle chasing down Jinx in the middle of the street. His lips twitched. "Well, since she saved his life, how about we try to keep Jinx's hijinks as far from Miss Brindle as possible, huh?"

Zoe hung her head. "Yes, sir." Her head was only down for a bare moment before she snapped it back up, a glitter of irritation in her blue eyes. "Pa says Jinx will learn to behave sooner or later, but I sure wish it would be sooner. He made me late for work too, so Belle got the fun job inside and I'm stuck out here mending socks. Ya see, when Jinx ran after that cat, he knocked me in the mud. I had to run home and change. Then Ma made me go pick berries with her, and we ran into this guy named Hank who—"

"My ma home?" Reagan indicated the house with a tip of his head. He hated to cut the girl off, but when Zoe got started on a tale, sometimes they dragged on far longer than he had time for at the moment.

Zoe looked a little sheepish. "Yes, sir."

As he whipped off his hat and opened the door, he offered the girl a wink to let her know he wasn't upset with her. "Best get back to repairing that sock so I don't get in trouble for distracting you from your work."

Zoe's soft smile was full of understanding. "Yes, sir."

Ma was leaning over her table, her lips clamped around the heads of several straight pins, when he stepped inside. "Morning, Ma."

She lifted her brows and gave him a nod as she laid a pattern piece over her material and smoothed it with practiced fingers.

He was glad to see her getting back to herself. He'd been worried about her for longer than he liked to think about.

It had been four years since Pa died, and for the first two of those years, Reagan hadn't been sure if he'd ever see his spunky, vivacious mother again. But slowly over the past several months, he'd seen her return to her happy self. It did him good to hear her humming as she pinned.

She was young, still in her early forties, since she'd birthed him at seventeen, and for the past couple years he'd been praying that the good Lord would bring a hardworking, decent, and respectable man into her life. Of course he hadn't dared breathe a peep about that to her, because in her estimation she was doing just fine on her own. But he'd seen the moments of loneliness in her eyes when she thought no one was looking. If the truth were told, he'd felt some of that emotion himself.

For some reason that thought brought to mind the vexing woman who had sent him here for advice in the first place.

Several deft movements later, all the pins had been put to use holding the pattern in place, and she turned to him with her familiar smile and arms outstretched for a hug. "What brings you to my place so early today? The pies are barely in the oven. They won't be ready for at least another forty-five minutes."

He grinned at her and settled one hand over his stomach. "I've become that predictable, have I?" Just about everyone in town knew that Ma baked fresh pies every Friday morning. And who could blame him for taking his bachelor self to his ma's place regular as clockwork on such days?

She reached up and pinched his chin. "You are a good son. Don't let my teasing get you down. Now, what can I do for you?"

Reagan tapped his Stetson against his leg. "I actually came by to talk for a bit. But"—he nodded toward the uncut dress on the table—"I can see you are busy. I can come back another time."

"Nonsense!" Ma stepped toward the kitchen. "You just set yourself down at the table, and I'll fetch you a cup of coffee. I can practically cut out a dress in my sleep. You won't be interfering a bit."

Just as Ma disappeared into the kitchen and Reagan was about to sit, Belle Kastain bustled out of the back room with her hands full of ribbons and buttons. "I think I found the perfect accessor—oh!" Her eyes widened, and her face bloomed pink when she saw him.

Reagan lurched back to his feet, feeling the discomfort he always felt around the girl. "Belle." He nodded and pressed his hat to his chest. "Morning."

One of these days the girl was finally going to believe the nonverbal messages he kept sending to her that he wasn't interested in a relationship. At fifteen she was nearly a decade younger than him, and he was no cradle robber, even if the girl was as pretty as Belle Kastain.

Belle hurried forward and dumped the buttons and ribbon into a little pile on the corner of the table, her hands trembling slightly. "Your ma must have just stepped out. Would you like me to get you some c-coffee?" She smoothed her hands over her hair and tucked some loose curls behind her ears.

Reagan tipped his head toward the kitchen. "Ma's getting it now. Thanks anyhow."

Belle fiddled with one of the tiny pink buttons. "I heard you rescued the new schoolteacher yesterday?"

"Just doing my job." Reagan tried to discourage her near-hero worship of him at every opportunity. "Joe did a great job leading the posse. He's actually the one who rounded up and captured almost the whole gang." At nineteen, Joe was a much better match for Miss Belle Kastain. And a lot more interested in her too.

But as usual, Belle efficiently dodged his attempt to interest her in Joe. "Oh posh! I'm sure the part you played was a sight more important than you make it out to be." She doodled one fingernail across the tabletop and batted her lashes coyly. "I prayed for you to be safe."

Reagan swallowed, feeling rather like a fly caught in the outer reaches of a web, unable to escape and watching the spider creeping closer. "I'm sure both Joe and Miss Brindle appreciate your prayers as much as I do." Where was Ma with that coffee?

Belle continued to follow the path her finger traced around one end of the table. "Will you be at the welcome party for the new teacher today?"

Had she just swayed her hips with that last step? Reagan cast an almost desperate look toward the still-closed kitchen door. "Yes. I'll be escorting the teacher to the party, in fact."

"I'll look forward to seeing you there, then." Belle rounded the last corner of the table and sashayed his way. "I made your favorite chocolate cake." Her gaze honed in on him like he was a blue ribbon and she was determined to be the lucky prize winner.

That did it. He could talk to Ma anytime. "Chocolate cake sounds good." He strode around the table in the opposite direction Belle was coming from. "Speaking of which. I really ought to go check McGinty's to make sure he doesn't need any help cleaning up for the shindig. Tell Ma I said thanks and I'll talk with her later."

He didn't even give the startled girl time to respond before slapping on his hat and making his escape out the door.

Jinx leapt to his feet with a yip at Reagan's sudden appearance, and Zoe startled in her seat. "Ow!" She sucked on the finger she'd apparently just jabbed with a needle. "Why are ya in such an all-fired hurry, Sheriff?"

"Sorry. Didn't mean to give you a start. You all right?"

Zoe pulled out her finger and examined it closely. "I'll live."

"Good. I'll see you this afternoon at McGinty's." And with that he hurried down the street before Belle could come up with a reason to tag along with him.

Charlotte felt a bit guilty about slamming the door in the sheriff's face. But only a bit. What kind of a town only had a stage come through one day a week? Of course it was hardly his fault that there would be no stage for several days. But it *was* his fault that he hadn't seemed to care a whit that Zebulon Heath was out there playing the shyster and tricking people into moving to his settlement.

Dixie Pottinger, looking fresh, clean, and well rested, stood across the room behind the front desk. She lifted her gaze, her expression placid. "Can I interest you in some breakfast now, Miss Brindle?" Dixie's soft brown hair enhanced her kind, cinnamon-colored eyes.

Charlotte was reminded why she'd immediately liked her when they'd met the evening before. She swept a hand to her ruined skirt. "Give me a moment to try to repair as much of this as possible? It seems my bags have not yet arrived in town."

Dixie's lips twitched, and humor sparkled in her gaze. "I'm thinking you must have met our Zoe and her Jinx this morning?"

Charlotte chuckled. "The very same."

Dixie gestured through the large square door to one side of her, through which Charlotte could see several tables and a few other patrons. "I'll have your breakfast waiting for you when you come back down."

"Thank you." Charlotte took the stairs to her room, and while she brushed off as much of the mud as possible, she considered what she was going to do with herself for an entire week. Idleness was the devil's workshop. Especially when it came to the mind. The last thing she wanted was several days of free time to do nothing but wallow in misery over the fact that Kent had been unfaithful. Keeping busy was the best way to get past disappointments. This was a lesson that had been ingrained into her from the time she was still in pigtails. She might not be staying, but that didn't mean she could just fritter away the hours between now and next Friday. She needed a project. Something to do between now and then.

She examined herself in the mirror and, with a little nod of approval, decided that the dress would have to do. Dixie didn't seem the type to stand on ceremony, so hopefully the few smudges she hadn't been able to vanquish wouldn't get her banished from the woman's dining room. And with any luck the sheriff would keep his word and deliver her cases before the welcome party the town was throwing in her honor at noon. Then she would at least be able to keep some of her dignity while meeting everyone. Providing she could avoid Jinx until then.

Taking up her reticule, she adjusted the angle of her hat and then stepped out into the hallway and paused to lock her door.

Perhaps Dixie would have an idea about a project that would keep her busy for the week. Charlotte glanced at the sadly misshapen bouquet of daisies on the hall's end table. While the rooms were perfectly clean, heaven knew the woman could use some decorating help.

Joe Rodante rode into town, bone weary and hungry as a bear fresh out of hibernation. He hated coming home with bad news, but he'd found no sign of Waddell downstream. Reagan wasn't going to like it. He swung down from his horse and headed into the livery.

"Joe?"

He paused, searching the dim interior for whoever had just called his name. It was only a moment before he saw Liora Fontaine peering out at him from behind a stack of hay bales. His brows lifted, and he actually glanced behind him. He'd been doing his best to stay as far from the woman as possible since she'd come to town and started working for Ewan. Surely she had to be speaking to someone else. But no one else was in sight. Cautiously, he led his mount farther into the barn. "What can I do for you, Liora?"

She checked the doorway behind him, as though to assure herself he was alone, before stepping out from her hiding place.

Joe froze. She wore a plain brown dress, no paint on her face, and the long blond hair she normally let flow freely about her shoulders was pinned up with only a few curls wisping about her face. He'd never seen her look...*unsoiled*...before. Truth be told, in all the getup that she wore at McGinty's, he'd thought of her as pretty, despite the sadness that always seemed to haunt her eyes. But like this...unadorned, natural, and soft... she was breathtaking.

He tore his gaze off her and forced himself to concentrate on unsaddling his horse. "What can I do for you?"

"Did you find him—the outlaw?"

He brushed past her and put the saddle on the rack, laying the blanket out beside it. "No." He pushed by her again. Led the horse into its stall, hooked on the tie rope, and set to brushing it down. What did she really want? Surely a woman like her hadn't sought him out to talk about an outlaw hunt.

"Joe, I need your help." Her words were soft and wheedling.

The brush stilled midstroke. His heart rate kicked up a notch. With a huff of disbelief, he forced himself to return to currying. He'd heard that cajoling tone in her voice on more than one occasion in McGinty's when she was urging a man to her room. She'd even tried it on him a time or two.

"I'm not the man you're looking for, Liora. Can't help you." He stepped around to the other side of the horse.

She sighed, and when she spoke, seduction no longer colored her tone. "I'm sorry. I didn't mean...I know you're not...that kind of man. Which is why I know I can trust you with my money."

"If you need something, just ask. Don't try to manipulate me."

"It's my ma. I need someone to take her my pay."

Once again her words, and her frankness, suspended his movements. He hadn't expected her to take his command to heart. He looked at her over the top of the horse.

She stood, head bowed, fingertips pressed together, and tears shimmering on her lashes. Her shoulders hunched. She seemed fragile and tense, like if he turned her down she might just crumble.

Tossing the currycomb back onto the shelf, he unhooked the tie, stripped off the harness, and swatted his horse's rump to urge it farther into the stall. Stepping out, he shut the gate and draped the harness on the hook next to the stall. Folding his arms, he looked down at her. He clenched his jaw. Were her tears just another form of manipulation?

"Why can't you take it?"

She looked up, her blue eyes seeming even larger with the

tears pooling in them. “Ewan won’t let me leave town.” She shrugged. “He’s afraid I won’t come back, I suppose.”

Joe clenched his teeth. Everything in him urged that he turn her down. And yet if she were any other woman asking for his help, he would agree without hesitation. “If you want to quit working for Ewan, you know the sheriff and I would help you, right?”

Something like hope flared in her eyes, but she didn’t take the lifeline. “You have to take Doc Griffin with you. Ma’s been without her medicine for near six weeks now. There’s a doc in the camp where she lives, but I’m not sure I trust him. Nothing he’s charged us for has helped her.”

Joe frowned. “You working for Ewan just to help pay for your ma’s medicines?”

Her jaw jutted to one side, and her eyes narrowed in a way that told him her business was her own. “Will you do it?”

He sighed. “Where does she live?”

“Camp Sixty-One.” She pulled an envelope from her dress pocket and held it out. When he took it, she released a puff of air, and her eyes dropped closed for a moment. “Thank you. You’ve no idea how much this means to me.”

He tipped his hat and headed for the barn door. “I’ll see when Doc has time to ride out.” With that, he left her inside, willing away the image of Liora Fontaine looking broken and needy. Looking like a woman who just needed a man to wrap her in his arms and assure her all would be well.

He lifted his hat and scooped a trembling hand back through his hair before resettling it.

Maybe it was time he paid Belle Kastain another call.

Dixie Pottinger eyed the table she’d just set and ticked off a list on her fingers. Yes, everything was in place. She smoothed her hands over her skirt and reminded herself to breathe normally and not to be nervous. Just because the new teacher was posh and perfect didn't mean Dixie couldn't make friends with her, and she certainly could use a friend in this tiny little corner of the Northwest, Lord knew.

She'd been doing her best to tamp down her excitement over the prospect of another single female in town, ever since Sheriff Callahan had brought Miss Brindle in and paid for her room the evening before. She hoped the woman wouldn't be averse to joining her for breakfast this morning. She probably shouldn't even think about imposing on one of her guests in such a manner, but she was so hungry for another woman to talk to that she simply had to try.

She'd finished setting the table at just the right time, because Miss Brindle stepped into the room at that very moment. She had done an admirable job of cleaning the watered green silk that brought out the exquisite green of her eyes and made Dixie all the more aware of her own plain features and dress.

For a moment she wavered, but the table was already set for two, and Dixie was not going to let a little thing like money and status derail her from making a new friend. Dixie motioned her over and boldly asked, "I hope you don't mind if I join you for breakfast?"

Miss Brindle blinked in surprise, but a ready smile immediately lifted her lips. "Of course not. It would be a pleasure." At that moment the woman's stomach rumbled loudly. A flush touched her cheeks, and she put one hand to her middle. "Oh, do forgive me. I haven't eaten anything since the tomato and hard-boiled egg I had for lunch yesterday."

Dixie offered her a grin. "Grumbling bellies are just exactly what we like to hear in this establishment."

Charlotte's eyes softened. "You're very kind."

"Please." Dixie motioned to one of the chairs, and Charlotte eased into it with a grateful smile.

Dixie tried not to be anxious as she sank to the seat opposite and lifted the silver lids off their plates. She was ever so thankful that Ma had offered to cook for her a few days a week so she could get some other things done around the place. Dixie lifted her fork and tucked into her food, and was immediately embarrassed when Miss Brindle's eyes widened a bit and she bowed her head in silent grace. But despite Dixie's obvious embarrassment, Miss Brindle offered nothing but a gracious smile a moment later when she lifted her head and picked up her own fork.

"So tell me what made you want to start a boardinghouse in a little town like Wyldhaven?"

Dixie nearly choked on the bite of egg in her mouth. She doubted the elegant, put-together Miss Brindle knew anything about running for her life or hiding from a man who had promised to kill her the next time he saw her. "Oh, you know, Ma and I sort of came to the end of the trail, and this was where we found ourselves. She's a passable good cook, and I knew how to run a house. I figured adding a few more bedrooms wouldn't be too hard." She offered what she hoped was a normal-looking smile.

Miss Brindle raised a forkful of Ma's ham-and-egg scramble with an appreciative lift to her brows. "She's more than a passable cook, if she made these."

Dixie felt her chest swell with pride. "She did." But that was enough about her and Ma. She needed to keep details about herself as vague as possible. It was time for a subject change. "So what made you want to come teach in a town like Wyldhaven, Miss Brindle?"

The woman wrinkled her nose. "Charlotte, please. And in answer to your question, I actually thought Wyldhaven was going to be quite different. More to the point, Mr. Zebulon Heath led me to believe Wyldhaven was quite different. I don't think I'll be staying."

Dixie's disappointment shouldn't have been so deep since she'd only known the woman for less than twenty-four hours, and yet it was. Somehow, now that she'd set her mind on having a friend in town, the thought of letting that go could not be borne. "How is it different?"

Charlotte's lips pursed in tight irritation, and she raised a finger. Digging through her reticule, she finally pulled a brochure from within and handed it across to Dixie.

Dixie studied the pictures. One panel portrayed a town much larger than Wyldhaven actually was, with a church on one end and a schoolhouse across the river in the field. Another panel had three sketches—one of quaint stone cottages, one of an arched stone bridge over the river, and the third of a beautiful range of mountains looming over Wyldhaven nestled in a verdant valley. The rest of the trifolded pamphlet talked about how Wyldhaven had been founded, its bustling economy, and its upstanding citizens.

Dixie actually chuckled at the audacity of it. She dropped the parchment back onto the table. "Well, he got the mountains and the upstanding citizens right. And I'd give just about anything to see those boardwalks actually built."

Charlotte didn't appear to appreciate her attempted humor, but she tried to smile anyhow.

"I'm sorry you were deceived into coming here, but that doesn't mean the children here need a teacher any less than they did when you thought they lived in a fancy little town. In fact, the children here might need you more than children like that." She tipped a nod to the brochure.

Charlotte seemed taken aback. "That's true, I suppose. It's just...it goes against my every grain to cooperate with deceit. And if I stayed, I would feel like I was..." She searched for a word. "...rewarding Mr. Heath."

Dixie swallowed her regret. She was going to lose this friend before she'd even made one of her. Still, she had to try and convince her. The children did need a schoolteacher. "Well, I hope that you'll at least keep an open mind until you've had a chance to meet everyone at the party this afternoon. I think you'll find that the people here are quite easy to love."

Charlotte's smile was thin, but she did respond with, "Okay. I can agree to that."

And in that moment, Dixie somehow felt all was not lost.

They ate in silence for just a moment before Charlotte spoke again. "Sheriff Callahan tells me there will be no coach through here until next week. I'll need a project to keep me busy until that time. Do you know of anything around town that I could help with?"

As soon as the question left Charlotte's lips, an idea popped into Dixie's mind. Until that moment she hadn't even considered trying to raise money to go toward the building of a church or school, yet... "As a matter of fact, I know just the thing. It's a project born on the spur of the moment, but what would you say to organizing a boxed supper as a means of raising money to build a combined church and school?" Not that she had much need of a church, considering the way God had abandoned her, but others generally seemed to take comfort from a religious institution, and it would be good for the town to have one.

Charlotte's eyes widened, and Dixie could see she was seriously considering the idea.

Dixie rushed on. "The coach comes through next Friday. We could set the boxed supper for Thursday night. And that way you'd at least be leaving the next teacher, and any minister that decides to settle here, in a better position than they are now."

Charlotte's eyes sparkled. "I like it!" She lifted the brochure and examined the drawing. She tapped the location of the church on the image. "I think the building should go here. It can be built more like a church, and the school can just use it during the week. Then once we—uh, the town—gets some more funds, an actual school building can be built in the location where it is in the drawing."

Dixie hid her smile by downing her last forkful of eggs. She had a feeling Miss Brindle was going to be staying in Wyldhaven longer than she anticipated.

Chapter Nine

Patrick heard the wagon coming long before it arrived. A man was whistling, but he heard no other voices, so maybe the man was alone, just as he'd hoped he would be. It was one thing to rob a grown man. It was quite another to rob him in front of one of his children. No man ought to be humiliated in such a manner.

He continued to lie still, conserving his energy. Willing himself to fight through the coming pain.

The wagon pulled up beside him. Trace chains rattled as the horses bobbed their heads. Boots thumped to the ground, and he heard a man's heavy stride coming toward him.

He felt his heart rate ramping up. This was going to hurt. He remained motionless. Appearing helpless was going to be a key element if his plan was going to work. He only hoped the man wasn't a Quaker or some such who didn't pack a weapon.

But as the man stepped into view and leaned over him, Patrick noted the Colt strapped to his hip, and he relaxed a bit.

The man assessed him from head to toe, rubbing a hand over a short graying beard. "Wife tells me you're in a bad way."

Patrick offered a pitiful smile. "I've been better." And he was about to be better again.

"Well, let's get you to the house so's you can rest and get some food in you. Sound good?"

"More than you know." Could he do this left handed?

The man reached down to help him up. "Name's William Kastain. My wife and the kids headed into town to a social to welcome our new teacher. But she's put on a pot of soup that should be ready by the time I get you back to the house and settled in. She also sent you some biscuits and jam. I'll give them to you just as soon as we get you settled on the blankets in the bed of the wagon."

The news couldn't get any better. He didn't plan to kill the man, and he'd been worried about having enough time to escape. Waddell had pictured the man running back to his house for a fresh saddle horse and sending one of his family to town for the law while he backtracked to chase him down. But with his family off to town, that would be that much farther the man had to go before being able to get word to the law about the incident and come after him.

Patrick accepted Kastain's hand and let him pull him to his feet, then he clung to the man as though he needed a moment to steady himself. Truth was, he did need that moment, because another wave of agony swept over him. But he couldn't take too long. Gritting his teeth, he reached with his left hand and snagged Kastain's gun from its holster before the man could pull away and start them toward the wagon.

"What in the—" Kastain thrust his hands into the air.

Patrick tipped his head. "Sorry. I just need the wagon and the horses."

Kastain's face paled, and Patrick realized he thought he was going to shoot him. He took a step back. Pain knifed through his leg, and he almost lost his balance when it threatened to give out from under him. He gritted his teeth and forced his body into submission. "Just stay back and you won't get hurt."

Kastain tilted his head. His eyes hardened as he swept a glance over him.

Patrick could tell the man was trying to assess just how injured he really was.

Kastain stepped toward him. “I can’t let you take my wagon and my horses. My family depends on those.” He inched a little closer.

Patrick shook his head. “Don’t do it. I don’t want to hurt—”

Even before he could finish the sentence, Kastain lunged toward him.

Patrick gasped. White bursts of light exploded across his vision as Kastain crashed into his right arm.

“Give me my gun!” Kastain grappled to yank the piece from his grasp.

Patrick knew he only had a moment before he was overpowered. He pulled the trigger.

Kastain froze. His mouth slacked open, and his face turned pale. He stumbled a couple steps back. Blood bloomed across the man’s shirt on his right side.

Patrick’s face scrunched into regret. “I’m sorry, man. I didn’t want to shoot you. I really didn’t. It was you or me.”

Kastain looked from the wound in his side to Patrick’s face and then back again. Shock still coated his features. “I came here to help you...”

Waddell’s conscience pricked him. That was true enough. But he needed to get out of here. Anyone could have heard the shot and be heading this way to see if someone needed help. “Listen to me. Listen careful now. Take off that shirt and press it as hard as you can against the wound.”

Kastain just stared at him, still in shock.

“You want to live? Do it!”

Kastain started fumbling with his buttons.

Waddell nodded. “Good man. Turn around and let me see your back.” He didn’t dare get close enough to the man for him to try for the gun a second time. They might both end up gunshot.

Kastain groaned as he stripped off his shirt and turned so Waddell could see his back. Waddell felt all the blood drain from his face, and he swallowed hard. The bullet had gone clean through, and a stream of blood already soaked Kastain's pants nearly to his knees.

A scene he hadn't envisioned for years flashed into his memory. His mother gasping for breath on the rug before their hearth, blood spurting with each beat of her heart from the wound in her chest. His father waving his gun. Cursing her. Spittle catching glimmers of firelight as he disparaged her from near the doorway to the cabin, screaming that it was all her own fault. And Patrick's own small hands slick and sticky with blood as he knelt on the rug by his mother's side and uselessly pressed against the wound in an attempt to stem the flow. His father had walked out that day, and Patrick had never seen him again. His mother had died only moments later.

Now, he scrunched his eyes shut and shook the memory away. No matter how badly he wanted to escape, he couldn't leave the man to die in such a manner. "All right, listen. See that red fir right there? I'm going to help you. But if you so much as move, I'm going to walk away and let you bleed out, you understand? So put your hands on the tree and stay still."

Kastain followed orders.

Waddell tucked the pistol into his waistband and took the shirt from Kastain's hand. He stripped off his own shirt and wadded it into a ball. Pressing that firmly against the hole at Kastain's back, he tucked the body of Kastain's shirt against the smaller hole in his stomach and then used the sleeves of the shirts to tie the compress into place. He stepped back and palmed the gun once more. "All right now, you walk home, and your wife will find you when she gets there. But don't move any more than you have to once you get there. You just lie yourself down and rest a mite, else you'll bleed out."

Kastain turned to look at him, disbelief in his eyes.

Waddell tilted his head. "I didn't want to shoot you. You should have just let me walk away."

A huff of disbelief slipped from the man's lips.

Waddell sighed. This was the thanks he got for helping the man? "Best get going."

Kastain's shoulders slumped, but he did start to walk.

Patrick nodded. The man would be fine. He'd done the best he could. He swung aboard the wagon and gingerly loosed the reins from the brake handle with his left hand. Driving one handed was going to be a trick, but if the horses were trained well enough, they ought to stay on the main path without too much need for guidance. He slapped the reins across the horses' rumps and clucked to them. "Go on. Gid'up now."

The matched pair started out. And the last thing he saw of Kastain was him leaning a palm to a tree as he maneuvered his way past it. Patrick shook off a prick of conscience. The man would be fine.

Charlotte spent a leisurely morning in her room finishing up *The Last of the Mohicans.* And just as she had feared, the story was as tragic as the book's title implied. She always hated sad stories. Tales from the author Jane Austen were much more to her liking because they didn't leave her feeling dull and gloomy.

Deputy Rodante delivered her cases around half past ten, and Charlotte had never been so thankful in her life to see a trunkful of clothes. Dixie had surprised her with a portable tub and plenty of hot water. And she almost felt like a new woman when she emerged. She exchanged her soiled green watered silk for a light-blue bombazine and brushed her hair dry in front of the potbellied wood stove in the corner before pinning it up.

There was still time before the sheriff was set to pick her up, so she spent the next few minutes doodling morose thoughts about Wyldhaven in her journal and thinking through how she was going to tell the townspeople their town founder was a crook of magnificent proportions. But then her pen turned to telling of the boxed supper. And as she jotted idea after idea for ways to raise the money and get the town excited, her doldrums fell away.

Thus when Sheriff Callahan arrived to fetch her for the dessert social, she was feeling quite distracted by excitement over the whole benefit.

As they left the boardinghouse, he crooked his elbow and held it out to her. Charlotte hesitated in surprise. Had Kent ever offered her his arm? He'd certainly escorted her plenty of places, but he'd always strode along beside her with his hands tucked behind his back. He'd taken her hand on rare occasions to assist her in and out of a coach, but even that he'd mostly left to the footman.

Realizing she'd left the sheriff standing with his arm protruding, Charlotte gave herself a little shake and slipped her hand into the bend. There was that scent of leather and spice again, wafting over to unbalance her with its allure.

Charlotte rolled her eyes at herself. In a moment she would be leaning toward the man and sniffing like a starving woman in a bread factory. She'd better come up with a distraction. "Dixie and I broke our fast together. She had an interesting idea." Charlotte took a moment to fill him in on Dixie's plan.

The sheriff looked down at her. "So you would spend time

raising money for our town, even though you don't plan to stay here?"

"I don't see why I shouldn't. I'm going to need something to keep me busy for the week I'm here. And as Dixie said, it will leave whichever teacher eventually *does* come to stay in a better place."

The sheriff rubbed his free hand over his chin. "Very admirable, Miss Brindle."

The compliment shot straight to her heart and bloomed like a lily in sunlight. She tamped down the pleasure and forced a sedate "Thank you, Sheriff. Now I have a question. What types of things would get the men involved in this boxed supper?"

He chuckled. "You ladies provide food, and we men will be there, certain sure."

"Yes. Yes. Of course the women will put together boxed meals for the men to bid on, but I was considering some contests perhaps? For instance, back in Boston we've done benefits where two baseball teams put on a charity event. Each man had to pay a dollar for his position on the team, and everyone else had to pay a quarter if they wanted to sit and watch. Do you think the people in this town would get excited over something like that?"

Sheriff Callahan paused outside of McGinty's Alehouse. He tipped his hat back and scratched his head as he stared down the street for a moment. "Not sure about baseball, Miss Brindle. But maybe some contests that have to do with logging? Since we are a logging town, and all."

Charlotte almost jumped up and down in her glee. "Yes! Yes, yes, yes. That's just the sort of thing I was hoping for, Sheriff! You are brilliant."

"Well now..." The man resettled his Stetson, then looked

down at her and smiled. "That's the first time anyone has ever told me so."

The world faded away, and her only awareness was of a pair of most mesmerizing blue eyes, the slash of a crooked dimple, and a nicely sun-browned face. Charlotte held her breath. This was not happening. She really ought to pull away, yet somehow she couldn't find the will to move.

The sheriff's face turned rather serious, and his gaze swept over her features and paused on her lips. His tongue darted over his lips.

"Reagan?" A woman's strident voice lacerated the moment.

Charlotte's first realization was that the woman who had said his name may as well have coated the word in ice before she spoke it. And her second realization was that somehow she and the sheriff were standing very close to each other—much too close for propriety.

On the pretense of adjusting her shirtwaist, Charlotte stepped back as casually as she could manage. She felt a swirl of lightheadedness. Hadn't she just this morning reminded herself that only three weeks ago she had thought she was marrying Kent? Hadn't she reminded herself that she in no way wanted to get involved with another man? And yet somehow, after only having known him for two days, the sheriff of Wyldhaven seemed to be able to jumble her thoughts into a veritable logjam of attraction tangled with frustration at that very attraction.

She was off her rocker. That was the only explanation.

Turning to face the woman who stood in the doorway of McGinty's Alehouse, she smoothed her hands over the front of her skirt. When her gaze settled, however, she realized the woman was more of a girl. For despite her pretty blond curls combined with a pair of fetching blue eyes, she couldn't be more than fifteen or sixteen.

If she wasn't mistaken, the sheriff sighed, but he did tip his hat. "Miss Kastain." He motioned to Charlotte. "May I present Miss Brindle? Miss Brindle, Miss Belle Kastain."

Charlotte offered the girl a curtsey.

But it was clear from the winter breeze Belle directed Charlotte's way that the girl had set her cap for the good sheriff.

"Shall we?" The sheriff swept his hat toward the door.

"Certainly." Charlotte lifted her skirts but paused to eye the building for a moment. "Is an alehouse the best place for this meeting, Sheriff?"

"This is the biggest building in the entire town."

Charlotte sighed. "I see. Well, there's nothing for it, then."

She put all her years of finishing school to good use and strode into the room ahead of the sheriff, even though in that moment she felt like she'd rather be just about anywhere else. She was dreading that she would need to be frank with the people about their beloved Mr. Heath and why she couldn't stay. And in truth, she always felt rather like a bug under a microscope when meeting new people. The fact that Belle Kastain was still glowering at her like she'd fully enjoy skewering her to a display board was doing nothing to dispel that imagery.

Just then Dixie bustled up. "There you are. I can't wait to introduce you to everyone!" Dixie rushed her away so quickly she didn't even have time to thank the sheriff for walking her over.

The next moments were a flurry of introductions. Every square inch of McGinty's Alehouse seemed to be filled with families eager to meet the new schoolteacher. Charlotte met so many people, she knew there was no way she was possibly going to be able to remember everyone's names.

Most of the men were big burly loggers, but there was the short and slender postman, Ben King, and his wife, Bertha, and the doctor, Flynn Griffin, with his dark complexion and dazzling smile. Charlotte noted a blush in Dixie's cheeks when she introduced him.

Before Charlotte realized what was happening, a hush fell across the gathering, and she noticed she was at the front of the room, with every eye on her.

Zoe Kastain—Jinx, thankfully, was nowhere to be seen—stood near the front of the group, two identical little girls on either side of her that Charlotte remembered were her younger twin sisters. Though she couldn't recall their names—something biblical and yet not *quite* biblical—they were still young enough to have large gaps in their smiles where teeth were missing. All three girls offered grins of adoration. Their older sister, however, stood at the back of the room, alternating between staring affectionately at the sheriff and scowling passionately at Charlotte.

Until this very moment, she had planned to tell the people what a crook their town founder was and then inform them she wouldn't be staying.

But for some odd reason, Charlotte was no longer certain it was the best idea. Right now she had something more important to talk about. She could let everyone know later that she wouldn't be their teacher after all.

She folded her hands together in front of her to keep them from fidgeting nervously. Her gaze found the sheriff's at the back of the room, and he offered her an encouraging nod.

She licked her lips. There would be no better time than the present to tell the people about Dixie's idea for a benefit. "First I want to say what a pleasure it has been to meet each one of you." She smiled at several of the women throughout the room and was gratified to receive smiles in return. "This morning Dixie Pottinger and I shared breakfast together. I have to admit to being rather appalled to learn there is no schoolhouse or church in town—especially since I was led to believe there were both by Mr. Heath before I came here." A low murmur rippled through the room. Charlotte held up her hands. "But Dixie had a fabulous idea, and I thought since we are all gathered together, now would be a good time to get the town's thoughts on it as well." She paused to give her next words their intended effect. And not even her many years of finishing school could keep the excitement out of her voice when she said, "What does everyone think of doing a boxed-supper benefit, with the money slated to build a church building?"

The low murmur turned into a low roar. Charlotte was gratified to hear underpinning excitement.

"At first the building could be used as both a church and as a schoolhouse, and then later a second building could be built for a school."

"I think that's a fabulous idea!"

Charlotte did remember that woman's name because that woman was none other than Mrs. Callahan herself.

Charlotte's face heated. Her gaze darted to the sheriff's, and though his wink was rapid and subtle, it did nothing to decrease the heat flaming through her cheeks. Would he ever let her live down the fact that she'd mistaken him for a married man?

Beside the sheriff, Belle Kastain fidgeted. "I believe Mr. Heath's plans were to build a bank next."

"Belle!" a woman toward the middle of the crowd chastised. "Let the adults make the decisions please."

Belle hung her head, but her frown of defiance didn't dissipate.

Charlotte felt sympathy for the girl being called out in public like that. “No, it’s okay. Belle has a right to bring up the other side. But should we put the proposition to a vote? Or what? How do you handle such things in this town?”

Humor lit the sheriff’s blue eyes, and he planted one shoulder into a post at the back of the room and looked like he was settling in to be here for a while.

Reagan’s uneasiness burgeoned along with the excitement in the room over Miss Brindle’s proposal. As he watched her enthusiasm grow with each passing moment, he had an unsettling feeling about the week ahead. Was it possible the lady might change her mind about returning to Boston? Would she be staying on as Wyldhaven’s teacher?

He settled his gaze on the Nolan brothers, who were gathered in one corner of the room with a couple other boys from the outskirts of town. They were watching Miss Brindle and speaking low behind their hands to each other, with a certain gleam in their eyes that sent a curl through Reagan’s stomach.

He transferred his gaze back to the woman at the front of the room and decided right then and there that he needed to do everything in his power to convince her that going back to Boston was the best possible solution for her. Because if she stayed, Reagan could see a lot of trouble for her—and in turn, himself—on the horizon.

And yet…rambunctious boys lived the world over. Would there be anyone in Boston to come to her rescue were she to face such a lad back there?

Reagan almost snorted when he realized the direction his thoughts had turned. *The woman is not your concern,*

Callahan. No. Keeping Wyldhaven on the even keel was his only worry in this whole situation.

Enthusiasm for Miss Brindle's proposition was building, and people were tossing ideas at her right and left.

Miss Brindle threw up her hands with a laugh. "We need to write all these down, or I'm never going to remember them all." She dug a pencil and a tidy roll of paper from the tiny bag tied to her wrist, then pegged little Zoe Kastain with a look and held them out to her.

Reagan's stomach dropped. *Don't—*

"Zoe? How about you help me by jotting down ideas as they are mentioned?"

Even from his position at the back of the room, Reagan could see Zoe's shoulders slump. The girl searched the room over her shoulder, near panic on her pale face, obviously looking for her mother's advice on what to do.

Reagan lurched into action. "I'll do it, Miss Brindle." He angled through the crowd and took the pencil and paper from her, yanking on one side of the ribbon tied about the pages.

Miss Brindle looked confused for just one moment, and then her own face paled and she placed one hand to her throat, her gaze darting back to Zoe. But after the briefest of moments, her smile for the crowd was back, and Reagan eased out a breath of relief that Zoe hadn't been too terribly embarrassed by the situation. Most of the people in the room probably hadn't even caught on that Zoe had never had the opportunity to learn to write yet.

"Of course, Zoe, I should have thought. You have your sisters to watch after. I apologize."

Reagan's estimation of Miss Brindle climbed a notch.

Charlotte continued as if nothing out of the ordinary had just happened. "Very well! Thank you, Sheriff. Now where were we? Oh yes, please jot down the idea for a log-sawing contest." Charlotte scanned the gathering. "What else?"

The ideas poured in fast and furious for the next fifteen minutes, and finally Reagan was out of paper.

Charlotte, who had already charmed the entire room, spread her hands and offered her tinkling laugh. "I think we'll have to stop there because one, we are out of paper, and two, I think I'm starting to see smoke wafting up from poor Sheriff Callahan's fingers, he's been writing so furiously!"

Laughter rippled through the room.

Reagan shook out his hand and blew on each finger as though snuffing out a candle, and the laughter mounted.

Dixie stepped up next to Miss Brindle and spoke to the crowd. "How about we say that anyone who would like to continue planning the event should show up at the boardinghouse tonight at seven? I'll make the dining room available, and I think if we spread the word about this to the surrounding communities, we can make quite a success of this benefit! Now, how about those desserts, folks?" She swept a hand toward the tables along one wall, which were filled nearly to overflowing with sweet treats brought to the gathering by the ladies of Wyldhaven.

As the crowd drifted over to form a line at the tables, Charlotte turned to face Reagan.

He held out her pencil and the pages.

Her expression was stricken, and her voice was low when she spoke. "Thank you so much for stepping in. I had no idea she couldn't write. I feel terrible to have embarrassed her!"

"Think nothing of it. You couldn't have known. And you covered it nicely."

Charlotte fiddled with the pages as her gaze drifted over the gathered people and lingered on each child for a moment longer than the rest. "They really do need a teacher here, don't they?"

Just not one like you... Out loud he reassured, "We'll find someone. Don't worry yourself about it. In fact, I give you my word that I'll do my best to find a teacher to replace you before the term starts two weeks from now."

Her gaze darted back to his, and her jaw jutted slightly to one side. "You sound like you would be quite pleased if I returned to Boston, Sheriff."

Reagan almost cringed. His tone probably had sounded rather relieved at the prospect of her leaving. He massaged a hand over the back of his neck. There was nothing for it but to be honest, he supposed. "I'll be the first to admit that I don't see someone like you as being the best fit for our town."

She tipped her chin up slightly. "Someone like me?"

Oh boy. He was digging himself a hole big enough for a grave, but maybe telling her how he saw things would be exactly what she needed to convince her that going home was indeed the right decision.

He eased out a breath. "Miss Brindle, I mean no disrespect to your abilities to teach. It's just that life is rough here in Wyldhaven. I can tell you've been raised with many luxuries that simply won't be available to you in our town. Not to mention, there will be boys who...well..." Seemingly of its own volition, Reagan's gaze drifted the length of her, but he pinned it to the toe of one of his boots before it could meander its way back up to her eyes. "You cut a fine figure of a woman, Miss Brindle, and you are a petite little thing. I just feel some of the schoolboys are going to need a bit of a firmer hand than you will be able to offer. And I don't have time to keep running to your rescue."

"Keep running to my—" Her voice had started to rise, but

she ended her rebuttal with a strangulated huff and lowered her voice to a whisper. "I've half a mind to stay, if only to show you what I'm made of, Sheriff Callahan!"

He felt his eyes widen. His gaze snapped to hers. She couldn't be serious, could she? "I think that would be a mistake, Miss Brindle." Not only for his town, but maybe for his heart as well.

"You do, do you? Well, I—"

"I've brought you both a plate of sweets." Belle's voice cut through the tension, and Reagan couldn't decide whether to be happy for the interruption or not.

He accepted the plate Belle held out to him with what he hoped didn't appear to be too stiff of a smile. "Thanks."

Behind them, the front door opened with the tinkle of the bell Ewan had hung above it. Reagan tossed a look over his shoulder. *King? What is he doing here?*

Reagan stepped back and offered a slight bow in both Belle's and Charlotte's directions. "I see Sheriff Timothy King just walked in." For Charlotte's sake, he added. "He's from Cedar Falls, a town a couple hours from here, but his son, Ben, runs our post office. I need to see why he's in town. Please excuse me."

If he wasn't mistaken, both women were drilling holes in his back as he walked away, because he could feel the heat of twin glares all the way across the room. Each for a different reason, he felt sure.

Chapter Ten

Charlotte glanced at the plate of desserts Belle had placed in her hands and felt her stomach do a slow curl. The thought of eating anything with her stomach already churning the way it was, made her feel a little green around the gills. But worse yet was the piece of chocolate cake smack dab in the middle of the plate. She always got a pounding headache whenever she ate anything with chocolate in it. Most kinds of tea and coffee caused the same thing. Still, it would be rude to refuse the refreshments the town had worked hard to prepare in her honor.

She met Belle's look with a smile and lifted the plate slightly. "Thank you."

"Ma and Zoe went berry picking this morning. Ma made the fruit salad you see there." She pointed. "But I made the chocolate cake." Belle's chin lifted in pride, and she gave Charlotte's plate a pointed look that communicated a clear message.

Charlotte wanted to groan. Of course the chocolate cake would have been made by the one girl in the town who already disliked her. Forcing a smile, Charlotte lifted the fork and took a small bite of the large piece of chocolate cake at the plate's center. She would pay for her desire not to offend the girl later, with a mountain-sized headache.

Belle folded her hands in front of her and tipped her head to one side. "Well?"

Charlotte felt a tingle of frustration at the girl's boldness. She dabbed at the corner of her mouth and swallowed. "It's quite delicious. Thank you."

Belle gave a satisfied nod. "Reagan likes my cake too." A glitter of challenge flashed in her narrowed blue gaze.

"I'm sure he does."

"Belle, dear." Mrs. Callahan stepped close and took Charlotte by the arm. "Why don't we let Miss Brindle sit at one of the tables and enjoy her refreshments? How about you fetch her a drink?" The woman looked at Charlotte. "Tea? Coffee?"

Charlotte darted her tongue across her lips. At this rate the town just might be the death of her. "Just water is fine, thank you."

Mrs. Callahan transferred an instructive gaze to Belle, who sighed and headed off, presumably to bring back a cup of water.

Charlotte had never felt more relief in her life. She'd been afraid the girl had planned to stand there and watch her down every last morsel of her piece of cake. Charlotte's desperation that the girl would be back at any moment drove her to clutch at the older woman's sleeve.

Mrs. Callahan, who had started to escort her to one of the tables, gave her a startled look and stopped.

Charlotte cast a desperate glance back toward Belle. She kept her voice low. "Mrs. Callahan, I wonder if I could impose on you to help me with something?"

The sheriff's mother quizzically offered, "Certainly. What can I help you with?"

"It's the chocolate cake, you see... Belle made it, and I do not want to offend her, but anytime I eat chocolate, I come down with a raging headache." Charlotte wondered if the woman could read the desperation on her face.

Apparently she could, because Mrs. Callahan threw up her hands. "That child! I suppose she practically forced you to take a bite?"

Charlotte didn't want to get the girl into any more trouble, so she held her tongue.

"Belle and her stubbornness, I do declare! I'll fix this. Wait here." The woman lifted her skirts and hustled straight to Dixie's side. She said something low to her, with a nod to where Belle was filling a glass with water from a pitcher. Dixie's eyes widened, and she in turn lifted her skirts and hurried over to meet Belle, while Mrs. Callahan practically dashed across the room to the sheriff's side.

At his mother's rapidly spoken words, Reagan's brows lifted and his gaze searched Charlotte out across the room. He grinned before covering the distance between them in several swift strides. Without a word, he slipped his own fork beneath the slice of cake, transferred it to the empty space on his own plate where his slice had already been devoured, and then gave Charlotte a two-fingered salute that was only slightly hampered by his fork, before returning across the room to resume his conversation.

Mrs. Callahan settled into the seat next to Charlotte, just as Dixie and Belle returned with a tray of water glasses.

"Dixie met me and suggested I bring all of us water." Belle's eyes lit with pleasure. "You finished my cake first?"

"You do make a delicious chocolate cake." Charlotte felt a bit of guilt traipse through her chest, but mostly it was drowned out by relief, and when the girl turned her besotted attention to the sheriff for a moment, Charlotte took the opportunity to mouth *thank you* to both the other women at her table.

Both of them grinned and offered her conspiratorial winks. And that was the first moment Charlotte felt like she might be able to be happy here in Wyldhaven—if she chose to stay.

But then there was the sheriff's opinion of her. Despite the fact that he'd just rescued her, she felt her irritation with the man come to the fore once more.

"The sheriff thinks I'm unfit to stay on as Wyldhaven's teacher." Charlotte nearly gasped. She scrunched her eyes closed. Whatever in the world had made her blurt that out? Especially in front of the man's mother?

"He what?!" Both Dixie and Mrs. Callahan dropped their jaws in disbelief.

Charlotte was gratified to see both women turn exasperated looks toward the man across the room.

She nodded. "He says I'm too small and proper and that I—" She snapped her mouth shut. Oh, when would she *ever* learn to think before she spoke? Mortification stole her breath, and likely all the color in her face too.

But it was too late now. Three sets of female eyes were drilling into her like their lives depended on it.

"And that you what?" Dixie prompted.

There was no way on God's green earth she was going to tell them that he'd said she cut a fine figure. Her mind scrambled for something else to replace the words she'd almost spilled. "He said he won't have time to keep coming to my rescue." She was just thankful she'd been able to come up with a truthful alternative.

Belle sighed. "Well, he is right about that. The sheriff is a very busy man. You should probably take his advice and return home."

Both Dixie and Mrs. Callahan inhaled sharply.

"What?" Belle didn't look a bit sorry for her candor.

Once again Charlotte found herself coming to the girl's defense. "No. It's all right. Truly. I actually knew from the minute I rode into town that going back home would likely be my decision. But I'm stuck here for the next week, so I might as well make the most of my time."

Mrs. Callahan rested one hand over Charlotte's on the table and leaned in. "If there's one thing I've learned over the years, dear, it's that a person can do anything they set their mind to do." She nodded firmly. "So if you decide you want to stay, don't let anything or anyone talk you into running back home." She punctuated her words with a pair of narrowed eyes angled in her son's direction.

Reagan could tell that Timothy King was reluctant to speak about the matter that had brought him to town. With so many gathered in the alehouse, Reagan couldn't blame him. So he offered the opportunity to step outside. "It's a mite warm in here, King. How about we take our plates out into the street?"

King nodded. "Don't mind if we do."

Reagan chomped down two cookies and slurped down half his coffee before King cleared his throat and got to the point.

"Wanted to let you know about something that might make your job a bit difficult."

Reagan shoveled in a big mouthful of Charlotte's piece of cake and held his silence.

"Word about Cedar Falls is that the Waddell gang is holding your new teacher responsible for Waddell's death."

Reagan just about choked. "Holding *her* responsible? *He's* the one who kidnapped her. And it was the coach horse that bucked him off into the river. And it was only providence that I was close enough to catch her before she followed in his wake!

Besides, last I heard, they hadn't even found the man's body yet." He hadn't had time to search himself, what with the paperwork he'd needed to send off about the arrests they'd made and a couple of scuffles he'd had to deal with out at the logging camp. But Joe had scoured the riverbanks for several miles downstream and found nothing. Neither had he received a telegram from any of the other lawmen, which he would have, had any of them found him.

King twisted his head in a gesture that said he agreed with Reagan but that wasn't how the Waddell gang saw it. "All I'm telling you is what I've heard. Word is, they're going to be gunning for her."

Reagan suddenly couldn't stomach another bite. He set his plate onto the top step and hung his hands from his hips. It was now more imperative than ever to convince her that returning to Boston was in her best interest. He held one hand out to King. "I appreciate you riding over to let me know."

King nodded, propped his fork on his plate, and shook Reagan's proffered hand. "I know you'd do the same for me."

Reagan picked up his plate, but he didn't return to the alehouse just yet. His mind worked a hundred miles a minute on the best way to convince Miss Brindle to return home. He'd glimpsed enough of her stubbornness that he didn't think coming right out and telling her a threat had been made against her would be the best solution. That might cause her to dig in her heels and stay out of sheer stubborn pride.

He would give her a few days to see just how isolated life could be here in Wyldhaven. Planning for a boxed supper was sure to bump her up against some limitations she wasn't foreseeing. And maybe that would be enough to convince her to return to Boston without him having to push any more. He would talk to her in a few days and gauge what her plans might be. Until then, he'd just have to make sure she was safe at all times.

A movement at the end of the street caught his eye. He squinted against the bright sunlight and put one hand to his eyes. A horse was walking into town, its rider slumped over its neck in a way that made it clear something was not right. He set his plate down once more and hurried to meet man and horse.

Wait... He recognized that horse! That was Will Kastain's horse! He broke into a run. When he got close enough to see a slick of blood had oozed from Will's side, over the saddle and across his horse's side too, his heart lodged in his throat.

"Hang on, Will. You made it to town. We're gonna get some help for you now!" Reagan grabbed the horse's reins and led it as quickly as he dared back toward McGinty's, where he knew Doc was still socializing. "Doc!" He was yelling even before he got to the door. He left Kastain astride and burst into the room. "Doc, come quick."

Flynn lurched to his feet and pushed his way through the crowd as quickly as he could. "What is it?"

Reagan felt his insides turn. "Gunshot." He tilted his head to where Kastain waited.

"Clear a table!" Doc Griffin yelled. "Everybody step back and make way." He dashed out to get Kastain.

Charlotte Brindle was the first to move, followed by Dixie. They made quick work of clearing away all the dishes on one of the tables.

Reagan searched the room, and when his gaze stopped on Susan Kastain, her eyes widened, and she put one hand to her throat. He heard Zoe give a little gasp, and when he darted a look at Belle, she had both hands pressed to her mouth. He returned his focus to Susan, his fists curling around the brim of his Stetson clutched before him. “It’s William, I’m afraid.”

“Oh dear Lord have mercy! Did that man hurt my Will?”

Reagan had started to turn back to the door, but he froze at that. The room had grown so quiet he could hear the pounding of his own heartbeat in his ears. “What man?” Come to think of it, Zoe had started to tell him about a man this morning, but he’d cut her off.

Doc muscled his way back through the doorway, his arms wrapped around the chest of Kastain. Joe followed, carrying the man’s feet.

“Pa!” Zoe cried out and lurched forward.

But Dixie, who was the closest to the child, reached out and wrapped her arms around her, holding her back. “Let Dr. Griffin do what he needs to do, Zoe.”

Flynn and Joe laid Kastain out across the table. A muscle flinched in Doc’s cheek. “What I need is for everyone to get out. Ewan, get me every lamp you’ve got. Light them and bring them close.”

No one moved.

“You heard the man.” Reagan slapped his hat back on and clapped his hands. “Everyone out.” He gently pushed Ben and Timothy King toward the door, knowing they would help him by leading the way.

When Dixie went by, she squeezed his arm. “I’ll take the Kastains over to Mother’s and my place. Come get them when you have news?”

He nodded. It was only a moment before he had the room cleared. Most everyone took it as a sign that the social was over, and, somberly, families started for their homes.

Reagan sighed and pinched the bridge of his nose. He would have to run out and check the Kastain homestead before too long, but first he needed more information from Mrs. Kastain about the man she'd been referring to. He had an inkling of suspicion that he wasn't going to like her answer one little bit.

Why had he cut Zoe off earlier?

Dixie and Rose's quarters were above the dining room of the boardinghouse. Charlotte sat in the front parlor with one of the twins, Sharon, on her lap, and the littlest Kastain boy, Aidan, plastered to her side. The other twin, Shiloh, sat next to him. Across the room, Mrs. Kastain paced, and Belle and Zoe were both perched stiffly on a single chair, arms wrapped around each other, even though another chair was just next to them. Tears tracked down Zoe's cheeks. Belle simply stared blankly at the floor.

Charlotte's heart pinched. *Dear Lord, please help Dr. Griffin to be able to save Mr. Kastain's life.*

She'd been using a slate to help distract the littlest children, and now she helped the twin on her lap erase the chalk drawing of a very sad kitten. "Let's give Shiloh a chance, shall we?" She urged the little girl to the floor and snugged the other girl in to take her place.

Aidan popped his thumb from his mouth. "I wanna tu'n."

Charlotte squeezed him close. "You'll get a turn in just a minute, as soon as your sister is done."

Seemingly satisfied, he plunked his thumb back into his mouth.

A knock sounded at the door. Dixie hurried to answer it. Everyone seemed to hold their breath, but it was just the sheriff, and he didn't have an update on Mr. Kastain's condition yet.

He looked at Mrs. Kastain. "Susan, I wonder if I might ask you a few questions about the man you mentioned."

Charlotte's stomach clenched. Somehow she had an inclination that she wasn't going to like what she was about to hear. She made a conscientious effort to relax so she didn't pass her tension on to the children near her.

Mrs. Kastain pinched at her forehead with fingers and thumb. A shadow seemed to cover the little light that remained in her eyes. "Yes. Go ahead. Ask me anything."

The sheriff rotated his hat through his fingers. "Instead of me asking, why don't you just tell me about your day starting from this morning."

Mrs. Kastain sighed, and her shoulders dipped in weariness. "Zoe had come to town to work, but Jinx knocked her in the mud."

The sheriff folded his arms and looked like he was trying not to be impatient.

Mrs. Kastain didn't seem to notice the sheriff's hurry. "She came home to change. Belle was already in town, and I thought, since Zoe was home, she could help me pick berries for a fruit salad to bring to the social. We had our berries and were almost home when we came across a man sprawled out on the ground."

Charlotte sucked in a breath and held it.

"He was banged up pretty good. Had a gash over one eye and a bigger one on the side of his head that disappeared around to the back. His arm was in a bad way—he'd somehow managed to splint it though. And he said he had a bum leg and couldn't walk. Will was going to drive us all to town, but we sent him back for the man and walked in instead. He said he would settle the man at the house and then come into town with the wagon. I should have noticed that Will was later than he should have been." A sob escaped her.

The sheriff's eyes darted in Charlotte's direction for the

briefest of moments, and he cleared his throat. "It's all right. This is not your fault. Can you describe this man's clothing to me?"

"His clothes were right dandy, though they were all wrinkled like. And he'd cut up part of his linen shirt for his splint, I think. But his shoes were those fancy kind that you see bankers wearing if you ever make it to Seattle."

Charlotte's eyes dropped closed. *Patrick Waddell.* When she opened them a few moments later, the sheriff was looking right at her, but he quickly dropped his focus to where the toe of one of his boots kicked at the floor.

"Did this man have thinning gray hair and look like he might have fallen in the river at some point?"

Mrs. Kastain frowned as though trying to remember, and Zoe spoke up for the first time. "Yes, sir, I'd say that was right. His clothes was still all damp."

The sheriff swallowed. He looked at Charlotte once more, opened his mouth as though about to say something, then snapped it shut again.

A tremor surged through her. He thought this was her fault! And he was likely right. Oh, *why* hadn't she just kept quiet on the stage the other day? The sheriff and his men would have swept in and captured Waddell and his gang then. But because of her interference, the man had gone free.

The sheriff seemed to have moved on from the idea of pointing that out to her in public. He tipped a nod to the ladies in the room before saying, "I'll come up and let you all know just as soon as Doc gives me an update." And with that he pushed his hat back on his head and exited the room.

Reagan clomped down the stairs, still unsure whether he should have offered a word of warning to Miss Brindle. If Timothy King had heard that the Waddell gang was gunning for Miss Brindle before this, she might be in even more danger now. Waddell was nothing if not calculating and vengeful. He would know that someone had betrayed him, and he wouldn't have to think hard to draw the conclusion that the person was from Wyldhaven and had tipped off his gang so they'd know he was going to be on that stage.

Waddell would certainly head to one of his hideouts. Unfortunately, it wasn't likely to be the one that Joe had followed Lenny to the other day. Though they would certainly check it out, as well as attempt to follow the wagon tracks to wherever he might be heading. But Waddell was smart. He'd only use the wagon for so long, and then he'd ditch it. It would be that much harder to follow his trail through their rocky mountain terrain after that. And after he'd healed up for a few days, he'd be heading this way. Reagan would bet his bottom dollar on it, if anyone asked. And he didn't like this feeling of impending trouble for his town. Not one little bit.

With a sigh, he pushed into McGinty's.

Doc still leaned over his patient on the table, a grimace of concentration on his face. "Hold the light higher, Ewan!" he snapped.

Ewan did as he was commanded, but heaved a sigh. "He's gone, Doc. Ain't your fault. But there ain't anything you can do 'bout it neither."

Reagan stepped over and lifted another of the lamps, holding it to cast more light on the wound.

Doc grunted. "He's not gone! He's still breathing." He angled his head for a better view and tied off a string that looked like fishing line, then used a rag to swipe away more blood. He seemed to be searching for any more areas that might be bleeding inside. "There, I think we've finally got it." He set to sewing up the wound on the outside.

Reagan felt his stomach turn and looked away from the needle piercing the man's skin. "Kastains are waiting over at Dixie's. Can I give them an update yet?"

Doc nodded. "This is the last stitch. He's pulled through till now. But it will be touch and go. He can't go back out to his place. Too much jostling for him in his current state. We'll carry him up to my bed for now. So you can tell them it's hopeful, but I'm making no promises just yet."

Reagan nodded and set down the lamp. "Need me to stay and help carry him?"

Doc shook his head. "I sent Ben for Joe. And"—he tipped a nod to Ewan—"between the four of us, we should be able to get him up there just fine."

"All right." Reagan clapped a hand on Doc's shoulder. "Good work."

Chapter Eleven

Charlotte heard the stair treads squeak and knew someone was coming. She bit her lip and stared at the door, waiting for it to open. If she was this worried about Mr. Kastain, she couldn't imagine how his family must be feeling. Of course, none of them probably felt the guilt of being the reason that Waddell wasn't behind bars right now.

A flash of light and a sharp pain in her head let her know she didn't have long before she would need to lie down. The pain ebbed to a tolerable level as the door opened and the sheriff stepped in.

He swept his hat off and smiled.

A collective release of breath brought a bubble of joy.

"Doc says to tell you he's made it this far. Surgery is over, and he feels he's gotten the bleeding stopped. He doesn't want him traveling back to your place right away however. The jostling might start the bleeding again. They've taken him up to Doc's room, and he'll stay here in town for a few days."

Mrs. Kastain strode to the sheriff's side and clasped his hand between both of her own. Tears of happiness streamed down her cheeks. "Thank you, Sheriff. Thank you ever so much."

He nodded. "Will's a fighter. I pray he'll pull through just fine."

Charlotte's mind caught and clung to his word "pray." Was the sheriff a believer? Had she ever asked herself that question about Kent? He'd attended church with her, so she'd always simply assumed he was. Now she had to wonder.

Another flash of light and a pain deeper than the first pulsed through her. She needed to get to her room before someone had to carry her there. Gritting her teeth, Charlotte urged a sleepy Aidan to lie against one of the twin's laps. They'd both moved around so much now that she'd lost track of which twin was which.

She stood and crossed to Mrs. Kastain and pulled her into a hug. "I'm so glad your husband is battling on. If you'll pardon me, I'm going to head to my room now." She turned to Dixie. "Please let me know if you need my help with anything." She hoped that wouldn't be necessary, because she knew that for the next several hours she wouldn't be good for much except to lie on her bed with a cold cloth over her eyes. Hopefully, this headache would be a short one and wouldn't go on for days, as they sometimes did. She lifted her skirts, nodded to the sheriff, and started for the door.

He stepped back and opened it for her. But then instead of staying in the room as she'd hoped he would, he followed her out onto the landing. "Miss Brindle..." He frowned and assessed her with a little worry in his eyes. "Are you all right?"

She brushed a lock of hair off her forehead and tried to smile, but feared it came out a bit wan. "I'll be fine. And I want to apologize. I know you think this is my fault." She tipped her head to the room they'd just left.

His frown deepened. "I feel no such thing. Why would you think that?"

"Oh..." She was at a loss. She'd felt certain that was the emotion she'd seen in his eyes before he'd gone down to check on the patient. "Well, you would have captured Waddell had I not been on that coach and done what I did."

Reagan stepped toward her. "That doesn't make it your fault. The blame for this lies solely with Waddell."

Unaccountably, she felt tears well in her eyes. She blinked them away in frustration. "Well, I wish I could share your feelings on the matter. I can't help but feel that had I not interfered, Waddell would have been safely behind bars and—"

Reagan held up a hand. "You are forgetting to consider that we didn't know you were in the coach with Waddell when we laid our plan for his capture. I think he would have taken you hostage no matter what you did."

She felt a bit lightheaded at that thought, but it did give her pause. And the more she thought on it, the more she felt he was probably right. "I hadn't thought of that." Another flash of light crossed her vision. And this time it was accompanied by such a flame of agony that she gasped and pressed her hands to her temples.

"Hey, what is it?"

She felt the sheriff draw a step nearer, even though her eyes were closed to abate as much of the pain as possible. A moment later when she could once more open her eyes, she waved a hand to dismiss his concern. "It's only a headache. I just need to lie down."

He took her by the elbow. "I'll walk you to your room."

"That won't be necessary, Sheriff." She gave her arm a yank meant to loose it from his grasp, but he held on.

A soft smile barely curved the corners of his mouth. "Nevertheless, humor me."

She gave in because fighting him would take too much time and energy. "Very well."

He walked her to her room and took the key from her and unlocked her door. Pushing the door wide, he held out the key and swept a gesture into the room with a gallant little bow.

When she reached to take the key, he withheld it from her. Her gaze darted to his.

He searched her face as though to assure himself she really was going to be all right.

She sighed and held her hand out once more for the key. "I'll be fine, Sheriff."

Slowly, he deposited the key into her palm. Then closed his hands around her fingers. The gesture was somehow much more intimate than he likely intended it to be. Her heart hammered, and for some reason she couldn't seem to pull in a full breath. All thoughts of the encroaching headache were momentarily banished.

He squeezed her hands gently. "I hope you know that if you need anything, you only need to send someone for me."

A warm wave of appreciation swept over her. And she couldn't seem to get even half a breath in that moment, so all she did was nod.

He stepped back, gave the brim of his hat a tug, and then spun on one heel and strode away without so much as a backward glance.

Charlotte couldn't help but notice how cold her hands felt.

As Reagan banged his way back into his office, he tried to banish the memory of the soft feel of Charlotte's small hands beneath his own. It was late, but he needed to head out to the Kastain place if he wanted to get a jump on tracking Waddell first thing in the morning. It wouldn't be the first time he'd slept in someone's barn to aid in the speed of a case.

"Sheriff, what's all the ruckus about out there?"

He ignored Horace Crispin and concentrated on the note he was writing to Joe. Joe had insisted Doc accompany him out to Camp Sixty-One to take a look at a sick woman he'd learned of, but they were due back this evening. Joe was a fine deputy and could cover things for him here while he went scouting. Next, he loaded up extra ammunition and pulled his warm jacket from the hook behind the door. Without so much as a word, he left the prisoners and stepped back out into the night. No sense in giving them the information that Waddell was still alive. Let them keep wondering.

It took him an hour to get his horse and get out to the Kastains, and then another hour to complete the evening chores that had gone undone due to the circumstances. The Kastains would have gladly invited him into their home, were they here, but since they weren't, he laid out a horse blanket on some hay in the loft and curled into his jacket.

He slept fitfully, and every time he woke it was to the memory of a pair of pretty green eyes, or pouty lips that could make a man forget which way was up, or soft, tiny hands that enticed a man's fingers to linger longer than was proper. He gritted his teeth in frustration and punched the straw into a more comfortable pillow beneath the horse blanket. There was no sense in going all loony over a woman who wouldn't be staying around for long.

When the rooster finally crowed, he lurched from his makeshift bed with relief. He milked the cow and then set a saucer down for the Kastain's tabby cat, and gave a bigger bowl to Jinx, who was tied to the clothesline. Then he set the bucket of milk on the back porch and covered it with a towel, took up his rifle, and led his horse in the direction of the river. By the time he arrived, the sun should be up high enough that he could start tracking.

The morning after Will Kastain arrived in town, gutshot, Liora stood behind the bar, willing herself to hold it together.

She knew all too well just exactly which sorry excuse for a human being had pulled that trigger. And Kastain a good family man, with little kids not even school aged yet. But what could she say? There was no information she could give that would help them catch him. The law likely knew more about his movements and activities than she had for the past several years. Until two weeks back, she hadn't heard his name in months.

She wrung out a rag and set to wiping down the counter. Again.

The bell above the door tinkled.

She didn't even look up. "We aren't open yet."

"I know."

She stilled. Lifted her face. Her heart stuttered.

Joe had stopped just inside the door and shoved his hands into his back pockets. For a long moment he stood there simply looking at her with an ocean of sympathy reflected in his gaze.

Was it the little clapboard hovel that Ma lived in that had him looking at her like that? Or the fact that Ma was an entertainer of men, just like she'd become? She tilted her head, studying his expression. The pain and sorrow reflected in his deep brown eyes. The compassion evident in the angle of his head as he met her, gaze for gaze. Maybe it was both. And maybe something else deeper too.

Her fingers knotted into the rag. "Did you find her?"

He nodded, a small furrow ticking his brow for just a moment.

"Did Doc look at her?"

Again, only a nod.

Something was wrong. She could feel it. She turned her back on him and dropped the rag into the bucket of soapy water Ewan kept on the back counter. A strange swishing sound rushed through her ears. "Thank you for taking her the money. I'm sure Doc asked a fair price and gave her just what she needed to get back on her feet." She lifted the coffee and poured him a cup. Pot clattered against rim. She thumped the pot back onto the stove. Dredging deep, she found her smile, pasted it on, and turned to slide the cup toward him. "Can I make you some ham and eggs?"

He switched his hands to his front pockets, thrusting them deep, hunching his shoulders high around his jaw. "Liora—"

"Maybe hotcakes instead?"

He sighed, hesitated, then finally sank onto a barstool. He tossed his black Stetson onto the bar, dragging the cup closer to him. "Sure. Whatever you've got is fine."

She busied herself cooking up hotcakes, ham, and eggs. But the whole time she could feel his eyes boring into her back. Feel sympathy rolling off him in waves. She fisted her hand around the handle of the spatula and clenched her eyes tight. She did not want some highfalutin deputy's sympathy. Just because he likely grew up behind a white picket fence with a ma who made him dinner each night didn't mean he had a right to feel sorry for her! Whatever he had to say could wait for another day. She didn't think she could stomach it today. Not after yesterday.

Scooping all the food onto a plate, she dug deep for that smile again and turned to face him. But the minute their gazes connected, she lost her will for pretense. The man could seemingly see right through her.

Pressing her lips together, she slid him the plate. "More coffee?"

"Liora." He reached out and grabbed her arm before she could move away. "Your ma is sick." His thumb grazed the inside of her wrist.

She yanked her hand back to her side. "I know that, of course. That's why I had you take Doc out to see her."

"She's real sick. Doc says there's nothing he can do but keep her pain as tolerable as possible till the end." His voice rasped. "I'm sorry. I felt you should know."

The corners of the room turned dark. Everything fell out of focus except for Joe's fathomless eyes, searching her, piercing to her very core, willing her to be strong. "But the last doctor said it was just a light case of influenza. That she just needed to take his tonic for six weeks."

Joe looked down at his plate. He stirred his fork through his food but didn't eat any of it. "Doc says it's something to do with her heart. It's not pumping her blood around like it should. She's all swollen up. Keeping too much water in her body, he says." He lifted his gaze to hers once more. "If you are going to see your mother again, you need to go now."

All the strength left her legs, and she stumbled to one side. There was nothing to sit on behind the bar, so she leaned her palms into the wood, hung her head, and willed herself to keep breathing.

Joe stood and dropped some money next to his plate. "I'll talk to Ewan. Maybe if I offer to escort you, he'll let you go." His boots barely made a sound as he crossed the room and stepped out onto the street, closing the door behind him.

She shook her head. Joe thought her shock was about Ma. And if she was honest, some of it was due to learning Ma was dying. But truth be told, she'd seen enough death in her lifetime to know that sometimes it was a boon. You couldn't live down in the squalor of humanity for very long without realizing that death and hard living went hand in hand. Despite that, she'd never before thought of it reaching out to touch them personally. How many times had she asked Ma to get out of her line of work, take them to a city where they could both do laundry or sewing? Ma had always declined. She said the pay was better in her line of work, which was a lie. They both knew the truth. John Hunt never would have let Ma go. She made him too much money.

All her growing up years, Liora had sworn she would never, ever become her mother. But then death had reached out its gnarled finger to touch them. Ma had taken sick. Yet hope bloomed when the first doctor had said they just needed his tonic. John wouldn't pay for it unless she became one of his girls. She shuddered even now at the memory of his eyes drifting over her and the lecherous smile that had raised his lip. Liora had told him just where he could spend eternity, and left for Seattle. Providence had smiled down on her for a few short weeks. She'd found work and felt renewed hope. And then the bank had been robbed. She'd lost Mrs. Pendergast's job. Ewan had been in Seattle picking up supplies for his alehouse when he'd discovered her crying in the alley behind the mercantile. When he'd told her what kind of job he was offering, she'd closed her eyes in defeat and given in. Maybe there was no grace for women like her.

She had only taken this job to keep Ma alive, and now Joe was telling her it wouldn't have mattered? She had signed her soul over to Ewan for a whole year, and it wasn't going to make a difference. Ma was still going to die.

If there was a God, he was somewhere up in heaven, laughing at her.

When Charlotte arrived in Dixie's dining room for the benefit planning meeting, which had been postponed to seven o'clock that evening, she was disappointed to see that despite all the excitement expressed about the box social at the afternoon gathering the day before, only seven women were in attendance, including herself, and two of those were Belle and Susan Kastain. She'd gathered from snatches of conversation heard through her door that they had stayed in one of Dixie's rooms the evening before to be near William.

The headache that she'd been babying by lying in her room with a cool cloth over her eyes since last evening pulsed a little stronger on the right side of her skull. It hadn't been so bad up in the dark quiet of her room, but the lanterns at either end of table gave her the feeling of blades being shoved into her eye sockets. She'd hoped that it would have abated more by now. She got them so rarely, now that she knew what foods to avoid, that she'd forgotten how debilitating they could be.

Dixie, who was sitting toward the head of the table near her mother, Rose, frowned at her. "Are you feeling well?"

Charlotte carefully sank onto the seat beside her so as not to jostle herself. "Just a small headache." Small was an understatement, but she would survive. She turned to Mrs. Kastain, who sat with Belle at the other end of the table. "How is Mr. Kastain?"

The woman smiled, but the worry couldn't be banished from behind her eyes. "Doc was over early this morning to report that he made it through the night. I've sat with him all day, and he's done nothing but sleep, which Doc says is right good. Doc's been giving him some pain medication to help him rest easy."

"I'm happy to hear it."

"Yes. It's good news indeed." She returned to the conversation she'd been having with Mrs. King when Charlotte had entered the room.

Since there were no eyes on her at the moment, Charlotte gave in to the urge to massage her temples.

Dixie laid a sympathetic hand on her arm and leaned close. "Remind me never to make you anything with chocolate."

Charlotte smirked and then winced. "Or coffee. Or tea."

"Can I get you a cold cloth or something?"

Charlotte shook her head, glancing down to where Belle doodled on a piece of paper with a stubby pencil. "That might raise questions, and I don't want to hurt her feelings."

"Well, you need something. You have about as much color as a barrel of flour."

Charlotte laughed, but the action sent a bolt of fire through her skull. On its heels, nausea surged so strongly that she looked around in a panic. There was nowhere private to run should she find the need. "Much as I want to be here, I'm afraid I need to go lie down again." She only hoped she would make it to her room in time. She stood, but the whole room swayed, and she leaned her palms against the table to maintain her balance.

Both Dixie and Rose surged to their feet, as though ready to catch her if she collapsed.

Rose nudged Dixie. "Bet Doc would have something that would help."

Dixie gnawed her bottom lip and studied Charlotte with a worried expression. "Have you been this bad all day? You should have sent for the doctor long ago, if so."

Charlotte's mind was so preoccupied with fighting off the agony and nausea that she couldn't form a reply. And despite the fact that all the women, including Belle and her mother, were staring in curiosity from the other end of the table, she was beyond caring about propriety at the moment. Why had she thought she would be okay to come down? "Dixie, I can't... Can you please help me back to my room?"

Rose put an arm around Charlotte's waist and nudged Dixie toward the door. "I'll help her. You go get Doc."

Without the need for more urging, Dixie hoisted her skirts and darted across the room. Only a moment later Charlotte heard the bell at the front ring, followed by the click of the door closing behind her.

There was no rushing her own movements. If she did anything too quickly, she was going to have an issue that would make all these women regret the fact that they'd made it to the meeting.

"Slowly, Rose. Please. Or I'm going to be sick."

Rose tsked. "Poor dear. You set the pace. I'm in no hurry."

The other women at the table leaned close in whispered conversation now, but all were still staring at Charlotte. Perfect. Just what she wanted—to be the topic of central interest. Maybe she could get them back on track. "I'm so very sorry," she murmured into a lull. "Please be sure to give me some assignments. I'll be feeling better again by morning."

"Come on, dear. Don't you worry none about that right now." Rose gingerly draped Charlotte's arm around her shoulders.

Charlotte gladly accepted the help. All she wanted to do was get away from the light and be able to stop moving.

From the other end of the table, she heard Belle sniff. "Pampered and sickly. Just what Wyldhaven needs in a teacher."

"Belle Kastain!" Susan's voice rang with indignation. "For shame. I'll not have a child of mine speaking in such..."

The words faded as Rose helped her into the foyer and they started toward the stairs.

Behind them the bell above the front door jangled again. "Dixie said you needed some help?"

Charlotte winced as much from recognition of the sheriff's voice as from the volume of it, which sent shards of light dancing across her vision and nearly took her knees from beneath her due to the surge of pain. That in turn reinvigorated her nausea.

"Rose..." She covered her mouth.

"Righto. Outside with you then." Rose turned them toward the door. "Sheriff, carry her please. Quickly. Outside."

The sheriff swept her up and cradled her against his chest. She might have protested the action if it wasn't taking all her concentration to keep from being sick all down the front of him.

"What's the matter with her?" Tension tightened the sheriff's voice.

Eyes closed to shut out as much of the world as possible, Charlotte could feel that they were moving, but everything felt sludgy and distant.

"From what I can tell, it was the chocolate cake she ate yesterday." Rose's voice was a near whisper when she spoke, bless her. "She told Dixie she gets these severe aches in her head when she eats chocolate."

"I'll be fine by morning." She tried to speak the words, but had a feeling they came out more like a moan.

Dixie folded her trembling hands before her and wished she'd thought to send one of the other women over for Dr. Griffin. The man had a way of looking deep inside her as though he could read all her secrets. And she would like to keep her secrets buried so deep they'd never surface again. But her concern for Charlotte had sent her out the door and running this way before she could even think twice about it.

Ewan looked up from behind the bar. He scanned her, doing nothing to hide the roving of his gaze.

Dixie squeezed two fistfuls of skirts and retreated until her back was pressed against the door.

Ewan smirked. He lifted a gray bushy brow in question.

"The teacher is right sick. We need Dr. Griffin. Would you mind going up and fetching him?"

Ewan tipped his head back and angled it toward the stairs. "Doc!" His yell could have lifted the roof off the place.

Dixie's heart jolted. She winced and covered her chest with one hand.

Ewan grinned unrepentantly at her, shook a long shank of gray hair out of his eyes, and then spat a stream of tobacco toward the spittoon he kept behind the bar.

It was only a moment before Flynn appeared at the top of the stairs. He leaned over the rail. "What is it?" His dark curls were disheveled, his eyes bleary. Had he already been asleep? She felt her heart constrict in concern, but immediately armored herself against it. What with taking care of Mr. Kastain, he likely hadn't slept much the night before. Flynn would be fine.

Ewan gestured to where she had maintained her position by the front door. "She needs you."

Dixie felt her face pale at the way Ewan had worded that, or maybe it was because of the way Flynn's blue eyes lit up when he noticed her. Nothing good could come of the attraction Flynn did nothing to hide from her. She gritted her teeth. *And best you remember that.*

She forced her gaze away from his face and focused instead on the middle button of his shirt. "It's the teacher. Something is wrong."

He started down the stairs, lifting his black bag that she just now noticed he'd already had in hand. "Knew it would be a patient. Only time Ewan yells for me like that is when I'm needed."

"Yes, well...I'll see you over there." Dixie made her escape. It would be best for the doctor—and for her—if she didn't encourage his feelings in the least. But a wagon passing down the alley between McGinty's and her boardinghouse slowed her flight.

"Dixie, wait!" Flynn caught up to her before she had gone two steps.

How did the man have the ability to make every inch of her feel helpless and yet hopeful simply by stepping to her side? She heaved a sigh, ready to rebuff whatever request he was about to make of her. He'd been making it plain for a couple months that he was interested in getting to know her better.

But all he said was, "What can you tell me of her symptoms?"

"Oh." Symptoms, yes she could tell him that. If her mind was functioning at the moment. She forced herself to concentrate. "Pains in her head. At the social yesterday—well, she says it's from the chocolate cake. She only took one bite to please Belle. Then she had Jacinda and I help her get rid of it so as not to hurt Belle's feelings. I kept Belle busy getting water, and Jacinda had Reagan take the cake from her plate, but—" She took a breath and literally clamped her teeth over her tongue. She was babbling like the drunken monkey she'd seen at the circus two years ago.

"I see."

A frown furrowed his brow, and she could tell he was attempting to diagnose Charlotte's symptoms. He had a dedicated focus when it came to treating his patients. Her admiration of his care and concern for others was one of the things she had to battle most often. She swallowed and looked away from him.

The wagon passed, and he put his hand to her back. "Lead on then, please."

She stepped out quickly. And if her rush was just as much to escape the warm shiver his touch sent through her as it was her concern for Charlotte, well, Dr. Griffin didn't need to know that.

Flynn curled his fingers into his palm, not missing the way Dixie quick-stepped to get away from him. She walked just ahead of him, and he took the opportunity to study the side of her face silhouetted in the light coming from the boardinghouse windows. Her jaw was hard and tense, and he had a feeling it was only partially due to the teacher being sick. There were moments when he thought she might be softening to him. Moments when he would catch her watching him across a crowded room, or hear her soft intake of breath when he stepped up beside her unexpectedly. But always she shuttered the softness away and turned stony, leaving him longing for just one more glimpse of it.

She probably thought to rebuff his attentions and make him move on to pursuit of someone else, but the problem was, the more she rebuffed him, the more he longed to get to know her. She laughed when she thought no one was looking. She sang when she thought no one was nearby. He'd even seen her dancing in the wildflower field just north of the creek one time, but he hadn't dared step out to let her know he was there. In the end he'd skulked home before she caught him watching her and figured him for an infatuated reprobate.

There was something more to her story. He only wished she

would trust him enough to tell him about it. Instead he had to content himself with the rare and few glimpses she allowed him of her real self.

He wasn't going to give up though. Not by a long shot. In fact, he figured it just might be time to ramp up his efforts at getting the fair Dixie to trust him.

But for now, he had a patient to deal with.

And some sleep wouldn't hurt either. If he tried to talk to Dixie now, he was liable to yawn right in the middle of his speech, and that would certainly send her the wrong signal.

Chapter Twelve

Charlotte's humiliation was complete. The sheriff carried her back into Dixie's and helped her sit on the bench in the foyer.

Rose pressed a glass of water and a piece of toweling into her hands.

"Thank you." She wiped her face and then took several sips of the water. Already the pain in her head had decreased quite a bit. She didn't know why, but emptying her stomach often relieved the pain somewhat.

She opened her eyes. The sheriff was squatting on his haunches before her, his hat pushed back on his head and a grave concern etching his angular features. It was in that moment that she realized she hadn't had her eyes open for several minutes, and the sheriff had guided her each step of the way.

Of course he would find her in this state. It would only add fuel to his argument that she ought not to stay. And was that such a bad thing since she was determined to go back home anyhow? She *was* determined, wasn't she? The water was cool and soothing. She took a few more swallows, looking away from him.

He was not to be put off, however, and leaned in to her line of vision. "Are you doing better now?"

"Yes. Much. Thank you. Were you able to find Waddell's trail?"

A muscle ticked in his jaw. "Lost it after he let the Kastains' team and wagon go. We'll keep looking."

The front door opened, and Dixie entered with Flynn Griffin. The doctor strode to Charlotte's side and sank down beside her on the bench. Dixie went to stand beside Rose, wrapping her arm through her mother's, a pinched expression of worry clinging to her. Charlotte squirmed under the collective scrutiny of so many pairs of eyes.

Flynn took up her wrist and pressed his fingers to the pulse point. "Dixie tells me you've had a severe pain in your head?"

Charlotte nodded. "But I've had them before, and I'm feeling a little better now. With rest, they always seem to diminish."

He didn't respond for a moment. He was staring at the ground, and Charlotte had a feeling he was counting her heartbeats. Finally, he lifted his head and released her. "I see. I'm glad to hear you are feeling better, but with your permission, I'd like to accompany you to your room and listen to your heart? Do a few other checks?"

Charlotte felt her trepidation rise. The money to pay for a doctor visit wasn't a problem. But what if he found something wrong with her that would prevent her from teaching in Wyldhaven? Then she'd be forced to go back to Boston. She gave her head a little shake. What was she saying? She *wanted* to go back.

Her face must have paled because the doctor held up both hands in a reassuring gesture. "Dixie or Rose can accompany us to your room, if you like? And I promise not to stay long. After doing the surgery on Will, I spent almost the entirety of last night delivering a baby and then took a run out to one of the logging camps to check on a sick woman, so I plan to return to my own slumbers just as soon as I make sure you're all right." He offered her a smile of assurance and camaraderie.

Charlotte liked the man. He had a manner that she suspected put most of his patients at ease. Yet she knew she didn't need to take up any more of his time. "Thank you, but I can assure you I will be feeling much better by morning."

Dr. Griffin smiled tolerantly. "Why wait to start feeling better till morning when I can likely give you something to ease the pain and you can get a good night's rest tonight?"

The sheriff stood. "Right. I'll carry her up. You and Dixie follow."

Before she could object, he'd once again scooped her up into his arms and started for the stairs.

"Sheriff, I must protest."

He looked down at her and offered a wink. "Sure. Have at it." There hadn't even been a hitch in his step.

She rolled her eyes, somehow knowing that he would simply ignore anything she might have to say. And she was still in too much pain to argue with him, so she chose, instead, to simply drop her head onto his shoulder.

Reagan's heart constricted in his chest, his concern mounting. He may not have known the woman for long, but he'd known her long enough to discern that giving in was not like her. She must be even worse than she was letting on.

He took the stairs as quickly as he could while still being careful not to jostle her. And when Dixie pulled back the covers of the bed and he laid Charlotte down, he couldn't help but notice how closely her complexion matched the sheets. Stepping back so Doc could have access to her, he whipped off his hat and crimped the brim into his palms.

Unaccountably, he could feel his heart beating a tattoo against the inside of his ribs. How had this slip of a woman worked her way into his heart in such a short amount of time?

Frankly, the realization terrified him. One of the reasons he was good at his job was because he didn't have a family to worry about. He didn't have to fear what those he was tracking down might do to loved ones. He could be a little more reckless because if he didn't come home, there would be no great loss to anyone.

Sure there was Ma. But she'd been the wife of a lawman before she was the mother of one. And she knew how to take care of herself—the derringer she kept strapped to the inside of her ankle was the proof of that.

But this...this was something else entirely. This feeling brought to mind a cabin of his own, all aglow in firelight when he rode up at the end of a long shift. A woman with dark curls and beguiling green eyes opening the door to greet him. Wrapping willing arms around his neck and offering him pliant lips to—

Dixie laid a hand on his arm. "She's going to be all right, Sheriff."

He cleared his throat and motioned to the door with his hat. "I'll just..." He exited without looking back.

He apparently needed a long dip in the snow-melt runoff that was Wyldhaven Creek.

It was dawn, almost a week after Patrick had hauled himself from the river. His right arm still pained him, but all his other cuts and abrasions were on their way to mending.

He rolled out of his bedroll and stood near the entrance to his cave, listening carefully. Birds twittered. The river burbled. Wind whispered through trees and grass. And somewhere in the distance he heard an elk bugle. But there were no sounds other than should have been heard on the back side of a Cascade Range mountain.

Satisfied that he was still alone at this particular hideout, he stepped through the cave entry and strode to the river to quench his thirst. The ice-melt water was so cold it made his hands ache and his face sting when he scooped some to his mouth and then patted his face to dispatch the last vestiges of sleep.

When he lifted his head, birdsong no longer embellished the morning. That was his first clue that he wasn't alone. Carefully he withdrew the Bowie from the sheath at his waist. Every sense attuned to the landscape around him, he sank to his haunches. Where was the danger? Behind him and to his left, he heard a twig snap. He shucked the pistol that he'd kept when he let the Kastain horses go free. He'd known someone would find them and return them to their owners. They'd likely be glad to get their wagon back too. Now he wondered if that hadn't been a mistake. Sure, he'd let the horses go several miles back just as soon as he'd assured himself he'd made it far enough from town to be close to several of his hideouts. But if the sheriff had tracked the horses to the spot where he'd let them go, it was conceivable he might be the one sneaking through the bushes right now.

He caught a flash of red above a white hand. He let the Bowie fly. It stuck fast into the tree trunk by the intruder's head.

A loud curse rang out. "Blazes, Waddell! You could have taken my head off with that thing!"

Lenny Smith stepped out into the open, hands raised by his head.

Disgusted at the fear coating his tongue with metallic prickles, Waddell thrust the pistol back into its holster.

Without a word he strode over and worked his knife from the tree. "You got word from town?"

Lenny shook his head. "I've been having to lay low too."

Waddell's curiosity piqued at that. Why would Lenny be having to lay low? He narrowed his eyes at the man. Was it Lenny who had betrayed him?

"You know? On account of the sheriff out hunting all of us down this week?"

The sheriff had been out looking for him, but he doubted he cared much about Lenny, who had only ever played a role of inconsequence in any job they'd ever pulled—like dropping the lamp chimney in the front aisle of the mercantile that day in Seattle so he could slip into the back room. He doubted the law had ever even heard of Lenny Smith. So why would Lenny care about staying out of the sheriff's sights? He needed some time to ponder.

He pointed the Bowie toward the cave. "I got rabbit."

"Sounds good. My belly's just about ready to run off and try to find another mouth to feed it." Lenny rubbed his stomach in anticipation.

Patrick sank down onto the stone he'd placed by his fire inside the cave and set to carving some of the rabbit he'd spitted and roasted the evening before. He offered the hind leg to Lenny and dug into his own portion while he tried to think. Lenny obviously hadn't been part of the ambush last week, or he would have been arrested along with the rest of the crew, but how many of his men were still free?

He licked a finger and glanced at Lenny. "How many have been arrested?"

Lenny shook his head. "You ain't gonna like it. That sheriff in Wyldhaven is smart. He set us up. They arrested Horace, Walter, and Dougal that first day."

Patrick narrowed his eyes. "That leaves you and me, McTavish, Shade, and VanFleet."

Lenny nodded. But he kept his gaze fastened to the meat he was voraciously consuming.

"How do you suppose the crew knew I was going to be on that stage that day? And why weren't you, McTavish, Shade, and VanFleet arrested with the rest?"

There was the tiniest hitch in Lenny's chewing before he caught himself and resumed. "You got me. I'd gone into Seattle to see if I could make me a little money at the tables in the Blue Moon. I think McTavish and VanFleet took a temporary job in the coal mines over near Black Diamond. Not sure where Shade ended up. Next thing I'd heard was the guys was rounded up. And I been lying low ever since."

Lenny never had been a very good liar.

Patrick moved swiftly. Before Lenny even knew what hit him, Patrick knocked the meat from his hands and pinned him to the wall of the cave. He tickled Lenny's jugular with the Bowie and leaned in, speaking real soft-like. "I don't believe you."

Lenny licked grease from his lips, eyes so wide they bulged. "All right." He cursed. "I'll tell you what happened, but you gotta believe me that I tried to talk the guys out of the ambush idea."

Patrick eased up the pressure just enough to let Lenny know he had permission to speak.

He gulped visibly. "I was in the alehouse down to Wyldhaven. The sheriff came in to eat dinner, and a few minutes later his deputy busted in to say he'd heard you were going to be on the next day's stage! I swear I had no idea it was a setup! I waited till they left, and then I went up to the Turkey Gulch hideout to tell Horace what I'd heard. I was thinking something must have happened to you down in Seattle and you were coming back to split the profits with us like you promised. But Horace, you know Horace, he was having nothing to do with that!" Lenny stretched his neck like he might already be able to feel the slice of Patrick's blade. "He's the one who said we ought to ambush you before you ever reached town. But I wanted no part of that. Mick, nor Van either. They said they wasn't gonna be part of it and took off for Black Diamond, just like I said. Bobby, well, he didn't say a word. Just up and walked out, and I ain't seen him since. You gotta believe me. None of the four of us were there! I swear. I stood up for you and said you was coming back just like you'd said. But like you know, the sheriff and his men were waiting. I still don't know how they knew for sure the guys was going to be at that exact spot."

Patrick cuffed him upside the head. "He had you followed, you idiot!"

Lenny's expression scrunched into one of confusion. "But if he did that, why wouldn't he have just arrested the crew and me at the hideout?"

Patrick rolled his eyes. "Because he also wanted me, dolt. And he needed proof—more proof than just poor innocent Tommy Crispin's story—that it was us who robbed the bank. Proof that Horace freely gave to him when he showed up and set to shouting at me about splitting the bank money fair and square that day."

"Oh, I see." Lenny truly looked befuddled that he hadn't thought of that before.

Patrick let the Bowie slide over Lenny's throat as he considered. Was Lenny actually naïve enough to believe he would have come back to split the profits? Or... He worked his teeth over his upper lip. Was he shrewd enough to set the crew *and* him up, and think he could come back now and have this territory all to himself?

Lenny trembled, and by the gray pallor of his face and the dots of moisture on his brow, it looked like he could pass out at any moment. "You gotta believe me. I never meant to set you up."

Patrick didn't have to believe him, but in either scenario he had to admire the man—in the one Lenny'd stood up for him, and in the other he'd tried to take over. And besides, he needed him right now. Because whether Lenny had wittingly or unwittingly set him up, the lawman had definitely been the one to lay the trap. And that meant he had some retribution coming. He'd decide what to do with Lenny later. He loosed the man and stalked back to his rock. "I've got a job for you."

Lenny's legs must have given out from beneath him, because he sank to the cave floor with his back still to the wall and scrubbed his quavering hands across his face. "You got it, Boss. Whatever you need."

"Tell me about this Wyldhaven lawman."

"I don't know much about him except that his mother is a looker that lives in town. She runs a dress shop, but word about town is she's as crack a shot with a pistol as she is talented with a needle and thread."

Crack shot wasn't exactly what he'd been hoping for. "Anyone else the sheriff might care about?"

Lenny swallowed. "I snuck through town last night because I had buried a small stash of cash next to the livery and I was running plumb low on funds. Anyhow, I got my money, but when I was heading out of town, I saw the sheriff carrying a woman into Dixie's Boardinghouse. She must be the new schoolteacher I've been hearing about, because I didn't recognize her."

Interesting. "She slender with the biggest bunch of brown curls you ever did see?"

Lenny pooched out a lip. "Seems about right. She had her arms draped around his neck, and her head on his shoulder, all cozy-like."

Very interesting. Patrick folded his arms and considered the woman who'd been on the stage with him. And boy howdy, considering on her was no hard thing at all. Crack shot definitely wouldn't be an issue with a woman like her. No sir. She was bone china, precious gems, and silk to her core. He smirked at the very thought of her with a gun.

He rubbed his hands together in anticipation. "Lenny, I do believe I have a plan. We just need to let the hullabaloo die down for a few days, is all." He stalked to his bedroll and sank onto it, angling his hat over his eyes to block out the daylight. A few more days of rest and healing would do him some good anyhow.

Doc Griffin had given her some powders that helped her sleep the whole night through, and when she woke the next morning, she felt like she'd been given a new head. The week passed in a flurry after that. Charlotte was pleased that the ladies had kept her in mind as she'd requested when assigning the projects, and there had been plenty to keep her busy.

Mr. Kastain had recovered well enough that he'd been allowed to travel home to his own bed just this morning. And Charlotte had been very relieved to hear the news. She hadn't been quite able to convince herself all week that it wasn't her fault the man had been shot, no matter what the sheriff had said.

She and Dixie had worked on decorations all week, and now

the day of the boxed supper had arrived. Wagons had been trundling into town since just after midmorning, and Dixie's dining room had fairly hummed during the lunch hour.

Reagan, with more than a little grumbling and muttering under his breath, agreed to organize both a lumber-sawing and a tree-chopping contest for the men. Each man would have to pay two bits to enter the contests, and anyone who wanted to watch would be charged one bit for a seat.

Women—including Dixie's mother, Rose—had been planning, cooking meals, and baking pies all day. And the town was fairly alive with mouthwatering scents wafting from stoves and propped-open kitchen doors. The pies and dinner baskets would be auctioned off to the highest bidders for this evening's meals. Charlotte's own basket was already packed—all except the pot roast that was still simmering on Dixie's stove.

There would be two tables of donated preserves, jams, jellies, and pickles for sale. As well as a dance following dinner, where two bits would be required for the use of the dance floor—which was naught more than a cleared section of field near the river that Ewan McGinty had worked to flatten and rope off, but the man had done an admirable job with the task he'd been given.

Now, Charlotte ventured into the boardinghouse kitchen. Both Dixie and Rose hovered over a steaming sink, their hands fairly a blur as they worked to diminish a pile of dirty dishes that stood shoulder high at one side of the sinks.

"Is there anything I can do to help?" Charlotte asked.

"Oh, I'm glad you stopped by." Dixie tossed a glance over her shoulder. "Still no more headaches?"

Charlotte resisted a growl of frustration. The last thing she wanted was to be treated like a glass doll. She'd already explained to Dixie numerous times that the headaches only seemed to come on after she ate certain foods. And she wasn't about to tell her again. "What can I do to help?"

Dixie gave her a chagrinned smile. "I'd planned to go pick some wild roses this afternoon to finish up the centerpieces for the tables. But"—she swept a sudsy hand toward the dirty dishes—"neither Ma nor I expected such a crowd for lunch. Do you think you could take that pail"—a tip of her head indicated a galvanized bucket by the back door—"and go and pick a few for me? There are scissors in the drawer to the right of the door."

"Certainly!" Charlotte was inordinately pleased with the task. All week she had wanted to get out and about to see the countryside, but planning for the boxed supper had kept her too busy. And since she was leaving on tomorrow's stage, this would likely be her last opportunity to do so. Charlotte strode across the room, found the scissors, and picked up the bucket. "Is there any specific place I should look for wild roses?"

"Take the road across the bridge and then just follow the footpath. The field is just about a mile down on the right hand side. You can't miss it."

"All right then, I'll be back after a bit. Happy dishwashing."

Dixie snorted, and Charlotte chuckled as she stepped out into the afternoon sunshine of what could not have been a more beautiful end-of-summer day. The sun hung high above the treetops, spreading gilded kisses on the mountains across the green valley, and birds chirped lustily as they darted through the air in an apparent game of tag.

She looped the handle of the bucket over one arm and took the path across the rickety bridge. On the other side, she paused to turn and look back at the town. A wave of melancholy washed over her.

Throughout the week, as she had met and worked with

women on various projects for the supper, she had tried to keep an emotional distance, knowing if she grew attached to these people it would make things all the harder when it came time to leave.

And yet despite her best efforts, she was feeling the impending arrival of tomorrow's coach with a great deal of dread.

Last night as she'd been lying in her room, pondering the doings that would take place today, Charlotte had rehashed all her reasons for staying and for returning home. She'd run into the sheriff yesterday when she'd gone to check that the area for the log-sawing contest was cleared and ready. He'd once again impressed upon her that going back to Boston was in the best interest of all.

Even now she gritted her teeth. It was one thing to know something herself. It was quite another to have a muleheaded lawman telling her she wasn't sturdy enough to survive in his town without causing him a lot of trouble.

So last night as she'd been lying in her bed, all her stubbornness had risen to the fore, and she'd longed to march right down to his office and tell him she'd changed her mind and would be staying whether he liked it or not! But reason had soon taken over—thanks to the many lessons she'd learned the hard way over the years due to just such rashness—and she'd soon recognized the foolishness in her desire to prove her mettle to the man at the cost of living in Wyldhaven.

With a huff, she put her back to the town and stepped out with purpose. "You make no sense, Charlotte Brindle. Just go home with your pride tucked into your satchel like a prudent woman would."

Reagan stepped out of his office and surveyed the street.

Wagons had been arriving in a steady stream since early this morning. Everywhere he looked, small clusters of people stood chatting and laughing. Looked like Dixie and Charlotte's idea was going to be a big hit. He hoped the fundraising went as well as the socializing.

Despite the happy occasion, a simmering tension had held him in its grip all day. This was just the kind of doings a man like Waddell might use to work some sort of trickery. And if not Waddell, then some other group of outlaws bent on taking over some territory, perhaps. He'd instructed Joe to be on high alert all day, and he planned to do the same.

Movement across the bridge caught his eye. A woman with a basket swinging by her side just disappearing into the shadows of the forested path. He narrowed his eyes. It was a yellow dress he hadn't seen her wear before, but he'd recognize that pert little stride anywhere. What was Miss Brindle doing, heading off alone into the forest on a day like today?

He growled low and set off after her. There was no time to fetch his horse from the livery, which lay in the opposite direction. She apparently needed someone to instruct her that strolling through the forest in these parts was not like taking a stroll in a Boston park.

All week he'd been doing his best to keep tabs on her and make sure she was safe, and all while keeping her innocent of the fact that some members of the Waddell gang had targeted her as responsible for Waddell's death. And now that Reagan knew the man was alive and hiding out in the area somewhere, the danger to her could be even worse. He'd spent the better part of two days trying to backtrack the Kastains' wagon and horses to the place they had been given their heads to return home, but a rain squall had made the task all but impossible. Waddell was still out there. Reagan wasn't taking any chances on what type of revenge members of the gang might seek to take. But neither did he want to make Charlotte fearful and feel like she constantly needed to be checking over her shoulder.

He'd learned rather quickly this week just how zealously the woman could flit from one project to the next, and it had taken more of his time and innovation than he'd thought possible to keep tabs on her, all while keeping her from realizing it. He still had a little paperwork to do because of the arrests they'd made last week, even though he'd been at it all morning. But he was certainly glad he'd stepped outside to take this quick break. It looked like the paperwork would have to wait.

She'd disappeared completely from sight now, and a premonition of impending trouble curled a fist in his gut.

He picked up his pace.

Chapter Thirteen

The path led Charlotte into a thickly treed wood, and as she stepped into the welcome cool of the shade, she continued her self-lecture. "Whatever in the world would make you want to stay in a town like Wyldhaven? Especially after the way Mr. Heath deceived you into coming!"

Well, she'd certainly like to show Sheriff Callahan that she was made of sterner stuff than he obviously thought she was. Charlotte groaned aloud as she navigated a fairly steep incline in the trail. She rolled her eyes and mumbled to herself, "Surely this melancholy arises from more than the desire to prove yourself to that man?"

That was when she thought of little Zoe Kastain and her twin sisters, who had never lived in a town where they'd had access to an education. Sure, Sheriff Callahan had promised that he would try to find another teacher to take her place, but what if she left and they could not find a replacement? The children would go another year or more without learning.

And then there were the people themselves... When she'd first arrived, she couldn't imagine what would make anyone want to live in a dirty, uncivilized town like Wyldhaven, but as she'd gotten to know several of the women this past week, she'd come to realize that each family was just trying to scrape out a living for themselves. They worked dawn to dusk, and not many of them had time to spend on building boardwalks or cobbling streets. They rose with the roosters and worked straight through at laborious work until they fell into bed in exhaustion at night, then woke up and repeated the process the next day. Special occasions like tonight's boxed supper gave them something to look forward to—something to break up the monotony of their days. And yet despite the grueling nature of their lives, Charlotte couldn't help but admire their work ethic and the commitment of women who stuck by their husbands, even when it meant living in a backwoods place such as Wyldhaven.

Relieved to know that her dilemma did have some substance to it other than a man with broad shoulders and alluring blue eyes, she rounded a bend in the road, and to her right a field opened up. A soft breeze whispered over the meadow, and Charlotte gasped at the beauty stretched before her. As far as her eye could see, there were wild roses bursting with magenta blooms, and here and there a splash of cobalt lavender where a butterfly bush broke through the monotony of pink. With the sun cascading through windswept leaves to create mottled patches of shadow and light, the sight quite literally took her breath away.

Her gasp must have revealed her presence, for suddenly, a woman stood from behind a rosebush not too far away. She quickly swiped at her cheeks and started to hurry past Charlotte.

Concern immediately filled Charlotte. The woman had obviously been seeking some solitude, and she'd disturbed her. She held out a hand to stop her. "I'm terribly story to have intruded on you." She lifted the basket. "Dixie Pottinger asked me to come pick some roses for the centerpieces on the tables."

The woman stilled, a look of surprise on her face.

Charlotte frowned. It was almost as if she hadn't expected Charlotte to speak to her.

She had blond hair braided into a delicate halo, and though her dress was a plain muslin, she had a very pretty face with large eyes and delicate brows. She was holding something in her hands, but Charlotte couldn't quite make out what the brown clump might be.

Charlotte stepped forward and held out one hand. "I'm Charlotte Brindle, the new schoolteacher in town. Though truth be told, I don't know how long I'll be staying."

The woman stared for a long moment before transferring the object she was holding to her left hand and reaching out to grip Charlotte's fingers. "Liora. Liora Fontaine."

Charlotte smiled. "It's a pleasure to meet you, Liora. If you don't mind my asking, what do you have there?" She tipped a nod to the object.

A hesitant smile transformed Liora's face from pretty to beautiful. She glanced down and then held the item out for Charlotte to see. "It's a sparrow's nest." She looked to the trees above. "Likely this is an old one and they are up in the branches weaving a new nest even as we speak."

There was something about Liora's expression that took Charlotte back to the year she was ten when Father had moved them from New York to Boston. Charlotte's first day to school had been miserable, uncertain, and lonely until Bonnie Blythe had approached her and offered to share her apple. Just that one simple act had been like the first ray of morning sunshine after an all-night storm. She and Bonnie had been fast friends ever since. And now as Charlotte studied the uncertain expression on Liora's face, she wanted to offer that same ray of friendship.

She reached out one finger and touched the edge of the

perfectly woven nest. "Amazing, isn't it? How the Lord gave the birds the ability to create something so intricate?"

Liora tilted her head. "If you believe in that sort of thing."

Charlotte felt a jolt of surprise. It never ceased to amaze her when someone claimed not to believe in a God whose fingerprints were so obviously visible in all His creation. "I do believe it. The Bible says not a sparrow falls that He doesn't see and care about. It goes on to say that if He cares that much about small sparrows, we can be sure to know He cares for us even more." She studied the girl's face, hoping her words might be an encouragement since she'd been so obviously distressed moments ago.

Liora studied the bowl of intertwined grass and twigs, one edge of her lower lip tucked between her teeth.

Charlotte assessed that she'd likely said enough on the subject for now. She glanced around. "It almost seems a sacrilege to pull out the scissors and start cutting, but I need to hurry back with the flowers if we are to get them arranged and on the tables in time for the supper. Would you like to help me? I only have one pair of scissors, but with one of us choosing blooms and the other cutting, it might go faster."

Liora tilted her head. She darted a glance to the path leading to town and continued to work the one edge of her lower lip between her teeth. "I'd really like to, but I have to get back into town myself. I'll be late for work if I don't get on."

Charlotte frowned. She didn't recall seeing Liora about town. "You work in Wyldhaven?"

Liora hung her head toward the ground. "Yes, and I've already been gone too long, so I need to scuttle. Nice to meet you." She dipped a curtsy and then turned and hurried down the path.

Charlotte debated whether to call after her, but decided to

let her go. Wherever did the woman work? She would make it a point to ask Dixie. Maybe even encourage Dixie to include Liora in a few of the town's social gatherings. The woman was obviously lonely and troubled. She would like to help her, even if she was heading back home on tomorrow's stage.

Right now, she needed to get Dixie her flowers.

Lenny watched from behind a tree at the edge of the wood as Liora left the schoolteacher standing alone with naught but a tin pail clasped in her hands. He checked the trail. Empty. This was exactly the opportunity he'd been searching for. Finally he would return to Waddell with the prize in hand.

The truth was, he'd known the story Reagan and Joe had spun was a trap from the first moment. He'd also known that Horace's impulsiveness would have him charging right into the trap. Which should have left Lenny with a nice free piece of territory for his own pillaging. What he hadn't counted on was Waddell escaping. And he could see the distrust reflected in the man's gaze each time they spoke. What he needed now was to regain some of the man's confidence.

The woman hummed as she made her way to the first bush.

Lenny ducked his head to keep out of sight as he crept from behind the tree and cat-footed to a row of grass between the rosebushes. He imagined the look of surprise and appreciation on Waddell's face when he returned to camp with the woman. This was exactly the ticket he needed to get back into Waddell's good graces.

Her humming grew louder. He parted the branches of one bush and could see the yellow of her skirt just ahead.

But just as he reached for the knife in his belt and decided now was his chance, she muttered something about butterflies, of all things, and sprang away to cut flowers from a blue bush several paces ahead. Too far to make a quick grab for her.

Disgusted, he let go of the branch he'd been holding. It sprang up and slapped him in the face, one thorn gouging so deep it was all he could do to withhold a howl that would alert her to his presence. He cursed softly under his breath and pressed his fingers to his chin. They came away bloody.

He cursed again and was just about to start forward for the second time when he heard boots crunching through the grass a few feet away. Boots that supported too much weight to be the slip of a teacher.

Carefully, he parted the branches again. He could no longer see the schoolmarm, who must have moved deeper into the field, but above a bush several feet away, he could see the broad shoulders of a man making his way through the field. The man turned sideways to slip between two bushes, and sunlight glinted off something on his chest.

Lenny jerked back and pressed his face to the ground. The sheriff! He wanted no part in that fight. He'd once witnessed the man bring down a jackrabbit at seventy-five yards.

Slowly, he slithered backward toward the relative safety of the dark woods. Waddell would have to wait a little longer to get his revenge.

And Lenny would have to hope he lived long enough to get back into Waddell's good graces.

Charlotte chose her clippings carefully, both so that she would have the best of the blooms for the tables, but also so that she didn't strip any one bush too bare. And a few minutes later she looked up to note that she stood in the middle of the field. Any direction she looked, there spread a fuchsia and blue ocean of beauty.

A thrill of joy zipped through her. "Father, Your creation is amazing!" She spread her arms wide, tipped her face to the sky, and spun in a circle, laughter spilling from her lips.

When she came to a rather dizzy stop, her gaze landed on the sheriff, who was standing in the middle of the field not far away, arms folded over his chest and Stetson tipped back as he watched her unashamedly. From this distance she couldn't see any laugh crinkles around his eyes, but something in his stance told her they were there.

Heat flaming through her face, she bent and retrieved her pail and dropped the scissors down between the stems. "Sheriff, what are you doing here?" As she made her way through the sea of flowers toward him, she scanned the area to see if any other people had witnessed her very unladylike display of giddiness.

His lips tilted into a slow grin when she stopped before him. "No one here but me, don't worry."

Charlotte's heart rate picked up. She remembered being dismayed at finding herself alone with him on her first day in Wyldhaven, but now she felt chagrinned to note that her uptick in pulse had nothing to do with dismay but very much an emotion of another sort. And that right there was both a reason to stay and a reason to run as fast as she could to get on tomorrow's stage. To run and not look back. She didn't know if she would ever be able to bring herself to trust her heart to another man.

So why was it she couldn't seem to stop herself from wondering what it might feel like to be wrapped in his arms? Especially since he had made it abundantly clear he shared no such attraction? He felt she would be inadequate as a teacher and wanted nothing more than to see her get on that stagecoach tomorrow.

She tore her gaze away and focused on one of the blooms in the bucket. "What brings you out here?"

His feet shuffled. "I saw you heading this way, and I figured I'd tag along to make sure you made it back to town safely. Quite a few newcomers around today. And what with the recent dealings with the Waddell gang..." He hooked his thumbs into his belt loops and settled his weight on one foot. "Just didn't want any monkeyshiners to find you."

Her brows arched in curiosity, and she couldn't suppress the humor that quirked one lip. "Monkeyshiners?" Definitely a term she'd never heard in Boston.

"Yeah, you know. Troublemakers. Wanted to make sure you were safe, is all."

Ah! So he was simply doing his job and naught more. Why, especially when she'd just been thinking she'd never be able to trust her heart to another again, was she so disappointed with that realization?

She swept a hand toward the path behind him. "Well, I was just heading back. So I won't keep you. I appreciate you taking time to check on me."

He stepped over beside her and took the pail but didn't retreat right away. With a crinkle of amusement at the corners of his eyes, he reached out and lifted a rose petal from her hair. He held it up for her to see, rubbing the softness of it between his thumb and first finger before he tossed it to one side. Still he didn't step back. His expression shifted to something more serious, and his gaze drifted from her eyes to her hair. From her hair it swept across both cheeks and then on down to linger on her lips. A muscle ticked in his jaw, and he returned his focus to her eyes.

"How's your head been?"

Heat hammering through her with each pulse in her veins, she folded her hands together. She couldn't seem to make sense of his question. Not when he'd just been looking at her like a man did when he was interested in a woman. Her mouth went dry. She must think. He'd asked her... She frowned, searching through the fog of the last few minutes, and then it hit her. "My head. Yes. It's been fine. No more pain. Thanks for asking."

Standing this close to the man, she noticed for the first time a small scar that started above his eye and angled back beneath his Stetson. Her fingers itched to reach up and trace it, but she clenched them together tightly to ensure they stayed put. He studied her further, the lawman in him likely trying to assess if she'd spoken truthfully, and yet she doubted any of his captives had ever felt the impact of his searching blue gaze quite as deeply.

Had Kent ever looked at her in such a way? She'd certainly never felt such knee-weakening force from any look he'd ever given her. Had never *wanted* him to look at her like this.

She could hear her heartbeat thumping in her ears, feel the prickle of awareness that raised every particle of her body to attention, hear the soft inhale and exhale that indicated she was still breathing even though the tightening of every muscle in her chest would surely cut off that ability at any moment.

He cleared his throat softly and stepped back. He stretched a hand toward the pine-needle-strewn trail. "I'll see you home safely, if you don't mind." The words were low and gravely, as though he might be having a hard time finding his voice.

Charlotte suddenly felt as though someone had lit a match to the brush just behind her. She hoisted her skirts and tried not to look as though she'd like to run through the rosebushes back to the trail. But all the while she could feel his gaze drilling heat into her back.

Once they reached the trail, he stepped up beside her, and that was not much better, for then she could feel the warmth of him through her sleeve each time they swayed near to one another.

After a few awkward paces, the sheriff said, "You've kept yourself rather busy this week."

Good. Something neutral. Maybe that would help her get her mind off this infernal attraction for the aggravating man.

She nodded. "I'll be glad to leave the next teacher in a better position, and though I've been disappointed with some of the limitations I've come up against in planning the benefit, I still think we are going to have a wonderful time tonight. It looks like there's going to be a good turnout, and perhaps with a church building, Mr. Heath will be able to talk a minister into settling in the town soon as well. I just hope he's more honest with a man of the cloth than he was with me!"

The sheriff chuckled. "So you've not changed your mind then? About returning to Boston?"

There was a hopeful note in his voice that set her teeth on edge. Skirts hoisted, she spun to face him, effectively blocking the trail. "You really can't wait to be shut of me, can you, Sheriff?"

He stopped and, cocking one hip to the side, hooked a thumb into a belt loop. "My concern is only for your safety, Miss Brindle. And for that of Wyldhaven." A glitter that bordered on challenge flickered in his blue eyes.

Charlotte's irritation rose. She took a step toward him. "Seems to me that your concern has more to do with the worry that if I stay, it's going to mean more work for you!" She reached out and flicked the star pinned to the front of his shirt.

He had hold of her hand before she could retreat even half a step. His thumb caressed the backs of her knuckles, and there was something distinctly similar to hurt in his gaze.

Charlotte's breathing hitched.

He released her and stepped back. "You seem set on making a villain of me." He loosed an exhale that came out just short of a growl. "I assure you my only aim in asking after your decision was to make conversation, though I stand by my belief that you will be safer in Boston, and I think you would be wise to keep to your plan of returning home. So I ask again, have you changed your mind? Or will you be getting on that stage tomorrow?"

She hesitated. Here it was again. The conundrum. Go? Or stay? Retreat? Or fight? Abandon little Zoe Kastain and the students like her? Or stay and put up with some less-than-adequate conditions in order to teach them? Back in Boston there were drawbacks. Here there were drawbacks, one of them the frustrating man standing before her at this very moment. Despite her desire to stay away from Kent, she longed to retreat to the safe familiarity of home. But if she did, she would be abandoning the children of Wyldhaven. Children who very badly needed an education.

And yet the sheriff *had* promised to find a replacement for her. "Have you found another teacher to take my place yet?"

He cleared his throat and looked like he wished he didn't have to answer that. "These things take time. But I can assure you that I will make it my highest priority to find a new teacher just as soon as I can."

There, you see? You needn't worry. Surely the man wouldn't deceive her in this. She could return home knowing that the children would still be in good hands. Yes. In the end, she was fairly certain that returning to Boston was the right thing for her to do.

She opened her mouth to tell him so, but she was prevented from speaking when from behind them on the path, Zoe Kastain called out, "Sheriff! Miss Brindle!"

A glance back revealed the little girl barreling toward them, her arm stretched full out before her and Jinx lunging at the end of a lead rope.

Charlotte stepped partway behind the sheriff. She'd planned to wear this dress to this evening's supper, but she hadn't counted on an encounter with Jinx.

Reagan met her gaze over his shoulder and laughed. "Don't worry. I'll whack him with the bucket if he gets anywhere near you."

Charlotte's face warmed, and she wrinkled her nose at him. So he had noticed the dirty paw prints on her skirt the other day.

Thankfully, Zoe was able to hang on to the dog's leash this time, and when Jinx gave a happy yip and lunged toward the two of them, tongue lolling like he'd be overjoyed to offer a sloppy kiss, Zoe yanked him back before he could make contact. "No, Jinx!"

With a whimper, the dog settled onto his haunches. Charlotte obligingly stepped from behind the sheriff and bent to give the dog's head a few pats.

Reagan chuckled. "You are supposed to walk the dog, Zoe. Not let the dog walk you."

Zoe grinned. "Jinx don't rightly *walk* anywhere. But Pa says he'll settle down a bit once he gets another year or two under his hide." Her gaze sobered a little at the mention of her father.

Charlotte's heart went out to her. "How is your pa?"

Zoe brushed a lock of red hair that had escaped her braid behind her ear. "Ma says he's strong and that he's going to pull through just fine." A smile lit her pretty blue eyes. "He even halfway sat up in his bed and ate dinner same time as the rest of us last night. I'm heading to Doc Griffin's right now to pick up some medicines Pa be needin'. I have to get back so's Belle can be on time for the supper."

As though reminded of her purpose, Zoe started on past them, but as she did, her focus darted to the pail full of flowers in the sheriff's hands. "You two been picking posies together?" A gleam of awareness sparkled in the gaze she darted between them.

Charlotte cleared her throat even as the sheriff hurried to say, "We have not. Miss Brindle picked these for the supper tonight, and I happened upon her and offered to walk her home for her protection. Nothing more." He lowered a stern expression toward the girl. "Understood?"

Charlotte felt a little miffed. He didn't have to be so all-fired adamant about it!

Zoe scuffed at a stone with the toe of one shoe, hanging her head like a chastised toddler. "Yes, sir."

"Good. Now would you like to accompany us back into town?"

The sparkle and enthusiasm immediately returned to the girl's demeanor. "I sure would!"

The rest of the way into Wyldhaven, Zoe chatted about how thrilled she was that school would be starting in just over a week and that she and her siblings couldn't wait to have their first day of schooling ever. "Well, Belle had some schooling when we lived down in Portland for a while. But we moved from there a few years after I was born, so she don't rightly remember much."

With each passing moment Charlotte's heart grew heavier. How could she return back home to her life of comfort and ease knowing she was leaving these children in such grave need of an education? And yet could she reconcile herself to living in such an uncivilized place? Especially after Mr. Heath's deception?

She sighed. She had less than twenty-four hours to decide.

When they reached the bridge, Charlotte voiced a question she had wondered about when she came over it earlier. "Sheriff, why is this portion in the middle of the bridge lower than the rest?"

"That's a spillway. In the spring, winter runoff fills the creek quite high."

"Why wasn't the bridge simply built a little higher?"

"I believe, if the drawing in your pamphlet can be trusted, Miss Brindle, that Mr. Heath intends to do just that with a stone archway. This bridge was only meant to be temporary."

Her ire rose at the reminder of the deceptive little pamphlet. "Well, I can assure you that Mr. Heath in no way mentioned that picture was how he *planned* for Wyldhaven to look *eventually*."

They had arrived at the boardinghouse now, and Sheriff Callahan paused and extended the bucket full of flowers with a little bow. There was an aggravating glint in his gaze that made her wonder if he thought she was making too much of Mr. Heath's deception. "I'm sure there was some sort of misunderstanding, is all."

She felt her chin lift slightly as she accepted the bucket from him, and the man had the audacity to chuckle as he settled one hand against Zoe's shoulder, lifted a wave of farewell, and walked away down the street.

"Sheriff!" Charlotte called.

He stopped and looked back at her.

"Don't worry. I've just as much desire to return to Boston as you seem to have to see me go!"

The sheriff looked relieved, but beside him, Zoe's eyes rounded, and Charlotte felt a prick of conscience for her impetuous, brash words, yet before she could amend her statement, the sheriff had prodded the little girl on her way and left Charlotte standing alone.

She stormed into the boardinghouse kitchen and slammed the bucket onto the counter. "Oh, that man positively makes my blood boil!"

Dixie, who was just wringing the last of the water from her dishrag and giving the counter one last swipe, gave her a startled look.

Charlotte took a breath. "Sorry." She waved a hand. "Sheriff Callahan is just as bad as Mr. Heath! He harbors no outrage toward the man for deceiving me into coming out here!"

Dixie tilted her head. "So which one makes your blood boil?" Gentle humor softened her brown eyes.

Charlotte threw up her hands. "Both of them. For different reasons."

Dixie laughed softly. "Yes. I'm sure the reasons are very different." She arched a brow.

Charlotte folded her arms and did her best imitation of a glower. She knew Dixie was implying that her frustration with the sheriff was due to an attraction, but she wasn't going to dignify the implication with a response.

Dixie chuckled. "All right. I can see you don't want to discuss that. So back to Mr. Heath... The thing is...none of us have ever known him to be deceptive like this before. What were his exact words to you?"

Charlotte huffed and stomped over to the vases that Dixie had set out on the counter. Roses she had earlier so carefully and gently snipped she now thrust into the vases with venom. "We only spoke for a few minutes in my parents' parlor, and

I remember almost word for word what he said as he handed that brochure to me! First he said, 'This will tell you a little about the Wyldhaven I have dreamed of building for quite a goodly sum of years.'"

Dixie's brows lifted. "'Have dreamed of building'?"

Charlotte stilled, a rose held frozen above the mouth of a vase. She felt a little lightheaded. "Well yes, he did say that, but he made it sound like his dream had come true!" She stabbed the rose in with the other flowers as though it were a dart she was thrusting into Mr. Heath's shoulder.

Dixie's expression remained passive. Charlotte couldn't help but notice that her new friend didn't look like she was coming around to her way of thinking.

"What else did he say? Anything?"

"He certainly did! As he was leaving, he said, 'Miss Brindle, I believe that if you compare Wyldhaven, the little piece of New England blooming on the wild frontier, to any other town, you'll find it will be the far superior place to settle one day. And we hope you'll grace us with your excellent teaching skills.'"

Dixie straightened. "'Will be'? He said it just like that? 'Will be the far superior place to settle one day...'?"

Charlotte felt her jaw go slack. And some of the starch seeped out of her annoyance toward the man. Had she really been misjudging him from the moment she'd arrived in town? She'd thought he meant she would settle in the town one day, not that the town would be far superior one day. Still... Her jaw jutted to one side, and she pinned Dixie with a look. "Yes. He did say it just like that. But surely he had to know the impression his words were leaving on me?"

Dixie hung her dishrag on the hook by the sink and then plunked her hands on her hips. "Honey, he's a man. Literal is the only language they speak. I'm sure Mr. Heath felt he was quite clear that Wyldhaven would one day be as depicted on that brochure."

Charlotte threw up her hands, but in that moment she was dismayed to note the excitement shooting through her at the thought of getting to be part of a project like that. Imagine! Taking a little scrap of a place like Wyldhaven and turning it into a beautifully warm and welcoming village.

Staying would also allow her to avoid the dread she felt each time she thought of going back to Boston and facing Kent again.

On the other hand, it also meant she'd have to resign herself to living in this backwoods squalor for some time to come.

Chapter Fourteen

The thrill of taking on a project like Wyldhaven didn't leave Charlotte for the entire rest of the afternoon. As she and Dixie put the finishing touches on the tables in McGinty's Alehouse, ideas of new school projects to add to her list kept flitting through her mind. But with each passing moment, her dismay at her new excitement rose a notch higher. Whatever was the matter with her? She felt like someone had stuffed every conflicting emotion imaginable into her and then given her a good shaking, to boot.

Families had started filtering into the room only a few minutes ago.

Charlotte stood to one side at the rear of the space and worked the kinks from her back as subtly as she could. Bending over the tables all afternoon, combined with sleeping on the slightly lumpy mattress in her room at the boardinghouse, had pain shooting through her lower back. Within a fortnight she could be in Boston sleeping on her own comfortable feather tick, and yet here she was, seriously considering not getting onto the stagecoach in the morning.

"I've a liniment that will make that feel better."

Charlotte startled at the male voice that spoke quietly from just behind her. She turned to find Dr. Flynn Griffin standing at the bottom of the steps that led to the upper floor of McGinty's.

"Sorry. I didn't mean to sneak up on you." Flynn swept his hat to indicate the staircase. "I rent a room from Ewan." He pinned her with a searching look. "No more headaches this week?"

"No." Charlotte shook her head and offered a reassuring smile. "And as for my back, I think I'll be right as rain given a few moments. I've just been bent over the tables for quite some time."

The doctor turned to scan the room. "Everything looks lovely, Miss Brindle."

But Charlotte noticed that the good doctor's gaze was not on the table decorations but instead rested on Dixie Pottinger, who was welcoming people near the door.

Charlotte leaned a bit closer to the man and lowered her voice. "Would you care for a little inside information as to the appearance of Miss Pottinger's basket, Dr. Griffin?"

His gaze darted to hers, and he blinked. "Whyever would you think—" But at Charlotte's lifted brows and wagging finger, his stance relaxed, and a slow smile turned up the corners of his lips. He dipped his head and scuffed at a mark on the floor with the toe of his boot, like a schoolboy caught spying on his teacher.

That was the moment Charlotte realized what a nice-looking man the doctor was, with his dark wavy hair, hazel-blue eyes, and closely shaven jaw.

His gaze skittered over Dixie once more before he angled it toward Charlotte. "Unfortunately for me, Miss Brindle, Miss Pottinger is quite set on remaining single, but if you care to share the appearance of *your* basket, I'd be happy to bid on the chance at spending an evening with you."

Charlotte chuckled. "The purple basket, Dr. Griffin. I think you'll find the contents rather delicious and the company more than tolerably pleasant."

The doctor tipped her a nod and stepped past her. "And now if you'll excuse me, Miss Brindle, I think I will mosey on my way before I get arrested."

"Arrested?" But the word was spoken to his disappearing back.

"Evening, Miss Brindle." Sheriff Callahan was suddenly beside her.

She dipped a curtsey, but her thoughts were still on the doctor's perplexing statement. She turned back to watch him slip out the door and onto the street. "Sheriff? Are you trying to arrest the doctor for some infraction?"

Sheriff Callahan pulled his head back and puckered his brow. "As far as I know, Doc is among the most upstanding of citizens, Miss Brindle. What brings such a question to mind?"

It was Charlotte's turn to frown as she puzzled over the doctor's parting words. "Oh nothing. Just something the doctor said as he was leaving just now."

The sheriff stood quietly by her side for a moment, his hands clasped behind his back, as he scanned the room. He looked rather nice this evening in a black suit. His coat was cut with tails, and his vest of blue silk brought out the striking blue of his eyes. He wore no hat, and his blond hair curled in rebellion to the pomade he'd used in an apparent attempt to control it, but instead of making him look unkempt, it gave him a roguish air that made her mouth dry.

Realizing she was staring, Charlotte felt her face heat. Before he could catch her, she followed his example and turned back to studying those gathered. Across the room, Dixie met her gaze, her brows lifted in humor. Charlotte wrinkled her nose at her, but then offered a smile and a small shrug. Dixie laughed, then turned to greet someone who'd spoken to her.

Thankful for another segment of quiet, Charlotte took a moment to pray that the benefit would be a smashing success.

All across the room, families conversed with one another, most of them laughing, a few of them oohing and aahing over babies they hadn't seen for a few weeks or a child who'd lost a tooth since the families had last visited. To their left, two men talked about the latest saw one had purchased from the Sears Roebuck catalogue. To their right, Belle Kastain stood chatting with a group of girls close to her age, but her gaze kept traveling to the sheriff. Charlotte tried to offer the girl a smile, but received only an icy squint in return.

At her side, the sheriff cleared his throat. "I wonder, Miss Brindle... Since you will be leaving on the morning's stage, would you consider breaking with propriety and giving a man a clue as to the color of your basket?" She could see a hint of entreaty pinching the corners of his lips, even though he hadn't faced her but kept his attention focused steadily on the goings-on before them.

First, in the wildflower field, the man had stared at her like he might want to kiss her. Then he'd taken her hand on the trail, and she'd felt certain he was going to kiss her. But he'd once again told her it would be best for her to go back home. And now he was asking to eat dinner with her? Charlotte felt her jaw go slack. But she managed to keep her lips sealed just in the nick of time to avoid the unladylike propensity.

He'd been standing next to her for several minutes now. Had he been working up the courage to ask her about her basket all that time?

Instead of being irritated, it warmed her through rather much more than it ought, to learn that the sheriff wanted to bid on her basket. Still, she wasn't about to reward the man, especially considering the way he kept pointing out that she wasn't suited to work in Wyldhaven. She suppressed a smile, feeling a little giddy wave of power. "I'm afraid a lady never reveals her secrets, Sheriff Callahan."

"Indeed?" Frivolity touched the edges of the word, though he still wasn't looking at her but fastidiously perusing the gathering. "More's the pity for the likes of me, then."

Just then a thought came to Charlotte that almost had her laughing out loud. "Purple is a beautiful color, don't you think, Sheriff Callahan?"

His gaze snapped to hers. "Purple is indeed a beautiful color, Miss Brindle."

Charlotte gave him a parting curtsy, for if she stayed, she was sure to burst out laughing and give her ruse away. "I bid you good evening then, Sheriff."

He offered the sketch of a bow. "And I, you." His attention had already turned to the table full of picnic baskets before she'd even taken two steps. And she imagined him searching out Dixie's purple one.

Oh, but this was going to be a fun evening. If only the decision over tomorrow's departure still wasn't weighing so heavily on her.

There was something about Miss Brindle's little chuckle as she left him that raised Reagan's awareness of her subtle deception. She hadn't actually said her basket was the purple one. She'd only pointed out that purple was a lovely color.

Reagan grinned and scrubbed a hand over his jaw. He studied the baskets. The purple one was likely one of the single ladies'. Perhaps Dixie's? Or... He shuddered. Maybe Belle's?

He darted a glance at Miss Brindle's back. Surely the woman wasn't so callous as all that, was she?

Speaking of Belle...

Apparently intent on taking advantage of the fact that he was standing alone, Belle sashayed to his side. She tucked her hands behind her back and cast a coquettish look toward the baskets. "Your favorite chocolate cake accompanies one of those dinners, Sheriff."

Reagan didn't dare dash Belle's assumptions about her chocolate cake, but to him, one chocolate cake tasted much like another. They all went down easy, no matter who baked them. And he wasn't about to sell his soul for a piece of cake—chocolate or not.

Still, if he guessed wrong about Miss Brindle's basket and accidentally ended up bidding on Belle's, that could prove disastrous. And he knew one deputy sheriff who'd be more than happy to know which basket was Belle's. So he ventured, "And I'm guessing yours is the orange one?"

Belle giggled and swayed her hips, causing her skirt to swish around her ankles. "Guess again."

Reagan scanned the baskets once more, and that was when he noticed one of the boxed suppers was tied with a large pink bow of the same material as Belle's skirt.

He coughed to hide the bark of laughter that almost burst forth. Subtle, she was not.

As soon as he'd composed himself, Reagan tipped her a nod. "I think I see it now, Miss Kastain. Now if you'll excuse me, I need to go see to the first round of the sawing contest." That was true enough, though he also needed to find Joseph Rodante and let him know which basket was Belle's, and a quick chat with Dixie to learn which basket was Miss Brindle's wouldn't hurt either.

As he made his escape, he pondered over the fact that he probably shouldn't even consider bidding on the schoolteacher's basket. It was bound to cause all sorts of ruckus about town, and not only with Belle. There was his mother to consider. And all the other clucking hens who had been trying to marry him off for the past several years. But what could it hurt? When he'd left her at Dixie's this afternoon, she'd all but promised she was leaving for Boston on the morning's stage, so all the fuss and bluster would have no foundation to build upon.

And a man certainly couldn't be chastised for hoping to spend a platonic evening with one of the most beautiful women he'd ever had the pleasure of meeting, even if she was a bit stiff around the edges.

Of its own volition, his gaze sought her out as he passed where she stood chatting with the Carlton family. The golden yellow of her dress, and the jaunty tilt of her flower-bedecked felt hat, enhanced her complexion to a rosy hue and brought out the golden flecks in those haunting green eyes.

Yes indeed. A picnic meal sitting across from her wouldn't hurt his feelings in the least.

Charlotte wished she could be in several places at once. But since that was impossible, she scurried from one event to another as quickly as she could manage.

First she stopped by the log-sawing competition—and tried to convince herself that she was only there to witness the fun and not because she might bump into a certain blue-eyed sheriff. But she needn't have worried. His back to the crowd, the sheriff was deeply engrossed in judging the competition where teams of two men each got on either side of a long, viciously-toothed blade with handles on each end and made quick work of sawing through logs as thick around as a wagon wheel. Charlotte was fascinated by how the team on the right worked so smoothly that it made their blade seem as if it were passing through softened butter. The team on the left kept getting their saw stuck, and at one point the blade buckled and nearly nicked the leg of one of the sawyers. The crowd gasped. But the two men on that team simply laughed and went back to work.

The woman next to Charlotte leaned close. "Those two ain't normally sawyers. But they can burl a log down the river without once falling off. They just joined the competition for the fun and to support the cause."

The crowd cheered as the team on the right made their last push and a round of the log toppled to the deck at their feet.

Reagan stood between them and lifted their hands high in the air. "I present to you tonight's first winners!"

Charlotte looked across the crowd. Their laughter and cheering brought a smile to her face. With a happy sigh, she went in search of the next booth.

The canned goods table was being run by Mrs. Callahan. Everything looked delicious. Charlotte paid two bits for a small jar of pickles and one of raspberry preserves. She would have bought more, except she was thinking of the long journey back to Boston.

Holding a jar in each hand, she stared down at them. A heavy weight seemed to be resting over her heart. Was she making the right decision? She lifted her focus to the street teeming with joy and joviality. She never would have expected it, but she found herself admiring these hardworking people who came together in support of a cause.

She glanced back down at the jars. Would they make it home without breaking if she tucked them carefully into her luggage in the morning? The thought dropped a rock into her stomach.

She took the time to run the jars up to her room in the boardinghouse and stood at her window for a moment, looking down on the flurry of activity on Main Street. The sawing contest was down near the livery, and the canned goods table was just across the street in the open lot, and more people than Charlotte would have guessed possible milled on the street between the two.

But now the people started moseying back toward McGinty's. It must be time for bidding on the suppers.

A beautiful blonde in a bright-red dress caught her eye. Not necessarily because of the color of her ensemble, but because of the way she sauntered up to the sheriff's side and threaded her arm through his. He pulled away from her in surprise, but when he took note of the woman's face, he seemed to relax slightly and even tipped his hat in her direction, though he didn't offer her his arm again.

As they walked closer, Charlotte squinted and leaned nearer to the glass. The woman was Liora! The girl who'd been crying in the wildflower field just this afternoon. Charlotte had forgotten to ask Dixie about her. Charlotte's gaze skimmed to the low cut of Liora's dress and the paint that heightened her features, and realization over why she hadn't known Liora worked in Wyldhaven washed over her. She felt a wave of revulsion, immediately followed by self-chastising guilt. Still, her ire reared its head as it always did when she thought about women like that. The ire was accompanied by an ugly feeling at the sight of Liora next to the sheriff. And the realization that the sheriff hadn't acted like she was a stranger. *Charlie, there's not a man alive who doesn't have his needs met by such a woman once in a while.* A sick sensation trembled through her, and her first instinct was to dash down and give the woman a solid and unquestionable piece of her mind.

But then, as if on a soft whisper, the image of Liora as she'd been earlier came to mind. She'd been crying, cowering behind a bush and dressed in a conservative brown. And she'd touched a place inside Charlotte that made her want to be her friend. Charlotte swallowed. Why would a woman such as that be crying? She certainly seemed happy enough right now. Charlotte's stomach twisted. She closed her eyes, willing away the familiar bitter enemy of her soul, the pride that didn't want to love the sinner.

She remembered the day that she'd discovered Kent had been visiting...women...behind her back. She'd told the Lord that she simply wanted someone to truly love her. Could it be that a woman like Liora only wanted the same? And yet—Charlotte's face heated—perhaps love meant something entirely different to a woman like her?

A visage of Pastor Sorenson's frown popped into her mind. She released a short puff of breath. Yes, even if the woman didn't understand what true love was, she deserved to have it offered to her. *Lord, I have so far to go before I'll be like You, offering true love to sinners one and all. Help me to be Your love extended to her in any way I can. Don't let my bitterness, disgust, or critical attitude stand in the way of Your love reaching out to her.*

Determining that she would try to offer friendship to Liora if the opportunity presented itself, Charlotte quickly locked her door and placed one hand to her stomach as she hurried down the stairs to join everyone next door.

Liora disguised her dread over the evening behind a bright

smile that she knew would deceive everyone. She knew it because it worked every other day of her life, so why wouldn't it work tonight also? The smile might be a little more difficult to maintain on this evening, however. Joe had stopped by just this morning to let her know Ewan had declined to grant her leave to see her mother. Ewan's refusal terrified her. Maybe because it was something so much like John Hunt would have done to her mother.

In danger of falling into melancholy, she hurried forward and looped her arm through the sheriff's again, but the moment they stepped through the door, he tipped his hat in a good-bye and pushed through the crowd. He hadn't said where he was going, and if she was honest, he likely only had one destination in mind—somewhere away from her.

"Evening."

The familiar voice, speaking from so close to her side, sent a jolt of awareness through her. She kept her working-girl mask firmly in place when she turned to him. "Good evening, Deputy." She trailed one finger over his chest.

He grabbed her finger. "Don't." He released her and propped his hands on his hips. A hard light in his brown eyes matched the clenching of his jaw.

Her mask slipped just a little. "I'm glad I bumped into you." She pulled in a breath, wishing she didn't need to impinge on his helpfulness again. "I have some more money to send to my ma. Would you be willing to take it to her?"

He studied her without reply for a long moment, something like disappointment in his eyes. Finally he said, "If you quit working for Ewan, you could take it to her yourself."

A tremor of wistfulness swept through her. If only she could. "I've contracted myself to Ewan for a year."

"I'd buy it out for you."

"You'd—" Her jaw dropped. No one had ever offered to do something like that for her. Ever. How much would Ewan even require to buy out her contract? It would be an astounding amount, she felt sure. But then she would be left still needing work. Even if Ma was dying, she would still need medicine for weeks, maybe months to come, wouldn't she? Liora shook her head. "And where would a woman the likes of me get a job besides"—she swept a hand around McGinty's Alehouse—"this."

He seemed unfazed. "I'd help you find something. You could do laundry for the crewman. Or start a cookshack." His lips tilted up at the corners. "You could certainly give Ewan a run for his money there."

She was too shocked to laugh at his dry wit. He was serious. "And where do you think I'd come up with the money to start such a venture?"

He glanced down and kicked at something on the floor, then lifted his gaze to hers once more. "I'd front you the capital to get started."

The man was crazy. That was all there was too it. How much money did he have anyway? "Why would you offer to do something like that? You barely know me."

A soft breath slipped from him. "Because I believe in second chances. I've certainly been given enough of them in my lifetime. You were created for better than this." He encompassed the room with a gesture that matched her earlier one. "You *deserve* better than this. And I know God would want that for you."

God. So there it was. She laughed. She couldn't help it. "Listen. I appreciate your kindness. I really do. But trust me when I say that God wants absolutely nothing to do with me. He's certainly proven that, time and again."

He shook his head. "If you believe that, you're deceiving yourself, Liora."

So matter of fact. So trusting. So deluded. How did a smart and kind man like this fall into such a pointless belief? She dug the envelope from her pocket and held it up. "Will you take it to her?"

With a sigh, he took the money and tucked it inside his suit jacket. "First thing in the morning."

"Thank you."

He only nodded before he slipped through the crowd, greeting people as he went, and she couldn't help but feel that she might have just given up her last chance at true happiness. What if she had held out for just a little bit longer? What if she'd come to town and asked for help instead of signing Ewan's stupid contract? What if she'd found a good man like Deputy Rodante to step in and lighten her burdens?

She pressed her lips together. It was too late for what-ifs now, and she knew it. She'd never have a good man like Joe in her life. Didn't *deserve* a good man like him in her life. Especially not now after the recent choices she'd made. If Ma hadn't gotten so sick maybe— She jerked her thoughts off that trail. What was done was done. She lifted her skirts and sashayed through the crowd, just like McGinty had instructed her, smiling and flirting with any man who would look her way.

Alan Trollick sat alone at one end of the bar, and she scooted up next to him, pushing down the roil in her stomach. "Alan..." She ran one hand over the man's shoulder. "How are you this evening?"

He grunted and scraped a look from her head to her toes before going back to his drink. She couldn't believe Ewan was serving alcohol still. She would have thought that he'd put a pause on that, at least for this one evening when the entire town would be crammed into his establishment. But she didn't get paid to think, just to serve. "Can I fill that up for you again, Alan?"

The door opened, and the schoolteacher stepped inside. Liora still couldn't believe the woman had taken the time to speak to her earlier today. But it had been obvious only a moment after they'd begun conversing that the woman had no idea what kind of job Liora held in the town. It would only take one look this evening for the teacher to put two and two together, and then the friendship she'd offered would be yanked back quicker than a blink, for none of the other women would tolerate a person of Miss Brindle's standing befriending her. And somehow that realization dropped a rock of dread into the pit of Liora's stomach. How she had missed having everyday conversations about silly things like fallen sparrows' nests.

She remembered the woman's words about the nest and snorted softly. Why was it everyone in her life lately seemed set on lying to her about how much God cared? If God had ever cared about her, it had only been to see how flat He could smash her beneath His heel.

The teacher seemed to be looking for someone, and in that moment their gazes connected. Liora couldn't have been more surprised when the woman smiled and lifted a hand in greeting.

She offered a nod in return but looked away before anyone noticed and she got the woman in trouble. Let her live in her dreamland of fallen sparrows that were noticed by a caring Creator a little longer. She would soon enough be jolted back to the reality that the rest of the world lived in.

Chapter Fifteen

Charlotte braced herself for whatever sight might greet her with regard to the sheriff and Liora when she stepped into McGinty's. She halfway expected that she might see them just disappearing from sight at the top of the stairs when she entered the room. But to her relief and surprise, Liora was standing near the bar, talking to an older man, and the sheriff was nowhere to be seen. In her relief she even managed to dredge up a smile for Liora, who gave her a brief nod before turning away.

Charlotte's relief over the fact that the sheriff had parted company with Liora had her trembling. She clenched her teeth. Wished she could summon as much indifference toward the man as he seemed to feel toward her. And reminded herself that she never would have suspected Kent of consorting with such a woman had she not seen the proof with her very own eyes. Just because the sheriff had walked away from Liora's obvious invitation this time didn't mean he would the next. Something in her throat cinched up hard and tight at that thought. It was best that she just put the man from her mind.

Ewan was preparing to begin the auction and urging people to gather around, and Charlotte's thoughts turned to the evening ahead. She wished she hadn't let Dixie talk her into making a basket of her own, but what was done was done. And now she would have to face partaking of her meal with whichever man won the bid on her basket. Now more than ever, she hoped the sheriff had fallen for her ruse about Dixie's basket, because now that she'd seen him conversing rather cordially with a woman of the night, affable dinner conversation might be more than she was capable of.

The married women's baskets went up for auction first, and without fail each husband bid until he won his wife's—with some good-natured raising of bids from other members of the community.

And then the first of the single women's baskets was placed on the podium. Ewan McGinty, who was serving as the auctioneer, grinned like a mule in an alfalfa field. "Gather 'round, gents! Never has there been such amazing opportunity to spend the evening in the company of a pretty lady and the delicious food she prepared!"

Charlotte swallowed as several burly loggers, who smelled like they hadn't seen the inside of a bathhouse since last month, brushed past her to get a better look at the baskets. Could she be stuck sharing her dinner with a man such as that? One hand went to her throat. Perhaps stilted dinner conversation with the sheriff wouldn't be so bad after all.

She searched the room. She hadn't seen him since she'd walked in. Was he even in here? She spotted Liora across the room, laughing with a man Charlotte didn't recognize, but she still didn't see the sheriff. Her disappointment was unaccountable.

"The flowers on the tables are right fetching, Miss Brindle." The sheriff's voice came from behind her, and her relief was such that her eyes dropped closed for a moment.

Sheriff Callahan stepped up beside her, close enough in the crowded room that she could detect his faint scent of leather and spice.

Liora laughed in a way meant to draw attention and then smiled seductively at the sheriff, but he didn't seem to be paying a bit of attention to her. And for some reason that added even more impact to Charlotte's relief.

Though he kept his gaze fixed on the baskets up front, he leaned close. "You did say 'purple' was a lovely color, correct?"

Her fingers fiddled with the lace of her high collar, and she swallowed again. My, how she wished propriety would allow her to just out and tell the sheriff that her basket was the green one—Dixie had claimed the evergreens, ferns, and tight green buds of the not-quite-budded holly bush blooms matched her eyes to perfection—but that would be too forward. So all she allowed herself to say was, "I did say that, Sheriff, yes." Her gaze skittered across the room. "Do you think Liora might have made a basket?"

The sheriff was so startled by her question that he actually jolted. "How do you know Liora?"

Charlotte studied him. Was it guilt that had made him start? Or simply the fact the she was bringing up a woman of the night like Liora?

"I met her earlier, when I was up in the rose field. She was crying. I got the feeling she might need a friend." She frowned. What had made her confide in the sheriff in such a manner? Liora might not appreciate her spilling out the truth about the state she'd been in, but the words were out now.

He folded his arms and darted a glance toward Liora. "She needs more than a friend. She needs a Savior, Miss Brindle."

Charlotte's surprise at his statement must have been evident on her face.

He cocked an eyebrow. "Wouldn't you agree?"

"Yes. I would." She was just astonished to hear a man saying as much. She'd never heard Father or Kent speak of spiritual things in such open terms. She looked back across the room to the woman. Her smile had dropped away, and she was staring into space. A deep sorrow seemed to cloak her entire frame. "I have a confession to make, Sheriff..."

He turned to look at her, waiting.

Charlotte pursed her lips and eased out a tremulous stream of air. Here she went again, blurting things she didn't mean to. She moistened her lips, darting a glance toward Liora. "Do you ever find it difficult to do what you know is right?"

"Never."

She spun toward him, only to find him grinning.

He spread his hands. "I believe that's the nature of fallen man. Yet failure is partly what reminds me I need a Savior."

Charlotte put one hand to her throat. Indeed. How was she with all her carefully concealed pride and conceit any better than a woman like Liora? Simply because her sin was less blatant? *Father, forgive me.* Her gaze settled on Liora again. Yes, she agreed that the woman needed a Savior. And what better way to introduce her to the Savior than by offering friendship? But how? She would be walking on very thin ice. "Sheriff, I want to be Liora's friend, but I'm not sure I know the best way to go about it."

The sheriff remained silent, a slight frown puckering his forehead. After a long moment, he turned to look at her. "You are quite extraordinary, Miss Brindle."

Charlotte's pulse quickened, but before she had a chance to question exactly what he meant by that statement, Ewan called out that the auction had begun.

The first basket lifted to the podium was covered with wild sweet pea blooms in fuchsia. Two loggers bid for the privilege of dining with a lovely looking brunette who stood to one side, blushing like a Georgia peach. In the end, the taller of the two men won, to many "huzzahs" from the crowd.

The next basket placed on the podium was Dixie's purple-bloom-festooned basket, tied with the lavender ribbon.

Dr. Flynn Griffin glanced back at Charlotte and lifted his brows.

Charlotte smiled softly, offering a subtle nod.

"One dollar!" Flynn called out, facing Ewan at the front once more.

"One dollar and two bits!" Sheriff Callahan raised the bid from beside her.

Charlotte's eyes fell closed. The sheriff was going to bid for Dixie's basket, and she was going to be left to eat with a malodorous logger.

"One fifty!"

"One seventy-five."

Flynn turned to give the sheriff a piercing look.

"Going once..." Ewan McGinty called, raising his gavel above his head. "Going twice..."

"Two dollars!" Flynn called out.

After a collective gasp of delight, everyone in the room seemed to hold their breath until Reagan gave the doctor a friendly smile and a little bow accompanied by the sweep of one hand toward the basket.

Raucous laughter filled the room as Ewan proclaimed the basket won by the good doctor.

Charlotte glanced over to see Dixie at the food table, straightening plates and napkins that were already straight, her cheeks as rosy as the wildflowers Charlotte had picked this afternoon. Charlotte smiled. At least someone would enjoy eating their meal tonight.

The next basket lifted to the podium was Charlotte's green one.

A murmur traversed the bidders, as they studied the remaining single women in the room.

Charlotte felt a little sick.

Beside her, the sheriff stood stoically, one fist resting over his lips. There was a sparkle in his blue eyes as he calmly watched the men try to figure out whose basket this was.

Mercifully, Charlotte was able to keep from fidgeting, but only barely.

Ewan bent over the basket and gave it a sniff before rolling his eyes as though in heavenly ecstasy. "Whatever is in this basket smells mighty fine, fellas. Who wants to give me the first bid?"

A paunchy logger at the front of the crowd called out, "Two bits!"

Beside Charlotte, the sheriff gave a little snort, but held his silence.

Charlotte's stomach rolled over and threatened to mutiny.

Another man Charlotte couldn't see hollered, "Fiddy cents!" at the same moment as another up ahead of her shouted, "Seventy-five cents, and I'll even throw in a kiss for whichever little lady this belongs to!"

Crows of delight traversed the room.

Charlotte did press one hand to her stomach this time, and yet despite her nerves over whom she would end up eating dinner with, she couldn't help but admire the friendly camaraderie of this community.

From across the crowd, the long-bearded man who had just offered the kiss as part of his bid turned and smiled right at her. His teeth were as yellow as a harvest moon.

Never mind. There was nothing lovely about the camaraderie after all.

The sheriff still remained quiet, and it was all Charlotte could do to keep from jabbing her elbow into his side.

"If'n anyone kisses the lady, it'll be me, Butch Nolan! One doller!" This from the first man who had bid.

Charlotte's feet shuffled.

The sheriff leaned close, a concerned expression tightening his features. "You all right there, Miss Brindle?" A spark of humor glinted in his gaze at the last moment.

Charlotte glowered at him.

And he laughed outright. "Three dollars!" he called loudly, punctuating it with a subtle wink in Charlotte's direction.

A sigh of relief slipped through Charlotte's lips in a long exhale, and she felt some tension release from her shoulders.

"Aw! Sheriff!" lamented the unknown voice from the back of the crowd good naturedly, "You gots to go little by little, so's those o' us 'thout much money can hang on to our hope fer a little while!"

"Speak for yourself, Gimpy!" Butch Nolan retorted with a flash of his yellowed teeth. "Three fifty!"

"I sure hope your dinner is worth it, Miss Brindle," the sheriff muttered to her in an aside. "Four dollars!"

Butch Nolan grumbled and emptied his pockets. He painstakingly counted his change while receiving much good-natured ribbing from his friends. Finally he proclaimed, "Four dollars and thirty-eight cents!"

Sheriff Callahan cupped his chin and pondered his response, a twinkle in his eyes. "This is getting to be an awfully expensive basket. Sniff it for me one more time, McGinty. Is it worth this price?"

McGinty made a show of inhaling and acting dazzled by the

scent. "Sure smells like it might be worth it, Sheriff. And the money's for a good cause."

"Hmmm, I guess that's true." Reagan massaged his jawline, deep in consideration, much to the delight of everyone in the room.

Everyone except Charlotte and Belle. Belle looked like she'd like to get her hands around his throat. Charlotte certainly wanted to smack him. Surely he knew this was her basket. He wouldn't consign her to eating with the fragrant and colorful Mr. Nolan, would he? And she certainly hoped that whoever won would enjoy her pot roast with potatoes and cabbage. It had been the meal she made that was most raved about by her classmates at the finishing school. Not even Miss Gidden had been able to find any fault with it. Though she normally liked to add some basil, and Dixie hadn't had any in her kitchen, she hoped it would suffice just this once, until she could order in some herbs.

Charlotte blinked. Until she could order in some herbs? What was she thinking? This once would be the only time she'd have to cook in this town, wouldn't it?

She scanned the room, her attention lingering on each child she could see. Children she would never get to know. Children who might never have another teacher if she tucked her tail between her legs and ran back east. Liora, who might never have a friend.

Across from Charlotte, Zoe Kastain and her twin sisters were jumping up and down and clapping in delight as the sheriff paced through several antics as though tormented over whether he was going to place another bid. And next to the girls, Belle stood, glaring at her passionately. Perhaps Charlotte had earlier been mistaken about just exactly which throat Belle would like to squeeze.

"Going once!" Ewan prodded. "Going twice..."

Charlotte closed her eyes and prayed she wouldn't get sick right here in front of God and everyone.

"Five dollars!" the sheriff finally called out.

Butch Nolan groaned audibly, and those nearest him offered pats of consolation to his shoulders as Ewan McGinty proclaimed the sheriff the winner.

Charlotte's legs nearly melted out from beneath her skirts, so great was the relief coursing through her.

The next basket lifted to the stand was the last one, and Sheriff Callahan's deputy, Joseph Rodante, started the bidding high and didn't relent until he had won.

With whoops and much applause, the crowd dispersed to find places to eat their dinners. The men who had won paid what was due, and each woman stepped up to acknowledge her ownership of the basket. Charlotte was painfully aware that Liora had not made a basket and was performing quite an act to keep up her smiles.

The sheriff grinned at Charlotte when she stopped before him. He tipped his chin toward the greenery on her basket. "I'm kinda partial to green over purple."

Charlotte felt her face warm and was about to respond, when Dixie practically plastered herself to Charlotte's side. "Perhaps you two would like to join the doctor and me for the meal?"

Charlotte's gaze drifted to Liora across the room. She'd planned to ask the sheriff if he'd mind if Liora joined them, but now... "That would be fine with me if it is fine with the sheriff?"

Reagan gave Dixie a slight bow. "We'd be pleased to have you two join us."

"Would anyone object if I invited Liora too?" The words blurted out of Charlotte's mouth before she could think twice.

Everyone sputtered for a moment, and none of them seemed to know where to look.

Charlotte felt a little foolish. She hadn't realized the idea would be so repugnant to them. "It's just that she seems so lonely, and I only thought—"

"Sure. Ask her." The sheriff looked a little surprised at his own words.

Dixie stepped to her side and squeezed her arm. "I think it's a lovely idea. Do ask her."

Dr. Griffin cleared his throat, exchanged looks with the sheriff, and then said, "We're not likely to have many more warm nights like this one. How about if I fetch a blanket and we eat outside?"

When Dixie only studied the floor near her feet and Reagan deferred to Charlotte with a lift of his brows, Charlotte agreed. "That would be lovely. Thank you, Dr. Griffin."

"Good. I'll be right back."

While the doctor retreated above stairs, Charlotte hurried across the room to where Liora stood wiping down the bar. She tilted a nod to where the sheriff and Dixie stood waiting. "We wondered if you would like to join us outside for dinner?"

Liora blinked. It only took her half a second to shake her head and turn away. "I don't know how they do things where you come from, but 'round these parts, you start associating with the likes of me and you'll discover right quick how easy it is to lose your standing, not to mention your job."

Deep in her heart, Charlotte felt the pain contained in those words. "None of us are worried about our standings or our jobs. Please join us?"

Liora strode purposefully to the other side of the bar. "Can't."

Charlotte cast a look back to where the others waited for

her. Doc Griffin had returned with a good-sized quilt over his arm. She couldn't leave them standing for much longer. She turned back to Liora. "Very well, but please know that you are welcome to come join us if you change your mind."

"Thank you." Liora didn't meet her gaze, just picked up a glass and started polishing it.

With a heavy heart, Charlotte returned to the others. They settled in a patch of soft green grass near the banks of Wyldhaven Creek, and Charlotte quickly realized that she and the sheriff were going to have to carry the conversation, for both Dixie and the doctor were staring in opposite directions with morose little frowns on their faces. But just as she was about to ask the doctor what had brought him to Wyldhaven, Belle and Joseph stopped by their blanket.

"Would it be all right if Joe and I joined your foursome?" Belle blinked coyly at the sheriff, and Joseph, still holding the basket that Charlotte now noticed was decorated with the same material as Belle's skirt, shuffled his feet uncomfortably.

Dixie was quick to respond to that. "Certainly." She swept a hand toward a small space at one side of the blanket. "Please, join us."

The sheriff scooted closer to Charlotte to make room for the new arrivals, but the doctor remained firmly seated a little distance away from Dixie.

Charlotte frowned and bounced a look between Dixie, who was once more studying her skirt, smoothing at invisible wrinkles, and the doctor, who was still staring sullenly out over the field.

Charlotte opened her mouth, but Sheriff Callahan cleared his throat softly and touched her hand, giving a little shake of his head.

Belle saw the gesture and gave a petulant toss of her curls.

Charlotte pinched off the questions begging to be voiced and asked Reagan to say the blessing over their meals. Once he had done so, she set to work dishing up a plate of beef, potatoes, and cabbage for the sheriff. She balanced two corn muffins on the side and then handed over the plate and a quart jar of the sweet tea she'd made this morning with a bit of wild mint she'd found in Dixie's garden. Dixie and Belle both dished plates also, and everyone tucked into their food quietly.

Charlotte tried to prod everyone to conversation several times, but with Belle only being interested in conversing with the sheriff, and Dixie's and the doctor's one-syllable responses, nothing she tried worked.

Finally, Dr. Griffin stood and offered a bow. "The dinner was delicious, as always, Dixie. Thank you. Now if you'll excuse me, I should ride out to the Ferndale place and check on the new baby that was born last week." With that, he hurried off.

Dixie packed up her basket after that and made an excuse of needing to get back to the boardinghouse for a bit.

"So how do you like Wyldhaven so far, Miss Brindle?" Joseph Rodante offered her a genuine smile.

God bless the boy for his thoughtfulness! "I've actually grown quite fond of the place, if I'm honest." Charlotte cast her focus back to the town and was more than a little surprised to find that the statement was true. Somehow the people of the town had already entwined themselves into her affections. She felt warmhearted at the realization.

Belle daintily nibbled on a piece of chicken as she cast Charlotte a look. "But you're still returning to Boston on tomorrow's stage? After all, no one would actually come to a place like Wyldhaven unless the good Lord Himself brought them here." She tinkled a forced laugh.

But her words were like a slap in Charlotte's face. Hadn't she prayed for God to guide her? And she'd seen Mr. Heath's ad only moments later. Some people might call that coincidence. But she didn't believe in coincidence. And in that moment of decision, everything around her snapped into sharp focus.

The possessive look Belle cast toward the sheriff after her question. The scrutinizing way that Joseph kept looking at Belle whenever she wasn't paying attention. The slump in Dixie's shoulders as she crossed the street. The happy sound of two little boys just downstream, whose parents had decided to let them wade in a shallow inlet. The crimp that no longer tightened her stomach like it had each time she thought about going back home and facing Kent Covington again.

With a huge sigh of relief, Charlotte knew that her conundrum had come to an end. "Actually, I've decided that I'll remain for the coming year."

Sheriff Callahan spewed the mouthful of sweet tea he'd just started to swallow. "You'll what?!"

But not even his disgruntlement could change her mind now. For the moment she'd said the words, Charlotte felt like the weight of the world had just slipped from her shoulders.

She nodded. "Yes. I quite like it here in Wyldhaven. I'm staying."

Chapter Sixteen

Reagan swiped the sticky liquid from his chin and stomped to the creek a few paces away to rinse his hands and get a grip on the rapid beating of his heart. He squatted to his haunches, nudged his hat back, and scanned the crowd gathered on both banks of the creek. Seeing nothing out of the ordinary, he skimmed the edges of the forest beyond. Even now, Waddell or his gang could be lurking somewhere, intent on doing harm to Miss Brindle. And she was as naïve to that threat as a baby to a wolf.

He tossed a glance over his shoulder. Charlotte laughed at something Joe said, and Reagan narrowed his eyes at his deputy. Joe glanced over and caught his scrutiny. When Charlotte turned to say something to Belle, he very subtly lifted his hands in a *you have no competition from me* gesture.

Perfect. So he obviously hadn't done as good a job as he hoped disguising his growing feeling from others. Reagan snorted. If he was smart, he'd want no part of this. Miss Charlotte Brindle was just about as stubborn as any female he'd ever met! His only thoughts should be on how to protect her, as one of the citizens of his town, and thus his responsibility.

Trouble was he was having lots of thoughts, and very few of them were in regard to her being a citizen of Wyldhaven.

He stared at the ground between his knees. Okay, so the woman was beautiful in a way that could stop a man's heart and muddle up every thought he tried to grab for. But she was bound to be a never-ending string of trouble for any man who invited her into his life. Just look at everything that had happened since before she even stepped foot in his town. And he hadn't even invited her!

But maybe part of this was his fault. He'd been doing his best to keep her in the dark about the dangers. Maybe it was time that he told her just exactly *why* he felt it would be better for her to return to Boston. Time to come out with the full truth, even if that scared her a little. If she knew the Waddell gang planned to kill her, maybe that would put some sense into that stubborn head of hers. He nodded, decision made.

He strode back to the group, still seated on Doc Griffin's blanket, and looked down at her. "Miss Brindle, may I have the honor of a dance?"

Charlotte's eyes widened, and he saw her swallow. She opened her mouth, and he had the distinct impression she was on the verge of declining him, but at that moment her focus honed in on something near the bridge. Reagan followed her gaze.

Butch Nolan was headed this way with a purposeful gleam in his eyes. Butch stroked one hand down his long red beard—which he'd braided sometime between the auction and now—and had the audacity to send a wink Miss Brindle's way.

Reagan folded his arms, leaned into his heels, and grinned down at Charlotte.

Charlotte scrambled to her feet like a mouse that had suddenly felt the breath of a feline. "Yes. Dancing sounds lovely, Sheriff. Let's go now." She clapped one hand to Reagan's arm and practically dragged him to the gate, where he barely had time to hand over the money for their dance tickets before she hauled him onto the floor.

But when the music started on Rose Pottinger's crackly phonograph, Charlotte held herself as far from him as possible.

Perhaps because of the way she tackled every obstacle with such zest, Reagan had forgotten just how petite Miss Brindle was. Her forehead barely reached his chin as they swayed across the open field, and her waist beneath his hand was so slender he had a feeling that were he to wrap his other hand around her also, his fingers could touch front and back. Tonight her mass of dark hair was pulled into a tight twist at the back of her head, but her curls must be as stubborn as she, for several had made an escape and wisped fetchingly about her cheeks and forehead.

Though he looked at her steadily, she fastidiously kept her face averted.

He sighed. Here was more proof that maybe the way he'd chosen to handle the threats against her hadn't been the wisest course of action. He'd hurt her with all his urgings to return to Boston. She felt certain he wanted her to go home because he didn't think she could handle the job of teaching in Wyldhaven and because he was a selfish boor who simply wanted to make his own job easier.

But she was wrong. Truth was, swaying across this field with her in his arms, he'd have given just about anything to have her stay. But if she stayed and something happened to her, he'd never be able to forgive himself. So for her own safety, though his heart was no longer in it, he ought to convince her. He fought against the urge to coddle and console her, and plunged in.

"I know you think you've made the decision to stay."

Her green eyes snapped.

He hurried on before she could interrupt. "But there are dangers here. I really must urge you once more to reconsider and instead return to the safety of Boston." The words cost him.

She still didn't meet his gaze, but her pert little nose tipped a fraction higher. "I assure you, Sheriff, I have carefully considered your multiple requests for such and have decided against your advice."

His jaw ached, and he realized his teeth had clenched together very tightly. "Miss Brindle, I assure you, you don't truly understand my reasons for requesting your leave."

"Don't I?" She turned limpid green eyes, full of hurt, on him. The tone of her voice said she knew otherwise.

He felt his throat tighten up. He'd had a string of words put together that he'd practiced several times. Words that would softly bring her around to seeing it was only out of concern for her that he was asking her not to stay on. But with her looking at him all petulant and full of wounded pride as she was, his mouth turned dry, and he'd be hornswoggled if he could remember anything, much less string two words together.

"As I thought." She looked away again.

He gave himself a mental shake. But before he could try to correct her misperception, she had somehow collected herself, thrown back her shoulders, schooled her features, and leveled him with another look. This time her expression held a hint of lava and smoke. "How do you know Miss Fontaine?"

"Who?" It took him a moment to associate an image with "Miss Fontaine."

Charlotte huffed and jutted her chin to one side.

"Wait...Liora?!" His feet tangled together, and they nearly bumped into the couple dancing next to them. He almost laughed. No one called Liora "Miss" anything. But the hurt that suddenly weighed down Charlotte's features kept his face straight.

Could *this* be part of the reason for her obvious peeve with him? But wouldn't that mean... The realization hit him like a plank to the side of the head. His mouth turned drier than sawdust. Charlotte Brindle, despite all her citified proper ways, harbored some feelings for him? His first instinct was to whoop with joy over the realization, which of course he didn't do, because the people of his town might just think he'd gone crazy and vote him out of office. But his second instinct was sheer terror. Because if she was already in danger all on her own, she would be in even more danger if he allowed her into his life. He had a dangerous job that could spill over onto any person he loved.

Loved? Whoa. Take a step back, Callahan. No one said anything about love.

But in that moment, Sheriff Reagan Callahan knew he was deceiving himself. For it was suddenly clear to him that he'd fallen in love with Miss Charlotte Brindle, likely the first moment he'd seen her when she stepped off the stage in that gaudy green feathered hat.

Charlotte sighed and blinked rapidly a few times.

He'd taken too long to answer her question. How was it he always seemed to be hurting this woman without even trying? "I assure you that I don't know Liora in any way except for the fact that I see her now and then when my rounds take me to McGinty's." At the very thought of what she was implying, irritation mixed with a great deal of hurt began a slow simmer in his stomach. "If the Lord should one day give me a wife, I'll want her to know she's enough for me just the way she is. I would have hoped you knew me well enough to at least understand that by now, Miss Brindle."

She swallowed visibly. "I'm sorry. Back in Boston..." She

started to pull away, but he firmed his grip just enough to let her know he didn't want her to flee.

He gentled his tone. "Back in Boston..."

She rolled her lips in and pressed them tight, but then must have decided to forge ahead, because she said, "There was a man who told me that not a man alive didn't...didn't at some point..." A blush swept over her face, and she couldn't seem to go on.

Anger curled a tight fist in Reagan's stomach. And this time it wasn't directed anywhere near Miss Brindle. "A man betrayed you, didn't he? By...consorting with such a woman?"

She released a puff of breath. Nodded.

He would like to get his hands around the man's neck for just a few seconds. And yet only a moment ago he'd watched her try to befriend Liora. She had a tender heart full of compassion. Was it any wonder he found himself falling in love with her? He lowered his voice. "Who was he, if I might ask?"

"His name was—is—Kent Covington. He is a journalist who works for the *Boston Tribune*." There was a dry, gritty, undercurrent of pain in her words. "I'd thought he was a godly man. And still after I caught him, he wanted me to marry him. He made it sound as though I had expected too much of him. And before Kent, there was Senator Sherman. He...well...that time it was Father's secretary."

Reagan suddenly wished they were in a much more private setting. He wanted to cup her face in his hands and make sure he had her full attention when he said the next words. He settled for leaning close to speak them right into her ear instead. "Any man who would cheat on you is a fool. A woman like Liora never has, nor ever will, fit into my...recreational plans." He leaned back slightly and tilted his head until he could capture her gaze. "Not because I don't see her beauty"—

Charlotte flinched a little, and he hurried on—"but because I value my relationship with my Savior too much to sully it with such idolatrous behavior."

She blinked. He felt her relax. "It is idolatrous, isn't it? Putting such desires above what is pure and right."

"I believe any desire that makes us long for it more than we long to please our Creator is an idol, yes."

Her gaze flicked to his. "For once we agree, Sheriff." A soft smile took any sting from her words.

He cleared his throat, his earlier thought begging to be voiced. "Even after a man betrayed you with such a woman, you still tried to befriend Liora?"

He felt Charlotte slump a little in his arms. "She looked so lonely and discouraged when I met her up in the field earlier today. I get the feeling she's a very sad person who puts on a mask of happiness, and I keep feeling the urge to befriend her." She huffed a little. "My finishing-school mistress, Miss Gidden, would tell me I'm being very unwise with my reputation. And perhaps that's one reason that, as I mentioned, I find it difficult to do what I know is right. But I suppose it's similar to what you just said a moment ago. I value my relationship with my Savior too much to waste it on petty meanness toward a hurting woman who needs to feel His love so much. Also, what you said inside earlier reminded me my sins are no less egregious than hers."

Reagan's admiration for the woman rose several more notches. "I would just encourage you to proceed with caution."

She angled him a look, one corner of her mouth tilting up into a small smile. "Does that mean you are going to relinquish your attempts to get me to return to Boston, Sheriff?"

Reagan swallowed. With his growing feelings for the woman, and the realization that she might even have some for him in return, he certainly wasn't going to keep urging her to return to Boston where a man waited who had treated her with such disdain. Yet neither could he let her stay without warning her of the local dangers to her person. "Miss Brindle, there are circumstances—"

"Mind if I cut in?"

Reagan's eyes fell closed. Blast if Flynn Griffin didn't have the worst timing. Reagan pegged the man with a glower, tightened his grip on Charlotte, and kept dancing. "Aren't you supposed to be out checking on the Ferndales' new baby?"

Flynn grinned. "You know, I ran into them over near the wood-chopping contest. Didn't think they'd come out, with the little guy being so new and all, but they had him wrapped up real good to keep any chill away, and he's put on at least half a pound this week. He's gonna be a strong little fella. Anyhow..." He shrugged and looked expectantly toward Charlotte. "Saved me the trip."

Reagan hesitated through several more beats. However, he couldn't seem to come up with a good excuse not to give the doctor a turn at dancing with the pretty new schoolteacher, so after only a moment more, he handed her off.

And Charlotte leapt into Flynn's arms like a frog lurching from a campfire frying pan.

Reagan stalked away. It was about time to get the ax-throwing contest underway. Maybe he'd even join in himself.

Too bad he couldn't put Flynn in front of the target.

Patrick heard Lenny slink back into camp and knew immediately that something had happened. Normally Lenny came all the way into the cave to give him the latest news he'd discovered while sneaking about town, but today his footsteps shuffled only as far as the fire built just inside the mouth of the cave to hide its light from searchers. Patrick heard him grouse beneath his breath as he sank onto one of the stones.

Patrick gingerly scooted off his bedroll. Curling his still-injured arm against his chest, he soft-footed to the cave front to peer at the man. Firelight danced along his face, revealing the sharp red line of a scratch along his chin. Lenny morosely stabbed a long twig into the coals and watched the stick burn.

Waddell cursed the man silently. He better not have done something to get himself noticed.

"What happened?" Patrick stepped out of the shadows and stood over Lenny, wanting to make sure to get a good read on his expression.

Lenny sucked in his lower lip. Shrugged. "Nothing."

If there was one thing he couldn't tolerate in his ranks, it was a liar. Patrick slapped him hard, open palmed. His broad, thick palm connected solidly, and Lenny hurtled sideways off his rock perch.

He cowered on the ground at Patrick's feet, arms curled over his head.

Patrick squatted beside him and leaned his forearms against his knees as casually as he could. It wouldn't do for Lenny to see that the slap had sent a ricochet of pain through him that made him glad to sink to his haunches. He pulled in a slow, steadying breath, willing away the shards of pain slicing through his arm. "Don't you lie to me. What happened?"

"I found her. Almost had her. But then the sheriff came along, and...I lost my advantage." Lenny tried to scoot away from him, along the ground.

Patrick leaned forward and pinched the man's face between his fingers, angling it toward the firelight to get a better look at the scratch. "How'd you get this? Were you seen? Followed?"

"No! I swear I wasn't. It was a rosebush." Lenny whimpered. "When the sheriff came up sudden like, I let go of a branch, and it smacked me in the face. But I wasn't detected. I was real careful-like."

Patrick sighed audibly to reveal his disgust. "Might have known you weren't competent enough to even bring in a slip of an eastern woman, Smith. I might have known." He stood and stalked back to the warmth of his blankets.

"I'll get her next time!" Lenny called after him. "I will. I have a plan and everything."

"You mess up again, Lenny, and you better pray they lock you in a deep, dark hole or else fill you with lead, because I won't be so understanding the next time, you get me?"

"I get you, Boss. I do." Patrick heard him scrambling to his feet.

Patrick stifled a moan and held his arm close to his chest as he eased down onto his bedroll. Some jobs were better done on your own, but this arm must have been busted up but good. He was still seeing white lights every time he moved it. He needed a little more time to heal. Just a little more time, and then the sheriff of Wyldhaven would rue the day he'd ever heard the name Patrick Waddell, much less tried to capture him.

Chapter Seventeen

Liora woke with a groan of pain. She covered her eyes with a trembling hand and inhaled slowly, trying not to wince. Exhaled equally slow. McGinty had assured her this would get easier. McGinty had been wrong.

She'd loathed herself for many years. But never had Liora loathed herself as much as she did this morning.

A knock sounded at her door, and she realized that must have been what had awakened her in the first place. She squinted at the window. The sun already streamed through and puddled on the floorboards. From the angle of the light, it must be close to ten.

Gingerly, she rolled from the mattress and made her way to the door. The last person she'd expected to see when she opened it was Deputy Rodante, but he stood on the other side nonetheless, hands crimping the brim of his black Stetson, staring down at the floor, an expression of sheer sympathy furrowing his brow.

He had bad news then. And he'd gone to see Ma this morning. She clutched at the door, bracing herself for whatever bad news he'd come to tell. There was no other reason an upstanding man like him would be outside her door at this hour of the morning.

But the moment he laid eyes on her, his expression shifted. He took in her face. "What happened? Are you all right?"

She'd momentarily forgotten the beating she'd taken last night. Before she'd gone to bed, she'd sat at her dressing table and met her gaze in the chipped triangle of mirror. One eye had already been turning black, and she hadn't even been able to inhale without shards of pain from ribs that had likely been broken. She probably looked a sight worse this morning.

Some men were rough. But McGinty's rules were that she had to simply grit her teeth and bear it unless she felt her life endangered. For those times he'd strapped a derringer to the underside of her dressing table. But it had come with the dire warning that if she shot a man, she'd never work for him again, no matter the circumstances.

She brushed aside Joe's concern. "There was a... misunderstanding with a...client. Ewan took care of him." The lie slipped free easily. She couldn't have the deputy tracking down Ewan's clients. Ewan would never stand for it. And she'd be the one to pay yet again.

Joe studied her for a minute but then seemed to accept her story. He sighed, hung his head, and gripped the back of his neck with one hand. "Listen, I have bad news."

She closed her eyes. *Please...*

"It's your ma. She isn't...wasn't...she was...gone when I got there this morning."

Liora's knees buckled, and though she clung to the door for support, it wasn't enough. She sank to the floor. She pressed her cheek to the smooth cool wood and just sat there. Empty. Broken. Numb.

When she opened her eyes again, he was squatting before her, arms propped along his knees, hat dangling from one hand and an envelope in the other. "I used some of your money to pay her final expenses. This is what was left." He held her envelope out to her.

She took it. Crumpled it into one fist. What did she care about money? She'd only taken this job so she could help Ma. And now... "She wasn't always a whore, you know."

He just looked at her, holding his silence. But his expression invited her to tell him more.

"When I was very young, my father worked the mines. But he was an"—she filtered through a list of several ready-to-mind curses and finally settled on—"intolerably cruel man. He left us when I was ten." She huffed. "Best year of my life." She flicked at the corner of the envelope with one fingernail. "Ma tried to make it as a laundress for a year. But...it was hard. I remember always being hungry."

Joe's hands clenched, and from the righteous indignation pouring off him, she got the feeling he would have liked to wring necks.

"Anyhow... After that first year...well...I suppose you've got a pretty good picture." She pressed her lips together. Why was she telling him this? She'd never talked to anyone about this before. "She did it for *me*."

He tilted his head, so much compassion in his eyes. "And you did it for *her*."

"And look how much good it did." She forced herself to her feet.

He stood with her, curling the brim of his hat as he rolled it through his fingers. "I'm very sorry for your loss."

"Thank you, Joe. You've been more than kind." The door clicked softly when she shut it, and she heard his boot steps disappearing down the hall. She fell onto the stool before her dressing table. Propped her forehead into one palm. Stared at the envelope.

She reached one hand under and fingered the cool wood of the derringer's grip. Unstrapped it, drew it out, and laid it on the dresser before her.

Such a small tool of destruction. Barely five inches from handle to barrel tip. She rubbed one finger along the cool metal and studied herself in the mirror once more.

And after she pulled the trigger? What would death feel like? Was it really the end?

Not a sparrow falls.

The words arrowed through her, seemingly spoken straight to her heart. Aggravated, she shoved back from the dressing table and marched across the room. Pain stabbed through her, and she folded her arms around her ribs in an attempt to lessen the shooting darts of anguish each movement caused.

Did God really see her fallen mother? Did He care what had happened to her? If He cared so much, why hadn't He stepped in to help them long before now? Before it was too late? *She's gone.*

The sobs hit her then. She collapsed onto her bed and curled onto her side, wishing she could believe in the fairy tale of a caring God.

If He cares that much about small sparrows, we can be sure to know He cares for us even more.

Her hand fisted into the blankets, and she wished she could get the woman's words out of her mind. She'd nearly gaped when the schoolteacher had come over and asked her to join them for dinner. Didn't the woman know anything about the way society operated? Didn't she care about keeping her job? Her reputation? It was ridiculous. The thought of Liora Fontaine eating in public with people like the sheriff, the doctor, the schoolteacher.

Yet now she had the foolish woman's words tantalizing her

with the fantasy that there was a God who actually cared for people. A God who saw even when the birds fell from their nests.

Would that it were true. Nothing in her life had indicated a God who cared for her more than for the birds.

Stop your whimpering, you little mongrel. No one's coming to your rescue, because no one cares. I'm leaving. And I want you to remember until the day you die that it's all your fault!

Liora closed her eyes against the memory.

Much more familiar words.

Much more truthful.

Much less comforting.

Reagan Callahan, boots propped comfortably atop one corner of his desk, sighed and tossed the stack of *wanted* posters back onto the blotter. He massaged fingers and thumb against the headache pulsing just behind his eyes, feeling the weight of his responsibilities to the people of Wyldhaven hanging like a heavy burden squarely around his neck.

The judge was due in next week for the trial of the Waddell gang. Reagan had hoped he'd have the rest of the gang rounded up by then, but he'd gone out hunting their trail for several hours each of the last three days and had come up empty. At least if he wasn't finding any tracks that meant that the outlaws weren't lingering around the outskirts of town waiting for their chance to dispatch Charlotte.

He still hadn't initiated a talk with her about the danger she was in. After Doc had interrupted their dance the other night, he hadn't gotten another chance to speak with her. He hadn't seen her again for the rest of the evening, and she'd been fastidiously avoiding him all week—he knew because just yesterday she'd seen him coming down the street and had quickly ducked into the post office to avoid meeting him. The action had hurt more than he would have thought possible. Maybe he'd just been imagining her feelings at the dance.

Reagan's feet slipped off his desk and thudded to the floor, effectively jolting him back to the present. He sighed and slurped another swallow of coffee. The coffee was stone cold—probably about the same temperature as Miss Brindle's leanings toward him. He grimaced at the sentimental thought. Great. Now he was going addlebrained.

Reagan snorted, wearily crossed the room, and poured himself another cup of the coal-black coffee that had been thickening on the office's wood stove since five o'clock this morning.

From one of the cells at the back of the room, Horace Crispin chuckled. "Feelin' a mite discouraged that you ain't found Waddell yet, Sheriff? Don't you worry none. He always shows up when you least expect him." The man guffawed and slapped his leg.

Reagan didn't even glance the man's way, but he couldn't help but realize Horace had just voiced his worst fear. Waddell or his gang could attack Charlotte just about anywhere, and what if he wasn't close enough to protect her? Feeling fatigued beyond belief, Reagan plunked the cup back onto his desk and fell into his chair.

With school starting first thing Monday morning, Reagan needed to track Charlotte down and make sure she understood the gravity of the danger she was in. Once school started, there would be an infinite number of suppers she'd be invited to, and Reagan couldn't have her traipsing all over the place without a guard, at least not until all the hubbub from the Waddell gang died down. Either that or he captured them all, and the chances of that happening before Monday were looking less and less likely.

Until a more permanent building could be erected, school was going to be held in Dixie Pottinger's boardinghouse dining room. School would start after the breakfast hour and end well before the dinner hour, so the only income Dixie would be losing was from her lunch crowd. And the school board had agreed to pay Dixie two bits per child per week to help offset the cost of the lunches she wouldn't be able to sell to her boarders.

That was likely where he'd find Charlotte, and he'd put off the confrontation with the town's new schoolteacher long enough. Reagan locked up the sheriff's office and made straight for the boardinghouse, but when he arrived, Dixie told him that Charlotte had gone across the street to the mercantile to pick up a few things for her "classroom." Reagan tipped his hat in thanks and headed over there.

The bell above the mercantile door tinkled when he entered, but neither of the room's two occupants seemed to notice.

Charlotte stood before the counter with both tiny hands plunked on her hips. "No chalk!? First you have plenty of pencils but no paper, and now you have a chalkboard but no chalk? Mr. Heath assured me that all the supplies for the school would be taken care of! I can't teach without paper and chalk, Mr. Hines!"

Reagan did his best to suppress a grin.

Jerry's freckles were almost an exact match to his curly red hair at that moment, and he rubbed the back of his flushed neck, looking very much like a schoolboy receiving his first switching. "I'm not sure how the chalk got overlooked, Miss Brindle. And I'm out of paper because of the oldest Kastain girl. She can draw a picture so pretty it could make your jaw drop."

Reagan couldn't see the look Charlotte leveled on the man, but he saw the tilt of her head, and the look must have been a doozy, because Jerry got right back to business.

"But I can assure you I've placed the order now, and the chalk and paper should be here inside a month. Six weeks at the most."

"Six weeks?!" Charlotte threw up her hands and spun around in exasperation. Her gaze landed on him, and she seemed to freeze for just a moment before she resumed her task. She bent and hefted a rather large crate of various items onto the counter. "Very well. I'll take these, and I presume it's okay if I charge them to the school's account?"

Jerry always kept a nub of a pencil behind his ear, and Reagan didn't think he'd ever seen the man move so fast as when he pulled the pencil down and set to tabulating. "Oh yes. Of course, Miss Brindle."

Charlotte spun toward Reagan, folding her arms and tilting her head. "Sheriff." There was still the slight sting of hurt in her tone.

Reagan hated that he'd been the one to put it there. He realized he was shifting his Stetson through his fingers and squeezed the brim tight to put a stop to the nervous action. "Charlotte. I wondered if I might have a word with you?" He swallowed. He hadn't meant to address her so informally.

She hesitated for a fraction of a second but must have decided to let his faux pas pass, because she said, "Actually, I'm really rather busy." She swept a gesture to the box of supplies. "As you can see, I'm just about to head back to the boardinghouse to finish up my final preparations before school starts. Since tomorrow is the Lord's day, I need to finish up tonight."

It was a dismissal, but he couldn't let her get away with it.

"Yes. And after school starts, you'll be even busier than you have been all week, which is why I really must insist you take a few moments to speak to me today."

She sighed and leaned into one hip, giving him a glower that he felt sure had made schoolboys confess secrets sworn to silence on blood oaths.

"The total comes to fourteen dollars and seventeen cents, Miss Brindle." Jerry nudged the crate back across the counter. "I'll put this on the school's tab. And you can be on your way now."

Reagan almost smiled at the hopeful, near-pleading note in the man's voice during that last sentence.

Charlotte started to lift the crate, but Reagan brushed her aside. "I'll get that. And we can talk on our way back to Dixie's."

She huffed but did tip him a nod of concession before she turned back to Jerry. "Thank you, Mr. Hines. You've been most helpful."

"I have?" Jerry couldn't have looked more confused if he'd tried. "Oh! Well, I'm always happy to be of service." He hurried around the counter. "Here, let me get the door for you." He yanked open the mercantile door, jarring the bell, and motioned for them to hurry along their way as if his life depended on it.

As Charlotte lifted her skirts and stepped down into the street, she wondered what had brought the sheriff out looking for her this time. His boots thudded softly into the dirt beside her, and she glanced over at him.

Ever since the night of the boxed social she hadn't been able to think about the sheriff without imagining the feel of them dancing together. She'd known dancing with the man was a bad idea in so many ways, especially for a woman who didn't want to risk her heart again so soon after having it crushed. Okay, the crushing had come with a lot of relief too, but still she wanted to give herself more time before falling for another man. Yet when she'd seen Butch Nolan striding her way, offering her that horrifying wink, she'd done the only thing a girl could do.

And now each time she thought of the sheriff, she remembered that tantalizing scent of leather and spice. The feel of his hand guiding her gently from her waist. The warmth of his palm against hers, and the gentle humor in his blue eyes as he tilted his head to tease her.

She forced her thoughts to the present lest she require the use of her fan.

Today the sheriff had rolled the sleeves of his blue twill shirt up to just below his elbows. No gentleman of Boston would ever be seen about town with his shirtsleeves rolled up! And yet she found she rather liked the glimpse of brown skin. And the way his forearms rippled as he adjusted his grip on the crate.

She'd done it now. Charlotte flipped her fan open and put it to good use. She really ought to look away.

As he maneuvered around the end of a logging wagon and stepped out into the street, he glanced back at her. "Coming?"

And it was only then that she realized her mouth had gone dry and she'd come to a complete stop at the foot of the mercantile stairs. She darted her tongue over her lips, snapped her fan closed, and lifted her skirts to hurry after him, willing away the warmth she could feel pinking her cheeks.

"Yes, Sheriff. Now..." With the hopes of covering for her embarrassing scrutiny of the man, she dove right into the topic at hand. "What can I do for you today?"

A muscle bunched in his jaw. “Reagan.” His blue eyes pierced hers.

Her heart thudded, and her mouth suddenly felt made of sandpaper. There was only one reason a man would want a woman to address him by his first name. And she just didn’t feel ready for that. Uncertainty kept her silent.

The sheriff’s brow lowered in consternation. He must have chosen not to press the issue, because he changed the subject. “I fear I have some news that may prove a bit alarming.”

“Oh?” Charlotte’s hands clenched her skirts more tightly.

“Yes. It’s regarding Patrick Waddell.”

At the mention of that man’s name, Charlotte’s feet refused to move an inch farther, no matter that they were right in the middle of the street. “What about him?” Fear lodged in the back of her throat.

The sheriff paused for a moment but then gestured with the crate for her to move out of the road. “Keep walking, if you would. A wagon is coming.”

Behind her she heard the jangle of the trace chains and the grind of wagon wheels over the corduroyed logs of the road. Oh for heaven’s sake, she was apparently determined to make a fool of herself today. She lifted her skirts and hurried to the other side, pausing once more in front of Dixie’s Boardinghouse. Her heart thudded against her breastbone at the mere thought of Waddell. What would the man have done with her if Reagan hadn’t come to her rescue?

“What about Patrick Waddell, Sheriff?” Charlotte willed herself to breathe normally. The outlaw’s violent actions had, quite frankly, terrified her. She really had no desire to ever see him again.

The sheriff took in her features and must have read the fear in her eyes, because he hurried to reassure her. “Please don't be concerned, Charlotte. Everything is going to be just fine, but can we"—he adjusted the carton of supplies in his arms and glanced around—"head into Dixie's parlor before we continue this discussion?"

Charlotte followed his gaze and noticed that practically every visible window in town had a face plastered to it. All of them taking great interest in her and the sheriff's conversation.

"Oh...o-of course." Charlotte led the way into Dixie's and pushed the door shut behind them. Did everyone in town know something she didn't know?

She led him through the foyer and into the dining room, and motioned to the table that would be her desk, come Monday morning. The sheriff deposited the carton on its surface and then removed his hat.

He glanced around the room. "I see you've already done much to turn the room into a school."

By the tone of his voice, she couldn't tell if he was impressed or simply surprised. So she merely shrugged. Thankfully, the crates that Father had shipped to her on the train had arrived just yesterday, and she'd spent a good portion of the night converting Dixie's dining room into a room that could suffice for both dining and educating.

Three small bookshelves, which she had scrounged from Dixie's attic, held both books and tea services, with a few dried flower arrangements scattered throughout. Two blue Mason jars on her desk held fountain pens and pencils, but she had draped swags of lace around them to disguise the utensils. The room held two large rolling chalkboards. (Thankfully, Mr. Heath had thought ahead and recognized the need for those.) And on the backs of each, Charlotte had hung copies of the Constitution and the Bill of Rights. On the dining room walls, Charlotte had put up educational prints—the landing of the

Mayflower, George Washington at Valley Forge, the arrival of the French fleet at the end of the Revolutionary War, and Charlotte's personal favorite, a painting of a woman helping slaves escape during the Civil War. Decorated with pretty frames and here and there a swag of dried flowers, the prints would serve as beauty for Dixie's patrons and lesson props for Charlotte's students.

But the sheriff—Reagan—wasn't here to see any of that.

Charlotte pressed her palms together. "What was it you wanted to tell me, Sher—Reagan?" She couldn't prevent a tremor from invading the question. And if it had just as much to do with her complying with the use of his given name, well, he didn't need to know that.

Reagan's eyes shone in a way that made her long to say his name over and over again. But after only a moment, he seemed to remember why he was here, and his face turned serious again. He crimped the brim of his Stetson and pressed his lips together. "Yes, I'm afraid I have some bad news—"

"Is he alive?" she interrupted.

Reagan hesitated a moment but then must have decided it was okay to answer, because he said, "Actually, we still aren't sure. Of course we know he was alive when he attacked William. But since then, no one seems to have seen him. At least no one that's talking."

Charlotte swallowed.

"But my news really has more to do with the Waddell gang than with Waddell himself. You see, I got word a couple weeks back... It seems that Waddell's crew has decided to hold you accountable for Waddell's...demise."

"Me!?" The word was naught more than a chirp. She felt her eyes widen. "Was that the reason you pushed so hard for me to return home?"

He nodded, his blue eyes full of concern. "One of the reasons, yes. The main reason, really."

Charlotte pursed her lips, still not sure she was ready to let him off the hook for being so adamant about her returning home, but with the knowledge that she could be in danger came the first niggling doubts over whether staying in Wyldhaven really was the right decision.

"So what does this mean for me? The fact that they 'hold me accountable'?"

"Well... For one, if you need to walk anywhere farther than the livery at the other end of town, I'd like to ask that you stop by the office for an escort. Either Joe or I will be happy to accompany you anywhere you need to go."

"What about field trips with my class?"

Reagan twisted his hat through his fingers. "Again, Joe or I will be happy to accompany you."

Charlotte lifted her hands in exasperation. "So because I had the unlucky fortune to end up riding on a stagecoach with a criminal who kidnapped me, I'm basically to be held prisoner in my own town?!"

Reagan tipped her a *be serious* look. "It's not going to be like that."

Charlotte folded her arms. Her feelings about one Patrick Waddell had just recast themselves into all-out anger instead of fear. "And how long must this go on?"

Rubbing one hand over the scruff on his jaw, Reagan seemed to consider his answer for a moment. "Oh, all the hubbub should die down in a few weeks' time. Let's just take one day at a time, shall we?"

"Bah!" Charlotte set to rather forcefully unpacking the crate of the extra fountain pens, inkpots, blotters, a map, and several books she'd chosen at the mercantile. "And Mother was worried I'd be killed by wild Indians! How little did she know!" She glanced up in time to see Reagan covering a smile, and let the loud sound of the dictionary falling to her desk reveal her pique.

He strode toward the door, tamping on his hat, and paused at the threshold to give the brim a tug in her direction. "Should you need anything, you know where to find me."

She only tipped him a nod and continued with her unpacking. But the longer she worked that afternoon, the more her agitation rose. Her anger was slowly seeping back around toward fear again. Should she pack it in and return to Boston? No, she couldn't do that. Hadn't she just decided the other night that the Lord really was the One to bring her here? She wasn't going to start doubting that now.

But what if she was attacked while walking through town? Or what if one of the outlaws broke in during school hours and threatened one of the children?

She tucked one fingernail between her front teeth and considered her options. And after only a moment, the truth hit her.

"I need to buy a gun!"

Yes! That was the perfect answer. Then even if Reagan or Deputy Joe were not around when the outlaws came for her, she would have something to protect herself with!

She dropped the last pencil into the blue Mason jar on her desk and looked around the room. Satisfied that the place was as ready as she could make it, she hefted the crate and made her way back out to the street.

Charlotte eyed the mercantile's sign as she marched toward it. Hanging crooked and misspelled as it was, it basically matched the rest of the town to perfection.

Mr. Hines stood behind the counter when she pushed her

way inside. At the jangle of the bell, he glanced up. Perhaps one of these days she'd find a way to tell him that his sign needed to be redone. But for now...

She set the crate on the counter between them. "I've brought back your crate." Charlotte tucked her hands behind herself and scanned the store, searching for the area where he might keep his guns.

Mr. Hines smiled. "Oh, that was right kind of you, Miss Brindle. But next time don't put yourself out. I could have had my son David bring it home from school on Monday." He removed the crate from the counter and turned toward a stack of other empty crates behind him.

"And I need you to sell me a gun."

Mr. Hines somehow lost his grip on the crate, and it landed on his boot. "Ow! Dadblame!" His face flamed as he hopped on one foot. "Forgive me, Miss Brindle. I ought not to speak that way in front of you."

Charlotte surprised herself by immediately waving away his concern. Mother would have been horrified at such a breach of propriety on Mr. Hines's part. And Miss Gidden certainly would have coached Charlotte to politely but succinctly put Mr. Hines in his place. Could she be adapting to the vulgarities of the country so quickly? She wasn't sure whether to be pleased or perturbed at that thought.

Apparently, the pain in Mr. Hines's foot had subsided enough that he could walk on it again. He limped over to the stairway that led up to the second floor. "David! Come down here a minute, Son."

A sprightly little redhead, the spitting image of his father and about ten years old, bounded down the stairs only a moment later. "Yes, Father?"

Mr. Hines pressed the crate into his son's arms. "Here, take this out back and put it with the other broken ones for me, would you?" Then Mr. Hines bent forward and whispered a few words into David's ear that Charlotte couldn't hear. Whatever he said caused the boy's eyes to widen, and he dashed out the door with the crate so quickly that Charlotte didn't even have time to introduce herself as the lad's new teacher.

She smiled at the cuteness of it, but a glance at the time on the clock above the counter told her she was going to miss dinner at Dixie's if she didn't get on with her purchase and get back to the boardinghouse. "Now about that gun, Mr. Hines? I'm thinking of something fairly small that could fit in a dress pocket. But it has to be a large enough…*bang*…to stop a grown man in his tracks."

"O-oh, m-my. That sounds s-serious." Mr. Hines's hands fluttered over the front of his apron, and he seemed to be looking at something out the front window of his store.

Charlotte tried to locate what had caught his attention but couldn't seem to see anything. "Mr. Hines? Do you have a gun that fits that description?"

"W-well. Y-yes, I do, as a matter of f-fact."

Since when had the man developed a stutter? He'd really been quite prompt with each request she'd made of him earlier this afternoon. Yet now his feet didn't seem to move any faster than a tortoise in mud.

Charlotte's impatience could no longer be contained. "Well, may I see it please? I'm sorry to be in a hurry, but I'm afraid I'll miss the dinner hour at Dixie's."

Yet no matter her urging, the man seemed to be operating with his wagon's brakes clamped into place. First he didn't have a key for the locked wooden cabinet behind the counter where he said he kept his guns, and he had to go upstairs to fetch it. But Charlotte had never seen someone climb a set of stairs so slowly in her entire life. He took an inordinately long time above stairs. Then when he returned below stairs, he once again seemed to be searching for something out on the street, and for the second time, Charlotte couldn't see what he might be looking at. It took him at least five tries to fit the key into the lock and get it to turn. Charlotte was just about to jump behind the counter and offer to help, when the key finally turned and the cabinet door swung open.

"Okay...let's see what guns I might have in here." He squatted very slowly before the cabinet, then lifted his face to look at her. "Do you have a price range in mind?"

Charlotte thought of the money that Father had pressed into her hands when she'd boarded the train in Boston. She hadn't touched it, and she felt certain there was enough there to cover the price of any pistol. "I don't think money is an object, Mr. Hines."

"Oh." He almost looked disappointed at that.

Charlotte frowned. Whatever had gotten into the man since he'd helped her so efficiently this afternoon? It was almost like he didn't want to sell her a weapon!

"Well, how about this one?" Mr. Hines laid a pistol nearly as long as Charlotte's forearm on the counter.

She eyed it dubiously. What if she picked it up and it went off? She didn't want to be the cause of poor Mr. Hines losing a limb! "Is it...does it have...bullets in it?"

The man's lips twitched, and he rubbed at them fiercely. "No, ma'am."

Gingerly, Charlotte reached out and tried to lift the gun. But she found she was loathe to touch it, and the two-fingered grip she put on it was only sufficient enough to raise it a few inches before its weight caused it to clatter back to the counter with a loud commotion. Charlotte slapped her palm to the pistol to keep it from dancing around any more than it already was.

"Ah, I think this one is rather larger than I was hoping for."

"Very well. Yes...I can see how it might be too large." The man ducked back down to peer into his cabinet, and for some reason he seemed intent on keeping his face averted at the moment. "Let's see what else I have in here."

Behind them, the bell above the door jangled. Mr. Hines lifted his head so quickly that he clipped the top of it on his cupboard.

As Mr. Hines gasped out a protest of pain, Charlotte turned to see Reagan striding through the door, with Mr. Hines's son David right on his heels.

"Sheriff!" Mr. Hines greeted, gingerly rubbing a hand over the top of his head. The word held so much relief that it was unmistakable. "Do you know that Miss Brindle here has decided to buy herself a gun! Ain't that something?"

Charlotte folded her arms and glowered at the man, not a bit fooled by his act. "And does every citizen in town need the permission of the sheriff to buy a gun? Or only those of the female persuasion?"

Mr. Hines's face turned almost as red as his hair. "Now don't go gettin' all kerfuffled, Miss Brindle. I only done called the sheriff over for your own protection."

Charlotte was afraid a breath might have hissed through her teeth. "And I'm only buying a gun for my own protection!"

Reagan cleared his throat. "I'm afraid this is some my doing, Jerry." He pulled Charlotte to one side, tilted her an *are you serious* look, and spoke low. "Do you know how to shoot? Did you carry a pistol in Boston?"

Charlotte raised an eyebrow at the man. "I can assure you, *Sheriff*, that I had no *need* to carry a gun while living in the civilized city of Boston. No one there ever decided I was the reason a villainous kidnapper went missing!"

A quick hint of humor tucked around the corners of Reagan's mouth, but he was apparently smart enough to manacle it before it could break free. He folded his arms. "Very well, *Miss Brindle*." He tossed her return to formality back in her face. "Buy your gun, but I can't let you carry it until you allow me to give you some lessons on how to use it."

Charlotte was opening her mouth to protest what she felt certain was likely discriminatory treatment, but then she thought better of it. This could be the answer to her problem. After all, she had no idea how to use a gun, and if Reagan was willing to give her some lessons, she really ought to take him up on the offer. So she transformed her protest into, "Very well, I accept."

Reagan loosed a sigh and stepped up to the counter by her side. "You still have that Webley and Scott British Bulldog revolver with the ivory grips, Jerry?"

Mr. Hines's eyes widened. "But that's a forty-four caliber!"

"It'll pack a wallop, that's for sure. But it's nice and compact, and will fit in the pocket of her skirt with no problem."

Packing a wallop. Charlotte gave a little nod. She liked the sound of that.

A moment later, Mr. Hines laid a gun no longer than the length of her hand on the counter. And Charlotte let out a sigh of pleasant relief. The gun was even pretty. She picked it up to examine it more closely. Nickel-plated, the very shiny silver gun was engraved all over with an intricate floral pattern that was quite feminine. And best of all, the gun wasn't too heavy and felt comfortable in the palm of her hand when she wrapped her fingers around the beautifully grained ivory handle. This was much better than the huge monstrosity Mr. Hines had showed her a moment ago.

She set the gun back onto the counter. "Yes. This one. I'll take it."

Mr. Hines glanced at Reagan as if for permission to sell her the weapon. Charlotte snapped her teeth together and tried not to be too irritated with the man. Perhaps he was worried she might shoot herself in the leg.

Charlotte's eyes dropped closed. Perfect. Now *she* was worried she might shoot herself in the leg.

"Add in two boxes of cartridges."

Mr. Hines must have taken Reagan's instructions as approval, because a moment later he laid two boxes next to the pistol and said, "The gun and two boxes of cartridges come to twelve dollars and fifty cents, Miss Brindle."

Charlotte couldn't resist. She looked at Reagan and lifted her brows. "Is it all right with you, *Sheriff*, if I pay Mr. Hines now?"

With a grin, the man nodded. He rubbed his jaw, the blond stubble rasping under his fingers. The look on his face said he wasn't quite sure what to do with her. And she supposed that ought not to be a surprise. There were days she didn't know what to do with herself either.

She paid for her purchase and then very deliberately picked the items up. It was a bit scary having something so small and powerful in her hands. Something that could bring about so much tragedy if she mishandled it. Without another moment's thought, she transferred the pistol and boxes to Reagan's hands. "I suppose you can keep me safe from murderous outlaws until you can find the time to teach me how to use this?"

He tucked the pistol into his waistband, holding the two boxes of cartridges in one of his large hands and propping his other hand on his hip. "You do one nice thing for a woman, and the next thing you know she's begging you to spend every last minute you have at her behest." The words were spoken so low Charlotte felt sure no one else heard them, yet still her cheeks blazed.

She lifted her chin and challenged, "Are you saying you can't, Reagan?"

He grinned at her and leaned closer. "Anything for a woman with beautiful green eyes who calls me by my given name."

She rolled her eyes at him but had to pinch her lips together to keep from smiling.

He didn't seem fazed by her pretended lack of appreciation for his flirtation. "How about we have your first lesson Monday afternoon after classes?"

Charlotte swallowed. She hadn't expected him to be able to teach her so soon. Truth be told, she was already having second thoughts about the need to carry such a weapon with her everywhere she went. But her pride made her bite her tongue and tip up her chin. "That should be fine. Thank you. I'll meet you at your office after I dismiss school for the day?"

He tugged on the brim of his hat. "See you then."

Oh Lord have mercy. What had she gotten herself into?

Chapter Eighteen

Liora stared at the derringer all day.

She'd put it back in its holster when Doc had come to look at her, but pulled it out again after he left. And since Ewan had given her the night off on account of her left eye being swollen near shut, and Doc confirming she had several broken ribs also, she'd stared at it a good portion of the night too.

Now the first rays of light streamed through her window. Her stomach rumbled, but she ignored it. She tucked her hands beneath the pillow and looked at the glint of gray metal across the room on her dresser.

She longed to silence the questions. The pain. She longed for an end. Oblivion. Rest.

She pushed back the covers, padded to the dresser, and lifted the cool metal of the gun into her hands. Back at the bed, she sat cross-legged and laid the gun onto the blankets before her. She folded her hands and rested her chin on them.

Looking.

Willing herself to courage.

How was it I was cursed to have an impudent child such as you? You're just like your imbecile of a mother. Get out of my sight. Life would be better if you'd never been born.

Liora trembled. She scooped her hands back into her hair and rocked.

Better if you'd never been born.

Better.

She reached for the gun.

Joe woke with a start.

Sunday morning's light was just beginning to stream through the window of the room he rented from Ewan McGinty. For the past several nights, ever since Liora Fontaine had come to him for help, he'd slept fitfully.

Knowing she was just down the hall. What Ewan was paying her *to do* just down the hall... He gritted his teeth and rolled to his side, putting his back to the light from the window. She wasn't his responsibility. But her story yesterday had found its way deep into his heart.

He huffed. He'd done more for her than he should have already, as evidenced by the fact that he was awake and thinking of her in the wee hours of the morning.

Liora...

He frowned. Sat up. Had someone just called her name? He listened but heard nothing. He swung his legs over the side of the bed and tugged his pants on.

He reached for his boots and held them a moment, listening again. Still, he heard no sound. But an uneasiness deep inside urged him to action. Something didn't feel right.

He shoved his feet into his boots and slung his Colt around his hips. His fingers fumbled with the task that was so familiar he should have been able to do it in the dark. Finally, he got the holster buckled. He grabbed his shirt and thrust his arms through the sleeves but didn't bother with the buttons.

Out in the hall, he paused to listen once more. Silence still permeated the building, but he couldn't shake the premonition that something was wrong. No light came from under Doc's door. Ewan's room seemed all quiet.

He reached down and unsnapped the strap on his Colt, settling his palm against the grip. Leaning over the rail at the top of the stairs, he searched the room below.

Empty.

A breath eased from him. He was jumpier than a treed coon.

Nothing was wrong, and he should try and catch some more shut-eye before his day began. Sundays were his day to take care of any complaints, feed the prisoners, and make the presence of the law visible about town.

He was turning back to his room, when he saw a shadow pass beneath Liora's door. His breath hitched. So she was up. Two steps took him to her door. He stood there for several long minutes. She likely wasn't going to appreciate him knocking on her door at this hour of the morning. But she'd taken that beating the other night. What if something was wrong?

His hands clenched into fists by his side. How had none of them heard her cry out that night? Surely she hadn't taken a beating like that in silence. Even the sound of the punches would have been loud.

Of course the night of the boxed suppers he'd walked Belle home and gotten in late. Doc had also said he'd ridden out on a call late in the evening. So Ewan had been the only one who might have heard anything. Surely he would have gone in to help her though?

Joe's eyes fell closed. He hated knowing she'd suffered. And yet it was her choice that had put her in a dangerous situation. He'd been speaking truth when he'd offered to buy out her contract. She could have been long gone from this place.

A muffled sound, something like a groan, came from beyond

her door. And then the unmistakable sound of a gun's hammer ratcheting back.

His pulse spiked. "Liora?" He knocked.

From inside came a soft gasp.

Shucking his gun, he leapt to one side of the door and crouched low. Was someone in there with a gun on her? "It's Joe, Liora. You all right in there?"

"Go away, Joe." There was a note of hopelessness in her tone.

"I can't do that." He flattened himself against the floor and peered through the crack under her door. He could see all the way to her bed, and there didn't seem to be another person standing in the room with her. His heart hammered in earnest then. Because if no one was in the room with her, it could only mean one thing. "I'm coming in, you hear me? You decent?"

Her laugh was dry. "Like it matters?"

"Matters to me."

Down the hall, both Doc's and Ewan's doors opened. They both stepped out into the hall, scrutinizing him quizzically.

"Good-bye, Joe."

"No!" Her door shattered beneath his boot before he'd even realized he was taking action.

She had finally worked up her courage to let go. The decision came with a great deal of relief. She wasn't sure what had brought Joe to her door at this time of the morning. Hearing his soft tenor voice had almost shaken her resolve, but she pushed past it. It would be one quick flash of pain, and then oblivion.

Quiet.

Peace.

"Good-bye, Joe," she said. And then she put the pistol beneath her chin.

"No!" The door shattered inward.

She flinched.

And the gun fired.

"Liora!" Joe rushed toward her across the room.

She stared at him wide eyed. And then she felt the warm seep of blood trickling down her forehead. Her ears rang. She gave herself a little shake. The bed was still beneath her. The chipped triangle of mirror still hung above her dresser.

"Liora, no!" Joe was at her side now, knocking the derringer out of her hand and kicking it across the floor. He grabbed her head, tilted it toward the light from the window. "How bad is it? I can't see! Doc! Get me a light!" He pressed her down against the pillow. "Liora, you stay with me, you hear? You stay!"

So much pain. Her eyes fell closed, but she could hear footsteps slapping across the floorboards. Only a moment later, light flooded the room.

"Move out of the way, Joe. Let me have a look at her." Doc Griffin's voice.

From somewhere near the door, Ewan cussed her. "What were you thinking?"

Familiar shame settled around her heart. She swallowed. Trembled. How was she still here?

Doc pressed something to her forehead and then lifted one of her hands to keep it in place. "Hold that there."

Ewan kept cussing.

"Ewan, shut up!" Joe snapped. She heard a scuffle and then the door shut, blocking some of the sound of Ewan's disapproval. "Is there anything I can do, Doc?"

She'd never heard that tremor in Joe's voice before.

"She's going to be fine, Joe." Doc's voice was as calm as you please. She heard him digging through his doctor bag. "She must have pulled back at the last moment. The bullet only grazed her cheek and cut a little deeper across her forehead. I'm going to put in some stitches."

"No." Liora tried to shake her head. Tried to push Doc's hands away.

She didn't want to be all right. She wanted to be gone!

A sickly sweet scent filled her nostrils. She twisted her head, trying to get away from the smell, but it stayed with her. Doc was still talking, but it seemed like he was getting farther and farther away, and she couldn't make out his exact words. Her head felt heavy. Her arms and legs felt even heavier.

Maybe the shot had done more damage than Doc thought after all. Maybe this was what death felt like.

Regret gripped her.

And then the world went black.

Liora's arm flopped out to one side, and Joe's heart nearly stopped.

Doc looked at him, his lips set in a grim line. "Don't worry. She's just asleep. I used some chloroform on her. It often helps to distance patients from a...trauma such as this. Gives them a little better perspective when they wake up."

Joe sank to his haunches. Ran his hands back through his hair. Willed himself to breathe.

Doc gave him a sympathetic look. "What made you get up to check on her?"

Joe shook his head. "I don't know. I thought I heard someone call her name. But..."

Doc bent and set to stitching her up. "Providence, likely."

Joe considered that. He'd be the last one to proclaim God had spoken to him, but maybe He had. It didn't matter. He was just glad he'd come. If he hadn't busted in when he had... Well, he didn't want to ponder on that. He pushed himself to his feet. "If you don't need me, I have some things to discuss with Ewan."

Doc nodded. "You do that. And while you're at it, you remind him that you and I are both rent-paying customers who can find elsewhere to live and who can encourage our friends to find elsewhere to eat and drink."

Joe appreciated knowing he wasn't alone in his sentiments. He stopped by his room first to grab the bag of cash he kept stashed beneath his floorboards, and then he banged on Ewan's door.

He didn't care what time of morning it was or if the man had already crawled back into bed. They were going to have this out now.

Monday morning, Zoe Kastain bent and gave Jinx's head a pat. "It's gonna seem like a long time to ya probably, but I promise I'll only be gone for a few hours. Aidan's too young for school, so he will come bring ya some scraps after lunch. And when I get home we'll go for a walk, and you can chase squirrels. But Pa says ya cain't come to school."

Jinx yipped and lunged at the end of his rope, looking none too happy to be tied to the clothesline.

Zoe felt guilty leaving him there, but no matter the wheedling she had tried over breakfast, Pa clung to his insistence that dogs did not belong in school. Truth be told, she hadn't wheedled too hard. Pa still hadn't regained his color. And he still had to be helped in and out of bed. Doc kept saying healing would just take time. But sometimes she laid awake at night wondering what might happen to them all if Pa didn't recover. If only she'd stayed to help Pa that day. Maybe she could have kept that outlaw from shooting him.

"Zoe! Come on! We don't want to be late on our first day!"

Zoe rolled her eyes when Belle turned to snap a similar order at the twins, who were just coming out of the house. Likely Belle just wanted to have time to say hello to the sheriff when they arrived. Because they weren't in any danger of being late.

And sure enough, as soon as they made their way across the bridge into town, Belle headed for the sheriff's office.

Zoe nudged the twins toward Dixie's. Despite her worries over Pa, she could hardly wait to experience her first day of school! She was so glad that Miss Brindle had changed her mind about going back to Boston. For a while Zoe had feared that her dreams of getting to attend school would never come true. But thanks be, Miss Brindle had decided to stay. Another thrill rippled through her.

"Let's go inside."

Shiloh did a little dance. "I need to use the necessary first."

Zoe wrinkled her nose. Her excitement over seeing her first classroom ever could wait a few more minutes, she supposed. "Fine. I'll take ya 'round back. Come on. Sharon, you oughta go too, so's ya don't have to ask to be excused before break time." Zoe shooed the girls toward the outhouse. "Go on. I'll be waiting right here for y'all."

Shiloh and Sharon had just disappeared behind the hedge that hid the privy from sight when Zoe felt a hand clamp over her mouth! Zoe rolled her eyes. *Washington Nolan!* She threw her elbow into her assailant's ribs, stomped her foot against the top of his boot, and twisted hard to break free. But the arms she'd been so certain of escaping only tightened around her.

"Be still, and no one has to get hurt!" Her attacker shook her.

Not Washington's voice! A jolt of fear sent tremors of weakness through Zoe's legs.

"Now come on. We are going inside to see your *sweet posy* of a teacher."

Eyes widening, Zoe did her best to scream, but the sound was clamped off by the meaty hand. Behind the boardinghouse as they were, no one would likely hear her scuffling.

A low chuckle escaped the man who held her. "Don't worry. It ain't you I'm after." The man dragged her through the back door of Dixie's, which led straight into the dining room, where they were to have school.

Miss Brindle looked up from something she was studying on her desk.

Zoe tried to signal with her eyes for the woman to run.

But Miss Brindle only jumped to her feet, one hand rising to her throat. "Unhand her at once!"

The man who held Zoe laughed softly, and it was not a pleasant sound. "I have a better idea. Let's make a trade. You come with me right now, and I won't snap this cute little girl's neck."

Little girl?! Zoe gritted her teeth and swung her elbow for all she was worth while at the same time thrusting the heel of her boot in a bid for the man's shin.

But again her efforts did no more than raise a grunt. "Be still," the assailant growled.

She would not be still! Zoe thrashed and twisted, but then she felt the cold press of metal against her temple.

She froze, panting hard and finding it difficult to pull in a breath around the man's hand. But it was the look on Miss Brindle's face that raised more fear in her than the feel of the gun to her head.

Miss Brindle's face was almost as white as the lace curtains at the window behind her. "Please. Don't hurt her." She stretched out one hand. "I'll come with you. Just leave the child be." A sheen of moisture glistened in Miss Brindle's eyes, and Zoe felt her desperation rise. How could she stop this outlaw from kidnapping Miss Brindle?

"That's right you will." The man's voice was gruff. "Now. You just sit yourself down in that chair right there where I can see you while I tie the girl up."

Miss Brindle moved to comply. "Why must you tie her up? She can't hurt you."

Zoe felt her eyes narrow. She bet she could hurt the man if he weren't holding a gun to her head!

"Can't have her running straight to the sheriff."

The man plunked Zoe into a chair, and before she could even draw a breath to scream, he shoved a bandana into her mouth. It tasted salty and foul.

"Hush up now." The man had a bandana over the lower half of his face, and his slouch hat curved down to cast deep shadows over his eyes. He set the gun near to hand and kept half an eye on Miss Brindle while he worked. With several quick movements, he had Zoe lashed to the chair good and tight.

Miss Brindle looked around like she hoped Miss Pottinger might come in, or even Miss Pottinger's mother, but Zoe knew they weren't coming, because she'd seen them only a bit ago riding out of town in a carriage together.

A moment later the outlaw, with his gun pressed firmly into Miss Brindle's side, poked his head out the back door to look both ways. And then Zoe watched helplessly as the man dragged Miss Brindle out the door and closed it behind them.

Zoe immediately tried to scream. But it was no use. The

bandana tied into her mouth prevented her from making more than the most pitiful of sounds. She yanked on her wrists and attempted to tug her ankles free, but was only rewarded with the tight leather thongs cutting even more firmly into her skin.

She stilled for a moment and tried to think. What would Pa tell her to do? And then it hit her! She needed to break the chair! But how did she go about doing that when her ankles were lashed to the legs? She couldn't stand... Maybe if she could tip the chair over, something would break.

She rocked hard to the right and then to the left until she felt the chair finally tip over the edge of balance and toward the ground. Her hopes soared! The chair crashed into the floorboards, smashing Zoe's arm between the armrest and the floor. Pain like she had never experienced before surged through her, bringing with it a wave of blackness and a shriek of agony that would have been loud if not for the gag.

Oh, this had not been her brightest idea! Because now she couldn't do anything, not even breathe, without sending torturous flames shooting up her arm from her wrist, which was still trapped between the chair and the floor.

Tears pooled and spilled over. Miss Brindle might die, and it would be all her fault because she hadn't been strong enough to stop that man.

Zoe didn't know how long she had lain there before she finally heard footsteps. She opened her eyes to see who was coming.

"Zoe Kastain!" Washington Nolan dropped the pail that he'd been holding and leapt to her side. His fingers fumbled with the knot at the back of the gag. "What happened?!"

Washington's knee bumped into her wrist just as he yanked the gag free, and Zoe felt her humiliation rise when a whimper that bordered on the edge of a shriek slipped from her.

"Sorry! I'm so sorry!" Washington leapt back.

Zoe pushed down the pain and managed to say. "Don't worry about me! A man kidnapped Miss Brindle!"

Behind Washington, his brother, Jackson, stepped into the room. Washington threw a look over his shoulder. "Get the sheriff! Now!" As his brother darted back out the door, Washington took a moment to assess her situation. "Okay, listen Zo. I'm going to have to lift your chair back to its upright position. It's probably going to hurt, but it will cause the least discomfort to your arm."

Zoe didn't even have the gumption to put him in his place about the shortened version of her name.

"Ready?"

Zoe nodded and gritted her teeth in preparation for the pain.

Washington picked up her chair in one smooth movement, and Zoe could tell he tried to set it down as gently as he could, but the bump of the legs hitting the floor still sent a jolt through her that had her seeing flashes of light.

He must have heard the air that escaped between her teeth, because he winced. "Sorry. Here, let me get you untied."

"A man took Miss Brindle."

"You said that. Sheriff's on his way." His fingers fumbled with the knots at one ankle, but his worried gaze skittered to her face. "Did the man hurt you any worse than...your arm?"

Zoe sniffed. "Did that to myself. Was trying to break the chair so I could get the sheriff. My arm got in the way." She tried to twist her lips into the grim smile he'd be expecting from her, but feared the expression was more of a grimace.

"Leave it to you, Zo, to break your own arm."

This time she didn't let him get away with it. "ZoEEE." She stretched out the last syllable of her name.

Sheriff Reagan burst through the door then, with Belle and Deputy Joe on his heels. "Zoe? What happened?"

Washington had finished untying all the knots now, and Zoe forced herself to speak past the throbbing in her arm. "I took the twins out back when we got to town. And while I was waiting for them, a man grabbed me from behind. He brought me in here and told Miss Brindle that if she didn't come with him, he was gonna snap my neck." Tears pooled in Zoe's eyes without her permission. She sniffed. "I tried to stop him, but he was too strong."

"Did you get a look at him?"

Zoe shook her head and felt her aggravation with herself rise. "Only a glimpse when he was tying me up. But he had his hat pulled low and a bandana up over his face."

The sheriff's hand settled on his gun. "Did you see which way they went?" His face looked like it had lost several shades of color.

Zoe scrunched up her nose as she shook her head. "Out the back is all I know. I'm real sorry, Sheriff."

Belle squatted by the chair, her eyes widening as her gaze fastened on Zoe's wrist. "Zoe needs Doc!"

"I'll get him." Washington dashed from the room.

Sheriff Callahan snapped his fingers at his deputy. "Joe, saddle our horses. I'll see if I can figure out which way they went." And with that the sheriff hustled out the back door as Joe headed for the livery.

Zoe let her eyes drop closed, not wanting to even breathe too deeply because of the pain, but at Belle's silence, she cocked one eye open to see what her sister was doing. Belle was swiping tears from her cheeks. "I shouldn't have left you. You could have been killed."

Zoe closed her eyes again. "But I weren't. I'll be fine." It was Miss Brindle they all should be worried about.

That and the fact that for the first time in her life, she'd felt relieved to see Washington Nolan. Yes. That was something to be very concerned about as well.

Charlotte's kidnapper forced her to run down the alley behind the buildings of the town, and then he bound and gagged her and made her climb inside a wooden crate in the back of a wagon parked right behind the jail.

Darkness closed in as he put the lid on, and then Charlotte heard a lot of other scuffling and thumping. Her hands were tied together, and her space was so cramped that she could barely move. Pressing down her panic, she tried to push against the lid, but it didn't lift even a little.

Her legs were also of no use to her. She'd tried to kick against the end of the crate, but it proved of little value when she could barely budge in the tight confines.

Now as she lay in the dark inside the crate and listened to the creak of the wagon wheels trundling her off to who knew where, she had to admit that the man's plan had been pretty smart. The last place anyone would be looking was in the vicinity of the sheriff's office at the moment it was discovered she'd gone missing.

She imagined the man driving out of town right in front of the sheriff and Deputy Joe, tipping his hat, and offering them a smile. Maybe they even knew who the man was and wouldn't question a thing!

And what about poor Zoe, tied up back there? The poor girl was probably terrified.

Lord, I'm trying to trust You here. But it seems like ever since

I placed foot in this town, bad things have happened. Wouldn't good be happening if she was actually where God wanted her to be? She had tried to befriend Liora, and look how that had turned out. When she'd learned yesterday evening what the poor girl had tried to do, Charlotte had felt so discouraged. Maybe she should have pressed harder to be her friend. And now Zoe had been a victim, and this time directly because of her!

Her asthma began to tighten a band around her chest. *Stay calm. Breathe slowly.* Tears pricked the backs of her eyes. *I'm right here, Reagan. Come find me, please, and I might even return to Boston, as you've so persistently requested.*

The September morning had been cool, but now the sun must be up and baking down on the crate, because Charlotte felt the air in the box pressing down on her, growing thick. The gag in her mouth sopped up any moisture as soon as it was produced, and her tongue felt like a dried stick. It also prevented her from being able to gasp for the air her lungs now so desperately craved.

She clenched her eyes closed. Willed herself to imagine fresh clean air. Inhale. Exhale. But as the weight on her chest seemed to grow heavier, her panic began to rise.

Reagan was shaking. His worst nightmare had just come true. If he lost her... He forced out a calming puff of air. *Concentrate.* Nothing good would come from panicking.

He stepped out the back door of Dixie's Boardinghouse and scanned the ground. The twins, Shiloh and Sharon, were just coming out from behind the hedge. "Go on into the schoolroom, girls." He motioned for them to be silent and to cut a wide arc around him so they wouldn't disturb any tracks. "Your sister Belle is inside waiting for you."

"But where's Zoe?"

"She's in there too. Go on now. And stay inside."

He turned his attention back to the ground. There! He squatted for a better look. Two sets of footprints visible in the dust, one small and delicate, the other larger and made by someone much heavier. The kidnapper couldn't be more than a couple minutes ahead of him, could he? Not if the twins had just finished at the outhouse.

Reagan jogged forward, pausing now and again to pick up the trail. There was one good thing about Wyldhaven's dirt roads...they were almost as good as a book for reading sign. When the trail came to an abrupt end directly behind the jail, he almost cursed. But a few moments of scouting led him to the alley where fresh wagon tracks could be seen between McGinty's and the jailhouse. Reagan jogged toward the main street and burst out onto it, glancing in the direction the tracks had curved.

There at the end of the street, just passing the livery, a wagon trundled out of town. But there was only one hunched-over occupant on the seat. Reagan narrowed his eyes. He spun back to look the other way just in case. No conveyances in sight.

Making a quick decision, he dashed for the livery, hoping Joe would have their horses ready. He needed to stop that wagon before it got out of sight!

Thankfully, Joe was just leading both their mounts out of the barn when Reagan sprinted into the yard. Reagan didn't even hesitate but grabbed his stallion's reins and swung into the saddle. "Wagon on the main road. Let's go!" He put his heels to his steed and galloped out to the road at full tilt. He could hear Joe right on his heels.

His heart hammered. What if this was a distraction? A lure to mislead them?

They easily caught up to the heavy vehicle only a few minutes later. Now that he was closer, he could see that Lenny Smith was the driver. He hadn't seen Lenny about town since that day in McGinty's when they'd laid their trap.

"Lenny, stop the wagon!"

"Ain't got time, Sheriff. I gots to get to Cedar Falls pronto," Lenny called over his shoulder. He looked stiff and agitated.

Joe gave Reagan a pinched-lip look.

"Keep a lookout." Reagan spoke quietly to Joe and motioned for him to stay behind the wagon. Then he shucked his Colt, urged his mount past the wagon, and pulled to a stop in front of it with his pistol leveled at Lenny's head. "I said, pull your wagon to a stop, Lenny!"

"Whoa!" Lenny's face was pale, and he hauled back on the reins so hard that one of his matched pair whinnied and rose up on its back legs. "Now, Sheriff, you got no call to be so persnickety! I ain't done nothin'!"

"We'll see about that. What you got in the back there?"

Lenny squirmed on his seat. "Nothing but some supplies for the mercantile over in Cedar Falls. Jerry Hines had some things that ol' Buzz ain't got. Figured to turn a little profit by sellin' Buzz some claptrap."

Joe spoke up from behind. "Then you won't mind if we take a look, will you?"

"I'd be happy to let you take a look if I had the time. But I'm on a deadline, of sorts. Have to beat Dan Waters from down Seattle way, else he'll be makin' a deal with Buzz 'fore I do!"

Reagan let the cocking of his pistol tell Lenny what he thought about that. "Step on down from that seat, Lenny."

"Awe, Sheriff, seriously now. It ain't nothing but food and supplies!"

Just then a muffled groan and several thumps emanated from the back of the wagon.

Lenny's eyes widened, and he slammed the reins down onto his matched blacks. "Get up!" The wagon lurched forward, but Reagan held his ground, knowing the horses were trained well enough that they wouldn't run him over.

They shied and came to a dancing stop just in front of his own mount, which bobbed its head in irritation at their close proximity.

Reagan reached out and grasped the chin strap of the nearest harness so the horses wouldn't be tempted to bolt again. "Lenny, if I have to tell you to get off that seat again, you're going to be wheezing air through a nice round hole in your chest."

Lenny threw his hands above his head. "All right! All right! But I just want to say, he made me do it! Weren't my idea, no sir!"

All Reagan could think about was getting to Charlotte and making sure she was unharmed, but he couldn't get too hasty and let Lenny escape. "Down on your belly. Hands behind your head! Now!"

Lenny complied.

"Joe?"

"I got him." Joe swung out of his saddle and grabbed his wrist irons from his belt.

Seeing that Lenny was taken care of, Reagan holstered his weapon, swung from his saddle, and leapt up onto the wheel to survey the contents of the wagon.

There! She must be in that crate! Kegs, casks, and boxes were piled all over the crate. He tossed them aside as fast as he could. "Charlotte, are you in there? Talk to me!"

The only answer was silence.

Chapter Nineteen

The lid was wrenched from her tiny prison, and Charlotte had never felt so thankful to feel the burn of the sun against her eyes. Or to hear Reagan Callahan's voice. She squinted blindly at the hands reaching in for her and battled the sunspots in her vision until her feet were solidly on the roadbed and she could close them for a moment.

"Oh, Reagan! Zoe—" Her words choked off.

"Zoe's fine," he rushed to assure her. "Doc Griffin is probably looking her over even now." He made quick work of the ropes binding her wrists and ankles.

Relief sapped the remainder of her strength. She clung to him and slumped forward until her face pressed against his broad chest. She fought for breath. "I...was so afraid you wouldn't...find me!"

One of his hands stroked over the back of her head. "I've got you now. Everything's going to be all right."

She gripped a double handful of his shirt and fought to pull the elusive oxygen into her lungs. "I...can't...breathe."

He smoothed her hands open until they pressed flat against his shirt, the firm muscles of his chest beneath. It wasn't proper for her to be touching him so, but her need for air took precedence over what should be shock at his impropriety.

"Feel me breathing? Breathe with me. Slowly. Here we go..."

He pulled in a long, slow inhale that she tried to match. "... And now out."

She pursed her lips as her doctor had showed her to do and forced herself to keep pushing air out even though she wanted to do nothing more than suck madly for every last morsel of oxygen she could capture.

"Good. In...and out..."

It was doing no good. Her lungs were not opening this time. Panic gripped her by the throat, and she started to tremble. Her hands fisted into the material of his shirt, and she felt herself stumble sideways a step.

Reagan gripped her by the shoulders. "Stay with me, Charlie darlin'. Just stay with me." He forced her hands to unclench and pressed them flat against his chest once more. "Feel it! We'll breathe a little shallower at first this time." He drew air in slowly.

She did her best to imitate him but ended up bent double and coughing. His hands tightened around her shoulders as he spoke soothingly and refused to let her go. Finally she was able to inhale. First one shuddering breath and then another.

"Good." He placed her hands against him once more. His chest moved beneath her fingers again, and she exhaled with him.

Slowly her lungs gave up their clench, and she sagged forward, feeling the cool imprint of one of his shirt buttons against her cheek. "Thank you." She wasn't sure if she was thanking Reagan or God, but hopefully both understood her appreciation.

She felt a tremor slip through the muscles beneath her cheek, and he whispered a few muffled words that might have been a prayer of his own.

Deputy Joe stepped up with a man in handcuffs by his side.

Reagan slowly set Charlotte back from him. And then he turned and slugged the prisoner right across his jaw!

Charlotte yelped and jumped back. “Reagan!”

The prisoner went to the ground like a sack of rocks that had just been dropped.

Reagan didn’t even spare Charlotte a look. He was glowering at the prisoner, who lay sprawled on the ground, gingerly assessing the damage to his lips and cheek. “You could have killed her!”

Wiping blood from his split lip onto his shoulder, the man spat. “I didn’t know she had a lung disease, Sheriff. Honest I didn’t.” A startled look crossed his face. “I ain’t gonna catch it, am I?”

Reagan grabbed him by his collar and yanked him to his feet. “I doubt you are going to live long enough to have to worry about that, Lenny.” He gave the man a shove toward Deputy Joe. “Joe, tie him to your saddle and walk him back into town, would you? I’ll take Charlotte on ahead in the wagon.”

Charlotte wasn’t sure whether to be flattered that Reagan thought enough of her to clobber his prisoner that way, or terrified of a man seemingly so prone to violence.

After he helped her onto the seat, he tied his own horse to the back of the wagon. She simply sat in silence. She offered a fleeting prayer of thanks to God that this apparently wasn’t going to be her last day on earth after all, and tried to remember what day it was that the stagecoach came through town. Surely she’d misheard God. All these bad things had to be Him telling her to return home, didn’t they?

After a moment, the sheriff climbed up beside her and set the wagon into motion. He shifted. “I’m sorry. I shouldn’t have hit him in front of you like that. Just…seeing you unable to breathe…” A muscle worked in his jaw. “That scared me. A lot.”

Charlotte darted him a look. "I would think a man in your position out here in the wilds of the West would have been faced by men much scarier than him."

"Oh, I have been. But it wasn't Lenny who scared me. It was the thought of losing y—" He broke off and cleared his throat.

Charlotte felt her eyes widen. Her heart thumped against her breastbone.

He glanced over and captured her gaze, and for a long moment they simply looked at one another. His vivid-blue eyes were soft and full of an emotion she couldn't quite put her finger on, but it made her mouth turn dry and her palms turn clammy. She tore her gaze from his and faced the road before them.

Her thoughts drifted first to Senator Sherman and then to Mr. Covington—both men who hadn't thought her worthy of fidelity. Would a man like Reagan be any different? She couldn't deny that she found the man attractive, but the realization that he might reciprocate the feeling filled her with apprehension. If they started courting, would he too one day betray her? The thought lodged a painful lump just below her heart. She hadn't known him long, but she would almost call Reagan a friend, and she hated the thought of one day feeling toward him as she felt toward Senator Sherman or Mr. Covington each time she thought of them now.

Yet she couldn't dismiss his comments from the dance about his Savior being more important to him. There had also been his murmured words... *Any man who would cheat on you is a fool.*

Her heart hammered at that memory. She clenched her hands atop her skirts. She could ponder more on that later. Right now she had a more pressing question. "Sheriff, have you ever thought you heard from the Lord only to later question if it were true?"

He looked over at her. "What did you think you heard?"

She shrugged. "Well… Before I came here, I prayed for the Lord to lead my steps. Then I noticed Mr. Heath's ad. And everything went so smoothly I just thought it must be God opening the doors for me. But now… My staying has put my students in danger."

He pulled the wagon to a stop in the middle of the road and planted his elbows onto his knees. Just ahead of them Wyldhaven stretched out, the livery on the near end and the river on the other. Several children were just now coming across the bridge, presumably headed for school.

The sheriff finally spoke. "I think we often make the mistake of thinking that if we are in the center of God's will there should be no troubles or hardship. But take the apostle Paul. He was warned that going to Jerusalem would result in his death, yet he also knew that was where he was called to go."

Charlotte's lips quirked. "Are you trying to say that staying might get me killed?"

He didn't smile as she'd thought he would. Instead he reached over and wrapped one of her escaped curls around his finger. He rubbed it with this thumb, studying it for a moment, and then finally he lifted his eyes to hers. "I certainly hope not. I'm going to do my best to ensure that doesn't happen." There was a softness in his gaze that made a tremor sweep through her. "The judge may require you to testify for a conviction."

She pushed away concerns about a looming trial for the moment. "I thought you would be elated if I said I was thinking about going back home."

He loosed her hair and scrubbed one hand across his stubbled jaw. "For the sake of your safety, I ought to be. However…" He turned to meet her gaze once more. “I find I’m loathe to give up the pleasure of your company.”

Charlotte smoothed a trembling hand over her skirts and tore her gaze from his. “You have given me much to ponder. For now I need to get back to my classroom and get on with my day.”

“No one would blame you for cancelling classes after what must have been quite a traumatic morning for you.”

Charlotte tipped up her chin. “I’m afraid it was probably even more traumatic for Zoe.”

The sheriff smirked. “I think you’ll find that Zoe Kastain is made of sterner stuff than you might realize. As are you.”

“I hope that’s true on both counts.” She pleated a piece of lace trim along her sleeve and offered him a smile. “Here I am late for my first day of classes, and I had a speech about the importance of promptness all planned.”

He slapped the reins against the horses’ rumps, setting them down the road once more. “I think kidnapping should be an exception to your rules.”

Charlotte glanced over at him.

He grinned and shrugged. “Well, don’t you?”

She laughed. “Yes. I suppose that’s as good of an excuse as any for tardiness.”

“You sure you should go ahead with classes today?”

She shrugged. “Sterner stuff, didn’t you say? And it will help me keep my mind off—” A sudden thought struck her. “You don’t think they would come back, do you? Today?” Her stomach pitched, and her lungs threatened to rebel from doing their duty yet again.

He adjusted his Stetson, a grim look crimping his lips. “I doubt it, but as soon as I get Smith settled in the jail, I’ll come over and sit in the lobby right outside the classroom door.”

Charlotte immediately felt chagrin for her fears. “Oh, you don’t have to do that. I’m sure all will be fine. I don’t want you squandering a day on account of me.”

He pulled the wagon to a stop in front of Dixie’s and came around to help her down. As he settled his hands around her waist and lifted her to the ground, he said, “It’s not a squander. I’d be doing the very thing I was hired to do—protecting a Wyldhaven citizen.”

Of course. The man was only doing his job, naught more. “Well then, I thank you, *Sheriff*.” She started to pull away, but his hands tightened about her waist.

Eyes widening, she lifted her gaze to his.

“Some citizens are a lot more pleasant to protect than others, *Charlotte*.” He let go of her then and stepped back, giving the brim of his hat a tug as one eyelid lowered in a quick wink. “And don’t forget about our shooting lesson this afternoon.” He leapt up to the seat, clucked his tongue to the horses, and left her standing, mouth agape, in a cloud of dust in front of Dixie’s.

The man had made “shooting lesson” sound like an evening of courting in a Boston parlor. “Oh for heaven’s sake, Charlotte. Pull yourself together. The man is nothing like Kent or the senator.” Maybe he was one of the reasons the Lord had directed her to Wyldhaven? The thought made her heart pound in anticipation.

She was still admonishing herself to come back to earth when she entered the classroom and found Dr. Griffin at the front of the room putting the last layers of plaster on Zoe Kastain’s arm. Charlotte came to an abrupt halt and glanced from the enraptured students to Flynn and Zoe.

“And that, children, is how you plaster an arm.” Smoothing the last piece of plaster-coated linen over Zoe’s arm, Flynn lifted one hand in a flourish like a grand master at a traveling circus.

The kids all laughed and clapped their hands in delight.

Flynn must have caught sight of her from the corner of his eye, because he spun to face her, his eyes lighting with pleasure. "And look who has finally decided to show up for school! None other than your teacher, Miss Brindle!" Flynn grinned in an obvious bid to put the children at ease, but his searching eyes and lifted brow contained volumes of sympathy and a question as to her well-being.

Charlotte strode purposefully to her desk, whispering to him on the way past, "I'm fine. Thank you for filling in." But his presence here had just given her a wonderful idea, so now she turned to face the class. "Did you enjoy Dr. Griffin's short medical lesson, class?"

A chorus of yeses greeted her.

"Wonderful. Perhaps I'll be able to talk the doctor into coming back from time to time to teach us some practical medical tips. How to clean and bandage a cut, for example, if you are out hunting and happen to injure yourself." She lifted her brows at Dr. Griffin, who was cleaning up his medical supplies from around Zoe's feet, and he smiled, giving her a covert nod of acceptance. Charlotte turned her attention back to the classroom, dropping her hands on Zoe's shoulders. "But I hope none of the rest of you will have to be an actual patient of the doctor's for our lessons." She leaned to one side and grinned down at Zoe.

Chuckles filled the room, Zoe's loudest of all, which gave Charlotte a sense of relief over the child's health.

Charlotte turned all her attention on Zoe then, squatting down in front of her. She lowered her voice. "I'm so sorry this happened to you."

Zoe shrugged. "'Tweren't your fault."

Charlotte gently squeezed the girl's uninjured hand. "How are you feeling? Do you think you need to go home and rest for the remainder of the day?"

Zoe shook her head emphatically, biting her lower lip. "I've been waiting to get to go to school for a long time, Miss Brindle. I'd like to stay, if it's all the same to you." She lifted her cast slightly. "This don't hurt near as much as the time I laid the inside of my arm against the stove door when I was loading the fire with wood."

Charlotte winced and cast another look at Flynn. "We better add burns to our list of medical topics to teach on."

Another round of laughter filled the room as Charlotte stepped out of Zoe's way and motioned her toward the tables that would serve as their desks. "All right, please take any seat for now. After I do some testing, we'll have assigned seats, but for today everyone is allowed to sit wherever they want. And do let me know if the pain gets to be too much for you, please."

Flynn appeared to be done cleaning up and heading out the door now.

"Class, please say thank you to Dr. Griffin."

"Thank you, Dr. Griffin," they chorused.

Flynn smiled and lifted a hand of farewell, and then Charlotte was left alone with her students.

The day passed in a flurry of tests and assessments as she tried to determine the closest levels of placement for each child. Too low and they would be bored. Too high and frustration with difficult assignments would set in. At lunch she was pleased to see that all the children seemed to play well together, and before she knew it, she had dismissed the last student from the room that afternoon and it was time for her shooting lesson with the sheriff.

All day he had sat near Dixie's desk in the lobby, reading a book. Every once in a while she had seen him walk past the door, and then each window, and she knew he was checking the perimeter. And not once during the school day had she felt nervous or fearful for her life or her students.

As she stacked the last of the day's tests and placed them in her satchel so she could grade them in her room this evening, she tucked her lower lip between her teeth. The man's presence might make her feel safe, but he simply couldn't be her round-the-clock guard. As she'd worked with her students, she'd managed to put aside her concerns, but what happened the next time he had to be called out of town? Would more of her students be injured because of her?

Maybe learning to use a weapon would help her protect the students if the sheriff or Joe couldn't be around. Then again, what if he taught her to shoot and then was counting on her to protect her students and she failed?

"You ready?" The very man of her thoughts pushed his head through the doorway.

She glanced up, feeling too much pressure. "What if I learn to use a weapon but then do something wrong if I ever need to use it? What if another outlaw comes into my classroom and I accidentally...I don't know...shoot one of my students while trying to protect them?"

He strode over and stopped before her. "Part of learning to handle a weapon is learning to use it safely." He touched her chin, urging eye contact. "You can do this."

She thought about the students and how eager they had been to learn today. Even Belle Kastain had been attentive and good natured. And she'd had a chance to grade a few of the tests. Zoe was still reading at a first-primer level, and she was nearly twelve years old! Perhaps more reasons why the Lord had directed her here.

Charlotte threw up her hands. “I’m willing to try.” She massaged circles at her temples. “I’ve never been one to back down easily.”

He smirked. “I never would have guessed.”

She wrinkled her nose at him. “I know the children here need me. But Zoe was hurt today because of me. What if I stay and that puts more of the children in danger?”

The sheriff cupped his chin in one hand. “If there is one thing I’ve learned, Miss Brindle, it’s that evil men can always find an excuse to perpetrate their foul deeds on a community. No matter who comes or who goes, there will always be evil men. The one difference we can make is in standing up against that evil. As you already mentioned, learning to use a weapon—wisely and with purposeful control—might be the very thing that will allow you to protect your students.” He paused as though hesitant to say the next words but then went ahead and said them anyway. “I get the feeling you think this is all your fault, but if it hadn’t been you Lenny attacked today, it could have been someone else.”

“I suppose that’s true. And yet...much as it pains me to say it, I’ve wondered, after all my stubborn insistence on staying, if maybe you weren’t right all along and I should go back home.”

“I think you and I both know you have a heart as big as the Cascade Range and you’ll never feel right about retreating to Boston.”

Charlotte sighed and picked up her satchel full of tests. He was right about that last. She’d forever wonder if anyone had arrived to replace her, or if her return to Boston had sentenced all the children of Wyldhaven to live forever uneducated. “Very well. I will come out and let you teach me to shoot. But I must say..." She couldn't resist teasing him a little. "You have renewed my faith in miracles, Sheriff."

He frowned. "I have?"

She smiled and led the way toward the foyer, tossing over her shoulder, "Indeed. I do believe you have twice today encouraged me to stay in town, when only last week you would have stood in the street and sang like a lark if it would have enticed me to return to Boston." She paused just inside the doorway and turned to see the expression on his face. "It's a miracle, wouldn't you say?"

He hooked his thumbs into his belt loops and chuckled softly. "Well, you do have a way of growing on a man, Miss Brindle." Humor danced in his blue eyes, but slowly his expression transformed from humor to something much more intimate and serious.

Charlotte swallowed and stepped back. She lifted her satchel. "I just need to run this up to my room. I'll be down in only a moment." She spun around to make her escape and ran straight into the doorframe. Her brow smacked against the wood with a loud crack. A groan of pain slipped free, and she cradled one palm over the injury.

Before she could take another step, the sheriff was right there crowding her in the doorway. "That sounded like it hurt. Let me see." He tugged her hand away from her eye, tilted her head to better capture the light from the window, and examined her closely.

All the oxygen seemed to have been sucked from the room, and it had nothing to do with her asthma. The sheriff's face hovered just above hers, so close she noted the small white scar that disappeared beneath his hat line, the smooth slash of his blond brows against sun-browned skin, the almost impossibly dark lashes lining those silvery-blue eyes of his—eyes that had quit examining her brow and were boring straight into her own now, while his hands remained wrapped around either side of her face.

Charlotte saw his throat work. "Doesn't seem to be cut, but you'll have a good-sized knot, it looks like." His voice rasped, and he tucked one corner of his lower lip between his teeth.

While his grip had been purposeful at the outset, now she realized it had gentled, and she felt one of his thumbs graze over her cheek. Heaven's mercy, she wanted nothing more than to close her eyes and lean more fully into his touch. Instead she forced out, "Clumsy me. I'll be fine, I'm sure." The words emerged as more of a whispered plea than a statement of fact.

His focus dropped to her lips.

Her eyes widened. "I'll be right back." She brushed past him before she could give in to the temptation to discover what it might feel like to have the man's lips pressed against her own.

Chapter Twenty

Reagan clucked to the horses to urge them over the last rise before the river bend where he'd decided to teach Charlotte to shoot. The ride out had been mostly quiet.

While they had both tried to make conversation, each time it had been stilted and fallen flat. For his part, every time he glanced at her he couldn't help but wonder how she had managed to usurp his focus so thoroughly. Only two weeks ago he'd been content to take each day as it came, and not much had captivated his thoughts except for doing his job, and doing it well. But now every time he laid his head down at night, enchanting green eyes swam in his memories, invaded his dreams, filled his first waking thoughts in the morning.

He let the horses have their heads, remembering the feel of her soft skin beneath his fingers, the way her eyes had widened when she'd noticed him watching her, the way her tongue had darted across her lips.

"Sheriff!" Charlotte squeaked from beside him.

He jolted alert and yanked the horses to a stop just before they plunged headlong into a field of succulent green grass next to the road.

Reagan gave Charlotte a sheepish look. "Sorry about that. I must have let my mind wander a touch." *A touch?* He'd been in a whole other galaxy. And he was a sheriff! He couldn't afford to let his mind wander like that. The slightest moment of inattention could mean the death of him or one of his citizens. He clenched his jaw. He really needed to get a grip on the crazy turmoil this woman had thrust upon his well-ordered life. "Almost there now."

He had picked the bluffs upriver from Wyldhaven to teach her to shoot. First, they were made of soft limestone, and he figured she could use some of that as chalk until Jerry could get her order shipped in. And second, the cliffs made a perfect backdrop for shooting into.

A few minutes later, he rounded the bend and pulled the team into the shady spot at the base of the cliffs. Setting the brake, he wrapped the reins around the handle and hopped down to assist Miss Brindle to the ground.

Much as he would have enjoyed lingering over the task, he very deliberately set her loose as soon as her feet were on the ground. *Business, Callahan. Strictly business.*

Her pistol and bullets were in a small wooden box beneath the wagon's seat, and he pulled them out now. First things first. "Let me show you how to load this." He opened one of the cartridge boxes and showed her how to insert the bullets into the cylinder. Then he looked up and met her gaze to ensure she heard his next words loud and clear.

"Never point this at anyone unless you intend to shoot them. Understood?"

She looked a little nervous when she nodded.

"Nothing to be afraid of. You'll be a top-rate markswoman in no time." He tried to give her a reassuring smile, but she only swallowed and clenched her hands into her skirts. He pressed on. "Now when you go to shoot it, you are going to line up the front sight here, with the rear sight here. You want a straight line between those and your target." He looked over at her to make sure she was taking in his instructions.

She nodded.

"All right then. Your hand is going to wrap around the grip, like so. And you slip your finger inside the trigger guard here." Another glance confirmed she was still focused and listening. "Your thumb levers back the hammer, like so. And after that, all that's left to do is aim and pull the trigger." He cocked an eyebrow to see if she had any questions.

She brushed a strand of hair from her eyes. "I think I'm following."

"Good..." He carefully released the hammer, then tucked the pistol into the back of his belt. "Now let me set up our target, and we'll get started." From the back of the wagon, he hauled down the old wooden barrel he'd brought and carted it over to the base of the cliff. Taking up a piece of the soft sandstone from the ground near his feet, he quickly scratched out a circle within a circle on the side of the barrel and then set the target on a flat-topped rock to bring it up to about chest height.

Back by her side, he pulled the gun from his belt and handed it to her.

She took it with two fingers like she might have lifted a dead rat by the tail. And the look on her face portrayed a fear that the thing might explode in her hands at any moment. He couldn't help but grin.

"Don't laugh at me, Sheriff. I'm really rather terrified." She hadn't taken her eyes off the pistol that still dangled from her finger and thumb.

Reagan swiped a hand over his mouth to bring it back into stoic submission, realizing a more drastic measure was going to be needed. "All right, well... Let's talk about grip." He stepped over behind her and reached around to guide her hands into the right position. He felt her stiffen, but continued as though he hadn't noticed. "You take this hand—"

"Sheriff, I'm sorry!" Charlotte thrust the pistol back at him. "I just don't think this is the right thing for me." She paced away from him and threw her hands into the air. "I was so certain I could do this. I've never backed down from a challenge in my life, but this"—she gestured toward the pistol dangling at his side—"and Wyldhaven"—she swept an indicator back toward town—"and outlaws, and outhouses, and a dismal lack of supplies!" Her shoulders drooped. "And Liora..." Tears pooled, and she dashed them away. "I'm still not certain if I could have done any more to reach her, or what that might have been."

He wanted to fold her in his arms and absorb all the pain and frustration she was feeling, but he held his ground. "Liora's pain started long before you came to town."

"I understand that." She folded her arms and paced a few more round trips from a rock to him and back before spinning on one heel to pin him with a look. "I just...I really think that the best thing for me would be to return to Boston on Thursday's coach."

She pulled in a breath as though the words had physically pained her, and there was such sorrow in her eyes that he knew she would regret the decision the moment the coach lost sight of Wyldhaven. But what could he do about it? This was partly his fault. He'd planted doubts that had now sprung to action.

He thrust the pistol into his belt once more, then strode over to fetch the wooden target. He gathered up two small stones and shoved them into his pocket, then hauled the barrel over and tossed it into the bed of the wagon. After that he paused by the bench and held one hand out to Charlotte. "I'll see you back to town."

The return trip was even more silent than the trip out had been. When Reagan pulled the wagon to a stop in front of Dixie's and helped her down, he once more tucked her pistol into the little wooden box with the bullets and handed it to her. "Listen. I know I've hounded you from the outset to return to Boston. But here's the thing. If this is where God wants you to be, then this is where you ought to be... Only you can answer that. But...would you read the first chapter of James before you make a final decision? Just the first few verses really."

She smoothed her slender hand over the lid of the box. "All right. What does it say?"

"Just read it." He gave her a nod and started to round the wagon but then stilled. "Oh, I almost forgot." He dug the rocks from his pockets. "I don't know if you'll still do classes for the next few days, but if you do, I thought you could use these as chalk." He dropped the pebbles of sandstone into her palm.

She rolled the rocks between her fingers and didn't look up till he'd already regained his seat on the wagon. Then she lifted the hand holding the stones. "Thank you."

He tugged at the brim of his hat. "My pleasure." And then with a slap of the reins, he left her standing there, and hang it all if he didn't feel like he'd handed her a piece of his heart instead of two stupid rocks.

Liora woke and opened her eyes. She stared at the ceiling, trying to make sense of where she was and why so much pain pulsed from so many spots. First she remembered the beating she'd taken from her last client. That explained some of the pain.

And then full memory flooded in.

Despite the fact that she hadn't moved or even tried to, she felt a swirl of dizziness. Had she really tried to kill herself? Her whole body quavered. What if she'd succeeded?

Not a sparrow falls...

This time instead of anger and annoyance, the words brought tears of wonder and hope. Was there really a God? Had He sent Joe to keep her from killing herself?

Exhaustion pressed hard against her eyes. She needed more sleep, but she was so thirsty. She tried to sit up, and gasped.

Instantly a face appeared above her own. *Joe.*

"Don't try to move. Doc says you need to just lie still and rest as much as you can."

She moistened her lips, but her mouth was so dry it didn't do much good. "Thirsty."

He disappeared from sight and returned a moment later with a cup of water and a spoon. With meticulous care he drizzled one spoonful of water at a time into her mouth. The water spread across her tongue and brought such relief that her eyes drifted closed.

She heard the spoon clink into the cup and felt the air stir as he started to pull away. She clutched for him. "Joe?"

"I'm right here." She felt the warmth of his hand settle over hers where it rested on his arm.

She swept her tongue over dry lips. Her eyelids were still too heavy to lift. "Thank you."

There was a beat of silence, and then he said, "Any time."

"How did you know to come?"

Another moment of quiet, then, "I think God brought me."

She let her hand fall back to the quilt.

I think God brought me.

How did one process that? It was too much for her to take in at the moment. It filled too many crevices that had been craving *presence* for far too long.

"Shhh, Liora. It's all right." She felt a cool cloth gently stroke her face and temples, and she realized that tears had slipped from the corners of her eyes back into her hair. But these weren't tears of sorrow or agitation.

Far from it.

For the first time since she could remember, she felt a sense of awe and wonder.

Joe dropped the rag back into the bowl of water on her nightstand and watched Liora sink deep into the oblivion of sleep. He hadn't gotten the chance to tell her he'd purchased her contract from Ewan and she didn't have to work for the man another day in her life if she didn't want to. But there would be time for that later. For now, he was just glad to see her resting easy. Glad to hear her thanking him for saving her life. Maybe she would find hope in her future after all.

Lenny hadn't come back.

Patrick stared at the ceiling of the cave, his good arm propped behind his head.

Lenny had left this morning with the promise that he'd be back with the schoolteacher in just a few hours, but it was late afternoon now. Something had happened. The man had failed him yet again.

So then... Patrick surged to his feet. It would be up to him. His arm wasn't fully healed, but it was good enough that he'd be able to handle that slip of a woman.

With slow purposeful steps, he started out for town. It took him the rest of the afternoon. And he was out of breath and exhausted by the time he arrived. *Too much lying about at ease.* His old body wasn't as spry as it used to be.

He leaned one shoulder into a pine, took a moment to catch his breath, and studied the town from just inside the cover of the forest. All seemed quiet. Not a soul was stirring.

Lenny had said the teacher was staying in Dixie's Boardinghouse, so he took the stairs at the back that led up to the balcony that circled the entire perimeter of the building. He shucked his Bowie and started peering in the windows. He wasn't quite sure what he was looking for, but when he came to the third window, it was the empty valise sitting against one wall that drew a smile from him.

"Bingo."

She'd been carrying that exact bag on the stage.

He slipped his knife between the window and the sill until he found the lock. It was only a moment more before he heard the satisfying click of the latch giving way.

He tossed a quick glance over his shoulder. All still lay in quietness.

Perfect.

He slipped inside to wait.

Charlotte made her way into the boardinghouse and wearily ambled across the carpet toward the stairs. Even though dinner was in full swing, she currently had no appetite. Her foot had just landed on the bottom tread when Dixie poked her head out of the dining room.

"Charlotte, there you are! Come in to dinner. Mother and I have been waiting to eat till you got back. We both want to hear all about your shooting lesson!" Dixie disappeared again before Charlotte could decline her request.

Weighing the desire to simply retreat to her room and mope alone against her aversion to hurting Dixie's feelings, she finally decided she could handle sitting at a table and picking at her food for a few minutes if it meant pleasing Dixie and Rose. She slowly stepped through the door to the dining room and sank into her seat at the table she'd shared each evening with Dixie and her mother.

It was only a moment before Dixie and Rose bustled out of the kitchen and joined her. Dixie set one steaming plate filled with fried chicken, mashed potatoes and gravy, and a helping of peas in front of Charlotte, and set her own similarly filled plate in front of herself. Rose carried a basket of rolls, which she placed in the middle of the table, and a third identical plate, which she set at her place.

"I'll just run fetch our drinks and the cherry pie I set aside for us for this evening and be right back." Dixie hustled away before Charlotte could even get out a peep about not being hungry.

And it was probably a good thing, because when the first tantalizing waft of fried chicken filled her nostrils, her stomach rumbled.

Dixie hadn't been back and seated for more than a few seconds when a table of loggers rose, dropped their money next to their empty plates, and then tipped Dixie their hats as they exited. Dixie took a quick bite of chicken and then dashed away to clear their dishes and seat the next group of men waiting for a table.

Rose watched her daughter as she shook her head. "It's a miracle that girl doesn't blow away in the wind. I don't think she's sat through an entire meal since we opened this boardinghouse. Sure was nice to picnic with her out by the river today. First time we've set down together and had peace and quiet in a long time. Your school is going to be good for more than just those children."

The forkful of potatoes that had been headed for Charlotte's mouth paused in midair as guilt swirled through her. She set the fork back down.

Rose broke off a piece of her roll. "What is it?"

Charlotte dropped her hands into her lap and loosed a breath. "I'm just not certain I should stay."

Rose gave her a sympathetic look. "You've had a hard day."

"It's more than just that. Before I came, my mother accused me of simply acting on impulse. And maybe she was right. If I leave, then maybe the Waddell gang will too."

Rose snorted most inelegantly. "If you think running back to Boston is going to stop the Waddell gang from churning mischief in these parts, well, you just don't know much about the Waddell gang. Honey, you are just an excuse for those no-goods to kick up their heels. If it's not you they use, it will be some other poor soul. Best thing you can do is learn to defend yourself and stand up to bullies like that. If you run, you'll only give them a stronger hold of fear on this community." Rose nodded emphatically, as though she may have just solved the world's problems, and then she leaned forward with a twinkle in her eyes. "Now tell me about your shooting lesson with the sheriff."

Charlotte felt her despair rise to the fore. "Well, it wasn't much of a lesson. The moment the gun touched my hands, I had this terrible sense of foreboding and fear. I cut the lesson short and told the sheriff I thought I would be heading back to Boston on Thursday's stage."

"What?!" Dixie dropped into her chair and gaped disbelievingly at Charlotte. "I thought you'd decided to stay." There was a little bit of distress in her eyes, and Charlotte felt sorry that she'd been the one to put it there.

Charlotte rubbed her temples and moaned. "I just don't know. I *want* to stay. I thought I should stay. But seeing Zoe

Kastain so hurt because of me...I'm just not certain it's the right thing anymore."

Dixie leaned across the table. "Nonsense. You listen to me. Zoe wasn't hurt because of you! She was hurt because of those no-good outlaws. They are nothing but a bunch of troublemaking thieves. And I'm begging you not to let them steal one of the best things that has happened to Wyldhaven since Zebulon Heath pounded its first nail—and that's having you in town as our schoolteacher."

Charlotte's heart soaked in the encouraging words. "That's very kind of you to say. But what if I can't learn to use a gun, and what if I fail to protect my students?"

Dixie blew a dismissive raspberry as she thrust her napkin back into her lap. "Any woman who can make her way all alone from Boston to the wilds of Washington can learn to shoot a little old gun."

Charlotte tilted her a look. "So do you know how to use a gun?"

Dixie's chin dipped. "I've shot a varmint or two in my day." Her gaze darted toward Rose, whose lips pressed into a thin line and whose face lost nearly all of its color.

A zing of curiosity zipped through Charlotte as she became aware of something hidden beneath the surface of the words, which she wasn't quite catching. She voiced the question lingering in her mind. "So what brought you two to the *burgeoning* city of Wyldhaven?"

If Charlotte wasn't mistaken, both of the women's eyes widened slightly. But Dixie was the first to respond. "We were looking for a new beginning. And we found one. I hope you'll find one too, Charlotte. Now"—she stood and lifted her skirts—"if you'll excuse me, I've a whole sink full of dishes waiting to be washed before I can take my rest."

Charlotte's gaze dropped to Dixie's barely touched food, and her curiosity flamed higher.

Rose tossed her napkin onto her own half-empty plate, stood, and started clearing the table. "I'll come help you, dear."

And with that, the two women bustled off, leaving Charlotte with the distinct impression that it was her questions they were running *from* and not work they were running *to*.

Curiosity still plagued Charlotte as she made her way up the stairs with the wooden box Sheriff Callahan had stored her gun in clutched to her chest.

She pondered Rose and Dixie's words. Maybe they were right.

She groaned. If only God would speak to her and tell her what to do. If she felt certain one answer or the other was right, she'd be able to rest in that. Maybe find some peace.

Her hand was on her door handle when she remembered that Reagan had asked her to read those verses. Her Bible was downstairs since she'd used it in a reading lesson earlier today.

She hesitated. Should she just read them in the morning? She pictured the look in Reagan's eyes when he'd made the request. Sighed. It would only take her a moment to run down.

She retraced her steps.

A few patrons were still eating in the dining room when she arrived back down, and Dixie and Rose hadn't yet returned the room to its classroom status. But no one was seated at the table Charlotte used as a desk. She sank into one chair, settled the box onto the corner, and tugged her Bible from the crate below the hem of the tablecloth.

"James..." She flipped through the pages until she came to the first chapter. He'd been right that she would only have to read a few verses. The words leapt off the page as though the writer of the book had penned them with only her in mind all those centuries ago. "If any of you lacks wisdom, let him ask of God, who gives to all liberally and without reproach, and it will be given to him. But let him ask in faith, with no doubting, for he who doubts is like a wave of the sea driven and tossed by the wind. For let not that man suppose that he will receive anything from the Lord; *he is* a double-minded man, unstable in all his ways."

She slumped against the back of her chair. *Unstable in all his ways.* Tears pricked her eyes.

This was so true of her. She'd asked God to guide her. And when He'd answered, she'd followed, but then because of a few hardships, she'd started doubting. Questioning. Thinking maybe she knew better.

Lord, forgive me. She dropped her forehead onto her hands as a wave of sheer joy and peace washed through her. God *had* spoken to her. She'd just been doubting. *No more doubting, Lord. If this is where You brought me, then I'll do my best to happily serve You here.*

Feeling like a burden had been lifted, she sat up. Returning her Bible to the crate below her desk, she gathered the wooden box into her arms and headed for the stairs. She couldn't remember the last time she'd felt so lighthearted. Wyldhaven with all its ruggedness and mud and outlaws and lack of schoolhouse or church was where the Lord had called her to serve. She would learn to live here and choose to be happy—she glanced down at the box in her arms—even if it meant learning to shoot a gun.

She snorted. Who was she kidding about learning to shoot? The moment the sheriff had put that gun into her hands, she'd had this terrible fear of the power of the thing. One mistake on her part and someone could lose their life! Would she even be able to point it at someone? Even an outlaw? She just didn't think so. Maybe that was one part of learning to live in the West that she could put off for a while.

After all, how much more could go wrong?

With a happy sigh, she slipped her key into her lock. She pushed into her room and latched the door behind her.

A hand clamped over her mouth! "Don't make a sound."

Terror clawed through her. One of the outlaws had been waiting in her room! How had he gotten in?!

Just when she'd decided she would trust the Lord, there came another test. But she wasn't going to waver this time. *Lord, I'm going to keep trusting. I know You brought me here for a reason. And I don't think I've done all You want me to do yet. So please help me.*

"You are apparently a hard woman to kidnap, Miss Brindle. I guess when I want a job done, I'd best do it myself." The man's fetid breath wafted over her when he pressed his mouth close to her ear.

Something tickled at the back of her mind. That voice! She'd heard it before. Where?

"Mmmm, don't you smell good." The outlaw made a grand gesture of sniffing her hair. "I guess I didn't get close enough to you last time to notice how lovely you smelled." He chuckled low. "Something I intend to amend this time around."

Charlotte's eyes widened. It was Patrick Waddell himself!

Waddell stepped around in front of her but pressed a pistol to her forehead to ensure her continued silence. "That's right… it's me. Surprised? I have to say…I've been thinking about you a lot over the past few weeks." His gaze trailed leisurely down the length of her. "And my memories didn't quite do you justice." He made a sound like someone enjoying a tasty pastry.

"We are going to get reacquainted, you and I, Miss Brindle. Very closely reacquainted."

Revulsion sent a shiver down Charlotte's spine, and she refused to look him in the eye, not wanting to see the lecherous grin upon his face. She stared instead at the place where the wall of her room met the ceiling at one corner.

She must think! How was she to make her escape? She must fight this battle on her own. And she must do so immediately. For if she let the man steal her away, no one would even know she was missing until she didn't show up for classes in the morning. And by then she would be much too far away for Sheriff Callahan to easily track her down as he had done this morning!

She stalled for time. "If you are here, then you obviously know I had nothing to do with your death!"

"Oh, my dear, of course I don't hold you responsible for my death!" He tsked as though she might be an unlearned child.

"What are you going to do with me?"

Again his lecherous gaze slithered over her, and Charlotte was ever so thankful for the box she still clutched to her chest. Even so... Cold terror clogged her throat.

"I'm here for an entirely different reason. You see, I've found over the past few weeks that I couldn't get the feel of you in my arms out of my mind." He ran the back of one hand down the length of her upper arm.

Despite the revulsion that threatened to silence her, Charlotte snorted. "I wasn't in your arms! I was slung in a heap over your saddle!"

"Well"—Waddell's lips lifted at one corner—"that's something I intend to rectify this time, my dear."

Charlotte's chin tipped up. "A gentleman never forces

his attentions on a lady!" She knew the words were silly the moment she uttered them.

Waddell threw back his head on a laugh. "Well, my dear, no one has ever accused me of being a gentleman!"

"No. I wouldn't think so." She rolled her lips in and pressed them together hard.

She'd pushed too far, because all levity left Waddell's eyes. "You have two minutes to pack a bag, Miss Brindle. Please bring what you need, because you won't be coming back."

The first bloom of hope poked its head above the soil of Charlotte's heart. He was going to let her pack? He obviously didn't know that the box she clutched so closely held a loaded pistol.

As if her very thoughts had directed the man's attention to the box, his gaze honed in on it. "What's in the box?"

Charlotte strode to her bed and tossed the box down as if it were of no consequence. "Just some things for my classroom."

"Well, you won't be needing those." He used the gun to gesture to her valise against the far wall. "Your two minutes is waning."

Charlotte's heart hammered as she retrieved the valise and set it on her bed next to the box. Her fear of the gun's power paled in comparison to her fear of this man, and she suddenly knew that if she could get her hands on her gun, she would shoot this lecher without hesitation. She just had to be wise in the way she went about it.

She strode to her bureau and withdrew a blouse, two petticoats, and some skirts, and then paced back to the bed and dropped them over the box next to the valise. One at a time, she lifted items, folded them, and slipped them into the bag.

Waddell watched her intently for a moment, but then, just

as she had hoped, he apparently grew satisfied that she was indeed packing as instructed. He stepped over to one side of the window and prodded the lace curtain aside to peer out onto the street below.

Charlotte slipped one hand beneath her clothes and eased open the lid on the box. She mentally ticked through the list of instructions the sheriff had explained to her. Lifting the skirt and the pistol together she used the material to shield the gun from Waddell's sight. She wrapped firm fingers around the grip, just as Sheriff Callahan had shown her, and slipped her finger into the trigger guard. *Be quick!* She cocked back the hammer.

Waddell flinched and started to spin toward her.

But not before she tossed down the skirt. The gun bucked in her hand. She blinked at the hole she'd just blown through the window. She'd missed!

Waddell bellowed and lunged toward her.

Charlotte adjusted her aim and fired again. A chunk of wood chipped out of the wall just behind Waddell's shoulder.

He kept coming, his own pistol once more directed her way.

Charlotte felt a puff of air pass her cheek, and then she heard a loud boom and saw smoke wafting from the end of Waddell's six-shooter.

A bullet had just barely missed her head! She blinked with the realization.

And then Waddell was before her with the warm barrel of his gun pressed once more to her forehead. "Don't. Even. Breathe," he wheezed out.

Her heart was hammering so hard, and her breaths coming in such rapid succession, that there was no way she could have obeyed his order, even if she had wanted to. Instead, she thrust her hands above her head. "All right. You win."

Despair swept through her.

Blast her faulty aim!

Chapter Twenty-one

Reagan Callahan had just entered Dixie's dining room and seated himself at a table when the first gunshot rent through the air, followed by tinkling glass.

He lurched out of his seat and was out in the lobby trying to assess exactly where the shot had come from, when the second shot rang out, and he realized it was coming from directly upstairs! "Dixie, get everyone out the back door!" he bellowed as he took the stairs two at a time to the upper floor.

Scuffling and more shots were coming from Charlotte's room! Of course it was her room! Who else's room would it be? He'd pulled his gun from its holster more times since she'd come to town just a few weeks ago than he had in the entire time he'd been sheriff before that.

Without another moment's thought, he lunged forward and kicked in Charlotte's door. "This is Sheriff Callahan!" He plunged into the room, and in that split second took note of Patrick Waddell with his pistol to Charlotte's head. His heart plummeted, but he put the first rule of any good lawman into practice. "Put down your weapon now!" Never let them see your fear.

Charlotte jolted around to face him with a gasp of surprise.

Patrick grabbed Charlotte and held her before him like a

shield, his gun pressed to her temple. His gaze was narrow and calculating.

Charlotte's eyes were wide as they met Reagan's across the room.

He didn't let his gun waver. "Let's talk about this, Waddell. What are your options? You shoot her, and I'm just going to take you down." The very words made his mouth dry.

Patrick removed the muzzle from Charlotte's temple and pointed it at Reagan over her shoulder instead, still clutching Charlotte as a shield. "How's this for an option? I shoot you and then take the china doll here straight out of town?"

Despite the threat in the words, Reagan felt relieved. Just as he'd hoped, Waddell had at least pointed the muzzle away from Charlotte for the moment. Now if he could just get Charlotte out of the man's grasp, even for a fraction of a second. That would be all he'd need.

"Why are you doing this, Waddell? She's never hurt you." Reagan sidled to his left a little, hoping to get a better shot.

But Waddell turned to keep Charlotte fully in front of him. The outlaw laughed. "You really have to ask that question, Sheriff? Don't you have eyes in your head? Look at this pretty specimen I've got in my arms right here." He gave Charlotte a little shake and tilted his head to peer out from behind her and pin Reagan with a look.

Reagan judged the distance between Waddell's visible eye and Charlotte's ear. Not enough room for a clean shot. *Just a little more, Waddell. Keep talking to me.* He took another small step.

Waddell angled with him, tucking his head in closer to Charlotte again. "Come on, Sheriff. Don't try to convince me you haven't noticed. In fact, I've heard that you and the little miss here have become quite close. That's the very reason I'm here. I've been lying awake nights pondering, you see. You set me up. Let the boys know I was going to be on that stage. This here"—Waddell grabbed Charlotte's jaw and jostled her head—"is payback, Sheriff. Plain and simple."

In that moment, Reagan decided to give him what he wanted. "You're right, Waddell. In fact, I plan to marry her, so I can't let you walk out of here with her."

Charlotte's eyes widened.

Reagan tipped her an apologetic look as he took another step to one side.

Waddell chuckled. "I might even feel a little sorry to disappoint you, Sheriff. You should feel this little gal trembling. I'm betting she didn't know you wanted to marry her." He turned them again, but this time one of his legs planted a little wide.

Reagan dared not look too closely lest he draw the man's attention to it. "Haven't you ever wanted a family, Patrick?"

There was a moment of pause before Waddell replied, "Had me a family once. Pretty little woman and a little girl that looked just like her." He huffed. "I'm afraid I wasn't much of a father."

Reagan held steady this time. "What happened to them?"

"Can't rightly say that I know. Liora would have been ten when I left them. Haven't seen them since."

Charlotte stiffened. "Liora? There's a woman named Liora who is a—she works for Ewan McGinty, just next door."

"What?!" Patrick's surprise was evident in the shuffling of his feet. One of his boots protruded just beyond the hem of Charlotte's skirt.

Reagan took the shot.

Waddell screamed.

Charlotte yelped and dove to one side. Her shoulder knocked Waddell's arm, and his reflexive shot went wide.

Reagan's focus found the front pocket of Waddell's shirt. He fired again.

Waddell's mouth dropped open, and he looked down at the crimson stain blooming across his chest. His hand fell limply to his side, and then the fingers went lax and his pistol thumped loudly to the floor. He took a stumbling step backward, and then his legs seemed to melt out from under him. He collapsed to the floor, his unseeing gaze pointed toward the ceiling.

Reagan quick-footed it to Waddell's side and kicked his pistol farther from his body. Bending, he felt for the man's pulse. Nothing. Reagan sighed but gave himself only a moment to absorb the reality that he'd just taken a man's life, before he thrust his own pistol back into his holster and hurried to Charlotte's side.

"Charlotte, I'm so sorry." He squatted down next to her and laid a hand against her head. "It's all right now."

Charlotte threw herself into his arms so forcefully that she nearly took him to the ground. "Oh, Reagan! I was so terrified!"

Reagan closed his eyes and tucked her head against his chest. She would certainly not change her mind about going back east now. The ache that had begun earlier this afternoon when she'd said she wouldn't be staying now burgeoned into a full-out pain.

But just then she pushed back from him, swiped at the tears on her cheeks, and pinned him with an almost desperate look. "You have to teach me to shoot!"

He blinked.

She gave a firm nod, her chin jutting off to one side. "I read the verses. You were right. I wasn't trusting what I knew to be true. I'm staying! And I'll learn to aim that blasted gun if it takes me a month of Sundays! I had the drop on him but missed twice!"

Reagan's heart still pounded, and he pulled her close again. He was actually glad that she wouldn't have to bear the burden of having shot the man, but he knew better than to voice that thought aloud. And it really would be safer for her if she learned to handle the weapon properly.

He spoke his next words directly into her ear, soft and low. "Yes, I'll teach you to shoot."

Trembling, she nestled in just below his chin, and he couldn't help but notice what a perfect fit she was in his arms.

Movement drew his gaze to the doorway. Dixie stood there, skirts still clutched in her hands, mouth agape.

Reagan cleared the emotion from his throat and gently set Charlotte back from him. He propped his hands on his hips and tipped his head toward the body. "Waddell was waiting for her when she got to her room."

Dixie's eyes rounded even more. "Is she all right?"

Reagan didn't respond. They both turned to look at Charlotte.

She twisted her fingers together, trembling visibly. And when she glanced over at Waddell, her face paled. As though she'd just lost all her strength, she sank onto the bed. Her focus shifted around the room until it rested on the pillow beside her. "I-I'm not sure I'll ever be able to sleep in this room again."

"I have just the solution to that." Reagan urged her to her feet and nudged her out the door. He prodded her down the stairs and out onto the street.

She looked around numbly, her hands fiddling nervously with the material of her skirt.

He placed one hand to the small of her back and turned her toward the alley. He prayed his mother would be home and not out on a delivery of some sort.

As they walked, he considered... Was he putting Ma in danger by bringing Charlotte to her home? The Waddell gang had put out the word that they held Charlotte responsible for Waddell's death when he wasn't even really dead. Wouldn't they come after her with even more gusto now that their leader actually *was* dead? Unless... He squinted. Could it be that Waddell and Lenny had been the last of the gang? There might be no one left to come after Charlotte now that Lenny and the other members who had been rounded up by Joe were in jail and Waddell was dead.

He scrubbed one hand over the back of his neck and thought through all the potential outcomes. And by the time they reached his mother's clapboard house at the back edge of town, he was satisfied that the danger to Charlotte from the Waddell gang had likely passed.

Even if there was a remnant of the gang's members, their time and thoughts would likely be taken up with vying for top spot in the new pecking order. Charlotte was most likely not going to be a priority any longer. At any rate, Ma knew how to protect herself, if it came to that. And Charlotte soon would too.

His mother's place came into view, and Reagan directed Charlotte up the stairs. When they entered the front door, Ma took one look at Charlotte, bounced a glance off him, and rose from the dining room chair where she'd been kneeling, hands folded, when they walked in.

Ma stretched her arms wide and enfolded Charlotte in her full embrace. "Come here, darlin'. Was all that kerfuffling something to do with you? I've just the thing! A hot bath ought to fix you up just right."

Over Charlotte's shoulder, Ma's worried gaze searched him from the top of his hat to the tips of his boots.

With a gentle smile, he spun around so she could see the back of him had no holes in it ether.

She rolled her eyes and shooed Reagan toward the exit, giving him a look that assured him Charlotte would be in good hands.

The next Saturday, Charlotte once again found herself riding on a wagon seat next to Sheriff Callahan as they headed out for her promised shooting lesson. The sheriff had arranged with his mother for Charlotte to stay in her spare room for the remainder of the school year, for which Charlotte was very thankful. She shuddered at the memory of Patrick Waddell's lifeless body on the floor in the middle of her room.

She and Reagan had been to visit Liora right after the incident. Considering that she'd only recently lost her mother, Liora took the news about the death of her father rather well. "Ma always said he'd be the cause of his own death" was all she'd said. Charlotte had been surprised by her lack of emotion, but then again, maybe a woman who'd been raised and then abandoned by a man such as that would feel more relief than sorrow at his death?

How sad.

Her face must have revealed her agitation, for the sheriff took one look at her and shifted on the seat next to her. "So tell me how you've been? Enjoying our crisp Wyldhaven autumn weather?" His tone was light. An obvious attempt at diverting her thoughts.

Charlotte glanced over at him. They had hardly spoken to each other since he'd left her in his mother's kitchen right after the shooting, but one thought had plagued her from that moment to this. Had he *really* meant he wanted to marry her? Or had he only been saying that to distract Waddell?

He'd stopped by her classroom yesterday, but he'd made no mention of the subject. He'd only stopped to see if she wanted to go shooting this afternoon. She presumed he'd been waiting till after the coach had come and gone to see if she really would stick with her decision to stay in Wyldhaven.

Despite the fact that she only wanted to discuss one subject, the better question would be to ask him how he was faring after taking a man's life—even if he was a low-down kidnapper and outlaw—so she turned his question back on him. "How have *you* been?"

His lips pinched in a way that told her he hadn't missed the real reason for her question. He scrubbed one hand over his jaw. "I've killed two men in my time as a lawman. Both of them were outlaws set on hurting someone. Despite that, it's never easy to live with the knowledge that you are the reason another human being is now walking in eternity." He shrugged. "The angst will pass. Even slept pretty good last night."

Charlotte was glad to hear he seemed to be handling it all right. She smoothed a hand over a pleat in her skirt. "I...I wanted to thank you for asking your mother to put me up." A shudder shivered across her shoulders. "I don't think I could have—" She cleared her throat.

The sheriff reached over and squeezed her hand. He didn't say anything, nor did he keep her hand in his, but the gesture was comfort enough to ease a sigh from her lips and to cause contentment to bloom to life in her heart.

Reagan reined the wagon to a stop and once again pulled her pistol out of its box. He studied her, wondering if the sight of the weapon would cause her anxiety, but her demeanor seemed steady and at peace.

While he'd been loading the gun, she'd dragged his old wooden barrel target into place against the base of the cliffs, so all that remained to be done was to once more show her how to hold the gun and let her begin to practice.

"Come here." He motioned her over right in front of him and turned her to face the target. He reached around either side of her to demonstrate the clasp he wanted her to use. He held the pistol in a two-fisted grip. "I want you to hold the gun like this. You take your right hand"—he spread open her fingers, trying to ignore how soft her skin felt beneath his own calloused ones—"and you tuck the butt of the pistol in tight against your palm like so." As he leaned around her shoulder to better see if she was following his commands correctly, a scent that reminded him of Ma's lilac bush tugged for his attention.

Business, Callahan.

He forced his focus back to his instructions. "And then you are going to wrap these three fingers around the handle, and this first one slips into the loop of the trigger guard, like so. Now..." He reached to guide her other hand up to support the pistol. "This hand just acts a little like a guide." He smoothed her fingers around her others and wrapped his own hands around the outside of hers.

With his face so close to her hair, the lilac scent practically danced in his senses now. He swallowed. Drew in another breath and let the scent linger before expelling it slowly.

Charlotte tilted her head to get a better look at him over her shoulder, which put her face within an inch of his.

He didn't pull back, because dash it, he didn't want to think about business at the moment. Hang it all, he didn't even want to remember that he was a sheriff at the moment. All he wanted to think about was kissing Miss Charlotte Brindle.

Her tongue darted over her lips, captivating his attention in a most alluring way.

He let his hands trail across the softness of her forearms to her elbows and then slip down to pry the pistol from her fingers. His focus never leaving her face, he stowed the Bulldog in the back of his belt. He wrapped one hand around her waist and angled her toward him.

Her hands skimmed over his chest and came to rest at each side of his neck. A glint of mischief softened her eyes, and she tilted her head to give him a coy bat of her lashes. "Is this part of learning to shoot a gun, Sheriff?"

He felt a slow grin bloom on his face. "Oh, I'm thinking about making it a regular part of our lessons, of a certainty."

A pretty blush that reminded him of peaches and cream shaded her cheeks.

Charlotte felt a tremor sweep through her. She'd known this man for only a few short weeks, and already she felt more for him than she ever had for anyone. The intensity of her emotions frightened her a little. She'd never felt this much for anyone before. She lowered her eyes from his so he wouldn't see just how much his words pleased her.

But he touched her chin and bent to reconnect their gazes. His thumb traced gentle strokes along the dip just below her lower lip. "I said something the other day, when Waddell had you. It was maybe a bit premature and brash."

Her hope plummeted. Of course he hadn't actually meant he wanted to marry her.

"But I meant every word of it."

She blinked. A quavering started in the pit of her stomach.

He hurried on. "I can see that I've shocked you. I don't want you to feel rushed or pressured. We'll take our time and get to know each other better. But I wanted you to know what my intentions are where you are concerned."

Charlotte felt a bit like her emotions were on a yo-yo, springing from the lowest of lows to the ultimate peak. Tears pricked the backs of her eyes. "Do you mean it?"

He frowned a little. "I do. But I'm not sure tears are what I was hoping to see right now."

She smiled and reached up to shush him with one finger. "Some tears are happy tears, Reagan Callahan."

A slow smile parted his lips. "Are they now?"

She let her finger trace his lip, his brow, and the tiny white scar that disappeared into his hairline. "Of a certainty. No wonder God brought me to the wilds of Washington. He knew my perfect match was hiding way out here in Wyldhaven."

"Indeed, He did." His voice was barely audible when he spoke. "Unless you have an objection, I think I'm going to kiss you now."

She ought to object. She silenced the voices of Mother and Miss Gidden, which both shouted that surely this was all happening too soon. Her heart hammered in anticipation, and her palms itched to pull his face closer. She wanted nothing more than his kiss in that moment, and that was sure. Charlotte reminded herself to breathe. "I have no objections," she whispered, tilting her face up to meet his.

She closed her eyes, and as his lips whispered against hers, a feeling of tranquility settled into the region of her heart. Contentment wrapped her in a cocoon of warmth. And a sense of belonging enveloped her.

This was bliss.

She curled her fingers into the silky softness of his hair,

feeling his hat tumble past her shoulder to land on the ground at their feet.

This was a glimpse at holiness—two souls connecting in a way that opened a celestial door to give just a peek into heaven.

His arms wrapped around her and tugged her closer. His lips skimmed her jaw, touched her earlobe, and then retraced their path.

Just a preview of what it meant to let go of self and truly love.

She curled her hands around both sides of his face, rested her thumbs against the corners of his lips, and pulled back just slightly. For a moment she simply breathed with him, searching his eyes. And then she gave herself to him again, lifting up on her tiptoes this time.

A picture of what it would be like to, for eternity, walk in harmony with the One who noticed, cared, and even hurt when sparrows fell.

Dear Reader,

I hope you enjoyed this first foray into the town of Wyldhaven. I'm looking forward to sharing more depth and history of Washington's logging industry with you in future stories.

It should be noted that the town of Cle Elum was not so named until 1908. Prior to that it was called Clealum. One of the largest mills in Washington operated in Cle Elum at this time in history. Many small towns sprang up around mills and in logging areas. Though Wyldhaven is a product of my imagination, there were many towns in Washington and other states across the nation that came into existence in a similar manner. Some were in optimal locations and are still in existence today. Many others were abandoned when the industry they were built around either failed, or needed to move to a new locale.

Keep reading to find an excerpt from *On Eagles' Wings*, book 2 in the Wyldhaven series, and to find some discussion questions for book clubs. There's also an opportunity to get one of my stories for free if you'd like to join my newsletter.

Until we meet again in the pages of another story, may the God of all ages protect and keep you as you walk along your way.

Wishing you God's greatest blessings,

Lynnette Bonner

Please Review!

If you enjoyed this story, would you take a few minutes to leave your thoughts in a review on your favorite retailer's website? It would mean so much to me, and helps spread the word about the series.

You can quickly link through from my website here: http://www.lynnettebonner.com/books/historical-fiction/the-wyldhaven-series/

Now Available...

You may read an excerpt on the next page...

Dixie Pottinger rinsed the last of the soapsuds from the sink and wrung out her rag good and tight. She glanced around the kitchen. Satisfied to see that everything was cleaned and put away as it should be for the night, she pressed both hands into the curve of her aching back.

She hoped Ma had been able to rest this evening. It had been telling when, two days ago, Ma agreed that it would probably be best if she didn't come down to help with the cooking. Even though she'd taken to her bed for the past two days, Ma had been coughing something fierce, and Dixie feared she hadn't been resting much. The work of cooking and cleaning for the boardinghouse was much harder on her own, but Dixie hadn't really noticed, what with her worry over Ma.

Thankfully, they had no guests in the boardinghouse tonight, so dinner had been a light crowd, and now she could go up to check on Ma.

She opened the warming drawer on the oven and withdrew the bowl of chicken broth and the biscuit she'd set aside earlier. Adding the pot of tea that had been steeping while she cleaned, a slice of lemon, and the jar of honey that Washington Nolan had come around selling last week, she hefted the tray and headed upstairs.

She could hear Ma's hacking cough even before she reached the door to their rooms. Carefully balancing the tray, she twisted the door handle and pushed inside. The main room was just large enough for a settee and a rocking chair. Ma's room was just to the left, and Dixie's own small room to the right. The only other room in their chambers was the small lavatory, a luxury Dixie was even more thankful for now that Ma had grown so sick.

She nudged Ma's door open and stepped into her room, then set the tray on Ma's dresser and approached the side of her bed. "Ma? How are you feeling tonight? I've just finished with the cleanup and brought you some soup. Does that sound good?"

The only response she got was a low moan and another round of hacking coughs. That sent Dixie's pulse skyrocketing. Ma had always been a hearty soul. Dixie never remembered seeing her this sick before.

She laid a hand to Ma's forehead, and her alarm rose even more.

Burning with fever!

That did it. Whether Ma would be upset or not, Dixie needed to go fetch Flynn.

She gritted her teeth at her impropriety. *Dr. Griffin.* Had he worked his way so far into her affections that she was thinking of him by his given name now? She must banish that propensity, posthaste!

She lifted her skirts and hurried down the stairs and out the front to the building next door.

McGinty's Alehouse was still quite busy for this time of day. Several men played cards at a table in the corner, a bottle of rotgut making the rounds and liberally shared by all. Several others lounged at the bar, chatting with Ewan McGinty, the proprietor.

Dixie hung back by the door until she caught Ewan's eye.

As usual, his gaze lit up and then drifted a lazy sweep down the length of her.

It made her stomach curl. Mostly because a look like that might have at one time turned her head.

Ewan aimed a stream of tobacco toward the spittoon he kept behind the bar. "Dixie, darlin'. What can I do for you?"

Dixie fiddled with the brooch pinned at the base of her throat. "Is Doc in? Ma's powerful sick."

"Doc!"

Dixie jolted. She should be used to the fact that Ewan never went up the stairs to get Doc from the room he rented, but simply hollered at the top of his voice. But she never seemed to be prepared when he did.

Flynn appeared at the top of the staircase only a moment later, doctor bag in hand. He descended the stairs rapidly, searching the room for who might be in need of his services.

His steps faltered slightly when he saw her by the door, but he quickly recovered and hurried to her side. "What is it?" A furrow of worry trenched his forehead.

Dixie felt a tremor course through her, and to her surprise, tears pressed at the backs of her eyes. She blinked hard. She was unaccountably relieved to see him. "It's Ma. I need you to come check on her. She's been sick for a few days. But her fever..." The words choked off, and she couldn't seem to say more.

Flynn held a hand toward the door and stretched the other, holding his bag, behind her to urge her forward. "Lead the way. I'm glad you came for me."

Dixie swiped at the tears that had now spilled over. Her fingers trembled.

Doc walked beside her, his worried gaze fixed on her face.

She huffed. "I'm sorry. I just... If I lose her."

"Hey." Flynn settled his hand in the middle of her back, directing her around a puddle in the street. "I'm going to do my very best not to let that happen. Don't borrow trouble and all that, aye?"

Dixie nodded. "Yes, you're right. I'm sorry. I just...don't like to see her like this." She lifted her skirts and took the stairs ahead of him.

Ma was coughing when they stepped into the apartment.

Dixie rushed ahead, leading the way to her bedchamber. She went around to the far side of Ma's bed. "Ma, I'm here. I've brought Dr. Griffin."

Flynn took over the moment he stepped into the room. He set his bag on Ma's bedside table and leaned over Ma so she could easily see his face without having to turn her head. He smiled in that special way he had with the infirm.

"Hello, Rose. It's me, Doc. I'm just going to listen to your lungs and do a little poking and prodding, all right? Don't mind me." He rested the back of his hand against her forehead, then lifted Ma's wrist in one hand and his pocket watch in the other.

Dixie's fingers plucked nervously at the pin on her blouse. There wasn't much space, but that didn't stop her from pacing first one direction and then the next. She kept her study focused on Flynn's expression, wanting to see if there would be any hint of despair or sorrow, but for now his face remained impassive.

From his bag he pulled a device that looked like a clamp of some sort with a bell on one end. He put the two prongs of the clamp into his ears and then bent over Ma and placed the bell-shaped end against her chest. He listened, first in one area, then moved the device to another area and listened again, then again, and again.

Dixie was practically holding her breath by the time he straightened and tugged the tubes from his ears. She studied his face, willing him to look at her. But his gaze was still trained on Ma.

Finally, after a long moment, his shoulders slumped, and he lifted his gaze across the bed to Dixie.

Her heart threatened to stop. She'd seen that look in his eyes before. She'd seen it on the day that Hiram Wakefield's son had been crushed by the logging wagon and died only moments after arriving in town. She'd seen it the day that the Kings' newborn had been born blue and cold and lifeless.

She shook her head, feeling the tears stacking up against her lids like thunderclouds on a horizon.

Flynn tilted his head and reached a hand to scrub the back of his neck, so much pain reflected in his gray eyes. With a jut of his chin, he indicated they should talk in the other room.

All she seemed capable of, though, was covering her mouth with one hand. Her feet felt rooted to the floor.

Flynn stepped to the foot of the bed and stretched a hand toward her, compassion and regret filling his expression as he motioned for her to join him.

There was something in the look that lent her strength, and she lifted her skirts and stepped past him and out into the sitting room of the apartment.

She heard him come to a stop just behind her. With a sigh, he set his doctor bag on the floor near his feet, then stepped around to look her in the face. "I believe she has pneumonia."

Dixie pulled in a breath. "That's bad, isn't it?"

Flynn sighed and folded his hands. "It's not good. We'll have to watch her round the clock to make sure her fever doesn't get any higher. We'll also have to keep fluids down her so she doesn't dehydrate. And we'll need more pillows to prop her up. Some studies I've read say there are better survival rates when patients are made to sit up in their beds. Steaming the room is also said to help. So we'll need to keep hot water going round the clock."

Relief eased some of her tension. "When I saw your expression, I thought..." She was unable to finish the sentence.

Flynn reached one hand to the back of his neck. "Listen. I don't want to give you false hope. The mortality rate for pneumonia is one in four. But I will be here every moment that I can and will do my very best to bring her through this."

Before she thought better of it, Dixie threw her arms around his neck. She felt him stiffen, and lurched back, face flaming. "I'm sorry. I don't know what came over me. I just— She means so much to me, and..."

Flynn folded his arms and tilted her a lazy smile. "Far as I'm concerned, you can throw yourself into my arms any time you want. But I think you know that already."

Dixie felt her face blaze, and she clapped both hands to her cheeks. This secret of hers had carried on long enough. Especially where Flynn was concerned. "Dr. Griffin...I'm terribly sorry that I've never told you sooner. But the truth is...I'm a married woman."

Flynn's eyes widened. He stepped back and propped his hands on his hips. "You're what?!"

Find out more about this series here:
http://www.lynnettebonner.com/books/historical-fiction/the-wyldhaven-series/

Want a FREE Story?

If you enjoyed this book...

...sign up for Lynnette's Gazette below! Subscribers get exclusive deals, sneak peeks, and lots of other fun content.

(The gazette is only sent out about once a month or when there's a new release to announce, so you won't be getting a lot of spam messages, and your email is never shared with anyone else.)

Sign up link: https://www.lynnettebonner.com/newsletter/

Book Club Questions

1. After Charlotte is betrayed by Kent, she prays and asks God to guide and show her what to do next. Do you believe God cares and has a plan for each step of our lives? What has made you believe the way that you do?

2. Charlotte's parents wanted a "good match" for her. They were so focused on Kent's outward appearances of wealth and good standing that they missed the lack of character beneath the surface. Have you ever misjudged someone in such a way? What measures can we employ to keep ourselves from being taken off guard by people like that?

3. Charlotte wanted to please her parents, and so against her better judgment, she decided she would marry Kent. Is it easy for you to stand and make your own decisions? Or are you a people pleaser like Charlotte? Of course, sometimes listening to others' counsel is an important and wise thing to do. What are some ways to ensure you are making right decisions for the right reasons?

4. Even after feeling she'd heard from God that going to Wyldhaven was the answer for her, Charlotte waffled about her decision. Have you ever found yourself in a similar situation? Why do you think it is so easy for us to fall into doubt?

5. After Reagan rescues Charlotte from Lenny, he makes the following statement: "I think we often make the mistake of thinking that if we are in the center of God's will there should be no troubles or hardship." What do you think about that? Have you ever been in a difficult or challenging situation and still felt confident that you were doing exactly what God wanted?

6. What do you think are some good things we can do to make sure we are walking in the center of God's will, hardships or not?

7. There is a lot of talk in our world today about police brutality. Did it bother you when Reagan punched Lenny? What about when he threatened to shoot the outlaws in his jail cells? Back in the days of this story, such tactics would not have even been questioned. Do you think the place where we are at as a society now is a benefit or a hindrance to law and order? Or maybe a little bit of both?

8. By listening to God's voice, Joe saved Liora from committing suicide. Have you ever been in a situation where you wondered if God was speaking to you and you acted or didn't act? How did that situation turn out?

9. Liora is looked down upon because she's a prostitute, but the townspeople aren't aware of why or how she ended up in that line of work. Have you ever judged someone without knowing his or her story? How did finding out more about Liora change how you viewed her?

10. Charlotte felt the Lord leading her to befriend Liora, even though she also felt the counter-pull of what society might think of her if she associated with a prostitute. Have you ever felt drawn to befriend someone who might have jeopardized your job or social standing in some way? Did you follow through? How did that turn out?

11. Why do you think Waddell was so determined to get revenge on someone—anyone—when he could have initially escaped and left the area?

12. What do you think Waddell would have done with Charlotte if he'd gotten away with kidnapping her?

13. Waddell's inability to let go of his thirst for revenge was the end of him. Are you currently unable to let go of anything despite the fact that holding on is hurting you or has potential to hurt you? What might help you let go?

14. At the end of the story, Charlotte asks Reagan how he is doing after he shot Waddell. His response is, "It's never easy to live with the knowledge that you are the reason another human being is now walking in eternity." He then goes on to say that time will help him move past it. Has your job or position ever required you to do something for which you later had to live with the consequences? How did that make you feel?

ABOUT THE AUTHOR

Born and raised in Malawi, Africa. Lynnette Bonner spent the first years of her life reveling in warm equatorial sunshine and the late evening duets of cicadas and hyenas. The year she turned eight she was off to Rift Valley Academy, a boarding school in Kenya where she spent many joy-filled years, and graduated in 1990.

That fall, she traded to a new duet—one of traffic and rain—when she moved to Kirkland, Washington to attend Northwest University. It was there that she met her husband and a few years later they moved to the small town of Pierce, Idaho.

During the time they lived in Idaho, while studying the history of their little town, Lynnette was inspired to begin the Shepherd's Heart Series with Rocky Mountain Oasis.

Marty and Lynnette have four children, and currently live in Washington where Marty pastors a church.

Made in the USA
Columbia, SC
14 November 2024

46160464R00205